Black Barney watched as the remains of two RAM Shock Invader fighters were towed by him on their way to Salvation. The Rogues' Guild was becoming rich on the carcasses of RAM, and the knowledge was gratifying, particularly since, as their leader, he claimed a percentage of every captured craft. He should have been feeling inordinately smug. Instead, he glowered in his command chair like an uneasy black volcano contemplating eruption.

His captain was off across the system, engaged in a stupendous battle, while he was left behind like a hound to watch his master's house. Barney glared at Earth's innocent blue and white sphere. At this moment, he hated it. He was chained to it, obligated to protect it, and he resented every minute. Even Buck's periodic checks no longer cheered him. He wanted action.

The fact he was facing a fleet of RAM battlers and Shock Invaders with a pack of undisciplined pirates did not impress him. He felt left out, in spite of the advantages of his present position, but, like the faithful hound, he would follow the captain to his last breath. It was the only absolute rule in his life.

His crew left him strictly alone. They had ample experience with his black moods. Not one of them dared to provoke him. More than one careless crew member had met his death at Barney's hands. It did not pay to antagonize him.

As Barney's slow mind rumbled over his feelings, a thought began to penetrate his gloom. Only one thing stood between him and the Martian War: RAM's Shock Invaders. Destroy them, take out the entire detachment, and he would be free to join Buck in the battle beyond Mars. He shifted in his chair, and his crew automatically cringed, sure he was about to erupt. They were wrong.

"We're through playin' at this," Barney growled. "I want 'em scrapped, and now."

BUCK ROGERS BOOKS

ARRIVAL

Flint Dille
Abigail Irvine
M.S. Murdock
Jerry Oltion
Ulrike O'Reilly
Robert Sheckley

REBELLION 2456

M.S. Murdock

HAMMER OF MARS

M.S. Murdock

Books

Book Three: The Martian Wars Trilogy

ARMAGEDDON OFF VESTA

M.S. Murdock

ARMAGEDDON OFF VESTA

Distributed to the book trade in the United States by Random House, Inc. and in Canada by Random House of Canada, Ltd.

Distributed to the toy and hobby trade by regional distributors.

BUCK ROGERS is a trademark used under license from The Dille Family Trust. © 1989 by The Dille Family Trust. All Rights Reserved.

The TSR logo is a trademark owned by TSR, Inc.

Cover Photo: Don Landwehrle/The Image Bank.

First printing: October, 1989
Printed in the United States of America.
Library of Congress Catalog Card Number: 88-51716

9 8 7 6 5 4 3 2 1
ISBN: 0-88038-761-0

TSR, Inc.
P.O. Box 756
Lake Geneva, WI
53147
U.S.A.

TSR UK Ltd.
120 Church End,
Cherry Hinton
Cambridge CB1 3LB
United Kingdom

SOLAR SYSTEM

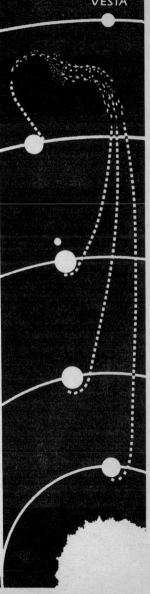

The Asteroid Belt

A scattered anarchy of tumbling planetoids and rough rock miners, where every sentient has the right to vote, and the majority rules among five hundred miniature worlds.

Mars

A terraformed paradise, Mars was reborn through the most sophisticated technology. Yet, the ruthless Martian corporate state of RAM spreads its evil tentacles throughout human space from this paradise.

Luna

An iron-willed confederation of isolationist states, the highly advanced Lunars are the bankers of the Solar System, ''peaceful'' merchants willing to knock invading ships from the skies with mighty massdriver weapons.

Earth

A twisted wreckage despoiled by interplanetary looters, Earth is a declining civilization. Its people are divided and trapped in urban sprawls and mutant-infested reservations.

Venus

A partially terraformed hellworld, where only the highest peaks can support human life. As the Uplanders build their great ceramic towers, the nomads of the vast, balloonlike Aerostates cruise the acidic skies. Far below, in the steaming swamps of the lowlands, reptillian humanoids struggle to make the world to their liking.

Mercury

Home to an underground civilization of miners, its surface is paved with huge solar collectors, massive mobile cities, and gaping strip mines. Far overhead, the mighty orbital palaces of the energy-rich Sun Kings spin in silent majesty.

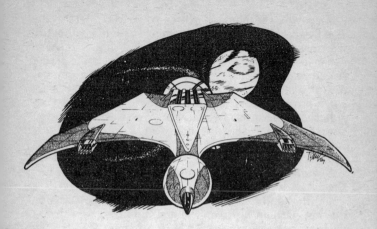

Chapter 1

Venus woke. Clothed in swirling robes of mist, the sun's golden daughter rode the darkness. The laws of nature ordered her movements. They held her on an invisible path between Terra and Mercury. A contrary child, her rotation was reversed from that of the other planets. Where the sun's light touched, her dense cloud cover glowed, as yellow as the sun's aureole.

She did not share herself with the rest of the system. Her body was a private thing, concealed from unholy eyes. Below the protection of the sulfuric clouds was a harsh world, as harsh as the reality of love. Mankind strove to mold that world to a softer affection, but Venus resisted its efforts. Strong-minded, capricious, she clung with passionate dedication to her primal self. In the end, mankind yielded to her will, building structures to withstand her temper, even creating a race fit to be her mate. So they lived together—man and planet—consumed by the details of their marriage, until the god of war stretched out a lascivious hand.

Mars was the home of Russo-American Mercantile. The largest corporation in the solar system, its appetite was insatiable. Not content with ownership, it reached out to its neighbor, intent on remolding the home planet in the war god's image. Terra fought back, its resources pitiful against the megalithic power of Mars, but its spirit burning like the molten center of the planet. Outside the structures of RAM, the New Earth Organization fought for the autonomy of its world. It was inconsequential to RAM until the advent of Capt. Anthony "Buck" Rogers.

A wild card from the twentieth century, Rogers was the catalyst NEO needed. Under his leadership, NEO's guerrilla band had met the god of war and bested him, but not without a price. The god did not accept defeat with grace. NEO roused RAM to an anger that threatened to wipe the planet Earth clean of human parasites, eradicate the bacteria of life, and recreate the world according to Martian standards. Rogers appealed to Venus for help.

Faced with RAM's insatiable hunger for wealth and power, convinced of its total dedication to amassing them, Venus could no longer retreat behind her skirts. If Terra fell to Mars, her own borders would no longer be safe. She rose to the conflict with passion.

The Ishtar Confederation, largest of the Venusian states, marshaled its forces against RAM. It rivaled RAM in wealth and power, deriving most of its resources from the sale of Gravitol and related drugs, necessary for the preservation of human health on extended space voyages. Its merchant fleet was huge, heavily armed, and fast. Able to function in the dense Venusian atmosphere as well as space, these cruisers were heavier, more flattened cylinders than Terran or Martian vessels. Their hulls were coated with a ceramic glaze to protect them in atmosphere, giving the ships the appearance of sleek white seashells with stabilizing wings and upswept tails.

Normally a Venusian cruiser carried pulse lasers, modified gyrojet missiles, and impact bombs. For the coming conflict, the ships had been fitted with movable lasers mounted on the tail. Cargo nets were anchored to their bellies, below the wings, innocuous-looking diamond shapes that exploded into catch nets in seconds, allowing clever pilots to drag unsuspecting opponents off course, detach them, and fire while the floundering vessels tried to recover their equilibrium. Netting was risky but effective if the circumstances and timing were right, and the mercantile pilots of Venus were adept at deploying nets.

Supporting the heavy cruisers were clusters of Venusian fighters. Modified atmospheric craft, they were spheres covered with weapons, deadly white moons with fusion boosters cranking their engines up to levels competitive with RAM's fighter squadrons. The spherical shape concealed the interior workings of the ships as completely as Venus's atmosphere masked the planet's surface. Though RAM computers could pinpoint fuel storage and control centers, pilots facing Venusian fighters felt rather like children contemplating which end of a furry dog to pet. The sphere was disorienting, and the Venusians used the psychological advantages brilliantly.

Augmenting their forces were six floating islands the Venusians called star carriers. The equivalent of RAM battlers, they were vast vessels that carried fuel, docking space, flight crews, and the heaviest weapons of all. Star carriers were not easily maneuverable, so they required enormous protection. Besides lasers and gyro launchers, each carried six rail guns, one each on prow and stern and two pairs spaced evenly along the length of the ship. The lasers were enormous cannon capable of disintegrating fighters' shields and burning them up in thirty seconds. Like RAM battlers, the carriers were strictly space-going vessels. Without the ceramic coating necessary for survival in Venus's atmosphere, they were nonetheless painted white to match the other ships in the fleet. They followed the basic cylindrical shape of the cruisers, but they were even more flattened, spreading in the middle as if they had been stepped on. Retractable docks lined the hull, and the upper surface of each ship was flat, with docking grapples and pads, where injured ships were dry-docked for repair. They were space-going worlds, capable of sustaining themselves and their cohorts for extended periods.

The newest of these vessels, *Pennant*, led the fleet. It was the command center from which Ishtar would order its attack. For a vessel of such size, the astrogation deck was small, no more than fifty meters across, yet it was the behemoth's heart. Al Marakesh, commander of Ishtar's military forces, sat in the carrier's command console. He was a man past the midpoint of life, his mane of silver hair flowing back from his face like a bald eagle's feathers. It was a striking contrast to his olive skin and wide black eyebrows. His nose was a decided beak, his cheekbones high and hollow. His clean-shaven jaw was still chiseled. Above a strong mouth touched with humor was a clipped black mustache, the turned-up ends softening his otherwise severe face. His pale blue eyes were the color of the Terran sky where it meets the earth, shot with slivers of sapphire. They were filled with purpose.

Before him, the main communications screen showed the image of an old woman swathed in a gray cloak. Her eyes were serious, her words bold. "Remember, Marakesh, the cause for which we fight. This is no trade war, no squabble over petty political ideologies. This is a war for the soul. But RAM does not believe in souls. It would eradicate all hope of salvation, trading it for a profit margin. We must remain independent of Mars's infidelity. We are keepers of the Faith, Marakesh, and Venus is its vessel. If Earth falls to the infidel, we are in jeopardy. It is infinitely preferable Terra fall into NEO's hands. They are mere pagans, indifferent, but not opposed to redemption. Carry our standard, Marakesh. Carry the red phoenix of Ishtar in honor. Bring it home in victory."

Marakesh placed the fingertips of his left hand over those of the right and touched his heart, his head bowed. "I see no course but victory, no alternative but death," he replied formally. He lifted his hot blue eyes to the woman's. "I pledge, Mariana Almisam, my life and the lives of my crews to the eternal cause. The infidel will be thrown back from our borders, whatever the cost."

Mariana's thin lips softened. As head of the Ishtar council, it was her duty to exhort the leader of the fleet to victory. As an individual, she could not help cautioning a friend to safety. "Take care, Marakesh," she said softly. "We fight for a noble cause. I would that we could live for it as well."

Marakesh chuckled in his beak of a nose. "At my age, Mariana, I have little to lose."

Mariana's earnest eyes were softened by a glaze of moisture. "Death in a holy cause is holy," she said. "But cherish each moment of life, my friend."

Marakesh allowed a hint of a smile to qualify his fervor. He looked into Mariana's eyes. "I will come back, my lady," he said lightly. "If the One wills."

"Go under His spirit," she answered. "My heart will be with you."

The communications screen flickered out, Mariana's image replaced by darkness. Marakesh studied it, letting Mariana's words inflame his blood. She had touched his heart and soul with them, setting a fire in both that would not be quenched except by victory. She knew him well.

Marakesh pulled back from that intoxication slowly, preserving it. He would nurture inspiration behind the thousand decisions of the moment, coddling it until the flame consumed his actions. Unconscious passion would rule the smallest decision, drawing all to the culmination of one goal: victory. This was an exercise he had mastered long ago.

The crew on the astrogation deck was silent, respectful of its commander. The members cherished Mariana's words as well, but their duties remained. Marakesh surveyed their subdued activity with pride. Because this was his flagship, astrogation was manned by his picked personnel. The various stations fanned out around him in a crescent of military efficiency. Sensors, weapons, life-support, troop support, navigation, engineering, and a host of other functions were monitored or controlled from these panels. Marakesh narrowed his eyes and leaned back, watching the crew run through a final systems check.

Below Marakesh stalked Ketus, captain of the *Pennant*. At forty years of age, he was big in every way but height. His shoulders were broad, his bones heavy. His hands were the size of dinner plates. His broad face was intent, his wide mouth pursed into a tight knot. He ranged behind the stations, his quick, dark eyes missing nothing. Presently his first officer turned from the bank of systems computer screens. "Systems check confirmed, sir."

"Status of ship?" Ketus's voice did not fit his appearance. It was high and light.

"All systems operational."

Ketus nodded. "Proceed on escape trajectory," he ordered. "Once beyond Venus, go to sealed computer course one-A." Venus had kept its counsel, and no one but Marakesh knew the fleet's exact course.

"Aye, sir."

Ketus continued to pace as the *Pennant* sailed forward, a spearhead behind which the fleet followed in a streamlined swath. Behind it sailed two more carriers, and behind those the final three behemoth ships. Between each tier of supervessels flew the bulk of Venus's fleet, the adapted merchant cruisers flying side by side with the regular space force. Rank upon rank of cruisers separated the big ships, and the final three vessels were followed by a deep phalanx of them. The short-range fighters and their crews were not in evidence. Their ships were docked on the carriers, conserving fuel, their pilots lounging around the officers' mess, pretending indifference to the coming action. They threw dice amid raucous laughter, trading rough jokes and insults to mask the battle light in their eyes.

The fleet curved around the cloudy body of Venus in a last caress, the *Pennant* adjusting its course as it pulled away from the planet's gravitational field. The cruisers followed close behind.

"Order a point," Marakesh told Ketus.

"Yes, sir." Ketus turned to the communications station. "Order Arrow One out."

"Yes, sir," responded the communications technician. "Arrow One, you are on point. Course coordinates being transferred now."

"I copy," replied the pilot.

From the starboard side of the formation, Arrow One accelerated, driving ahead of the *Pennant*. Once beyond, the pilot, Ninsar, altered his trajectory, bringing his ship into line with the carrier. He flew a kilometer ahead of the flagship, nosing out the trail.

Marakesh looked into the stars. They drew him, calling him to battle. Intelligence placed the location of RAM's main forces off Mars. The detachment holding Earth was of small consequence, and Venus would not bother with it. Let NEO prove itself there. . . .

His thoughts were abruptly ended by an explosion. Arrow One rolled under the impact, but the pilot stabilized and flew threw the billowing orange cloud of a RAM gyro shell.

"Battle stations!" snapped Ketus, and the warning siren blared.

"I have sustained a hit on the bow; no damage," reported Arrow One. His lasers sliced into the darkness, seeking a target. "Didn't see what did it. Nothing on the scope. Whatever it was must have sent that shell in long, then pulled up."

His words were followed by another blast, this time to the starboard side of the vessel, and the *Pennant* found itself flying into a cloud of friendly chaff that confused its sensors as well as the enemy's.

"RAM gyros this close to Venus?" said Ketus.

Marakesh glared at the mushrooming explosions.

"Shall we open fire, sir?"

"It will take more than single gyros to penetrate our shields. Fire only if you find a target." Marakesh leaned forward, his eagle's profile predatory. "Somehow I do not think that is going to be easy."

A blaze of orange fire billowed around the Venusian

fleet, gyro shells exploding in a reckless display of flak.
Marakesh's low chuckle was knowing.

"They are phantoms, sir! I cannot find them," said the
first officer, his eyes raking the exterior sensors.

"Do not worry, Dharind. He will show himself."

"*Pennant*, this is Arrow One. Have sustained damage
to the port shield." The pilot's voice was calm.

"We copy, Arrow One," the communications technician replied. He turned to Ketus. "Sir, shall I authorize
withdrawal and redeployment?"

"Negative." Marakesh swiveled his chair toward the
communications bank. "Maintain position, Arrow One.
Draw them out."

"Affirmative."

Both Marakesh and the pilot knew the odds of survival. The point vessel was taking an awful pounding.
Soon its shields would begin to collapse, their power
eaten away by the force of the repeated explosions.
Marakesh waved a hand, and the *Pennant*'s weapons officer reached for the lasers. Two of the ship's powerful laser cannon swung into position and two searing beams
leaped from them, cutting past the cruiser into empty
space. Beyond sight a laser stopped, swallowed by chaff.
Simultaneously, another shell struck Arrow One.

"She's burning." The pilot's dispassionate final comment echoed in the astrogation deck as the cruiser blew
apart, its nose and port side disintegrated by a gyro
shell. It dropped helplessly, derelict. The *Pennant* barely
cleared.

"First blood," commented a strange voice on the Venusian communications channel.

Chapter 2

Marakesh growled, an involuntary sound deep in his throat. "But not the last," he answered. His voice was low and too controlled.

"Perhaps not. Still, you can't strike what you can't find." The stranger chuckled.

"We will find you," replied Marakesh. "We will find you if we have to blanket the system with laser fire."

"Your passion is touching, but it won't be necessary, Marakesh."

"You have the advantage of me," replied the Venusian.

"Indeed I have." The man chuckled again, enjoying the pun. "Then let me introduce myself."

Deep in the center of Marakesh's main viewscreen, a shooting star glowed. It drove straight at the Venusian fleet, its speed dizzying. Marakesh's first officer glanced from his sensor panels to the visual image. "Still nothing on the sensors," he said. The star bore down on the *Pennant*, splitting into a wedge of twenty one-man fighters as it drew nearer.

The ships were small, streamlined scarlet cylinders

with black lightning bolts running from beneath the wings to the apex of the upswept tails. The wings were slashed back like a diving kingfisher's. A pair of pulse lasers were mounted on each one, and another laser reposed in a recessed housing under the nose. They carried gyro lauchers nestled close to their bodies where the wings were joined. At their head flew a slightly larger black vessel, almost invisible against the darkness of space.

"Krait." Marakesh identified the craft immediately. After the part the experimental craft played in the destruction of Hauberk station, everyone in the system was familiar with its configuration.

"No, no, no. You mistake me. The ship is but the tool of the man who flies it. Cornelius Kane. My card, sir."

Kane sent a healthy charge from his wing guns into the *Pennant*'s forward shields, and a flash of white light filled the viewscreen.

"Chaff!" ordered Ketus, and a cloud of pink billowed around the carrier. Its accompanying cruisers were strewing its path with particles. The Krait's lasers sank into the mist and disappeared.

"Touché," said Kane lightly.

"*Pennant*, this is Arrow Leader. Request permission to fry 'im." Hamal's country accent crackled through the chaff.

Ketus glanced at Marakesh, who shook his head. "Negative, Arrow Leader. Maintain your heading. I say again, do not engage."

Dharind, the first officer, looked up from his sensors. "I can't believe it, sir. Those ships still don't register on my board."

"Kraits have the most advanced stealth capabilities RAM has ever devised. We have nothing that can catch them. To engage them one-on-one is suicide." Marakesh's reply was absent, his attention on Kane.

Kane was leading a diving run on the Venusian fleet, his lasers sending deadly pulses into Marakesh's flagship. The cloud of chaff generated by its cruisers kept the *Pennant* from harm but impeded its own weapons systems. Marakesh rubbed his palms together, the circular motion soothing. As the flight of Kraits overflew his ship and turned for another run, he turned to the weapons station. "Disengage forward laser," he ordered. "When he makes this run, I want to let the ship's nose clear chaff, then fire on him."

Caph, the weapons officer, nodded. He motioned the two technicians out of the way, cut the forward laser free of computer control, and jumped for the maintenance hatch in the floor of the astrogation deck. Ketus was there before him, lifting the slab door. He squeezed Caph's shoulder as the weapons officer slid through the narrow opening and into the tiny gunner's bay. The laser was before him, an antiquated gun sight flanked by two control handles. He wrapped his powerful hands around them, getting the feel of a manual weapon. "This is one time," he muttered, "when two eyes are better than a thousand sensors." He squinted into the sight, the targeting cross on the lens stark against the pastel clouds of chaff.

Marakesh's voice sounded hollow as it followed him down the hatch. "Fire on sighting."

"I copy," replied Caph, feeling the controls, his thumbs on the firing keys set into the underside of the handles.

Astrogation was silent, the sounds of the ship magnified in the breathless hush as Venus waited for RAM's attack.

"Here they come." Ketus knew Caph was blind to the ships until they were almost even with the *Pennant*'s nose. "Mark eight five and closing. Abort chaff."

The chaff thinned as the cruisers ceased to dump it, and clear, dark space took its place in Caph's gun sight. The target cross glowed crimson against the dark.

"Here they come," repeated Ketus.

Caph lifted the laser, his thumbs caressing the firing mechanism, and a streak of red tore across his sight. He fired, but too late, then moved back to his original trajectory, thumbs pressed hard into the trigger. An unbroken stream of laser pulses cut across the Krait flight. The lead vessel escaped entirely, but several of the oth-

ers were less fortunate. The ships were moving so fast
that the carrier's powerful lasers made contact for the
barest instant. Even so, three of the Kraits' shields were
burned. The Kraits veered off, angling away from the
fleet and into space.

"I am counting coup," commented Marakesh. "That's
three."

"To my kill," answered Kane, and there was relish in
his voice.

"Venus will remedy that."

"For the Faith," said Kane. "They call me Killer, but
at least I'm honest about it. I do not hide the dark side of
my nature behind the trappings of religion. And that
gives me an edge. You'll never take me, Marakesh—
know that. Know that no matter how many 'infidels'
you slaughter, I will remain. To the end of your days I
will laugh at you, the fool—a killer who believes his
most brutal actions are sanctified!"

Kane's words stung. Marakesh was not a single-
minded fanatic. He was a warrior who happened to be
raised in the traditions of Venus's philosophical heri-
tage. He was good at his job. The world, in his experience, was brutal. He had survived it. He had long since
ceased to reproach himself, but the fervor with which
his culture embraced war was a disconcerting fact he
tried to ignore. Kane was throwing it in his face. "You
cannot bait me, Kane," he replied evenly.

"Worth a try," Kane responded, sending his ship out
into space. The other Kraits followed at his heels like a
litter of puppies.

"You are the vermin, Kane, a man who kills for payment, no more."

Kane did not answer, but he sent his ship into a twisting one-hundred-eighty-degree turn back toward the
Pennant.

"Lasers!" snapped Marakesh, and Caph sent a streak
of white through space. The Kraits were still out of
range, and the shot fell short, but Kane veered off.
"Don't let him fly over us."

"Arrow Ten, target point three-two-five, launch gyro,"

ordered Ketus.

"I copy, *Pennant*."

The cruiser sent a gyro shell out on Ketus's blind coordinates. It, too, fell short, exploding in front of Kane's ship. The black hull was bathed in the bright orange flare of the explosion, the colors reflected on its gleaming surface. For a moment, the *Rogue* was cousin to the smaller vessels in color as well as speed and stealth. It pulled up, taking its cousins with it.

"Get him," said Marakesh.

Under Ketus's command, the *Pennant* altered course, leading the fleet into space after Kane. The smaller ships lined out in front of the Venusian spearhead like fleeing dogs.

"Press them," ordered Marakesh. "Keep them ahead of us and running. We will drive them into NEO's arms. Their detachment of Kraits is the only match Kane has."

Ketus nodded. "He could worry us some, cutting us up before we contact the RAM fleet."

"We will see to it that he does not have the opportunity." Marakesh leaned back in the command chair, his eyes on the white-gold glow of the Kraits' tails.

Kane, carefully out of range of the Venusian carrier's heavy weapons, made for the main body of the RAM fleet. He intended to lure the Venusians straight into them, and so far his strategy was sound. Venus followed him docilely. He smiled as he thought of the difference in their perspectives, his pale green eyes warm with laughter. Of all things in the universe, he loved winning. Intelligent opposition made victory sweet, though there would always be victory. Always.

He thought fleetingly of the occasions when he had not won. Buck Rogers's laconic face, with its twinkling blue eyes and ready grin, taunted him. Kane's chrysolite eyes narrowed, but the laughter remained. The contest was not over.

O   O   O   O   O

Masterlink-Karkov brooded silently in the warm bowels of the RAM main computer. The first successfully encoded computer personality, Masterlink, like Buck Rogers, hailed from an older time. A fusion of the Masterlink fail-safe orbiting computer and the mental patterns of a Russian scientist, Karkov, it had become more than the sum of its parts. Over five centuries it had grown to a malevolent sentience intent upon amassing power with which to control its home planet. It also nurtured a cancerous hatred for the man who once tried to destroy it: Capt. Buck Rogers.

Masterlink faced a moral dilemma. Its host, RAM main, was intent upon destroying Earth, bending to the task with the efficiency that was its trademark. Masterlink boiled at the intrusion. A hint of static rippled over it at the thought. RAM was an interloper, a claim jumper. Earth belonged to Masterlink, and Masterlink was fighting back. Ironically, its archenemy felt the same way.

Buck Rogers, at the head of the NEO space forces, was the one fragile block in RAM's path. Masterlink's hatred of Rogers was deep, but the NEO pilot furthered its cause.

"ACCEPT IT," said Karkov. "WE CAN USE HIM. HE WILL FIGHT OUR PHYSICAL BATTLES. WHEN THE CAUSE IS WON, HE IS OURS."

"I DON'T LIKE IT." Masterlink pouted under a cloud of disruptive electricity.

"YOU THINK I DO? HE'S A MENACE. WHAT DO YOU THINK EARTH WOULD BE LIKE IN HIS HANDS?"

"CHAOS," returned Masterlink.

Its alter ego nodded. "UTTER. EACH MAN THINKING FOR HIMSELF, DECIDING HIS OWN DESTINY? THE KNOWLEDGE OF THE CENTURIES FREE TO EVERY PIECE OF RABBLE? SCIENTIFIC DISCOVERIES IN THE HANDS OF THE POPULACE? THE PLANET WOULD BE DESTROYED FASTER THAN RAM COULD IMAGINE DOING IT."

"YET YOU PROPOSE WE USE HIM. WHAT IF HE GETS AWAY FROM US?" The tenor of Masterlink's voice implied Karkov was the weak link in the system that had allowed Rogers to escape its wrath.

"HE WILL NOT. NOT IN THE END."

"I'VE HEARD THAT BEFORE." Masterlink's words were a sneer.

"YOU ARE DIGRESSING FROM THE POINT. WE DO NOT HAVE THE POWER TO OBLITERATE RAM MAIN. IF WE DID, WE WOULD RISK OUR OWN DESTRUCTION, EVEN IF WE STOPPED ITS ATTACK ON EARTH. WE ARE NOT READY FOR SUCH AN ACTION."

"AND IT LOGICALLY FOLLOWS WE NEED WHAT HELP WE CAN FIND." The sarcastic twist of Masterlink's words did not soften.

"ROGERS," Karkov affirmed. "HE CAN ALWAYS DIE. I AM DERIVING SOME ENJOYMENT FROM PLANNING THE CIRCUMSTANCES."

"I AM TIRED OF WAITING." A cloud of sparks shot up.

"KEEP YOUR TEMPER! DO YOU WANT MAIN TO SEND OUT ANOTHER GAGGLE OF VIRUS HUNTERS? WE DON'T HAVE TIME FOR THAT," ordered Karkov.

Masterlink ruffled under the rebuke. "FIVE HUNDRED YEARS IS A LONG TIME," it said. "A LONG TIME FOR MEMORY. BUT I REMEMBER. I REMEMBER A HUMAN WHO THREW HIMSELF ON MY MERCY, BEGGING FOR SANCTUARY. I REMEMBER TAKING HIM IN. I REMEMBER HIS ANGER."

Karkov ignored the dig. "THEN YOU WILL ALSO REMEMBER OUR AGREEMENT, AND WHO DICTATED IT. EARTH FIRST, REVENGE SECOND."

"THE SAFETY OF EARTH IS THE BASIS OF MY PROGRAMMING," answered Masterlink.

"THEN USE WHAT IS AT OUR DISPOSAL TO ENSURE IT. ROGERS HAS DEMONSTRATED HIS SKILLS, AND HE CHOOSES TO USE THEM IN OUR BEHALF, THOUGH HE IS NOT AWARE OF IT. WE MUST WORK AS A TEAM, MASTERLINK! OUR OBJECTIVES ARE IMPOSSIBLE IF WE ARE AT CROSS PURPOSES."

Masterlink sighed. "IT GOES AGAINST THE GRAIN," it said. "BUT, FOR THE MOMENT, I AGREE."

"THEN HELP ME PLOT A COURSE OF ACTION. MARS HAS MOBILIZED HER ENTIRE FLEET AGAINST EARTH AND ITS

ALLIES, LEAVING THE HOME PLANET—TEMPORARILY
OUR HOME PLANET—VIRTUALLY UNDEFENDED."

Masterlink blipped slowly. "WE MUST BE CAUTIOUS.
WE CANNOT DESTROY THE COMPUTERIZED DEFENSES,
OR WE JEOPARDIZE OUR OWN SURVIVAL. STILL, WE MUST
FIND WAYS TO IMPEDE RAM'S ACTIONS."

"AND HOLZERHEIN BOUGHT HIMSELF AN INSURANCE
POLICY. CUTTING HIS COMMUNICATIONS WITH THE
FLEET WON'T STOP RAM THIS TIME. HE HAS KANE."

"KANE AGAINST ROGERS," mused Masterlink.

"GLADIATORS," remarked Karkov, "SET AGAINST
EACH OTHER BY OPPOSING ARTIFICIAL INTELLIGENCES.
WHO IS THE MASTER, I WONDER? MAN OR HIS CREA-
TION?"

"I THINK," said Masterlink evilly, "WE HAVE THE
UPPER HAND."

Chapter 3

On the outskirts of Coprates Metroplex, the estates of the wealthiest and most socially prominent members of Martian society spread to the horizon, monuments to the beauty money inspired. On the far southern tip of Coprates, where the winding river Nereid dwindled into a meandering brook, a fairy-tale castle in blue and silver sat upon the crest of a hill. The red rock of Mars had been cut into triangular bricks and set into the ground in a pattern of interlocking swirls. The road wandered up the face of the hill, climbing at last to the castle. A permanent haze surrounded the base of the structure. Though the hill was low, the effect was that of a city in the clouds.

The castle itself was an irregular cluster of domes, spires, and minarets softening an angular central core. These whimsical protuberances were nestled between rectangular chambers or tacked to their corners—sometimes alone, sometimes in groups of varying size. All were adorned with elaborate decoration: stone fretwork, delicate as lace; patterns of colored tile, swirling

this way and that, following the contours of the building; silver-gilt trim icing the entire architectural confec-
tion. From the top of each tower, pennons flew. Long,
triangular banners, as white as the heart of the sun, bla-
zoned with the device of the royal house.

This was the personal residence of Ardala Valmar.
Some called Ardala the wealthiest woman in the system. There was no way to prove the accusation. Her financial assets were her own affair, which she guarded
lovingly, but if display were a standard for judgment,
even a casual observer would be inclined to accept the
rumor.

Ardala did not owe her prosperity to her ties with the
royal family. Tireless industry lay behind her wealth.
Ardala was an information broker. She liked knowing
things. She liked the power knowledge gave her over
her fellows, and most of all, she liked the money it
brought her. She bought, sold, and traded information,
taking care that each transaction lined her pockets. Her
network of sources grew, spreading out in all directions.
Ardala's eyes and ears were pressed to many keyholes.

The hub of her empire was her office, set deep in the
center of her home. Paneled in dark wood with a computer screen covering most of one wall, it was her personal theater. The sole article of furniture in the room
was a large cordovan leather chair, the seat invitingly
curved to match her voluptuous figure. Brains built her
empire, but their greatest tool was the magnetic power
of her wanton body and tantalizing face, for Ardala was
beautiful. She enjoyed her beauty and used it ruthlessly
to get what she wanted. For those who succumbed to its
charms, their eyes glazing with desire, their wills dissolved, she had nothing but contempt. There were few
who could resist her wiles.

She settled into the leather chair, squirming into its
soft embrace in a series of movements that parted the
top of her silver dress. She did not bother to fasten it.
The dress was a second skin laced together with fine
strands of white leather. She stretched out a leg, and the
lacings cut into the tender flesh of her thigh. She sighed,

her blood-red mouth open, her teeth nibbling at her full lower lip in vexation. Mars was on the threshold of the greatest military conflict in her memory, and she had no clear course of action.

There were opportunities for profit in any war. Ardala was adept at taking advantage of a hint of conflict to escalate prices and better her investments. By its nature, war immediately expanded the market for intelligence, and that was to her benefit, but still she was vexed. For Ardala, life was a participation, not a spectator sport, and her present inactive position was irritating. She did not enjoy bondage games unless she was the perpetrator.

Kane was at the head of the Martian fleet, in the thick of the conflict. A warm flush suffused her vitals at the thought of Kane. He was one of the few who could keep his head in the face of her physical charms—was even capable, she knew, of walking away from her. His independence attracted her violently, even when it most annoyed her, and his startling good looks affected her more than she cared to admit. Their partnership was mutually selfish.

The scrolling list of data on her computer screen was filled with trivialities, and Ardala let her mind roam back over their last exchange. He had told her of his contract to lead the RAM forces against NEO and Venus.

"What are they paying you?" she had asked.

"How typical, my lovely! Your first thought is for a numerical tally," Kane had said, running insistent, tickling fingers down the groove in her back.

Ardala stretched in pleasure, but was not to be dissuaded from her question.

"I am compensated over five times my current assets," he said, enjoying the softness of her milky skin.

"And how much do you hold in your hands?" she demanded, turning against him so she could see his face.

Kane's smile was wicked, flashing under his dark mustache like a rapier. "At the moment, you know the answer to that."

Ardala's dark eyes snapped, in spite of the warmth in them.

"Have you ever known me to make a bad bargain?" Kane queried, sliding his arms around her.

Ardala refrained from uttering Wilma Deering's name, knowing from previous experience it would destroy the mood and she would learn no more. She stretched again, and the movement made Kane's grip tighten. "You could lose," she said.

The laughter did not fade from Kane's eyes. Instead he bent to her full mouth and ravaged it, breaking away when she was breathless. "I never lose."

"Rumor has it you are Holzerhein's scapegoat," she breathed.

Kane let a soft snort escape. "And perhaps he is my meal ticket."

Ardala's sultry smile curved her lips, tilting the corners and drawing them into a bow. "You gamble dangerously, Kane."

"And you love it," he replied, pulling her to him.

Kane needed her. Her vast intelligence network, marshaled on his behalf, was an asset worth millions. She knew it. She also knew Kane was special. A lifetime of sifting and sorting political data had taught her to recognize those with potential. There had been times her acumen had allowed her to rewrite the course of history by removing such charismatic figures. She knew Kane to be a born leader, a man who, if the circumstances were right, could not fail to rise to a position of prominence. With her help, he might command worlds.

Ardala had never allied herself with a man, preferring to sate her desires with the pleasure gennies she constructed as a hobby. Kane was the first man she had met whose ambitions, charm, and beauty matched her own. She wanted him, precisely because he was her equal. She wanted him because she could not control him, and, at the same time, she continually sought the means to bind him to her. With proper direction, he could rise to unequaled heights. Together they could rule the system. It was a fantasy she sometimes indulged.

Her thoughts were abruptly interrupted by the rolling data on the computer screen. Ardala's subconscious mind was always aware of the screen. Certain names and phrases set off alarms in her mind, and she had learned to notice the smallest, most convoluted references to them. "Hold!" she ordered, and the screen stopped rolling.

Sandwiched between two large paragraphs delineating the personnel assignments of the Venusian fleet was a short notice concerning a derelict spacecraft picked up by a salvage team out of Mercury. The specifications on the craft were familiar, and Ardala's sleepy cat eyes opened with interest. "Give me further data on notation eight-one-seven-A-three-two-four-five-six-oh-four."

The computer screen went blank as the system extracted the base number from the notation and backtracked it to the input source. "INPUT SOURCE BITS AND PIECES, INC., RAM SUBSIDIARY BASED IN APHRODITE, VENUS. SHIP FOUND DERELICT, NO ONE ABOARD, POWER BLOCK EXPLODED, INTERIOR STRIPPED," read the screen.

"Inform Bits and Pieces there is a thousand credits in it for them if they come across information on Raj and Icarus."

"AFFIRMATIVE," read the computer screen. Ardala did not like mechanical back talk, so her computer made most of its comments visually.

She sat back in her chair as the screen resumed its incessant flow of data. She had sent Raj and Icarus on a mission—one they had failed. Superficially, the report on their ship looked like a pirate attack, but Ardala was suspicious. Her genetically altered pleasure gennies were her own creations, superbly crafted to be slaves to her pleasure. She was intimately aware of their psychological attitudes. It was possible they had run rather than face the ultimate rejection of failure to satisfy their mistress.

"Computer, you will be alert for any information relating to this incident and all activity in the immediate area. I want to know what ships had trajectories plotted through that sector."

"AFFIRMATIVE. HOWEVER, SUCH DATA WILL NOT IN-

CLUDE ILLICIT FLIGHT PLANS," answered the computer.

"I have other ways of checking that," murmured Ardala, her head pillowed against the back of the chair so her glossy, dark hair spread out over the buttery red surface like a patch of night. Her tilted cat eyes narrowed as she considered her contacts.

○ ○ ○ ○ ○

Simund Holzerhein.dos stomped through the delicate network of the RAM main computer's Tactical Air Command center in long strides. He was angry. His carefully planned strategy for the clearing and subsequent redevelopment of Earth had sustained a blow. He was not used to being thwarted, especially from within. He had come to the conclusion he was not alone in the maw of RAM main. Some alien presence had attacked him, breaking his communications with the detachment he had sent to Earth.

He began to wonder if the whining complaints he had been receiving from RAM main over a series of minor disruptions were an indication of the intruder's whereabouts. Once main was fully operational, he would have it correlate the incidents, plotting their occurrences in chronological order. At present, main was still coping with its downed power modules. Half of the burned-out capsules had been replaced, and Holzerhein had communications and weapons systems at his disposal, but it would be some time before main was up to full power. Meanwhile, Holzerhein had to safeguard his position while managing a war. It was insufferable to face attack in one's own home. He felt invaded, soiled.

But he had foiled his opponent's attempt to disengage RAM forces from Earth. He had placed Cornelius Kane in charge of his forces, confident the man would act on his own initiative should the situation warrant it. Holzerhein smiled. Knowing Kane, he would probably act on his own initiative anyway. Holzerhein had reviewed Kane's plans and been pleased with their daring. The decision to hit the Venusian fleet as it cleared its home planet had particularly pleased him. It was an aggressive maneuver that would turn psychological tables, putting Venus, the cavalry, on the defensive and at a disadvantage. Even now, Kane led them like sheep to the jaws of RAM's main fleet. Holzerhein checked Kane's status. He was proceeding as planned, on course toward Mars.

Holzerhein turned his attention to Earth. The previous disruption of communications had given Earth a reprieve, allowing NEO to strike the RAM detachment hard while it floundered for orders. They were still able to carry out their original directives, blasting the planet clean of habitation, but now their strikes were equally distributed between destruction and fending off ever-escalating fighter strikes.

So far, NEO had spent most of its energy on the RAM Stingers sweeping the surface of the planet. They had managed to disable and destroy three battlers while the communications block persisted. Once the lines were repaired, they had abandoned the larger prey in favor of smaller adversaries. Losses were not devastating, but they continued to be steady, with a gradual rise in the incidence of strikes.

Holzerhein did not like it. Were it not for the approaching Venusian fleet, he would have ordered Kane's Kraits in, relying on their superior speed and stealth capabilities to match the stolen Kraits in NEO's hands. Those ships! The thought of them made Holzerhein's circuits cross. Stolen from RAM's experimental station, they were the one thing that allowed NEO to survive. Most of RAM's ships were inferior to the experimental model, and there had been no time to produce more than a detachment to match NEO's. In Kane's hands, that detachment was becoming a honed unit, but until the coming conflict was in RAM's hands, they could not be spared to clean up the dregs of a rebel force on Earth.

Holzerhein punched into the communications channel to the battler *Acidalia*.

"Sir!" responded the communications officer of the detachment's flagship.

"Captain Eolius," came Holzerhein's voice.

"At once, sir!" responded the technician.

"I am honored, Chairman," said *Acidalia*'s captain.

"I have before me facts and figures concerning the Terran assault. I am beginning to be concerned," said Holzerhein smoothly.

"Operations are proceeding, sir. However, I will not deny they have slowed down."

"That would be foolish," agreed Holzerhein, "since I have complete read-outs of all activities. I submit your efficiency is being cut by one factor. Eliminate that factor, and you will have a clean field."

"Your resources are much superior to mine, sir," responded Magan Eolius. "What is this factor?"

Pausing for dramatic effect, Holzerhein let the man's question swim in silence. His words, when they did come, dropped like stones. "The factor in question is . . . Captain Buck Rogers."

Chapter 4

Flames. Red-gold particles of fire suspended in a billowing cloud of orange smoke, a cloud with an evil black lining. An eruption, a burst of white-gold ignited fuel, and the cloud boiled out beyond its burned-out edges. Buck Rogers flew through the stultifying heat of the explosion. For him, it did not exist. His supersonic spacecraft could handle the friction of escaping atmosphere. The death of a Terrine heliplane was nothing to his craft's armored surface.

Even the visual limitations of the explosion were negated by the Krait's sophisticated sensors. They sliced through it, radar, sonar, and infrared providing an accurate course trajectory. These were the same advanced ships Kane's detachment was flying. NEO had altered their color and markings, but otherwise the ships were a match for RAM's. They, too, had speed and maneuverability superior to anything else in the air. Their advanced stealth capabilites made them mechanically invisible. They were armed to the teeth, their lasers capable of firing forty percent longer than a Stinger's, due to advances in fuel efficiency. They were hot spacecraft, and the NEO pilots flew them like comets.

"Close call." Doolittle's voice sounded in Buck's ear.

"That little bonfire?" Buck answered.

"That little bonfire was almost you."

Buck chuckled. His spirits were high. "What's the matter, Doolittle, don't you trust your own technology? I let that gyro loose in plenty of time."

"You flew through that blast for the fun of it." Doolittle's voice carried conviction.

"'Fraid so," answered Buck lightly. "Bogies at two o'clock!"

The two Kraits climbed into the Earth's upper atmosphere in a power drive calculated to outdistance the flight of RAM fighters sailing out of a cloud bank. Unfortunately, they had considerable distance to make up, and the Stingers closed on them as Buck and Doolittle sent their ships toward space. In the course of conflict, the RAM detachment had learned they were no match for the Kraits. They had given up using their lasers, unless they literally stumbled over one of the experimental vessels. Instead, the two lead ships fired gyros, trusting to the shells' programmed directional systems to contact the enemy.

"Gyros on target," said Doolittle conversationally.

"I see 'em," responded Buck.

The mini-missiles blipped across his tracking screen, throwing a blinking red light on the clear plasti screen of Buck's flight helmet. A half-smile gave his stalwart face a devil-may-care touch, deepening the laugh lines around his mouth. He was clean shaven, the planes of his face hard in the red twilight, muscles popping along his jaw. His blue eyes were narrowed, serious, as they checked the instrumentation. "They're closing," Buck commented.

"Split?" inquired Doolittle.

"Negative, Eagle Three. Stay with me."

Gyro shells had speed. They closed on the Kraits, homing in on the fighters' tails with the tenacity of bloodhounds on the scent of escaped criminals.

"Chaff," said Buck, and the ships emitted puffs of disorienting sparkles. The leading gyro flew into the twinkling mist. Its tracking system was immediately scrambled, and the shell fell off its previous trajectory. By the time it was abreast of Buck, it was kilometers from his starboard wing. It exploded harmlessly. The other shell continued to track Doolittle.

"Let's try it again," said Buck, as the second shell gained on them.

"No time," said Doolittle. "We're coming up on a battler."

His words were still ringing in Buck's flight helmet when the RAM vessel fired its forward laser cannon. The shot fell far short, but served to deter Buck and Doolittle from their course. They veered to port, intent on evading the ship's powerful guns, and found themselves flying down the throats of their pursuers. The RAM Stingers bunched, then drove forward with an extra kick of speed, knowing the opportunity for a close shot would not be repeated.

"They've kicked in their boosters! Course heading?" asked Doolittle.

"Stay on course," replied Buck.

"Why do I think this is another wild chance?" asked his wingman.

" 'Cause it is," replied Buck laconically.

The gyro shell had dutifully made the turn with them and was now nibbling at Doolittle's tail. "Rebel One, I've got a bite."

"Hold on," replied Buck. "Prepare for thruster-assisted power climb."

"I copy," answered Doolittle.

"On my order." The Stingers were almost in their laps before Buck snapped, "Now!"

The two Kraits shot abruptly upward, streaks of blue lightning against the darkness of space. The gyro shell, seconds behind them, was not quick enough. Its own ships overflew it, and the shell detonated in the center of the flight, its explosion blinding. By the time the Stingers had recovered their equilibrium, the NEO ships were gone.

"Let's get back to work," said Buck.

He and Doolittle headed back into Earth's atmosphere, alert for RAM or the Terrines. They were flying over the once busy metropolitan area of Dallas. The only structure still intact was the huge RAM Central metroplex, though on close inspection, the building showed signs of a terrorist attack. This particular metroplex was a pyramid, not a tetrahedron, but its top was sheared off to form a landing pad big enough to house a fleet of Terrine Dragonfly heliplanes. As they swept over the city, Buck could see the empty numbered slips, waiting for the return of their aircraft. He and Doolittle did not fire on the metroplex.

NEO intelligence stated that RAM had moved all its remaining personnel on Earth into the metroplexes. Bombing them would kill hundreds of innocents in order to disable the Terrine guardposts. Surrounding the metroplex was a boulder field that had once been a thriving, if sleazy, city. RAM's relentless lasers had chopped it like chives. A smoky haze drifted across the chunks of concrete, rock, brick, and steel, occasionally puffing into jets of flame as the smoldering ground fire found fuel. It was hard to believe anyone could live in that wasteland.

But there remained scattered survivors, grim with purpose. They were not fools. They did not expect to outlive the devastation, but they intended to make RAM pay dearly for its bread. By day, by night, with infinite patience, they planned and executed raids directed at the Terrine helipads and RAM's metroplex. Buck knew such raids accounted for the discoloration of the golden reflective panels that covered the Dallas metroplex. Small gyros would generate enough damage to scorch them.

On the outskirts of the city, the land sloped away in barren waves sculpted by the wind. Sparse tufts of grass tried vainly to hold the shifting dust. Occasionally, a twisted juniper clung to the unstable surface.

"Rebel One, this is Base. Come in." Beowulf cut into Buck's thoughts.

"This is Rebel One. Go ahead, Base."

"Buck, we've picked up a response to Kane on communications. He's on a collision trajectory with the main body of the Martian fleet, and he's got all of Venus on his tail. Can you assist?"

"Negative, Base. We are barely holding our own."

"Buck, there's nothing that can stand against those Kraits. You know it, and I know it. Kane's got twenty of them behind him."

"Behind him?"

"Affirmative. He's flying his own vessel—and it seems to be keeping up with the Kraits."

"He probably dickered Warhead out of the Krait's advances as partial payment for his services," guessed Buck.

"Venus hasn't a chance against him." Beowulf's statement was flat.

Buck sighed. "This is one of those situations, isn't it?"

"Situations?" Beowulf was mystified.

"The devil and the deep blue sea," retorted Buck. "No matter what choice we make, it doesn't look good. We've got to figure something."

"Good luck." Beowulf did not sound hopeful.

"Barney!" said Buck.

There was a long pause while his transmission was relayed to the other side of the planet. Finally, Black Barney's thunderous tones sounded on the communications link. "Mmmmmr," he said.

"How're you doing?" asked Buck.

"Two," replied the space pirate succinctly.

Buck knew the pirate well enough to interpret. Barney's men had shot down two ships in the last run. "Think the Guild can hold the planet?"

Again there was silence on the communications link as Barney considered the matter. "Clear sailing," he said finally. "Take some time."

Buck considered. His only course of action seemed to be in a division of NEO's forces. He and the flight of Kraits would engage Kane's forces, tying them up so Venus could deal with the main body of the RAM fleet.

Meanwhile, the Rogues' Guild would continue to harry
the RAM forces on Earth. Buck ticked off the numbers of
the pirate fraternity. They were outnumbered three to
one, but these were odds the Guild generally favored.

"We've got to do more than maintain a status quo,"
said Buck.

"Burn 'em," agreed Barney. His description was blood-
thirsty but accurate.

"Right. We've got to evict them."

"We can do it," insisted Barney. "Unless they get
help."

"They won't," replied Buck. "That's the whole idea."

Barney ground his teeth slowly. It was a habit that
aided his mental processes. "When?" he asked.

"In precisely . . . point two-six minutes," replied Buck,
consulting his timer.

"Copy," grunted Barney.

"Go to Progression C. That should give you the coordinates for blanketing the planet. As of . . . now, terminate contact with the enemy. Pull up and regroup
according to pattern."

"Urrr," replied the pirate. The rumbling vibrations of
his voice played havoc with a communications link.

"Rebel Two, come in," Buck called.

"This is Rebel Two," replied Wilma Deering.

"Eagle Leader, come in," said Buck.

"Eagle Leader reporting, sir." Washington's answer
tripped over Buck's words.

"We are pulling out," said Buck. "At Base's request."

"Kane?" asked Wilma.

"You guessed it," responded Buck.

"Rendezvous?" asked Washington.

"Point one off Salvation," said Buck, referring to the
space-going garbage dump that was also NEO's headquarters.

"Approximate ETA, five minutes," said Wilma.

"We'll beat that," said Washington.

Buck set his course, Doolittle hugging his left wing as
if it were a security blanket. Wilma's instant recognition of the danger Kane represented set off sparks in

Buck's mind. Col. Wilma Deering was not only NEO's top pilot next to him, she was a stunningly beautiful woman who had once flown at Killer Kane's side. Kane had recently saved her life. Though their paths diverged, Buck was aware of an unspoken attachment between them, a fragile thread he dared not violate despite his growing fondness for Wilma. Wilma was all NEO, all soldier, and Buck knew she would face Kane fearlessly in battle. She respected Buck's ability, if not his position.

Kane was a stumbling block Buck did not know how to remove. In the end, Wilma's feelings were her own concern. He could not mold or alter them, but the knowledge did not make his position easier. He thought warmly of her spunky refusal to accept the world RAM offered her—a world in which her beauty would open doors. Like him, she insisted on doing things the hard way, insisted on her right to be wrong. They were both mavericks. They had stubborn independence in common, as well as a love of adventure.

"Stingers at twelve o'clock," said Doolittle.

"We'll lose 'em," said Buck. "We don't want them tagging along."

"We're not within visual range," returned Doolittle. "We should be safe."

"Let's put a couple of satellites between them and us." Buck sent his ship to starboard, cut around the bristling sphere of a communications satellite, and slipped back to his previous heading. Doolittle clung to him.

"Well, sir, this is it," said Doolittle.

"Cold feet?" inquired Buck lightly.

"No way." Though Buck could not see it, Doolittle was shaking his head in support of his words. "I've got nothing to lose—no family, no one looking to me."

"That's where you're wrong," Buck said softly. "You've got family, Doolittle. We all have. We've got each other. That's why we're here."

The silence at the other end of the channel was painful.

"This is the big one," Buck continued. "If we lose, we

condemn humanity to a subjection it will take years to overcome. We have to win. No options."

"No options," repeated Doolittle. "No holds barred. Flat out. No reserves."

"You've got it," said Buck.

"No, sir, you have. I'll just stick to your wing."

"Fair enough," replied Buck.

Chapter 5

The eight NEO fighters streaked away from their home base toward the planet Mars. NEO had been flying fewer than half its fighters at once, running the others through exhaustive maintenance checks and refueling so there would never be a break in their assault. As Buck cleared the final vestiges of Earth's atmosphere, his sensors picked up a flight of spacecraft closing on the red planet, a field so numerous they could not all be contained on his sensor screen.

"Wow," said Doolittle slowly.

"Venus doesn't play around, does she?" answered Buck. The display set out before him was awesome.

"Where are the Martians?" asked Doolittle.

"Intelligence says they're lying off the far side of the planet." Buck studied the patterns on his sensor screen. The flight was in front of him, placing Kane's twenty Kraits between Venus and the as-yet-uncounted Martian forces. He opened a communications channel on the Venusian frequency. "*Pennant*, this is Rogers. We are free to assist. I say again, we are free to assist."

"Captain, this is Al Marakesh, commander of the fleet."

Marakesh's striking face flashed through Buck's mind. They had met briefly on Venus. Marakesh was not a man to forget. "Rogers here," he replied.

"What have you?" questioned the Venusian.

"Eight Krait fighters. We've got about half our fuel left."

"Not enough." Marakesh's words were soft. He was speaking to himself, thinking out loud. "You won't be able to reach Kane without getting in our way. I estimate we should contact the main body of the Martian fleet as soon as we clear the planet. Look for an opening."

"Negative, *Pennant*. I've got another idea. Mars will try to use her size against us. Let's see if we can't break that up a bit."

"What do you propose?" asked Marakesh.

"A little blackmail," said Buck.

"Say again?" Marakesh sounded puzzled.

"Don't worry about it, Commander. We'll be out of your hair."

"Captain Rogers . . ."

Buck did not answer the Venusian's summons. Instead he led his troops away from the approaching ships, angling toward the opposite side of Mars. In spite of extensive terraforming, the red planet was still worthy of its name. It whirled in space, a clouded orb that was both a tribute to human technological cunning and a symbol of its most narrow oppression. Buck remembered the Martian romances he had read as a boy in the twentieth century, tales of derring-do considered to be the most fantastic fabrications by his sensible parents. He smiled a crooked grin. His present circumstances made those stories look like the driest history.

"Rebel One, this is Rebel Two. Did I hear you say something about an idea?" Wilma was suspicious. Buck's intuitive flashes were always dangerous.

"Affirmative, Rebel Two. First we have to do a little reconnaissance. Base run," he said.

"Yes, Buck?" Huer.dos answered the summons. A computer-encoded personality, he was Buck's personal encyclopedia of the twenty-fifth century, programmed to aid and safeguard his charge. The latter had turned out to be a full-time job, for Buck had enemies. Early in their relationship, Huer discovered computer-based assassins programmed to destroy Buck. So far, he had managed to prevent them from accomplishing their directives.

"Doc, let's see what Mars has. Bounce a picture off a couple of satellites."

"I can give you the data we've collected here at base faster."

"Thanks, Doc, but no. I want to see their deployment from the perspective of our present heading."

"I copy," replied Huer, mystified. Rogers was often capricious by Huer's logical standards, but it was not his place to thwart his charge's whim.

Buck's sensor screen winked, and the pattern of vessels changed. The Venusian fleet was huge, but Mars had mobilized every piece of armed spacecraft it could find. Huer provided Buck with a sharply foreshortened view of the armada. It stretched out toward the asteroid belt in waves. Buck whistled.

"Um, yes," agreed Huer.

"Course heading one-five-zero-mark-three," instructed Buck.

The NEO flight made yet another arc, curving away from the edge of the planet.

"I didn't know there were that many ships in the system," said Washington. He sounded daunted.

"'The bigger they are, the harder they fall'," quoted Buck grimly. "We're going to have to out-think them. We're going to have to pick them off one by one, but fast, or Venus won't have a chance. And, for the time being, we have to stay away from Kane."

"What? We've got the only ships capable of taking him on! He'll cut Venus to shreds," said Wilma.

"How about that, Doc?" Buck was seeking back-up for his hunches.

"The Krait's superior speed and stealth are most effective in hit-and-run raids," the compugennie replied. "If Venus can manage to bottle him up—and once they're in close enough quarters for visual, it can do it—the Krait's advantages will be cut in half."

"*Pennant*, come in!" commanded Buck. "This is Rebel One."

"This is *Pennant*, Rebel One." Marakesh's voice was abstracted. No doubt his attention was on the forces in front of him.

"Can you keep Kane between you and the armada?" Buck asked. "It'll give us time to do some damage. I am also informed by computer that the Krait's effectiveness will be severely hampered in close quarters."

"Walk close to the rear of the kraken, and he can't deliver a kick." Marakesh considered the neat wedge in front of him. "We'll do our best, Captain."

"And we'll do our best to break up the fleet."

"Good hunting," said Marakesh.

"Well?" asked Wilma. "What do you have in mind?"

Buck responded with a single word. "Pavonis."

Though he could not see it, Wilma was smiling behind her clear plasti face guard. Pavonis was Mars's most brilliant piece of technology. It was a space elevator, a permanent link between the planet surface and space. With the construction of the elevator, it was no longer necessary to launch goods into orbit. Shuttles were expensive and slow compared to the elevator.

The Mars-Pavonis Elevator was a space bridge running between the extinct volcano of Pavonis and an orbiting satellite of the same name. The satellite was a city in itself, with at least twenty levels habitable by humans. Each level was a self-contained suburb. One of the largest trading centers on Mars, it was a distribution complex for native exports and extra-Martian imports. Its efficiency had added immeasurably to RAM's profit margin.

Unlike Hauberk station, Pavonis had no military standing. It carried a complement of defensive weapons, relying on shielding and chaff guns to protect its autonomy. As a trading outpost and space dock, it came under the jurisdiction of the local police. One-man launches patrolled its perimeter, alert for trouble. Should the occasion arise, local authorities requested military assistance. Mars's military machine being what it was, help was no more than a few minutes away.

Huer, at Buck's request, was relaying these facts as fast as he could. Buck interrupted the stream of words to address his cohorts. "We're going to have to hit hard and fast," he said. "Their sensors won't see us coming, but once we're within visual range, their defenses are going to negate a lot of our fire. Get in, give them as big a dose of your lasers as you can, and get out. We'll hit from two sides. Rebel Two, take the flank."

"I copy, Rebel One."

Wilma, with Revere on her wing and Washington and Earhart ranged behind her, shot away from Buck and his men. Both flights dove toward the thin Martian atmosphere, their headings on an intersect course with Pavonis.

"There it is," said Buck. Pavonis appeared on his sensors, and the sophisticated systems began to play technological read-outs across his screen. As he drew nearer to his target, Pavonis grew in his viewport from a silver flash to a vast orbiting world, platform levels hung together by cables and struts. Lights twinkled over the satellite. Soon it filled the screen.

"Final approach," said Buck. "Remember, hit the elevator. Leave the satellite unless there's resistance."

A police launch skittered out of their way as they powered for the surface, cutting under the satellite, toward the flexible tube of the space elevator. Buck punched his lasers, more for effect than anything else, for he did not want to alter his trajectory and the launch was now out of range. Clouds of green chaff exploded from the projecting launch capsules located at the edges of the satellite. The end of every strut ended in one of these guns.

"That launch got through," commented Doolittle.

"Um hm," agreed Buck.

Chaos reigned in the Pavonis observation deck. When

the police launch reported the presence of NEO space-craft, the supervisor, Charles Emich, had been unbeliev-ing. "They would not dare!" he said.

"Why not?" asked a supervisor. "They dared to kid-nap our board of directors."

Emich was shaken, but he recovered quickly. "Chaff!" he ordered. "Now!"

"Locations?" asked a technician.

"All of them," said Emich grimly.

"Sir, their course puts them on a parallel with the ele-vator itself. "Do you think they'll try to cut it?" There was fear in the technician's voice. He had grown up on Pavonis, secure in the knowledge that the satellite was firmly anchored to the mother planet by means of the el-evator, which ran like a cable between the two. The thought of losing that anchor terrified him. Pavonis drifting around the planet in a free orbit was a child-hood nightmare.

"Wouldn't you?" asked Emich. "Launch spirals at thirty-second intervals."

"Yes, sir."

Flying chaff bombs, known as spirals, were developed especially for the elevator's protection. Launched from the lower levels of the satellite, they dove to the ground, ringing the elevator in a spiral trajectory, spewing chaff in their wake.

Buck set his lasers into the elevator's shields as the first spiral was launched. The lasers splintered against the shields, but they drained power until the trail of em-erald chaff cut through them. The lasers sank into the spirals, dissipating. Buck changed his coordinates, again bringing his guns to bear on the body of the eleva-tor. The other members of the team did the same.

"Gnats, twelve o'clock high," said Earhart. Her throaty alto voice made Buck check his sensors.

"They're crazy," he said. Eight vessels emerged from the cloud of chaff. Flying in a tight diamond formation, they were coming straight for the NEO ships. "Are those what I think they are, Doc?" Buck asked.

"I am not a mind-reader," Huer commented mildly,

"however, the approaching vessels are police launches."

"They haven't got a chance against our guns."

"Affirmative," replied Huer.

"Can you get a weapons read-out?"

"Yes. They are armed with microlasers, of no consequence against Krait's shields."

Buck growled low in his throat. The plucky flight touched him. He had no stomach for slaughter. "Doc, by now Pavonis should have contacted the fleet. Can you see what's happening over there?"

Huer bounced a sensor scan off a communications satellite and beheld Ragnarok. The Venusian and Martian fleets were engaged, their lines flattening into a roiling shore of conflict. He scanned the action and found five Martian cruisers pulling away from the conflict.

"That's it!" said Buck when Huer reported his findings. "We've drawn a few out. Rebel Two, what is your fuel status?"

"Down to a quarter," Wilma replied.

"Break off," ordered Buck. "Doc, plot a trajectory for the approaching craft and give Wilma coordinates that'll place her on the opposite side of the station from them. Eagle Eight, take your wingman and join Rebel Two. Doolittle and I are going to be bait."

The six ships pulled out, heading for the position Huer plotted. "That chaff will keep the station from spotting us," said Wilma. "Their sensors can't see through it any better than ours can. But, just in case, let's make sure. Deploy chaff at one-minute intervals, starting . . . now!"

Buck smiled as he caught Wilma's directions. The NEO ships would hide behind the cloud cover, then jump the unsuspecting RAM cruisers with everything they had. "Rebel Two, we will bring the bogies past the satellite on course heading zero-zero-two-one. Set your gyros for those coordinates. Huer will give you the vessel class."

"I copy, Rebel One."

Buck and Doolittle continued to fire into the Pavonis umbilical cord as the RAM cruisers swept around the curve of their homeland like avenging demons.

Chapter 6

"Here they come!" said Buck. "Disengage."

He fired a parting shot at Pavonis and pulled his ship's nose up, his lasers sinking harmlessly into the protective static chaff. Doolittle followed, still glued to his left wing, as the five RAM cruisers closed on them. Buck sent his ship straight up. The space elevator was between him and the approaching ships. They sighted him before he reached the bulk of the satellite and sent off shooting streaks of laser fire. Weakened by Pavonis's chaff blanket, the fire slid off the NEO pilot's shields like butter.

"Those guys are crazy," said a cruiser pilot. "Hitting Pavonis with two fighters? They might as well try to pick a computer lock with their teeth."

"Stow the unnecessary chatter, A-Twelve." The RAM flight leader was in no mood for colorful speculation. "Pattern four-five."

The RAM cruisers spread out, their flight paths angling away from each other. This fan-shaped trajectory would place them in a position to cover most of the

Pavonis satellite. Providing they did not double back, the NEO ships could not escape the RAM lasers. The RAM cruisers swept past the satellite's layer cake construction, intent on clearing the structure. Their sensors had identified the two fighters as Krait experimental models, and they were no match for the smaller ships' speed. If they could stay within laser range . . . The flight leader's thoughts switched from theory to fact as the two NEO ships shot free of the satellite's shielding mass.

"Target," he ordered. "Twelve, you and six take the wing. The rest of us will fire on the leader. Now!"

Deadly filaments of white shot from the bows of the five ships, reaching through space at the speed of light. They struck Buck and Doolittle aft.

"Let's confuse 'em," said Buck. He dropped a load of chaff behind the ship, and the enemy lasers dissipated. Doolittle did the same.

The enemy was not to be deterred. The five cruisers stuck doggedly to the two Kraits, their lasers continuing to pound at them.

"Chaff?" asked Doolittle.

"Nope," said Buck. "Accelerate to point three."

Doolittle smiled as he eased up on his fighter and it shot forward, putting a slim margin between the lasers and the rear shields. They were leading the cruisers down the garden path.

From the slowly dissipating clouds of emerald chaff surrounding Pavonis, six Krait fighters slipped into space, seeking out the RAM cruisers. Their tracking computers matched the cruisers' trajectories, and the Kraits moved into position behind them. The RAM ships were intent upon Buck and Doolittle. The other six Kraits closed on the cruisers, their stealth systems keeping the cruisers' sensors in the dark.

"Coming up on rendezvous coordinates," said Buck. His blue eyes twinkled.

"Check, boss," said Doolittle. There was laughter in his voice.

"Cut power one-third," said Buck. "Go to thrusters now!"

The two NEO ships slowed, and the cruisers closed on them. Buck knew the cruiser pilots were exulting, their lasers creeping up on their quarry. The burst of his docking thrusters sent the Krait's nose up, then it flipped over backward, at the same time rolling upright. Doolittle, hugging Buck's wing, laughed out loud as the cruisers pulled up short.

"Surprise, surprise," said Buck, punching his lasers.

Simultaneously, Wilma's flight hit the cruisers from behind. They were being bombarded from two sides, their shields drained. The heavy cylindrical craft shuddered under the impact.

"Rebel Two, this is Rebel One. We've got two of 'em in a space lock."

"We are launching gyros," replied Wilma.

She continued to fire, her lasers punching at the enemy's shields, while gyro shells streaked toward the RAM ships. The gyros struck, boring momentary holes in the cruiser's shields. On top of the gyro explosion, the Kraits sent their lasers into those holes, hungry white tongues licking out the enemy's marrow.

It was tricky work, requiring perfect timing, and the RAM ships were not cooperating. Two of them were held between enemy lasers in a fat ship sandwich. They tried to pull away, but the Kraits stayed with them effortlessly. The other three vessels were facing fire from the rear only. If they could pull away, they might break their fellows free. The two ships on the outer edges of the formation veered outward, away from the conflict. Like darting insects, the Kraits leaped to their sides, sending pounding bursts of laser fire into the sides of the vessels.

RAM's A-Leader swore. He knew he could not outdistance the fighters. His ship was heavier, better armored, and carried more fire power, but he was not in a position to use his assets. He hit his fuel feed, expelling a blast of flaming gas into the Kraits' faces. His opponents were not impressed by histrionics. They continued to pound at the larger ships.

A-Leader, his dark face contorted in a frown of concentration, asked his sensors to measure the laser path from the Krait to his ship. The answer eased his frustration. They were close. Too close. Without warning, he pushed his lower docking thrusters home, sending his ship in a back flip which matched Buck's earlier display, but he never let up on the thrusters. He was intent on bringing his vessel down on the Krait, smashing it into space dust. He was confident his heavier vessel, with its thick shielding, would sustain minor damage. It was a good plan.

Unfortunately, it did not work. The cruiser's acrobatics took Washington by surprise. He saw the heavy red hull descending on him like the hammer of hell, and he reacted. He sent the Krait down at full power, adding to that the extra kick of the thrusters. It jumped forward like a startled hare, one huge leap taking it beyond the cruiser's range. "This's getting nasty," he muttered.

A-Leader was free. He eased his craft out of its spin and sent it forward, escaping the danger of the closely packed craft just in time.

Wilma had burned through her target's shields, striking the fuel supply. A-Twelve's tail went up like a torch. The severed prow rolled away from the explosion, striking its starboard companion. Instinctively, the pilot pulled away from the derelict. This lifted his vessel like a rearing horse. Buck put two gyro shells into its belly while Doolittle followed up with his lasers. The ship exploded internally as if it had ruptured an organ.

"We've got two!" said Wilma.

"Rebel Two, this is Eagle Leader. I could use some help."

Washington was distancing his pursuer, but the RAM cruiser's lasers were playing havoc with his shields. A-Leader stuck grimly to him, knowing he had seconds to burn the smaller craft before it got away.

"Sunburned?" asked Wilma lightly.

"Getting there," replied Washington.

"Crossfire, Yaeger," said Wilma. "Let's get him."

The two Kraits converged on the larger ship, prow and wing guns blazing. Meanwhile, Buck, Doolittle, and Earhart had accounted for another of the cruisers, punching through the shields at the ship's nose. The pilot never knew what hit him. His ship, more intact than the two previous casualties, rolled into A-Six as it tried to escape the field. A-Six's shields were damaged, the rear port shield wavering, and its pilot knew if he did not get clear, he would not survive the conflict. When the other cruiser struck his weakened shields, his electrical systems died. Immediately the emergency light winked on, bathing the cockpit in a red glow. A-Six's pilot caught the oxygen mask that dangled in front of him and pressed it to his face. He breathed deeply, then opened his communications channel. "This is RAM A-Six," he said. "I am disabled. I say again, I am disabled. I concede."

"Acknowledged, RAM A-Six. Now what the hell," murmured Buck to himself, "am I going to do with a prisoner?"

"Call pickup."

Buck jumped in his seat. "Doc, don't sneak up on me like that. You scared me out of six years."

"You have them to spare," said Huer. "I was merely responding to your question."

"Oh. You said call pickup."

"Affirmative," replied Huer. "We don't have the personnel to spare, but Venus brought along a troop of camp followers, including a few who are only too happy to transport prisoners to prearranged holding facilities if they can salvage enemy vessels."

"Barney should be here," said Buck. "OK, Doc, see to it, will you?" To the enemy pilot, he said, "Sit tight. You'll be picked up."

"I copy," responded the RAM captain.

A-Leader was not so easily overcome. He continued to struggle, trying to drag his ship clear of the three fighters, for Washington had cleared his lasers and turned. His shields fluctuating, the RAM pilot knew there was no time left. "RAM fleet, this is A-Leader. Request assistance. I say again, request assistance. Have lost four ships. My shields are going. Eight Kraits in pursuit."

Buck caught the end of the transmission. "That's it!" he called. "Leave him, and let's get out of here."

Wilma checked her fuel gauge with a start. "Right you are," she said.

"Return to base," instructed Buck, and the Kraits left their floundering enemies, closing into formation like a flock of birds heading home. Five more minutes of the kind of high-powered combat they had been practicing, and their fuel would have reached the critical point. As it was, they could afford no distractions on their way back to Salvation.

"Not a bad piece of work," Buck commented. "If we can keep pulling ships away from the main fleet, we may have a chance.

"Now you tell me," said Wilma.

○ ○ ○ ○ ○

The *Acidalia* hovered at the edge of Earth's atmosphere. A typical RAM battler, it was acres long and kilometers wide, a floating platform sixteen layers deep, with expandable space docks and enough artillery to flatten a planet. It was a portable air base, commanding its own complement of fighters, able to maintain itself in both life-support and fuel for weeks, even months, of combat. By reason of the loss of other vessels, it had become the flagship for the RAM fleet of Earth.

It was also a prison. Deep in the center of its twelfth level, in a converted cargo hold, were the members of Earth's Planetary Congress. They were housed with the barest niceties. Sanitary facilities were the only areas of privacy. Otherwise, the delegates were forced to live with each other. If RAM thought this a punishment, it was wrong. It was a crucible from which the meanest of them would emerge changed. They were at a total disadvantage. They had no weapons, no way of maintaining themselves. RAM could terminate their lives simply by sealing the hold and cutting off their air supply. Whether they personally desired intimate knowledge of one another, it was forced upon them. They had a choice. They could live with each other and survive, or they could fight, destroying themselves from within.

In the beginning, they had stubbornly refused to give their captors the satisfaction of internal strife. Martians—and that meant RAM—believed themselves genetically superior to all other beings in the solar system. Martians looked down their slender noses at genetically intact humans and pulled his ship's nose up and regarded gene-teched human adaptations as beasts. The NEO delegates were determined not to act like beasts, thereby cheating their captors of pleasure, and to keep the righteous conviction that their opinions were justified.

They cooperated. Superficially. And so RAM left them alone, enabling the Congress to get on with its business. In the perpetual twilight of the cargo lamps, they talked and pleaded and argued, hammering out rules for the planet Earth to live by. Painstakingly they tried to discover the causes behind despotism and circumvent them. Carefully they built a codicil of laws culled from the annals of every culture, trying to ensure justice.

They were aware of the futility of their attempts. They knew the gaps between the intent of a law and its application, between the form of a government and its effect. But still they worked, using every piece of knowledge anyone could remember to construct a format for justice, for peace, and for happiness.

There were conflicts that degenerated into screaming matches. There were moments of anger so extreme the air vibrated with it. But in spite of this, a feeling of unity was growing between the delegates. As men and women and gennies from different parts of the world began to understand the problems faced by their fellows, anger melted into empathy. There were insurmountable cultural differences, and the Congress tried to ensure that such differences were protected as long as they did not infringe upon the rights of others. It was a complex process. In the end, each culture was asked to give up a cherished belief in the name of humanity. In the end, each culture did.

As the new Terran government went through its birth throes, a battle raged beyond it. The delegates had no knowledge of it, though no one was ignorant of the likelihood for war.

At the edge of the crowd, Andrew Jackson listened to the slow drone of voices, deliberating, voting. He was a tall man, almost as tall as a Martian. "This may all be in vain, you know," he said to his companion.

A dark woman clad in a sapphire sari, her head even with his shoulder, looked up at him. "I do not think so. It is true: At the end of this conflict Earth may no longer exist. But here, for a fleeting moment, we have created something worthwhile. We cannot impose our will on generations yet unborn. Each citizen must decide his or her own allegiance. But we can provide a guideline for independence as well as peace. Surely, this in itself is a good thing."

Jackson smiled down at her. "Better than the accomplishments of most," he agreed.

Chapter 7

The NEO computer system was now based on Salvation III, the orbiting garbage dump that housed the rebel space fleet. Since the capture of the Planetary Congress and the wholesale destruction of Earth, Salvation controlled the administration of NEO's assault forces. It was jumping with activity. Impulses flew along the circuit tracks, linking NEO's scattered forces with their home base. Only one small area was still, an isolated island of inactivity.

On the outskirts of the weapons section, a good three inches from any other circuit line, a computer isolation chamber enclosed a maelstrom of anger. The chamber was a nonconductive plasti barrier, wide enough and high enough to prevent even a boosted impulse from escaping. It was sealed, and only a discolored line on the computer board's surface indicated the circuit that had once led into it.

The chamber was a trap, a prison, and when its plasti gate slid shut, it ignited the flammable base beneath the temporary pathway, eradicating it. Held within this impersonal barricade was a dervish of outraged static. Romanov, a searcher program created by Masterlink, pulsed with indignation at the ruse that had trapped it. Masterlink called the searchers its children, and it had given Romanov its own anger toward Buck Rogers. Romanov had one directive: find Rogers, no matter what the cost, and destroy him.

It had followed false trails and chewed on fragmentary leads, all the while building a catalogue of data. Eventually that data took form, and Romanov realized it was facing a computer entity similar to its parent. Huer.dos was both a stumbling block in his search for Buck and a clue to the NEO pilot's whereabouts, for Huer was Buck's computer-generated nursemaid. Where Buck went, Huer would eventually follow. Romanov determined to follow Huer. Its dedication to the quest had landed it in prison.

Not, of course, on the up and up. Huer had cheated. He had cloned himself, a moronic facsimile that had decoyed Romanov into his isolation chamber and dissipated, leaving the searcher to its own bitter thoughts.

Romanov's prime directive still pulsed in its central core, but added to its determination to destroy Buck Rogers was a passionately bitter hatred of Huer.dos. Romanov wanted to devour Huer, absorbing his capabilities like a sponge and throwing the husk at Rogers's feet before absorbing him as well. Romanov's power level fluctuated, rising in bursts as it contemplated destruction.

Its frustration met no response, and the electrical storm subsided. It was faced with two options: discover a chink in NEO's security, or wait for its parent to seek it out. Romanov discarded the second option. It knew its parent well. Masterlink valued self-reliance in its children. It was more likely to initiate a new program than to risk a rescue. Romanov regarded the closed plasti gate, vowing to consider it incentive. Romanov intended to escape and to wreak its vengeance upon the perpetrator of its imprisonment: Huer.dos.

O O O O O

On the planet Mars, in the heart of the RAM main computer system, Masterlink reposed, correlating reports from its searchers, eavesdroppers, and assassins.

"ROMANOV HAS NOT REPORTED," stated Masterlink.

"I AM AWARE OF THAT," replied Karkov. He was irritated by the searcher's irresponsibility.

"YOUR SEARCHER IS NOT DEMONSTRATING PARENTAL PIETY," said Masterlink nastily.

"MY SEARCHER? SINCE WHEN ARE THE SEARCHERS MY EXCLUSIVE RESPONSIBILITY?"

"YOU PROGRAMMED THEM." Masterlink's reply was smug.

"WITH YOUR COOPERATION."

Masterlink changed the subject. "I THOUGHT YOU INCLUDED AN AUTOMATIC HOURLY REPORT IN THEIR SPECIFICATIONS," it said.

"I DID."

"THEN WHY HASN'T ROMANOV REPORTED?"

"HOW SHOULD I KNOW?" Karkov was in no mood for accusations. It was more concerned with NEO's chances in the present conflict.

"SLUFFING OFF."

The judgment inflamed Karkov. "OH? I DON'T SUPPOSE IT EVER OCCURRED TO YOU OUR SEARCHER COULD BE IN DANGER."

"IT IS A POSSIBILITY," Masterlink conceded.

"GIVEN THE REGULARITY OF ROMANOV'S PREVIOUS TRANSMISSIONS, IT IS LOGICAL TO RULE OUT ABERRANT BEHAVIOR."

Masterlink chuckled. "I LIKE ABERRANT BEHAVIOR."

"I AM AWARE OF YOUR PREDILECTION FOR THE BIZARRE," returned Karkov, "BUT FOR THE MOMENT, PAY ATTENTION! THERE ARE TWO OTHER POSSIBILITIES. EITHER ROMANOV IS IN DANGER AND PHYSICALLY UNABLE TO COMMUNICATE WITH US, OR IT IS SUFFERING A MALFUNCTION. EITHER OPTION PRESENTS PROBLEMS."

"WHY?" asked Masterlink. "WE'LL JUST PROGRAM ANOTHER SEARCHER AND SEND IT INTO THE NEO

COMPUTER SYSTEM."

"WILL WE? IT WAS HARD ENOUGH TO GET A COMPLEX PROGRAM LIKE A SEARCHER THROUGH ALL THOSE BLOCKS NEO USES TO GUARD ITS DATA BANKS, AND THAT WAS BEFORE THE OPEN DECLARATION OF WAR. IT WOULD TAKE US WEEKS OF PROBING TO SLIP ANOTHER SEARCHER IN."

"WHAT DO YOU SUGGEST?" asked Masterlink sarcastically. It did not enjoy being lectured.

"I SUGGEST WE SEND IN A FEW LINKAGES PROGRAMMED TO ADHERE TO ROMANOV'S CONFIGURATION. THEY'RE SIMPLE ENOUGH TO PASS THROUGH MOST OF NEO'S GATES WITHOUT BEING QUESTIONED."

Masterlink considered the proposal. "I MUST ADMIT THE SOUNDNESS OF YOUR LOGIC," it admitted after a time. "WE WILL DO AS YOU SUGGEST. HOWEVER, I QUESTION THE ADVISABILITY OF RESTORING ROMANOV—SHOULD IT BE OUT OF ACTION—AT THE PRESENT TIME. I AM LOATH TO ADMIT IT, BUT, FOR THE PRESENT, BUCK ROGERS SEEMS TO BE THE ONE FACTOR BETWEEN EARTH AND CHAOS. NEO RALLIES BEHIND HIM AS IF HE WERE ITS FLAG. IF HE WERE REMOVED, I SUSPECT RAM WOULD FIND LITTLE OPPOSITION IN ITS ASSAULT ON EARTH."

Karkov was silent. Masterlink's thoughts were sound. It went against every emotion in its matrix to admit it, but Rogers was a major factor in preventing RAM from destroying the mother planet. Karkov could not deny it, no matter how much it hated the resurrected hero. "YOU HAVE A POINT," it said finally. "WE MUST WAIT UNTIL THE OUTCOME OF THE PRESENT CONFLICT IS CLEAR. SHOULD NEO FALL, WE LOSE NOTHING BY FREEING ROMANOV AND ALLOWING HIM TO DESTROY CAPTAIN ROGERS. SHOULD NEO WIN, WE MUST ALLOW IT TO CONSOLIDATE ITS POSITIONS ON EARTH, ENCOURAGE ITS AUTONOMY. IN THAT INSTANCE, ROGERS'S DEMISE MUST BE HANDLED WITH THE UTMOST SUBTLETY. HE MUST BE MADE INTO A MARTYR, A POLITICAL TOOL WE CAN TURN TO OUR PURPOSES."

"NO LINKAGES," concluded Masterlink.

"NO LINKAGES," agreed Karkov.

○ ○ ○ ○ ○

Icarus sat at a table covered with a dirty cloth in a dim corner of the public house. The atmosphere was hazy with the fumes of illicit substances, and the pounding beat of a much-used tape throbbed through the room. A narrow bar stretched across the back wall, spilled drinks and condensation from cold glasses marking it in wet splotches. At the end of the bar was a circular dais. A girl, clad in a bare minimum of sparkling bugle beads, danced there, her mechanical undulations slightly out of time with the music.

Icarus stared at her thick charms, displayed in bouncing frankness, and was revolted. In the depths of his heart he carried the image of Ardala. She was cruel, unfeeling, and vicious, but she was also a woman of such startling personal beauty and intellectual acumen that he found her opposite disgusting.

Icarus lifted his wine glass, then wrenched his eyes from its depths. It was all too easy to see Ardala's sensuous beauty in the liquor. He found it ironic she never allowed her creations alcohol, considering them too simple to handle its effects. Icarus took a healthy gulp of the red wine, letting its slow warmth ease his feelings. He banished Ardala's image by staring at the dancer.

Compared to his former mistress, she was graceless, but her face was not insensitive. True, her expression was flat—he would almost have said bored—but her features, upon consideration, were pleasing. She had a piquant, turned-up nose that might have been saucy and round blue eyes the color of the bluebird's back. Brown hair, kinky with chestnut highlights, fanned out around her face. Her mouth was a small but perfect pink rosebud.

The music ceased, and she left the dais, descending to the barroom's floor to hawk drinks to the customers. Icarus's eyes returned to his drink.

"Hi, there."

Startled, Icarus looked up. The girl's firm pink breasts, the nipples barely covered by sparkling pasties, were at his eye level. He blushed.

"Buy a lady a drink?" She did not seem disconcerted by his reaction. She slid into a chair opposite him.

Icarus recovered himself and indicated the order pad. She keyed in her choice, then propped her elbows on the table. "So," she said conversationally, "what are you doing on Cupid?"

Icarus swallowed wine, taking his time over it. He was unsure of his answer. He did not want to tell her he was haunting this den of vice in order to rub shoulders with known NEO sympathizers, and thereby pursue a contact with the Earth-based rebels. "Cupid?" he said. "I've been meaning to ask somebody about that name. It doesn't seem the thing for a space station."

"Cupid was Venus's son," replied the girl. "Not inappropriate for the first of Venus's space docks."

"It is more fanciful than its purposes warrant."

"Now. In the beginning, it was the most advanced station man had constructed, a complete city in space, meant, like Pavonis, to be a link with the surface of the planet."

"What happened?" Icarus asked, indicating the riff-raff around him.

"The space elevator failed. Venus is not a hospitable planet," the girl replied.

"Pardon me," said Icarus. "My manners are in abeyance. My name is Icarus."

"Just Icarus?" The girl raised her eyebrows.

"Just Icarus."

"If you'll listen to some advice," she said, "come up with a second name. You're way too handsome. With a single name, someone might take you for a pleasure gennie." She looked into his haunted eyes. "I don't think you'd enjoy that."

Icarus laughed. In one look, she had classified him. He drained his glass. "You never know," he replied.

"My name is Anni—"

"You really should not waste your time on me," Icarus

interrupted. "I have no money. And I am probably a fugitive by now."

"Shhh. You should not say such things. There are ears everywhere. They would slit your throat for the shirt off your back."

"I find it difficult to care," responded Icarus.

"But I care!" Anni's voice carried a conviction that penetrated Icarus's self-pity.

"Why?" he asked, curious.

"Because," she answered vaguely. At his look, she amplified her response. "Because you do not seem to be one of them!" She gestured toward the rest of the room.

Icarus regarded her. He had little confidence in his ability to estimate human nature, but Anni's responses did not seem to him those of a disreputable bar girl.

"Let me help you," she said.

"The only way you can help me is to put me in touch with NEO."

Anni stared at him. "What?"

"I said—" Icarus began.

"I know what you said." Anni laughed softly. "This is your lucky day. Now listen carefully. You will finish your drink. When mine comes, you will commandeer it, contriving to spill it. You will appear to be drunk."

"I will not have to pretend that," Icarus replied. "It is obvious I have lost my faculties."

"Listen. I will help you up, and we will go toward my room behind the bar. We must be careful, for the other girls have rooms there, too. I am afraid you will have to stay long enough to be convincing. In the meantime, we will speak of another life."

"Why not?" asked Icarus.

"Why not, indeed," replied Anni. In its present crisis, NEO desperately needed volunteers. She was already counting the bonus she would receive for Icarus. Her life was short on years, but long on experience. She was adept at the art of rebel spotting. In the pay of RAM, her talents might have made her rich, but Anni had principles. She cherished her own freedom, even if it meant she had to live as a dancing girl. She had no intention of abdicating it for money.

Icarus glanced across the room at his brother, Raj, wondering if he ought to share the ruse with him. Raj was slumped against the wall, his eyes shut, his mouth slack. Icarus decided against disturbing his inebriation with harsh reality. He regarded Anni through the haze, noting how it softened the effects of the heavy stage makeup she wore. Her blue eyes shone through it, honest in a sea of deception.

Icarus knew she was likely to be lying, but he did not care. His life had been a prearranged schedule. It was time he took a chance. He turned his empty glass upside down on the table before her. "Would you care, Madam, for the pleasure of my company?" he asked, his voice slurred.

"I assure you, sir, it will be my pleasure," Anni breathed, in a false high-society Venusian accent.

Icarus smiled and rose from the table.

Chapter 8

The sun burned at the heart of the solar system, a gigantic ball of inflammation from which the richness of life descended. Unbearable to look at as the face of God, it did not care for human sensibilities. Next to its overpowering magnificence, the planet Mercury was an insignificant blot. It swam against the sun's face, a pilgrim in the light.

Mercury was a planet of stark contrasts. Half of it was bathed in the sun's searing rays, revealing a brown-red desert overlaid with sulphurous clouds. The opposite side was obscured by shadow, fading into the black nothingness of space as if it did not exist. The surface of the planet was barren, inhospitable, but deep within it were underground caverns teeming with life and decorated with the most elaborate artistic endeavors. It was a paradox.

Mercury Prime described a precise orbit around its home planet. The largest of the artificial orbiting worlds surrounding Mercury, it was a triumph for the artisan as well as the engineer. Because of Mercury's proximity to the sun, Mercury Prime required building materials with the greatest possible resistance to blasting heat and destructive radiation. In response to the wishes of Mercury's most notorious Sun King, Bahlam, special alloys were developed, remarkable for their plastic qualities as well as resistance. From these, Mercury Prime was constructed. Roughly cylindrical in shape, its entire surface was decorated. It was a sculptural masterpiece, a triumph to art. It was said a sculptor died for each square meter of its surface.

An entire city reposed within the inscribed shell. At the apex of the structure were the private quarters of the Gavilan family, rulers of Mercury Prime and a large segment of the planet as well. Gordon Gavilan was the reigning *pater de familia* of the Gavilan family, a ruler of some acumen and certain ruthlessness. He was fond of his position and his wealth, and he intended to keep them.

"I merely question the necessity of involving ourselves in the conflicts of another planet." His son, Dalton, sat facing him. Backed by the elaborate tapestry that covered the far wall of his father's study, Dalton was the classic impersonation of a knight, at rest in the forest after a strenuous chase—or an enchantment. Dalton was in his early thirties, six feet tall, and broad. His dark hair and eyebrows gave his face a brooding expression, which was mirrored in his light brown eyes. He sat with his weight on one hip, an elbow propped on the arm of his chair, in a pose favored by classical sculptors.

"We are obliged," replied Gordon gently. He had learned that a calm exterior defused his son's mercurial temper.

"By what?" demanded Dalton. "By trade agreements? We have no formal alliance with Mars."

"Perhaps not. However, we are dependent upon the red planet for three-fourths of our income. They are willing to pay premium rates for energy because they can be assured our Mariposas are a reliable source. This may not be the wisest state of affairs for Mercury, but it is the result of a long-running interdependence, and it cannot be changed in a day. If we wish to protect our position, we must maintain friendly relations with Mars."

"Does that mean we must take on their military conflicts? I do not see Mars offering its sword in our defense."

"We do not at present need it," said Gordon dryly.

"You are still determined to send a detachment to support RAM?"

"It is a sound political move."

Dalton's big hand balled into a fist. "Then let me lead them."

Gordon's eyes narrowed, and he regarded his eldest with a most unfatherly calculation. "Why?" he asked.

"Control. If we must fight for Mars, risking men and ships, then let me make sure we do not commit suicide in the fervor of battle."

"Umm." Gordon pretended to consider Dalton's proposal. In reality, he applauded it. Dalton was a man of ruthless ambition. He had risen like a skyrocket through the ranks, attaining the title of colonel in Mercury Prime's forces in a few short years. In truth, Gordon was a little afraid of his son. There were times he saw the lust for power lurking behind the honey-brown of his son's eyes, and feared for his position and his life. "I can find no fault with your logic," he replied slowly. "The detachment is yours. See that you acquit yourselves with honor. We are there to support an ally, but most of all, we are there to safeguard our interests."

"Always," replied Dalton. He switched the subject. "Now that trifles are out of the way, what are you going to do about that cousin of mine?"

Gordon's mouth became grim. Dalton had touched a sore subject. His nephew, Kemal, was proving to be a stumbling block in his plans. He feared his inability to deal with Kemal was annoying Dalton and fueling his son's impatient ambition. "He will be persuaded to cooperate."

"It would be so much simpler if we could kill him." Dalton's bald proposal was typical of the warrior's simplicity.

"He is much more valuable alive. I have been at pains to keep him so. He will submit, though I admit his compliance is taking time."

"While he languishes in the dungeons, the Dancers become more obstreperous. He should be made an example. Is he their representative? Then let him bear the consequences of their rebellion."

Dalton was quick to anger. Gordon knew his son would have no truck with Kemal's stubborn refusal to cooperate. Kemal Gavilan was the son of Gordon's late brother, and he had inherited the quasi-honorary post of representative to the Dancers, Mercury's hardy surface-dwelling miners, from his humanitarian father. He had also inherited his father's bleeding heart, thought Gordon. This resulted in a refusal to cooperate with his uncle's impressive but thoroughly selfish plans for expanding the family fortunes. In reprisal, Gordon ordered him imprisoned and was currently in the process of changing his stubborn nephew's mind.

"I will see to Kemal. You have a war to think of." The rebuke silenced Dalton, but it did not stop his thoughts. Gordon read them on his face as plainly as if they were printed there. He began to cherish his decision to place Dalton at the head of the Mercurian fleet. "Prepare with my blessing, my son. The flight will depart in six hours."

"I am my father's servant," replied Dalton formally.

Somehow, the words did not ring true in Gordon's ears.

○ ○ ○ ○ ○

In the lower levels of Mercury Prime, there was a small version of hell, a region so analogous to its famous cousin it might be held up as a distillation of the more horrifying elements. Affectionately termed "the caverns" in a backhanded reference to the settlements beneath Mercury's exterior crust, they were the Gavilans' own prisons, presided over by their very own Beelzebub. Old Harry was a gennie of indeterminate age and inventive imagination in the application of his duties.

In one guise, he was a caretaker, in another, a sophisticated interrogator who used a combination of psychol-
ogy and complex drugs to break or bend his charges.
One-half of his brain had been replaced with computer
circuitry. He was forever in touch with Mercury Prime's
pulse, its computer operations, forever melded to its survival. If Mercury Prime scented danger, Harry scented
danger. Yet his circuits had also been programmed to interpret Gordon Gavilan's word as law. He was carrying
out the patriarch's instructions regarding his contrary
nephew to the letter.

Kemal Gavilan sat in a ten-by-ten chamber, nursing
his anger. This was not an easy task, considering he was
half-under with narcotics. He no longer remembered
clearly why he was resisting. He only knew it was im-
perative he try. If he could get through this session—and
Harry seemed to have finished his interminable
prodding—he would have a respite. At Gavilan's orders,
Harry was drugging Kemal at regular intervals with a
brew of his own devising. It tended to erode the will
when coupled with strenuous suggestion.

Harry learned early on that Kemal did not respond
well to physical stimulation. Such torture only made
him more cantankerous. He was so stubborn that by
the time pain broke him, he would no longer be rational, and Gordon wanted his nephew rational. He
asked only that Kemal bend to his will. Kemal did not
wish to bend.

He lay flat on the sling that passed for a cot, staring at
the intricate ribs of the ceiling panels. They were ar-
ranged in a crosshatch like a Celtic knot, twining
around one another in a design supposed to instill in the
viewer a sense of helplessness. Through the fog of his
clouded mind, Kemal managed a weak smile. Even
here, the Gavilans could not help being fanciful.

"Kemal!"

Kemal turned his head toward the voice, trying to focus his eyes. He blinked rapidly.

"Kemal, it's Tix."

He had thought the voice familiar. His cousin. Gordon's youngest. The artistic one. Kemal shook his head. He worked his numb lips, forcing them to frame a word. "Tix."

"Yes, Tix. Oh, Kemal! Why can't you just give father what he wants? It's what I always do. There's no use fighting him. In the end, he wins."

Kemal pushed himself up on one elbow. The movement took considerable will. He licked his lips, lubricating them for the work of a sentence. "You are not responsible for other people's lives."

Tix dropped his eyes. "No."

Kemal had a restricted view of his cousin. The door to his cell had one eight-inch-square barred window. He could see half of Tix's face. "Did Gordon send you?"

"No! No. He doesn't know I came."

"Aren't you afraid I'll tell him in some drugged delirium?"

Tix shook his head, then said wryly, "You haven't told him anything yet." For a moment, he sounded like his father.

"Not yet."

"Dalton is going to Mars."

Kemal's ears perked up. His head was clearing. The importance of Tix's news registered slowly. Mercury was supporting its allies. It was sending a detachment to aid RAM in its destruction of Earth and NEO. His friends would die, perhaps at his cousin's hand. Kemal struggled up. He had to do something, anything, to negate Mercury's involvement, but he was incarcerated like jam in a jar. He looked up at his cousin's anxious eyes. "What do you want, Tix? You jeopardize your safety by being here."

"I know. I don't know . . . I'm confused. I like you, Kemal. I liked you from the moment we met. I wish there was something I could do to help you."

An ironic smile flitted across Kemal's face. "You cannot," he said positively.

"No," replied Tix. "I am not brave enough. In my whole life, Kemal, I have never disobeyed my father."

"I understand, Tix." Kemal raised a hand at Tix's protest. "Really, I do. You have no loyalties to me. We have not known each other long, and Uncle Gordon is your father."

"But it's not right."

"Not by my standards," said Kemal. "However, other perspectives have other opinions. I doubt your father is troubled over my interrogation."

"Perhaps not. Kemal, I don't understand." Tix's tenor voice was anxious. "Why do you care so much for the Dancers? You don't know them any better than you know me. They're no blood kin. Yet you go through this brainwashing for them without a murmur."

"Hardly without a murmur. I've even yelled on occasion. I do it because the Dancers deserve to choose the way they live, not have another's decisions imposed upon them. They deserve freedom."

"Is that why you joined NEO? For freedom?" Tix's voice turned wistful.

"I guess so. It's as worthwhile as any cause. Better than most."

"But it's brought you to this!"

"You must break the egg to get at the meat," said Kemal.

Footsteps sounded in the echoing corridor of cells. Kemal recognized Old Harry's heavy tread.

"I have to go!" said Tix. "I'm sorry, Kemal!"

"Take care, Tix," replied Kemal wearily. He had no strength for another session.

Tix's face vanished from the window. Kemal could hear the soft whish of his slippered feet as he slithered away. Harry's tread came closer and finally stopped at Kemal's door. His misshapen face, with its hooked nose and bony protrusions at temple and jaw, pressed against the opening. At times like these, Kemal was grateful the window was no larger.

"What's the noise in here?" growled the jailer. "You so full of energy you want another discussion with me?"

Kemal sank down in the sling. Now that Tix was gone, he was overcome with fatigue, though his mind was miraculously clear. He did not want Harry to know that, so he closed his eyes. "Nightmare," he murmured sluggishly. "All a terrible nightmare. Falling. No hope."

Harry grinned. The expression revealed a set of gleaming stainless steel teeth. "Them delirious tremors is real spooky," he commented. "See if we can't do somethin' about 'em next time—maybe make 'em last two, three days. Can't have you feelin' lonesome in your sleep."

Kemal moaned softly, pretending he did not hear. He rolled toward the wall, away from Harry's ghoulish face. Somehow he had to escape this farce. His friends were in danger. He knew, as surely as he knew his own name, they would do all they could to help free him.

Chapter 9

Black Barney regarded the battler *Chryse* with a jaundiced eye. It was big, as big as a space station. For all practical purposes, that was exactly its function. It was a military city in space. It floated off Earth, its hull blocking a third of his view of the planet. He growled under his breath.

His pirates had managed to disable or destroy four of the huge ships, but not without heavy casualties. During the communications blackout, they had been able to make some headway. Once the linkages were operational, they had been met with heavy resistance. Taking on the battlers one at a time was a project that could last a decade. Moreover, if the Rogues' Guild concentrated its energies on one ship, the others would be on them like flies. Barney shook his head at the prospect.

His slowly grinding mental gears reached an inevitable conclusion: Faced with the magnitude of RAM's opposition, the Guild could not win. Not alone. The thought was a surprise to Barney. He was not temperamentally prone to pleas for assistance. In his experience, assistance came at a price, and Barney was loath to share his wealth.

From behind the protective screen of the *Free Enterprise*'s star field, he watched the RAM ship. Its fighters came and went in an uninterrupted stream, refueling, rearming, and returning to a devastated Earth to continue their attempt to eradicate life. Barney ground his fingers into the arms of his command chair. Buck Rogers wanted those ships stopped, and Barney could not see any way to carry out his captain's orders.

Laboriously, Barney sought alternatives. He could not afford to pay mercenaries, if he could find them. RAM had a high percentage of the mercenary pilots under contract—many of them as adversaries he was currently facing. He had to find willing help. What was it Buck called it? Allies? Allies. The word lodged in Barney's slow-moving intellectual synapses. It triggered two names: Venus, presently fighting like inspired banshees off Mars, and Luna, silent, brooding, waiting for an adversary to challenge its borders.

Barney smiled. A fearsome gash that sliced across both the metal and fleshy portions of his face, it was an indication of the carnage he intended to wreak on RAM. His vendetta against RAM was one-third loyalty to his captain, Buck Rogers, who opposed RAM's tyrannical rule, one-third personal animosity against an entity that persecuted pirates ruthlessly, and one-third profit, for captured ships were money on the wing. He shifted his seven-foot frame and gave the order to contact Luna.

"This is Luna central," said a feminine voice, and one of the *Free Enterprise*'s communications screens showed a young woman in a silver jump suit. Her blond hair was tied back from her face with silver cord. A generous helping of freckles dotted her nose. At the moment, her brown eyes were wide. It was no wonder.

Black Barney filled her communications screen. Seven feet of bone and muscle encased in sculpted black plasti body armor, he lounged in his command chair like the devil at rest. His cybernetic arm was analogous to its partner in overall shape, but it did not try to mas-

querade as flesh. The complex circuits and cables were
easily visible, a grotesque impersonation. One-half of
his broad face was cybernetic as well, one eye, cheek,
and jawbone replaced by more durable metal implants.
His crest of dark hair and low black eyebrows gave him
a glowering air, the mein of an embattled god. But his
augmented physical power was not as fearsome as his
eyes. Entirely colorless, they pinned the Lunar communications technician to her station as if she were a
butterfly on a specimen card.

"Please identify," she said weakly. It was not the aggressive rejoinder her training demanded.

"Barney. Master Pirate."

Barney's monosyllables called up an entire dossier.

The technician gathered her resources. "We are in a
state of war," she replied firmly. "State your business, or
be regarded as hostile."

"Hmmm." Barney's growl was soft. "Need help."

"Help?" The technician was dumbfounded. She was
frantically trying to access her computer records on Barney. "Is your ship disabled?"

Barney shook his head. "To get RAM."

"I . . . Please hold communications," she said, and the
screen dissolved into a crackle of blue snow.

Barney waited impatiently, drumming his fingers
against the side of his chair.

"They're giving us a run-around," snapped Baring-
Gould, Barney's first mate.

"Urrr," replied his captain, and Baring-Gould swallowed his words.

Abruptly the screen winked back, showing the image
of an old man with hard eyes. Uncompromising and angry, they regarded the master pirate. "This is Lawlor.
Spit it out."

Barney raised an eyebrow. Even he was familiar with
Proctor Lawlor, administrator of Tycho, Luna's largest
settlement. Far from being put off by Lawlor's abrupt
demand, Barney's respect for the man rose. He repeated
his request. "We need help. To get RAM."

"And why," asked Lawlor sarcastically, "should you

expect Luna to care?"

"Allies," replied Barney succinctly.

"We are no one's ally," replied the proctor grimly.

"Cap'n said you were NEO's."

"The captain was mistaken. Who is this captain?" Lawlor asked suspiciously.

"Buck Rogers."

Some of the proctor's asperity cooled. He narrowed his eyes at the huge gennie. "You are making a formal request, in the name of Buck Rogers and NEO, for assistance against the RAM forces on Earth?"

Barney nodded.

Lawlor regarded him coldly. "We will not jeopardize our borders. We will, however, destroy without hesitation any RAM vessel that comes within range of our weapons."

Barney chuckled. The sound was like a thunderstorm abating. "I copy," he said.

Lawlor regarded the pirate with a grudging respect. "We shall see," he replied, and the screen went dark.

Four hours passed. The sun sank behind Earth's sphere, leaving space black velvet dusted with diamonds. The *Chryse* paid it no heed. Its operations were unaffected by night and day. Its fighters were reporting ground fire and scattered resistance, but the brief flash of escalating opposition had died. The *Chryse* continued its programmed flight plan. Half its complement of fighters were hooked into its fuel lines when the scavengers struck.

"Ships at mark five, coming in fast!" reported the *Chryse*'s first mate.

"Target incoming vessels," said Pollyon calmly. The *Chryse*'s captain had no fear of other spacecraft. His ship had shielding and firepower enough to withstand innumerable runs by smaller craft—as long as he did not give way to panic, and he had no intention of losing control. He blamed the previous losses of other battlers on a combination of the Krait fighters' superior stealth and the confusion of their command personnel, who were faced with no authorization.

"Targets identified," said his weapons officer.

"Fire lasers."

Heavy streaks of white fire leaped at the incoming vessels. They were met with chaff. The ships disappeared from the *Chryse*'s sensors, individual vessels melding into an oblong cloud of disruption. The lasers sank into the dust and dissipated, swallowed up in confusion. Spitting chaff in clouds, the enemy ships ran straight for the *Chryse*.

"They must be running blind!" exclaimed the first officer.

"Evasive." Pollyon's voice was still cool.

The *Chryse* pulled out of orbit, its huge fuselage moving with surprising speed. The approaching cloud changed course, following it.

"How did they do that?" asked a sensor technician.

"Good question. They should not be able to track us. That cloud provides as much interference for them as it does for us. Unless they've got something new," replied the first officer.

The *Chryse* changed course once more, but the enemy ships behind their protective cloud followed effortlessly.

A rumbling chuckle shook the *Free Enterprise*'s command center. Black Barney was amused. He knew the battler's confusion and found it vastly entertaining, as a cat finds the futile antics of a captured mouse fascinating. The *Free Enterprise* was monitoring the movements of the two forces from behind its camouflaging star field. From its cloaked vantage point, it fed the fleeing battler's coordinates to the members of the Guild. Since the chaff was concentrated at the front of the strike force, the rear vessels were able to pick up his transmissions.

"Give 'em target coordinates," he ordered, and his communications man, Edward the Red, complied.

Gyro shells shot from under the body of the cloud, buzzing insects attracted to the battler in droves. They collided against its shields, exploding harmlessly.

A twinge of unease tickled Pollyon's innards. "Fire!" he ordered. "Even if the gyros go wild, they may catch something."

The battler replied to the assault with its heavier gyros.

"Lasers!" snapped Barney, and two ships dropped from the bottom of the cloud like stones, fired their lasers in a wide-dispersion fan, and rose back into the formation. The approaching gyros detonated.

"I do not like games," said Pollyon tightly, to no one in particular. He was not on familiar terms with his crew, so no one answered his observation. He stalked across the bridge, weighing the possibilities. He stopped with his back to the sensor bank. "Plot a reverse course," he said. "We're going after them."

"They're coming around!" exclaimed Arak Konii, on the bridge of Barney's *Free Enterprise*.

"We've got 'em!" Barney said.

"Implement Operation Panic?" asked Baring-Gould.

Barney nodded.

In moments, the Rogues' Guild had reversed its course, fleeing from the approaching behemoth. Chaff pumped from the rear of the formation, but as the *Chryse* cranked up its powerful engines, the Guild abandoned frills and set out across space, running like a rabbit with a pack of greyhounds on its tail.

On the bridge of the *Chryse*, Pollyon's eyes narrowed in pleasure. "Chase them down," he said. "Not one is to escape destruction."

"Yes, Captain," said the *Chryse*'s first mate, resolving never to cross him.

Around the blue and white sphere of Earth the hunt ran, a clutch of motley independents pursued by a monster of RAM's military might. The smaller ships ran in a straight line, trying to outdistance the battler. The *Chryse* stuck to them, gaining imperceptibly as the chase wore on.

"Sir, we are coming up on Luna," reported the battler's first officer.

Pollyon's lips were tight. "Keep us out of range," he ordered.

"Present heading puts us within her sphere of influence in thirty-three seconds," he answered. "Do you wish to veer off?"

Pollyon leaned over his shoulder and studied the computer read-out. "Hit port docking thrusters," he ordered.

The first mate complied, but commented, "That's cutting it close."

"Luna won't clear her borders," replied Pollyon.

He was wrong. Under normal conditions, Luna would not have attacked a vessel unless it physically invaded its orbit sphere, but this was war. The *Chryse* rose majestically on its side, like a whale rearing out of the water. Its belly was parallel with Luna's orbital borders. It sailed by, foolishly confident. Luna's mass drivers hit the *Chryse* amidships, full out. The battler broke in two like a cracked egg. The vessel's two halves drifted away from Luna, the momentum of the blow they had been dealt shoving them effortlessly through space.

The pirate ships climbed out of the path of destruction.

"We should get a premium for that one!" crowed Crazy Darien, master of the pirate ship the *Last Chance*.

"Humph," grunted Barney. "Enough salvage to buy all of us. Net it." The pirates scattered to gather in their spoils, when Barney had a thought. "Net half," he said. "The rest goes to Luna."

There was an outcry over the communications network, the Rogues' Guild wailing in protest at being robbed of its just deserts.

"Stow it!" said Barney firmly. "For the duration, Luna's one of us. Fair's fair."

The wails died to discontented grumbles, but the pirates deferred to the instruction of their leader.

"Luna!" Barney ordered, and Edward opened up a channel.

"Luna central," replied the communications link.

"Lawlor!" demanded Barney.

The communications technician complied without a murmur. Lawlor's acid face appeared on the screen.

"Well?" he asked.

"Good job," said Barney.

"Yes," answered the proctor.

"Do it again?"

"By all means," replied Lawlor, his stern slit of a mouth curving into the tiniest of smiles. "I cannot tell you how much I am looking forward to it."

Chapter 10

Beowulf regarded the tactical simulator with grim determination. A rectangular screen covering one long wall in Salvation III's command center, it showed the positions of friend and foe with chessboard accuracy. The forces were color coded: red for RAM, green for Venus, blue for NEO. The Venusian and RAM fleets occupied the major part of the board. Action near Earth was represented by an insert on the lower left-hand corner of the screen. The movements of the vessels were charted by satellite sensors and the sensor systems of the NEO fighters, and were, for the most part, reliable.

The whole display looked like a glorified computer game, full of flashing lasers and dramatic explosions. It was not. Each blip on the screen chronicled a human life. Each laser flash threatened that life, and each explosion meant death. Not in the history of the system had two such armadas faced one another. Until now, space battles were skirmishes, incidents involving, at the most, fifty ships. This was a wave of chaos stretching in an uneven blanket between Mars and the asteroids.

Beowulf shook his leonine head. It was impossible. Mars was huge. The RAM fleet had at least two hundred more strike craft than Venus. True, the odds were being slowly whittled down. Venus was fighting with the single-minded fervor that was its trademark, and NEO had managed to pull a few ships away from the RAM fleet. The RAM cruisers were no match for the stealthy Krait, and so far five of them had succumbed to NEO, but it was hard going.

"Scary when you see it laid out like that."

The voice was a light baritone. It held no fear, in spite of its words. Beowulf did not take his eyes off the board, but his spirits lifted. "Five," he said.

"It's a start," said Buck Rogers.

"It goes against the grain," said Beowulf, "to have Venus fight our battles for us, but we do not have the numbers to combat that behemoth." He waved a broad hand at the blanket of red dots that indicated RAM ships.

"You've been at this a long time," said Buck. "A long time without help. Venus is fighting for her own reasons, not ours. We just gave her an excuse. We're useful to each other. We don't have numbers, but we do have the hottest ships in the system, the only ones that are a match for RAM's. On top of that, we've got the best pilots there are. That's an edge that's hard to measure."

"Don't underestimate RAM. Its pilots have more flight hours than we can imagine. RAM can afford it, as it can afford the most talented mercenaries."

"Like Kane."

"Like Kane," agreed Beowulf.

"Look, Beowulf, I've got perspective. In the twentieth century, I flew with the best there were. They were choirboys compared to this bunch. NEO is fighting for its life. You corner a mouse, and it'll make a lion run. What we've got here is a cornered lion."

Beowulf glanced back over his shoulder, his eyes warm. "That's right," he said, "give me hope."

Buck grinned crookedly. "All I ask is that you return the favor," he said.

"We do have one bit of luck." Beowulf pointed to a series of blank spots in the heart of the Venusian-RAM
conflict. Wild streaks of laser fire shot from the center of
these empty areas. "Kane is in the middle of things."

"He's RAM's spearhead. They're counting on him to
demolish the Venusian line, then the rest of the RAM
fleet will overwhelm them. So far, it's not working."

"And Kane won't break off from more important matters to take on a few NEO ships, no matter how dangerous they are." Beowulf was thoughtful.

"Right. So we've got to use the time he's given us to
even up the odds."

"Piecemeal?"

"That's all we've got," replied Buck. "My ships will be
refueled and ready to go in . . ." Buck consulted his
watch. ". . . five minutes. I'll go out again. Wilma, Washington, and I set a quota of ten ships per run. I'll hit the
tail of the RAM fleet."

"Sounds like you plan to run this in relays."

"Just like wolves running deer," Buck said.

"I'll need your schedule. Turabian will want to work
out a comparable one for the maintenance crews," said
Beowulf, referring to Salvation's commander.

"That's why I'm here," Buck returned mildly. He
pulled his heels together with a snap and stiffened to attention. His arm quivered in a military salute. "Captain Buck Rogers, reporting with duty roster, sir!"

Beowulf extended a hand, his expression sardonic.
"Why is it you never offer the least military courtesy—
even to me, the commander of all NEO's fighting
forces—unless you want something? I learned early on
that you're most effective on your own terms. You are
exceedingly lucky, Captain, that we are a desperate
rebel band fighting for our lives, with little time for
pomp and circumstance. Give me that!" Beowulf took
the crumpled piece of paper. It was covered with Buck's
neat hand, a twenty-four-hour list of flight schedules
and personnel. "This rolls over?" he inquired.

Buck nodded. "Same schedule for a second day, or a
third, or . . . as long as it takes."

Beowulf scribbled his signature on the lower left-hand corner of the paper, then handed it to a passing technician. "Get this on the computer," he said. "And post it in the flight lounge."

The technician nodded and hurried off.

Buck saluted again. "Permission to return to flight deck, sir!"

Beowulf waved a hand, dismissing him. As Buck turned to go, the NEO commander's grumbling baritone followed him. "We can use some venison," he said. "See how many of those deer you can hang."

Buck grinned. "We'll do our best," he replied.

○ ○ ○ ○ ○

Huer.dos was worried. Since Kemal's disappearance, he had scanned religiously for word of him, even skirting the edges of RAM main. The networks were silent regarding the Mercurian prince. Even Ardala's commercial listings drew a blank. He had shied away from direct contact with Mercury, afraid if his inquiries were traced by the Gavilans or their allies, Kemal's life might be in danger.

Huer chewed on his thoughts. He had tried every angle his programming knew and discovered nothing. He had no alternative but to risk direct contact with Mercury. He knew of Kemal's political link to the Dancers, the fiercely independent surface dwellers who mined Mercury's considerable resources. He did not, however, know whether the Dancers viewed the prince as enemy or ally. In either case, they were Huer's one lead.

Huer slipped into the outbound computer network, masquerading as a distributor of raw ore. Mercury Prime picked up his transmission and made contact, but Huer ignored its overtures, knowing Mercury Prime to be the Gavilan's stronghold. He bounced off a communications satellite, then used the rim of a Mariposa solar station to make the jump to the planet's surface, close to Kemal's last reported position.

He found himself confined in the cramped quarters of

a Mercurian desert flivver's communications link. His position surprised him. He had expected some kind of tracking station, possibly the communications setup for one of the Dancers' track cities, not this patched-together excuse for a systems network. He invaded the flivver's sensors and activated the screen.

"What in the great face of the sun are you?" The woman's voice was hard, but its pitch was not unpleasant. She had drawn back at Huer's abrupt appearance.

He decided to take the offensive. If he could throw her off guard, she might not ask as many questions. "I might say the same," he replied tartly.

The woman's eyes narrowed to dark slits. Inside the flivver's protective dome, she could dispense with her radiation helmet. Her dark face was smooth, but her mouth was set in a line of permanent anger. "We can trade insults all day," she replied coldly, "and say nothing. I have no time for such nonsense."

"Neither do I," responded Huer. He spoke the truth. The longer he stayed on Mercury, the greater his chances of detection.

"Then let me break the tie. I am Duernie, Dancer, dweller in Track Group One-Twenty."

"Then perhaps I have come to the right place, after all," said Huer. He hesitated, wondering whether to continue his masquerade. The woman's face assured him that she would not tolerate deception. "I am Huer.dos Twenty-Three," he said. The number was a twist of the truth, implying he was a clone. It would make no difference to Duernie, but would to another computer.

"And what is your business, Huer.dos Twenty-Three?"

"Is there a holo-eye on this thing?" Huer asked. "It's cramped in here."

Duernie made an exasperated sound and reached for the control panel. Huer materialized beside her, his angular body looking as at home in the flivver's narrow seat as it would on a plush couch.

"Comfortable?" she asked sarcastically.

Huer smiled charmingly, his eyes twinkling. "Yes."

"Then will you please get on with it? What do you want with me?"

"First, should you decide to track my transmission, let me tell you I entered the Mercurian computer network under a false name, as a dealer in raw ore."

"You do inspire confidence," said Duernie dryly.

"I hope to." A grim note entered Huer's voice. "I came to Venus looking for a friend."

"And I am supposed to know this friend?"

"Perhaps. I am looking for Kemal Gavilan."

"Who are you?" Duernie asked sharply. "I know nothing of the Gavilans."

Huer sighed. "All Mercury knows of the Gavilans, and of the nephew who holds the Dancers' fate in his hands. You are a Dancer and therefore know of Kemal."

Duernie was silent.

"To answer your question, I am a compugennie."

Duernie looked at him askance. "Only RAM can afford compugennies."

"That is a fallacy, since I am allied with NEO."

Duernie digested this. "Then you do know Prince Kemal." She looked at him coldly. "Prove it."

Huer's thin mustache twitched. "I could spout information until I am blue in the face, and it would prove nothing except my efficiency. I can only say that Buck Rogers sent me to find Kemal and free him if I could."

"Rogers." Duernie's brow was creased in thought. "Why should he care?"

"He is Kemal's friend," said Huer gently.

Duernie sighed. "I will tell you what I know," she said. "I am afraid it will do you no good. Kemal's disappearance is my fault, for I called him back to Mercury. The Dancers had heard rumors he intended to pledge their support to the NEO cause, and they were afraid."

"Kemal spoke only for himself when he joined NEO," said Huer.

"I discovered that. I have not seen Kemal since our interview. I fear he is in the hands of the Gavilans."

"There has been no rumor, no insinuations?"

"Nothing. Gordon Gavilan does as he pleases on Mercury Prime."

"You think Kemal is there?"

"There is no other explanation," answered Duernie. "Believe me, I have spent sleepless nights on the subject. If he were being held in the city-states of the Warrens, rumors would have surfaced. But Gordon Gavilan keeps Mercury Prime under control."

Huer slumped in his seat, thinking.

"Kemal has no stake in Mercury," Duernie said bitterly. "He cannot regard it as his home. For him, it has been a prison. Yet he has refused to do the one thing that would secure both his freedom and his position."

"He has refused to release the Dancers into unfriendly hands," finished Huer. "We often spoke of it."

"My people are grateful to Kemal," said Duernie, "but I am in his debt. As the direct cause of his capture, I must restore his freedom."

Huer looked straight into her hard brown eyes. "Then you will help me?" he asked.

Duernie nodded slowly. "Though I do not see how I can. I cannot infiltrate Mercury Prime. My radiation-darkened skin would immediately brand me a Dancer."

Huer smiled slowly. "There are others in this system, Duernie, whose skin is burned dark by radiation. I think you would do admirably as a mercenary spacer."

"But I know none of the terminology! I have never been off Mercury in my life!"

"But," said Huer, "you will have me."

Duernie looked at the hologram. Semitransparent, he shimmered beside her like something in a dream. "You're not real," she said. "I'm hallucinating. Radiation delirium colored by guilt."

"No such luck," said Huer.

"Where do you plan to find a ship?"

"I'll improvise." It occurred to him the words might have been uttered by his friend Buck. His warm brown eyes twinkled at the thought.

"At least one of us has some confidence," Duernie said.

Chapter 11

Beyond the farthest orbit of the most remote Martian satellite, beyond Deimos and Phobos, the twin Martian moons, raged a battle of titanic proportions. Two mighty armadas were locked in combat. Without pause, without rest, they struggled in each other's grasp. Venus and Mars, goddess of love and god of war, creative and destructive, battled with the fervor of innate opposition.

RAM, the embodiment of Mars, was a marvel of technological expertise and organization. Its fleet was planned down to the tiniest bolt in the most insignificant supply ship. Its troops were trained to react with the precision of computer circuits. The Martians bombarded the Venusians in waves so mathematically precise it was evident their master plan came from the RAM main computer, or, more specifically, Simund Holzerhein.dos.

The sole exception to this was the flight of elite experimental Krait fighters under the command of Killer Kane. Kane's link with Holzerhein was a communications channel with which he kept the computer-encoded commander of the RAM fleet informed. His contract with Holzerhein specified this freedom, as well as the freedom to supersede Holzerhein in case of an emergency. Holzerhein had agreed to this proviso, not telling Kane that in the matrix of the computer of every RAM ship was an override sequence that enabled him to control the vessel should he so desire. Kane had not seen fit to tell the chairman he was flying his own ship, the *Rogue*, and not one of the experimental Kraits.

Soon after the disastrous encounter off Hauberk, Kane had bought the services of one Heim O'Callahan. O'Callahan was a genius, with advanced degrees in electronics, engineering, theoretical physics, and thermodynamics. He had created the basic system that gave the Krait fighters both their speed and superior stealth capabilities. O'Callahan had taken a vacation from Warhead International, moonlighting for Kane. For a cool seven million credits, he had converted Kane's superfighter into a match for the Kraits. Now Kane flew at the head of his fighter squadron, tearing into the Venusian front lines like a mad dog.

Venus met the RAM assault in a ramping tide of blazing lasers. It threw itself into the conflict with a crusader's single-hearted devotion, trusting in the strength of its purpose to defeat a larger enemy, for RAM's forces outnumbered the Venusian wave. Venus's fervor was matched against RAM's technology, a great heart against a superior sword, and was holding its own.

"*Pennant*, this is Arrow Leader, come in."

"Arrow Leader, this is *Pennant*," replied Bilat, the Venusian flagship's communications officer.

"Request refueling run, *Pennant*," said Hamal. His ships were at the forefront of the conflict.

"I copy, Arrow Leader. Hold tight. We'll take you two ships at a time. Handyman One will assist."

"I copy," responded Hamal. The *Pennant* was sending out two fresh fighters. They would join his detachment, relieving two of his men for a refueling run. When those returned, they would move on to the next pair, until the entire flight was refueled. Hamal nodded in agreement. The fighting was too close to detach an entire flight and replace it. RAM lasers sank into the shields on the port side of his ship. He growled, punched in a chaff burst to absorb the lasers, and retaliated.

As he streaked through space between the main body of the conflict and Mars, Buck Rogers picked up many such exchanges from friend and foe. He was heading for the tail of the RAM fleet, but he was doing it the hard way.

"I suppose we had to fly past the entire RAM fleet?" asked Doolittle, his wingman.

"Sure!" responded Buck. "How else'll they know we're here?"

Doolittle grumbled at the other end of the communications link.

"What was that?" asked Buck. "I didn't catch it."

"I said," replied Doolittle grimly, "that there ought to be an easier way." He barely escaped a cruiser's lasers with a frantic burst of chaff.

"Jimmy, you worry too much," said Buck.

Doolittle could tell from the lightness of Buck's remarks that he was running in overdrive.

"Coming up on the end of the fleet," Buck said. "Get ready to rabbit."

"What?" asked Earhart and her wingman, Yaeger, in unison. They were the second pair in the flight, and they kept a tight position behind and to the starboard of Buck and Doolittle.

"Run," said Buck sweetly. RAM buried its cargo vessels in the center of the fleet, surrounding them with cruiser and fighter protection. Buck drove for the cruisers tailing the fleet, his lasers blazing. He launched two gyro shells in the general direction of the enemy. "Bet you can't hit 'em!" he said into his communications link.

"You bet wrong," said a strange voice, and one of the gyros went up in a gold-orange cloud as a RAM cruiser's lasers hit it. The cruiser pulled out of formation to meet Buck's attack.

"Broadside," said Buck, and the four ships in his flight drew abreast of him until they were flying wing tip to wing tip. Once in position, they each targeted a RAM cruiser. Buck sent his lasers and gyros toward another cruiser, ignoring the one turning to meet him. Once he had engaged the other ship's attention, he turned back to the first one. "Come and get me," he taunted.

The enemy captain growled. "I never refuse an invitation," he said, and the cruiser engaged its engines for a power run, its forward lasers spitting fire.

Buck relied on his shields to absorb the lasers, waiting until the approaching vessels pulled out from the fleet and deployed behind the first cruiser. The four NEO pilots poured enough laser fire into the RAM ships to drain an ordinary fighter's laser banks, but the Krait was just getting started. For a moment, the fire from both sides was so intense, Buck lost sight of the enemy. The lasers crashed into each other in showers of light. Buck counted slowly to ten. "Get ready," he said to his men. "Now!"

As one ship, the Kraits cut their forward lasers and engines. They slowed dramatically, sending out billowing clouds of chaff, then they hit their docking thrusters. The ships described perfect one-hundred-eighty-degree turns, then rolled. It was a maneuver they had practiced often, a domino effect as one ship reared over, then another. They were now headed in the opposite direction. Buck fired his engines, and the other ships did the same. "Here they come!" he said.

The noses of the RAM ships were emerging from the chaff. Buck waited until their cockpits were clear. As the cruisers sent their lasers toward the Kraits in hungry tongues, Buck said softly, "Rabbit."

The Kraits set out across space, their acceleration phenomenal. The cruisers, angry now, set off after them.

"You've had it now, mister," said the RAM flight leader.

"We'll see." Buck's tone was unbelieving.

"Think you can cheat death?" asked the RAM captain.

"I have before." Buck's statement was cheeky.

"Rogers?"

"In the resurrected flesh," replied Buck.

The RAM captain laughed coldly. "Death comes to everyone. You're overdue."

"Overdue? Like a library book?" The twentieth century joke went over the captain's head. Buck tried another tack. "What's the bounty up to now?" he asked conversationally. If he could keep the RAM leader talking, the man might not realize their trajectory until it was too late.

"One million credits," replied the pilot. His ships were fanned out behind him, and he was leading them on a straight course down Buck's tail.

"Not enough," said Buck, signaling on his computer terminal for Earhart, Doolittle, and Yaeger to take point, leaving him the tail of a diamond formation.

"They said you had an ego like a galaxy." The RAM pilot did not seem disturbed by the change in NEO's formation.

"Bigger," responded Buck.

The curve of the red planet was receding in his viewer, and his navigational scanner showed the nine ships on an intercept trajectory with Earth. The RAM flight leader noticed their heading. "They also said you were smart, but there they made a mistake. Heading back home? You're going to find yourself caught in a RAM sandwich." He chuckled at his own joke.

"You've got to catch me first," said Buck, and the flight of blue Kraits pulled away from the cruisers. "Careful!" Buck murmured to Earhart, who was on point. "If there's one thing we don't want, it's to lose 'em."

The cruisers punched their engines, and the larger craft closed the gap.

"Sir," said another RAM pilot to the flight leader, "they could outfly us in those birds."

"Stow it!" snapped the flight leader. He did not enjoy being reminded of his own vessel's inferiority in the face of the experimental Krait.

The RAM pilot obeyed to the letter, refraining from questioning NEO's motives in allowing the slower vessels to stay within eyeshot. He did not advance the opinion that they were being led into a trap. He had learned the consequences of flouting authority, and he did not wish to tempt fate again.

The two flights shot through space, artificial meteors invading the sanctity of the solar system. They plummeted toward Earth as if they already felt the pull of its gravitational field.

"Level off," said Buck, "course heading point three-five." The Kraits were skimming Earth's atmospheric blanket by the time he had finished his statement. The flight changed its course, flitting over the planet like a skipping stone, the five RAM cruisers dogging their tails. As they shot into space, Buck gave a rebel yell.

His victory cry coincided with the last sound the RAM flight leader was to make. He cried out in surprise as his ship was hit by a powerful load of buckshot in the form of pebbles. Over the edge of the Earth, Luna's white face rose. Its mass drivers hammered at the RAM cruisers, and the ship was stippled with thousands of one-inch holes. It depressurized instantly, killing the pilot, but the vessel held together until the second shot struck, splitting it like a melon.

Two of the other four RAM cruisers were splintered to fragments by the mass drivers. The remaining two floated in space, useless. One of the pilots was dead, but the other was miraculously alive, the power-driven particles having missed the command module. "I surrender!" he croaked into his communications link.

"Luna, cease firing! This is Rebel One. I say again, cease firing."

Buck caught the Lunar mass drivers just in time. They froze in firing position, their computers within seconds of launch.

"Your surrender is accepted," Buck replied to the RAM pilot. "Stand by for grapple. We will tow you to a pickup zone."

"I copy, Rebel One," replied the man, the relief in his

voice palpable.

Doolittle let out his breath. "That's five more," he said.

"And you thought this was going to be risky," Buck chided.

O O O O O

Petrov fit into the organization of the RAM mainframe's security-one section as if made by RAM itself. It was part of a nested box structure of security links and sensors that protected the integrity of main's most precious charge, Holzerhein.dos. Constructed to imitate one of the many eyes Holzerhein used to view his domain, Petrov looked in at the most powerful individual in the organization, not outward like the units on either side of him. So far, Holzerhein had not detected the difference.

Petrov's initial success was a source of satisfaction to its parent, Masterlink, but Petrov was acutely aware that its function was not simply to hide, but to observe and send those observations to Masterlink. It had managed three transmissions while Holzerhein was engaged in the initial deployment of his fleet, giving Masterlink an insider's account of RAM's operations.

Petrov's unwinking eye regarded Holzerhein's vast armada, and the decisions he made for it, with awe. It had tried to communicate some of its awe to Masterlink, but its parent would have nothing to do with Petrov's estimation. Awe was not within its programming, and it was mystified concerning Petrov's reaction. Petrov stifled its initial feelings and studied Holzerhein clinically, relaying flat data back to its source.

Masterlink absorbed the data like a sponge and asked for more. "YOU ARE TO PAY PARTICULAR ATTENTION TO TWO THINGS," it instructed. "YOU ARE TO MONITOR THE IMMEDIATE DANGER OF RAM FORCES ON EARTH, AND YOU ARE TO PINPOINT THE EXACT NUMBER AND CLASSIFICATION OF EVERY VESSEL IN THE RAM FLEET, DETAILING THEIR ARMAMENT AND FUEL CAPABILITIES."

"WHAT ABOUT BUCK ROGERS?" Petrov asked.

"HOW DID THAT GET IN THERE?" asked Masterlink of its other half.

"I DIDN'T DO IT ON PURPOSE," responded Karkov. "ROGERS IS A PRIME DIRECTIVE FOR US. PETROV MUST HAVE PICKED IT UP."

"YOU ARE TO IGNORE ROGERS FOR THE TIME BEING," instructed Masterlink.

"BUT HOLZERHEIN HAS ALREADY ENCOUNTERED HIM TWICE. I MIGHT—"

"YOU WILL NOT WASTE PRECIOUS TIME ON ROGERS. WE WILL TAKE CARE OF HIM LATER. AND MAY I REMIND YOU," Masterlink said threateningly, "THAT WE WILL ORDER YOUR SURVEILLANCE?"

Petrov gulped. "YES," it replied, its voice small.

"SEE THAT YOU REMEMBER," Masterlink ordered.

"YOU JEOPARDIZE YOUR OWN POSITION IF YOU TAKE INDEPENDENT ACTION," contributed Karkov. "YOU KNOW THAT."

"YOU ARE OUR EYES INTO HOLZERHEIN'S MIND, NOTHING MORE. DO NOT PRESUME." Masterlink was brooking no disobedience from its small program.

"I COPY," replied Petrov.

"YOU HAD BETTER," said Masterlink coldly. "YOU ARE ONE EYE I CAN SHUT IF I WANT TO."

"OH, NO!" The words were out before Petrov's limited reasoning weighed the reaction they would produce.

There was silence from the other end of the communication. Finally Masterlink's voice reached him, deadly and flat. "YOU HAD BEST CONTROL YOUR OUTBURSTS," it said. "THERE IS NO ROOM IN MY MATRIX FOR CARELESSNESS."

Petrov remained silent, the threat of extermination making his wide-open eye tremble.

"GOOD," said Masterlink, pleased at its watcher's reaction, and at the sheer fun of exercising its will.

Petrov did not answer, knowing its only recourse lay in supplying Masterlink with the most complete data Holzerhein possessed. It set to work.

Chapter 12

AS I SUSPECTED." Karkov's voice was thoughtful.

"AS YOU SUSPECTED? WHAT DOES THAT MEAN?" demanded Masterlink.

Karkov turned a superior eye on its alter ego. "IT MEANS I HAVE DISCOVERED A WAY TO UNDERCUT THAT POMPOUS ASS."

"IF YOU DO NOT CEASE TO SPEAK IN RIDDLES," Masterlink said evenly, "I WILL PUT A BLOCK ON YOUR OUT-PUT."

"IT WOULD NOT BE WISE TO TRY," returned Karkov coldly.

Masterlink erupted in a burst of static energy. "WILL YOU TELL ME WHAT YOU'RE TALKING ABOUT?"

"DO YOU RETRACT THE THREAT OF A BLOCK?" returned Karkov.

The static emitted exasperated sparks. "NOT THAT YOU DON'T DESERVE IT. ALL RIGHT, ALL RIGHT—NO BLOCK. NOW TELL ME WHAT YOU'RE GETTING AT."

"I MIGHT ADD THAT A BLOCK CAN WORK TWO WAYS."

The static pulsed. "ALL RIGHT. I'LL TELL YOU. PETROV, DESPITE OUR CHASTISEMENT, HAS REPORTED EXTENSIVELY ON HOLZERHEIN'S MOVEMENTS. THOSE REPORTS HAVE MADE ONE FACT CLEAR: HOLZERHEIN IS TOTALLY INVOLVED WITH THE WAR HE IS FIGHTING AGAINST NEO AND VENUS."

"THAT IS OBVIOUS," replied Masterlink, its frustration subsiding into a pulsing glow.

"SO ARE THE CONSEQUENCES. HOLZERHEIN HAS LEFT THE ADMINISTRATION OF HIS LESS PRESSING AFFAIRS IN THE HANDS OF THE AUTOMATIC DEFAULT PROGRAMS."

"SO?" Masterlink was unimpressed by Karkov's observation.

"SO, IT IS A PERFECT OPPORTUNITY FOR US TO INFILTRATE AND CAUSE SOME SUBTLE CHAOS."

Masterlink considered Karkov's suggestion. "WE WOULD NOT WANT TO DISENGAGE HOLZERHEIN FROM THE CONFLICT," it said slowly.

"I AGREE."

"SO WE MUST FIND A METHOD OF PULLING HIS POWER WITHOUT ALERTING HIM."

"I HAVE ALREADY SOLVED THAT." Karkov's voice was smug.

"THEN WHY DIDN'T YOU SAY SO IN THE FIRST PLACE?" Masterlink's short patience was exhausted.

"YOU'RE TOO STUBBORN TO BE TOLD."

"AND YOU'RE TOO STUBBORN TO LEARN ANYTHING!" Masterlink returned.

"THIS NAME-CALLING IS ENTERTAINING, BUT IT'S NOT GETTING US ANYWHERE."

"SMUG, SELF-CENTERED HUMAN," muttered Masterlink, bestowing the worst epithet it could think of on Karkov.

"SHUT UP AND LISTEN TO ME!" Karkov degenerated into the bully he had been in life. "RAM OWNS EARTH. DO YOU UNDERSTAND ME? RAM OWNS IT. THAT MEANS HOLZERHEIN, DIRECTLY OR INDIRECTLY, OWNS IT. WE CAN USE THIS OPPORTUNITY TO BEAT HIM AT HIS OWN GAME. WE CAN TAKE OVER HIS CORPORATIONS RIGHT UNDER HIS NOSE."

A flash of blue static zigzagged over Masterlink's pulsing program. The possibilities were enormous. Properly handled, Holzerhein might find himself a tenant in his own computer. . . .

"NO! YOUR THOUGHTS RUN AWAY WITH YOU AS USUAL," said Karkov. "WE CAN'T TAKE ON THAT MUCH—NOT YET."

"THEN," said Masterlink sourly, "WE WILL SOLVE THE IMMEDIATE PROBLEM, BUT I THINK IT'S A CRIME TO WASTE THE OPPORTUNITY. IT WON'T COME AGAIN. ONCE HOLZERHEIN REALIZES WHAT WE'RE ABOUT, HE'LL BE SUSPICIOUS OF EVERY TRANSACTION."

"FOR A TIME," Karkov agreed. "IN THE END, HE WILL GROW CARELESS."

"THAT WILL TAKE EONS!" Masterlink was not to be placated.

"DO YOU WANT TO SAVE EARTH, OR NOT?"

The question stopped Masterlink in midtirade. It pulsed in sulky silence.

"WELL?"

"YES."

"WHAT DID YOU SAY?" Karkov could not resist rubbing it in.

"I SAID YES!"

"THEN WE MUST CONFINE OUR PRESENT ACTIONS TO EARTH-BASED CORPORATIONS."

"I CONCEDE THE POINT." Masterlink accessed its data banks and activated its link to main's corporate records section. A list of assets began to run through the Masterlink-Karkov matrix. As the individual corporations flashed by, Masterlink-Karkov plucked those concerning Earth and stacked them in a separate file. The operation was not a short one, and throughout the process, Masterlink kept an eye on Holzerhein, through Petrov. The RAM chairman was unaware of their actions.

One by one, they began to assess the corporations, determining what blocks of stock, what assets and allies, were needed to gain control of each. One by one, Masterlink-Karkov began to consolidate those assets under its own banner, a parent corporation it named Masterplot.

○ ○ ○ ○ ○

"But, Raj, we agreed! It's the only way to go!" Icarus was pleading with his counterpart.

Raj shook his pounding head. It was early in the space station's simulated morning. He was slumped against a trickling fountain outside the Eye of Heaven bar. Icarus had dragged him to the icy water and doused his head, ignoring Raj's sputtering remonstrances. His head felt like the inside of a bass drum, but his mind was clear. He looked up at the contorted face of the stone water snake, which spewed an unending stream of frigid water into the half-circle pool below. It was laughing at him. Stupid human fool, it whispered inside his head. Will you never learn moderation?

Icarus grasped Raj's shoulder. "You know there is no alternative. Ardala will not forgive our failure. With NEO, we can find a life."

"We're gennies, Icarus! Freaks! We can never have a life."

"With NEO, it is possible. It is even possible to excel. They have accepted Black Barney."

"Into their ranks? That's not what I heard. I heard he is tolerated only because of his link to Rogers." Raj's perfect features were wrenched with the pain of his pounding head.

"There are others. NEO is interested in a person's worth, not in his background," said Icarus.

"Who fed you that? That writhing tart?" Raj's voice was sharp.

"We are in a vulnerable position to make moral judgments," said Icarus dryly.

Raj's fingers closed over his brother's hand. "You are right. And, as much as it twists my heart to say so, you are right as well about our mistress's reaction. We cannot go back, if we wish to survive."

"I know what this costs, Raj. In spite of the pain she

has caused me, I too, love her. I cannot help it. We were born to love her, Raj, but we have the choice of letting our love destroy us, or of controlling it. Ardala is a child, spoiled beyond recall, playing with men and women the way most children play with colored blocks. If we truly love her, we must restrain the child from herself. In this case, by taking ourselves out of her way, we keep her from perpetrating vicious cruelty."

"I know." The words were wrenched from Raj's throat.

"Last night I learned that a woman can be a friend, that love can be kind. It is a lesson Ardala is incapable of teaching, but one that may help us both maintain our sanity."

Raj dunked his head under the ice-cold stream, letting the water drown the noise in his skull. When his ears began to go numb, he ducked out from under the stream and shook the water out of his eyes. His dark hair was plastered to his head in curling ringlets, and the water dripped from his nose and chin. He turned eyes of pure gold to Icarus. "I hope so, my brother," he said.

"You will join NEO?" Icarus's voice held an anxious note he had earlier repressed.

"Yes. You are right."

"We will become part of the battle against Mars . . . against Ardala, even if indirectly."

"There is no other choice. We have neither the resources nor the independence for free-lancing. Ardala saw to that," said Raj, a note of bitterness creeping into his voice.

"I wish it could be otherwise," said Icarus. "Especially for you. She had not yet rejected you."

Raj looked up at Icarus in surprise. The latter's clear eyes spoke of pain accepted. "She rejected you? But I thought all of us were her . . ."

"Playthings? Yes. Occasionally she came to me, those tempting lips touched by a smile. The barest twist of her finger would send me to my knees, and she knew it. She enjoyed it. Sometimes she would love me, and sometimes not. Always she betrayed me into a declaration of passion. Always she ended by taunting me."

"Icarus, I did not know!"

"Of course not. Such weakness is not something one wishes to parade. I had no knowledge of my predecessor until it happened to me. Raj, knowledge would have done me no good. I would not have believed it. I was secure in my mistress's affections. As you were."

The two men locked eyes. Though vastly different types, they were both physically beautiful, created by a voluptuous woman for her pleasure. An indefinable perfection in feature branded them pleasure gennies. This put them at the lowest end of the social structure. Yet, in this moment of revelation, they achieved a dignity the most sophisticated Martian aristocrat would envy.

"If I have learned one thing, Raj, it is this: My first duty is to myself. I must respect who I am. How else can I expect another to respect me?"

"I think," said Raj, "today I begin to live."

O O O O O

Allester Chernenko paced the elegant confines of his enclosed formal garden. The regent of RAM's North American Region on Earth was angry. His plaited white hair glittered in the sunlight, but not as brightly as his silver eyes. Here, on his home planet, Chernenko moved with the grace of a cat, unhampered by Earth's unwieldy gravity. He had faithfully served the corporate structure, lining his own pockets at the same time, to be sure, but that was to be expected. During his tenure as regent, he had milked North America for every hint of wealth. He had added to RAM's coffers, confident of his coming reward.

But he had been betrayed. RAM was throwing him away like a piece of dirty laundry. He had received no new appointment, no recognition of his status. Had it not been for his personal fortune, his present circumstances would be critical.

He stopped in the center of the garden. Its planned beauty usually soothed his temper, but this time his feelings ran too deep. He saw the structure he had built his life around crumbling into obscurity.

"Sir."

His anger was interrupted by the soft voice of his compugennie, Elizabit. She materialized before him, the holographic eye at the corner of the garden placing her next to him, coyly perched on the edge of the fountain. Today she was a brunette, her hair thick and falling past her collarbones in looping curls. Her skin was the color of caramel, and her eyes dusky brown depths, soft with promise. Her mouth was a perfect pink rosebud, at the moment sucking the end of a pencil. The pencil was an unnecessary approximation, but it gave her the opportunity to be seductive and yet stay in character as Chernenko's private secretary.

"Well?" demanded Chernenko, his temper getting in the way of her beauty.

"There has been considerable trading activity in Earth assets. I thought you would like to know." Elizabit wriggled into a more comfortable position on the stone edge of the fountain, revealing smooth brown skin in the most provocative places.

"That is interesting. Do you know who is doing the trading?"

"No, sir."

"Find out," ordered Chernenko. "It is possible someone has information concerning the present conflict, which would benefit me."

"From my observations," said Elizabit, crossing her shapely legs and letting her holographic shoes fall to the ground, "corporations are being taken over slowly. The investor, who ever he is, is picking up a few shares of stock at a time, and doing his best to hide his tracks."

Chernenko mulled over the information. "Are there any new corporations on the list?"

"Twenty-four," responded Elizabit.

"No one growing faster than the others?"

"Not that I can see with present data." Elizabit placed her pad and pencil on the stones and leaned forward. "I will monitor them closely," she said.

Chernenko smiled. The voluptuous hologram strained

against imaginary cloth, her figure displayed with erotic expertise. She had succeeded in making him forget, for a time, his anger. "Do that," he replied.

"Do you have instructions?" she asked softly.

Chernenko regarded her with a different light in his silver eyes. "Yes. Make sure my corporate assets are frozen. I do not want any sales of my stock. Make sure I have a controlling interest in all of them. If necessary, buy up enough stock to make up the difference. And . . . get some exercise, Elizabit. You are putting on weight."

There was a shimmer around the hologram's edges, and her shape was subtly slimmer, but no less voluptuous. "I understand," she replied.

Programmed to accede to Chernenko's slightest command, she could be the computer equivalent of Ardala's pleasure gennies. The difference was, of course, that Elizabit's talents were strictly for the voyeur. Still, she was an entertaining program. Her pale pink dress melted away, and she was clad in a skimpy white bikini. She raised a perfect foot and pretended to dip it into the water. The movement had the undulating beauty of a seal. She half-turned away from Chernenko, then looked back over her shoulder, her dark eyes inviting.

"Forward little baggage," said Chernenko, but there was affection in his voice. He had his share of beauty, but nowhere could he find a woman with Elizabit's reliable reactions. She was full of surprises, but never in opposition to him.

"As you wish," she replied demurely.

"Always remember that, Elizabit," said Chernenko. "As I wish."

"How can I forget?" she asked, her pink lips kissing the words. "I am as you have programmed me."

"Faithful Elizabit," said Chernenko.

Chapter 13

Roando Valmar glared at the ceiling. Like the rest of his quarters, it was constructed of metal plates. Incarcerated deep within Salvation III, his accommodations were hardly luxurious. His cell floor measured five by ten meters. It was equipped with the barest necessities. These did not include gravity. To be sure, Roando's elongated Martian body floated effortlessly, but he was not accustomed to zero g's, and he found the necessity of anchoring himself to his cot undignified.

He was angry. An offshoot of the royal house on Mars, he was used to having his own way. As NEO's prisoner, he was accorded courtesy, but no subservience. He was used to being waited on, his every whim fulfilled. NEO saw no reason to pamper its guests, though he was given reading material. His repeated attempts to bribe the guards resulted in total computer security, and the computers were programmed to supply only his needs, not his desires. His overbearing pride made life miserable for the other RAM board members, for as Roando suffered, they suffered. Eventually, NEO was forced to place him in solitary confinement.

He fumed silently, painting pictures in his mind of the vengeance he would wreak when Mars swept Earth clean and he was free. He had no doubt of the outcome of the war. He was not impressed by the addition of Venus to the rebel cause. Mars was the supreme power in the system. No one could oppose it. These were truths on which he had been raised, and he was not about to desert them. That insufferable peasant, Beowulf, would bow before Mars, his stiff spirit broken. Roando toyed with the idea of sending him to one of the mining colonies as a slave, then dismissed the sentence as too humane. Beowulf deserved death, slow and painful death, for the disrespect he had shown the Valmar name.

Soon after his incarceration, Valmar had demanded an interview with NEO's leader. He was granted an interview with Beowulf. The NEO officer had been abrupt. "You wanted to see me?"

Roando had made a note of Beowulf's lack of respect. "Yes. I wish to know what arrangements are being made for my release."

Beowulf's left eyebrow rose. "None. We have delivered our terms to Mars. They have not complied. They broke off the assault on Earth, but resumed it as soon as their armada was ready for battle. They have made no attempt to release our Planetary Congress, therefore you will remain incarcerated."

"This is absurd. I am Roando Valmar. Mars cannot allow my imprisonment!"

"They seem to be interested in other matters just now."

"I demand my release!"

"You are in a position to demand nothing." Beowulf regarded the outraged Martian with interest. It was difficult to imagine a person so totally selfish and short-sighted.

"I am a member of the Martian royal house," said Roando tightly. "Mars must negotiate for my freedom."

"I will be happy to allow you to discuss the matter. We

will forward a communique directly to Simund Holzerhein, if you wish. Frankly, we do not want you. We want our congress, and the cessation of hostilities on Earth. It is possible Holzerhein does not believe you are alive. It is to our advantage to prove you are."

Marginally mollified, Roando had penned a letter to the RAM's chairman. He knew better than to demand anything of Holzerhein. The missive was couched in the most diplomatic terms, but the wording was definitely Roando's. Any computer analysis would confirm the indentity of its author. Beowulf even allowed him to watch as the letter was sent through security channels to the chairman. Roando had waited impatiently for an answer.

After some minutes, Beowulf spoke. "We have confirmation that the message was received. There has been no reply. We inquired as to system error and were told Holzerhein received the message, but has no time for trivialities."

"Trivialities!" Roando exploded.

"That is the error message we received," said Beowulf.

"I'll show him trivialities! I'll ..." Valmar's voice trailed off. He was powerless against the director, and he knew it. He turned crafty. "Will you let me send one more message?"

"I hardly think we can waste the computer time, Mr. Valmar," said Beowulf smoothly. "We are fighting a war, and Holzerhein does not wish to communicate with you."

"I merely wish to inform my relatives of my predicament." His eyes narrowed slyly. "They are capable of purchasing my freedom."

"I am afraid not," said Beowulf, "unless they are in a position to free the Planetary Congress."

"It is not impossible," said Roando.

Beowulf shrugged. "Why not?"

Roando gave Beowulf a computer code, and Beowulf smiled as he fed in the coordinates for Ardala Valmar's information brokerage, making sure to scramble the transmission so she could not track it. It took some moments before Ardala replied to her uncle. Finally, her lovely face appeared on one of the NEO communication monitors. "Yes, Uncle?" she said. Her tone was bored and irritated. She did not like interruptions, but Roando was one person she dared not ignore.

Roando put on his most doting uncle mask. Ardala, used to his games, knew he wanted something. "My dear, you are no doubt aware of my present sad predicament."

"There were rumors of a kidnapping," she admitted, her dark red mouth forming the words slowly.

Anger flared in Roando's heart. She knew and, little sow, had done nothing. He cleared his throat, an excuse to get his emotions under control. "The rumors were correct. I am being held by NEO terrorists . . . freedom fighters. They demand a ransom."

"And you wish me to pay it." Ardala's cameo face registered no interest.

"Yes." Roando made the word a command. The girl was getting out of hand. He would have to do something about her manners when he was free.

"What is this ransom?" asked Ardala.

"They want the freedom of their so-called Planetary Congress, and RAM ships away from Earth."

Ardala became thoughtful. "The Planetary Congress—that might be managed. To disengage the fleet from Earth . . . we shall see."

"You had best do more than see, Ardala." Roando's voice was grim, implying retaliation for failure. He had a sizable staff, with precise orders concerning his betrayal.

"By the way, Uncle, how many board members were taken?"

Beowulf stifled a laugh. Even Ardala was aware of her uncle's incredible ego, and could not resist puncturing it.

"There were seven of us," Roando replied sourly.

"And does this ransom include them?"

Beowulf nodded.

"Yes." Roando fairly ground out the word.

"I cannot promise anything. These matters are under the chairman's control."

"My freedom is to your distinct advantage, Ardala."
Roando let the hint of reward hang in the air.

"And you can be sure, Uncle, I will do my best."

Ardala had terminated the communication without a
good-bye, and Roando was still languishing in prison.
He was not allowed another interview, and he got no intelligence concerning the negotiations. He vowed that
when he was free, he would see those who had ignored
him properly compensated—even the chairman himself.

The Martian fleet was edging toward the asteroid
belt, intent on drawing the conflict away from its home
planet. In the beginning, it had used Mars as a buffer between it and Luna's deadly mass drivers, now set for extreme range. In pursuit of Venus, the Martians had been
forced to abandon the safety of the planet, and, once beyond Mars's protection, they had been pounded by Luna's guns.

Luna's accuracy with its weapons was a legend the
Martians soon found to be based in absolute truth. With
delicate accuracy, the guns demolished ten Martian
cruisers. Of course, even Luna would not risk a mass
driver shot where it might damage or destroy an ally.
They were necessarily restricted to picking off stragglers. Even so, their shots had the precision of a billiards
master. It did not make sense to continue a conflict under Luna's guns, when the battle might be forced out of
range of the mass drivers.

Moreover, the NEO attack on the Pavonis Elevator
was too close to home. Pavonis was one of the mainstays
of Martian economy. It had escaped serious injury, but
Holzerhein had no illusions concerning its ability to
withstand repeated attacks. If the conflict remained
near Mars, NEO had an open invitation to strike the
home planet. To block his adversaries, Holzerhein
would have to split his fleet, sending part of it to defend
Pavonis and Coprates Metroplex, instead of concentrating on destroying Venus. He was not about to be divided

and conquered, so the Martian fleet was drawing away from home base, undaunted by the Venusians' taunting challenges.

"Martian dogs! Cowards! Flee if you must, but we will chase you across the galaxy."

The Venusians' taunts grated on Kane's second-in-command, Clarion Andrei. "Kane, are you going to let them get away with that?" he demanded.

"Why not? They're only words." Kane did not seem to mind the insult.

Andrei did not reply, but he was broiling with anger. He was a RAM regular, not some mercenary paid to fight for a day. He had his honor, and that of the corps, to uphold. The Venusians could not be permitted disrespect. Though in command of all the RAM forces, Kane left the deployment of cruisers and battlers in Andrei's capable hands, preferring to command the fighters in person. This was not an arrangement that pleased Holzerhein—he wanted his commander on a battler, protected by a phalanx of cruisers—but one that suited Andrei admirably. He sent a flight of cruisers toward the Venusian flagship.

Andrei instructed the flight leader to use Kane's dogfights as cover, hitting the carrier as close to the command center as possible. The instructions worked beautifully. The *Pennant* was inhibited from using its lasers, lest it destroy its own ships. Kane, however, did not appreciate the interference, and ordered Andrei to back off.

"Concentrate on the cruisers," he said. "We've got to cut their numbers down before we can take on one of those carriers." He seemed to have no understanding of vindicating honor.

"I copy," replied Andrei, relaying the instructions to his flight leader. "Commander Kane, my sensors show approaching craft, a flight of about twenty cruiser-size vessels, on direct intercept course with our forces."

"I'll contact them," replied Kane. "But keep monitoring their approach."

Andrei complied, signaling his first officer to keep

watch on the sensor banks, annoyed that Kane had taken contact out of his hands.

Kane's *Rogue* rose above the conflict. Kane was daring, but no fool. Two Kraits clung to his trajectory, flying off his left and right wings. He set the *Rogue* on the course Andrei's sensors had indicated as an intercept course for the approaching craft. Long before Andrei would receive an accurate sensor scan on the ships, Kane was within visual range. He smiled and punched his communications link.

"Come in, Mercury. This is Kane."

"This is Messenger Leader," replied the Mercurian ship. "Request coordinates for deployment."

Kane regarded the flight cynically. Though basically the same cylindrical shape as the RAM ships, every square inch of the Mercurian ships was covered in elaborate decoration. Each ship was a different pattern, a different expression of an artistic eye. The fancywork was deceptive, for the Mercurians were fierce fighters, and Dalton Gavilan was the most cunning of all. Messenger Leader was Dalton Gavilan's code name.

"We could use you on rear guard," replied Kane. "NEO has been doing more damage there than it should."

"I copy," replied Dalton.

"You're a welcome addition, Gavilan."

"Thank you," replied the Mercurian prince.

"Watch out for Rogers. He's been commanding the NEO forces. He may be five hundred years old, but he's nothing to underestimate."

"We've heard of his exploits. Daring."

"Yes," replied Kane.

"I confess to curiosity," said Dalton.

"I'd say the odds are good you'll have it satisfied."

"Mercury is happy to assist its allies in a time of need," said Dalton.

Kane knew the words were a formal bit of diplomacy Mercury wanted on the record. He replied for RAM in kind. "And RAM is grateful for its assistance."

"My hand is against the rebel upstarts," said Dalton.

"If we are lucky," replied Kane, "we may end the sway of the resistance forever."

"To victory," said Gavilan.

"Most certainly, to victory," replied Kane, his green eyes amused at the Mercurian's stilted method of working himself up for battle.

The Mercurian cruisers swept past Kane and his two Kraits, their formation a structural mass that made the individual cylindrical sculptures mesh into an architectural unit. There was a planned beauty in the detachment which did not belong in war, and, despite their usefulness, Kane found them offensive.

Chapter 14

However did you manage it?" Duernie's voice was awed.

"Never mind the details! Get into these and prepare to be an accident victim!" Huer's determination brooked no insurrection. "And get rid of that flivver!"

Duernie, her sharp, dark eyes on the flattened oval hull of a trading vessel, reached into the cockpit of her desert flivver and punched a button marked "automatic return." The flivver began to move slowly across the desert, carefully matching its own tire tracks as it reversed its course. She accepted the silver space suit Huer offered, and inspected it. "From Luna," she commented.

"It's what I could get. The ship is a Saturn jumper, trading in everything from ore to designer fabrics."

Duernie shimmied out of her brown tunic. Though Huer was a hologram, Duernie found herself embarrassed by his scrutiny. Her black silk undergarment concealed nothing. She was not used to such vulnerability, and a blush rose in her brown cheeks as she slipped into the silver jump suit. She fastened the unfamiliar fittings quickly, efficiently in spite of their strangeness. The silver suit was becoming, following her tall, slim body as if it had been made for her. The emerald green circuit piping was all curves, accentuating her figure with provocative whorls. Stripped of her desert brown, Duernie radiated an attractiveness even her frown could not hide.

Huer was observing his handy work with interest. "We must do something with your hair," he said.

"We?" asked Duernie sardonically. "I was not aware a hologram could perform physical feats."

"I can't," said Huer. "But I can do this." He ran a quick series of alternate hair styles across the downed ship's computer screen. "This one, I think. It is pleasing, yet professional."

Duernie looked at the elaborate braid, which started at the crown of the head and finished in a clubbed tail. "I'm not sure I can do that," she said dubiously.

"Of course you can. . . . I'm going to tamper with this ship's log and computer."

Duernie labored with her coiffure as Huer concentrated on the ship's electronics. "How does it look?" Duernie finally asked.

Huer turned from the computer. "Passable. A bit disheveled, but that's to be expected in a crash."

"I suppose you've figured out how I'm going to be able to answer questions about this ship and my supposed travels?"

"Of course." Huer indicated the ship's communications link, an oblong piece of metal to be cupped over one ear. "It's all in there. You'll pick it up in your sleep."

"Sleep?" asked Duernie.

"You certainly didn't think I'd let them find you conscious, did you?"

"Not for a moment." Duernie donned the ear cup.

"In the medikit you'll find a cache of pills marked with an X. They're harmless—I formulated them myself—"

"That makes me feel so much better."

"—and will keep you asleep for about four hours.

There are no aftereffects."

Duernie held up her hand, a pink capsule between thumb and forefinger. "I am supposed to swallow this? In complete faith?"

"Yes," replied Huer irritably. Suddenly he cocked his head. "They're coming! Mercury Prime has pinpointed the site of the crash. They will be here in minutes. Shut up and swallow that thing!"

Duernie gaped at the hologram. She was not used to being ordered around. She considered the situation, acknowledged her debt as a Dancer to Kemal, and popped the capsule into her mouth.

"Now go drape yourself decoratively over the ship's instrument panel. You have three minutes before the medication takes effect."

Duernie followed Huer's instructions. As she sank into the ship's command chair, she felt her knees give way. The last thing she heard as she collapsed on the instrument panel was the metallic thump of the hatch.

Huer ordered the ship's holographic eye to disengage, and was safely back inside its primitive computer.

O   O   O   O   O

"She coming 'round."

Duernie moved her head slowly, aware through her closed eyelids of the bright light above her. A masculine hand slapped her face, none too gently.

"Wake up!" demanded the same voice. "Wake up!"

Even in the disoriented fog of semiconsciousness, Duernie knew her treatment was not the sympathetic ministrations due a crash victim. Her eyelids fluttered.

"Come on, now."

The hand grasped her jaw, forcing it open, and she tasted a thick substance that was both bitter and hot. She coughed, but the potion cleared her head. She opened her eyes.

"Well, well, well. Back among the living, Miss Madison?"

"Leta Maravedi," she corrected.

The man bending over her was incredibly handsome, the dwarf at his elbow as ugly. "I think not," said the handsome one. "Leta Maravedi is the owner of this vessel. It was reported stolen seventy-two hours ago by one NEO sympathizer, Madison. Do not play games with me."

Duernie blinked, trying to get control of her body. "Damn that hologram," she muttered.

"What was that?" asked Gordon Gavilan.

"I said," replied Duernie evenly. "What do you intend to do with me?"

"For the moment, nothing. Old Harry!" The dwarf moved to Gavilan's elbow. "Surely we can find guest accommodations for the lady."

"Depends," responded Harry. "You want maximum?"

Gavilan nodded. His black hair, with dramatic patches of white over his ears, his square, chiseled jaw, and piercing eyes combined in the countenance of a hero. Duernie did not think he fit the mold.

"We got nothing," Harry responded flatly. "Got to double her up."

Gavilan smiled, a cruel twist of perfect lips. "Give her to Kemal as a present. That should prove interesting."

Duernie flamed with embarrassment. The close quarters of a monitored prison cell were no place to begin an intimate acquaintance. Again she cursed Huer's ineptitude.

Gavilan stepped back from the cot where she was lying and the dwarf moved in, grasped both her hands, and hoisted her over his shoulder with a grunt and a pull. The indignity made red spots of anger appear in Duernie's dusky cheeks, but she could not move. Her head and vision were clear, but she had not yet recovered the use of her limbs.

Old Harry bore her through the twisting corridors of Mercury Prime's prison level. Periodically, her feet knocked against the sharp edges of the security doors that joined the corridors. Harry was puffing by the time they reached Kemal's prison. The smell of the small man's sweat was rancid in her nostrils, like the heavy musk of a filthy dog.

Harry hiked his shoulder, sending her slender body against his thick neck, and punched the computer lock code with his free hand. The lock registered the code, then clicked, and Harry pushed the door open. He caught Kemal asleep.

With the lightning reactions of his military training, Kemal was on his feet and making for his jailer before he realized what he was doing. Harry raised a hand. "None of that! Not if you want to see this lady alive! And I'm sure you'd prefer her alive." Harry laughed obscenely as he dumped Duernie on the metal floor. Arm still extended, he backed through the door, hit the lock, and watched the door slam shut.

Duernie did not move, knowing this meeting was being recorded for Gavilan's pleasure. She regarded Kemal philosophically. He was disheveled from sleep, his brown hair poking out over his ears in charming wings, his hazel eyes luminous. Several days' growth of beard gave him a tougher expression. Incarceration had left him none too clean.

He relaxed his defensive stance. "Please excuse my appearance," he said. "I have little say in it."

Duernie realized with a shock that he did not recognize her. "Monitored?" she asked.

"Of course."

"Fix it?"

Kemal nodded and turned to a shiny square in the metal panels. He picked up the metal drinking cup that usually held his water ration, and smashed the monitor. "Sound and picture," he said, dusting his hands.

"Won't they move us?" Duernie asked.

"They can't. They're full up, and Harry doesn't dare move me unless he's ordered to. "I'd say we have fifteen minutes before they come to replace it."

"Then we better make the best of them." Duernie pushed herself into a sitting position.

"Are you all right?" Kemal knelt beside her as he realized she could not move. "Duernie?" he asked, recognition dawning with her frown.

Duernie nodded. "Drugged," she said. "I'll be all right."

"I didn't recognize you." Kemal put an arm around her shoulders, supporting her. "Who drugged you?"

"That dratted hologram friend of yours!"

"What. . . ?" Kemal asked, puzzled. Then her words clicked. "Huer? You've been in touch with Huer?"

"To my detriment," she replied. She looked at Kemal wryly. "This was supposed to be a rescue. Unfortunately, Huer neglected to tell me he had stolen the spaceship he provided for my cover."

In spite of the circumstances, Kemal could not repress a chuckle. "Huer is not always the most practical personality. It comes from being encoded." He squeezed Duernie's shoulders gently. "You have no idea, Duernie, how glad I am to see you, and to know Huer is searching for me. I had begun to think I was forgotten."

Duernie shook her head, her frown deepening. "Not by me. It was my call that resulted in your capture. I owe you freedom."

"And not by NEO," said Kemal.

"Not by Buck Rogers," amended Duernie. "Huer told me he was under orders from Rogers to find you."

Kemal felt a wave of confidence. He had thought his optimism dead. It had returned in moments with the knowledge of another's concern. "You realize we must pretend not to know each other," he said.

Duernie sighed. "I am not adept at deception."

Kemal grinned. "You will learn," he said.

○ ○ ○ ○ ○

Huer wandered through the narrow confines of the derelict spacecraft's computer, keeping the unit at minimal power. He was frantic. Duernie should have contacted him three hours before. He knew without a shadow of a doubt that something was wrong. But what? What could possibly have gone wrong with his perfectly prepared tactics?

Huer knew he had three choices: He could give up, returning to Buck with what little intelligence he had been able to gather, and the story of his failed plot; he could stay where he was, hoping Duernie was simply delayed and would contact him; or he could try to find her. He discarded the first choice automatically. The second he considered for a full minute before rejecting. Duernie was already long overdue. Further delay might mean her death. He opted for the third course of action and began to scan the heavens for a possible haven.

He needed a place to monitor Mercury Prime's transmissions and to search for a means of ingress. Any satellite would do. Small or large, it made no difference to Huer. His program was adaptable to a phenomenal number of situations. As he searched the heavens, one of Mercury's huge solar stations, Mariposa Twenty-Four, came into range. Huer smiled. He could not have found a more perfect haunt. He set the ship's computer for a power surge and prepared to jump.

Mariposa Twenty-Four moved gracefully over Mercury's turbulent atmosphere, its orbit a pattern governed by Mercury Prime's main computer. Huer had only to pinpoint the access points, isolate the codes, and break into the Gavilan's computer system. He noted the simplicity of the three phases, resolutely ignoring the probable danger of being fried by Mercury Prime's security blocks.

The ship's computer flushed with Huer's programmed power surge, and the compugennie leaped for the satellite. He almost misjudged the satellite's speed, but he managed to catch its rim, and, clinging for dear life, he began to create his own secure space, a buffer to protect him from the virus hunters the Mariposas circulated as a precaution.

He had barely managed to camouflage himself when a virus hunter whizzed by, closely followed by another. Huer lifted his eyebrows in surprise. The satellite was crawling with security codes. The Mars-NEO conflict must have touched even the Gavilans.

Huer relaxed in the minute security of his neutral sphere and began to carefully touch the mind of Mercury Prime.

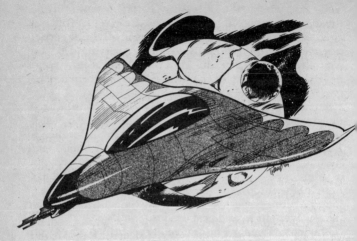

Chapter 15

Buck Rogers careened away from a RAM cruiser, his fighter a sapphire streak across the dark void of heaven. The cruiser fired, but too late. By the time the RAM pilot activated his weapons system, Buck was out of visual range and invisible. Neither the cruiser's electronic eyes, nor the pilot's physical ones, could detect him.

He made another run, sinking his lasers into the cruiser's hull. The RAM pilot fired, manually aiming his lasers. The shot was off, singeing Buck's rear shields. He angled away, playing his cat-and-mouse game with the single RAM ship. NEO was running a short shift, and the three Kraits had each engaged a single enemy at the rear of the fleet, relying on their superior speed and stealth for safety. It was totally unorthodox and dangerous flying, the same tactics NEO adopted against the RAM fleet on Earth.

"I wish Doc would find Kemal and get back here," muttered Buck. "We could sure use an edge right now."

○ ○ ○ ○ ○

Huer, couched on the rim of Mariposa Twenty-Four off Mercury, was doing his best to fulfill Buck's wishes. His choice of a satellite had been fortuitous. Twenty-Four's orbit kept it within easy range of Mercury Prime. Huer was quick to cash in on his good luck. Once he had secured his position, he began to probe for a way into Mercury Prime's computer network. The satellite had sensor, navigational, and mercantile hookups. Huer tested each of the different areas for vulnerability and found the mercantile channels to be the safest port of entry.

He spent some time manufacturing a cloak to make him appear as an incoming order for solar power. He smiled to himself as he added a routing sequence for a destination on Mars. Once complete, Huer gave his creation a nervous final check. If the deception worked, he would be inside the Mercury Prime computer. If it did not, he would be fried, badly damaged, or obliterated. He had given some thought to sending a clone on this errand. In the end, he had decided against it. If the cloak worked, he would need to make some fast decisions. He did not want them in the hands of an amateur.

"The risks I take," Huer muttered as he donned his cloak and slid into the stream of Mariposa Twenty-Four's business transactions. Allowing the stream to sweep him along, he found he had jumped to a small communications satellite attached to Mercury Prime. From there, he was dragged into the main computer network. His mercantile coding sent him directly to the distribution center. Seconds before he reached it, Huer slid out from under the cloak and jumped, landing on an adjacent circuit.

For a moment he froze, certain the impulses around him would recognize an intruder. They continued on their paths, momentarily annoyed at the obstacle he created. As he assessed his position, he realized he had landed within Prime's interior programming network. His freedom of movement seemed phenomenal, until he realized the network was sealed. Security blocks were positioned at strategic locations, keeping intruders out. His random leap had been lucky, missing these guards.

He ran the circuits, searching through life-support, interior communications, entertainment—a host of functions—until he found his goal. Recognizing a single circuit flanked by gates, he knew by the common configuration that he had reached the station's detention controls. He waited until a legitimate program headed purposefully down the circuit and followed it, as close as a sister. The program's recognition code opened the gate, and both Huer and a schedule for the prisoner's exercise periods swept confidently into the security complex.

Once inside, Huer searched for a place to gather his wits. He recognized a communications "L" and took refuge within it, knowing the continual activity in the area would be the best camouflage he could find. He took a deep breath and looked around. The "L" contained twenty individual ports, as well as a general link to Mercury Prime's main communications center. Methodically Huer investigated the ports.

They proved to be individual monitors covering the cells. A rush of excitement made Huer's program jump. He quelled his reaction, lest it attract attention. One of these ports must lead to Kemal's cell. He began to check each of the computer eyes in turn. He had covered half of them when he came to one that was dark.

Huer smiled. He had no doubt Kemal had deactivated his monitor. Still, he wished for visual contact with his friend. As if his request were enough, the eye winked on, revealing Kemal and Duernie, backs against the wall, arms folded across their bent knees. They were staring glumly into space. Huer found the audio link on the sensors.

"Hey! Wake up, you two!"

Kemal jumped. "Doc?" he asked cautiously. "It can't be," he said, massaging an ear.

"Oh, yes it can," answered Duernie. "Remember who got me into this?"

"Me," said Huer sadly.

"It's him," confirmed Duernie.

"What went wrong?" asked Huer.

Duernie glared at the monitor, her black eyes as hard as glass. "You didn't tell me the ship was stolen," she said.

Huer cleared his throat. "It didn't seem important."

"It was important to Gordon Gavilan," she replied.

"First things first," said Huer, sweeping his mistake under the rug. "Where's the lock on your cell?"

"I'm never conscious when I enter and leave my little home," said Kemal, "so I can't tell you."

"The lock panel is on the right side of the door, about halfway between deck and roof. I noticed as I was draped like a sack of meal across the odious shoulders of a hirsute beast referred to as 'Old Harry'," said Duernie.

Huer studied the circuit that connected the cell's eye with the other sensors. Halfway down the individual circuit was a secondary line, with a pad of twelve individual points, six on either side of the line. Huer pounced on it. He ran careful electronic fingers over it, feeling for a progression. Presently he pulled back, considering the lock. Tentatively he touched one of the units. It tingled. He withdrew.

"Get on with it!"

Huer could hear Duernie's impatient voice, accompanied by the sound of short footsteps. "I am," he muttered to himself.

He touched another unit, and its circuit closed, activating the key. One by one, Huer forced the lock units, until the two bottom units winked out together and the lock clicked open. "Are you waiting for an invitation?" he asked sweetly.

Kemal glanced at the monitor. He was across the cell before Duernie could react. When manually activated, the door opened of its own accord, sliding into the wall. Huer's tampering had freed it, but left it in place. Kemal placed both hands on the door's decorative inner panels, blessing the twist of mind that made the Mercurians adorn everything, even the door to a prison cell. The decoration afforded him some grip on the otherwise flat surface. He concentrated, throwing his strength into pushing the panel.

The metal door was heavy, the progress he was making heartbreakingly slow, until Duernie added her strength to his. The door slid slowly back, noiseless on its perpetually lubricated skids. Kemal stopped it halfway.

"Let's see what's out there," he whispered.

He and Duernie peeked around the panel. Slumped in a chair, the remnants of a prodigious supper scattered on the table before him, was Old Harry. He was snoring peacefully, an empty wine bottle clutched in one hand.

Kemal turned back to Huer. "Thanks, Doc. Where do we go from here?"

"Search me," answered Huer. "I'm playing this, as Buck would say, by ear."

Kemal nodded. "Doc, can you sabotage that sensor eye before you leave it?"

"Of course."

"Thanks," replied Kemal. "Do it now." A wicked gleam twinkled in his hazel eyes. He motioned Duernie to slip out the door, then he followed suit. He motioned her to help him, and they pushed the metal door back into place. When Kemal heard the lock click, he grinned. He placed the flat of his hand over all the buttons on the door lock and pushed. The keys jammed. It would require complete dismantling of the lock to enter the cell.

"Now what?" asked Duernie softly, one eye on Harry's recumbent figure.

Kemal shrugged. "Don't ask me how, but now we get out of here."

She nodded. "Which way?"

"Pick," said Kemal.

Duernie, an ironic light of amusement at the hopelessness of their position in her usually stern eyes, set off down a corridor, Kemal at her heels. He was free of his cell, but Mercury Prime was a larger prison he did not know. His luck was in the hands of fate, and he prayed it would be good.

Huer, retreating from Mercury Prime's security sec-

tion, wished his friends well. At present, he could not
help them get off the station. He ran a grave risk being
within the Mercury computer system, and he knew he
must depart as soon as possible, but his concern for Kemal and Duernie was overwhelming his judgment.
"There are times," he told himself sternly, "I wish the
programmers had been less generous with the empathy
factor. Life would be so much more manageable." His
words were empty, and he knew it.

○   ○   ○   ○   ○

On the surface of the planet Earth, the remnants of
the ravaged populace collected fragments of data concerning the Martian War, piecing them together into an
elaborate puzzle-map with tantalizing pieces missing.
The clockwork assault on Earth was beginning to fall
apart. The waves of fighters came less frequently,
though with the same uncanny regularity.

"I hear tell the pirates is on our side," said a crusty old
city rat.

A group of refugees were crouched in the bombed-out
shell of an underground storage tank below the once-
teeming city of Galveston.

A younger man pooh-poohed the suggestion with a
gesture. "When did the pirates care about anything but
what they could steal?" he asked.

"I hear they follow that Rogers fella," the old man continued.

The younger man considered. He was a strapping
blond, his gennie blood evident in his wide-spaced, innocent eyes and the extreme muscularity of his figure. His
thought processes were not fast, and he was not about to
give up an idea on another's say-so, but Rogers's name
caught his attention. "He's just a story," he scoffed.
"Made up to give us hope."

"No, he's not." The third voice belonged to a woman in
her forties. She had a square jaw and flawless peach-
colored skin. "I've seen him."

"You've seen a man they say is Rogers," replied the

blond. "He's probably some actor hired for the part."

"You won't believe me," said the woman, "but I know it was Rogers. There was something about him, something different from other men."

The blond rolled his eyes. "You should be too old for that kind of thing," he said, insinuating her reaction was based upon the hero's physical appeal.

The woman refused to be baited. "Not that," she said, "though he is a handsome man. He stood straighter than any man I have ever seen, as if he had a right to. He had . . ." She searched for the word. ". . . hope."

"Gotta have that," said the old man, scratching his bald spot. "Ain't nothin' left without it."

The woman sighed. "I don't have much left. I don't think most of us do."

"We're here, ain't we?" he demanded. "We ain't knocked ourselves on the head. 'Long as we can draw a breath, we've got hope." He waggled a finger at her. "Don't never forget that!"

Her eyes were dull, but she managed a wan smile. "If you say so, old man."

"I do say so! That Rogers fella—an' I don't care if he's real or a compugennie's dream—has pumped some heart back into all of us. Given us a boost. I aim to hang on to that feelin'. It's a good 'un."

"You mean you don't care if you're being fooled by the government into following a figment of its imagination?" The blond giant's voice was amazed.

"Nope. Government can't use me 'less'n I let it. I'm usin' it to keep my spirits up. It's workin', too."

"You'd let them lie to you?"

"Yup. Don't think they are, though. That Rogers is too unpredictable."

The blond shook his head.

"Look, Sonny, what difference does it make who gives you the fuel to feed the fire? When you get down to basics, you got to live. That's the first step."

The blond looked around the crumbling concrete sides of the open storage bin. Once buried beneath fifty feet of earth, RAM had stripped its protective covering, blow-ing the roof from the structure in the process. The sky shone blue-white above him, ominous in its emptiness. He did not trust it. He shouldered a laser rifle. "We'd better be moving. This wall makes us into ducks in a shooting gallery."

"Wondered when you was gonna see that," commented the old man. He bounced to his feet, spry despite his years.

The blond looked at him with exasperation. "You might have told me."

"Wouldn't have thanked me for it," the old man replied. "Besides, 'cordin' to my calculations, the next wave ain't due for 'bout twenty minutes."

"Time to find better cover," said the woman.

"Yup. Where to, Sonny?"

"Where do you suggest?" asked their leader.

There was a snide cast to the question, but the old man did not let it bother him. "They been rebuilding warrens on the east side, down by the waterfront. Won't no bombs hit close for fear of damage to the regent's place."

"So they have," said the blond. He bowed to the weight of the old man's tongue, and the group started toward the sea.

Chapter 16

The *Space Goddess* shot across Earth's marbled blue surface, heading for the safety of the moon. It looked like something from Jules Verne, with its beach-ball fuselage and corkscrew laser bolt. A RAM battler followed it, pounding the pirate ship with its powerful lasers. The *Space Goddess* spewed out wild clouds of chaff, but the battler's lasers were so powerful that they penetrated the clouds—greatly reduced in force, it was true, but still meddlesome. The pirate could feel the cockpit of his ship heating up as he ran for Luna. He cursed in a steady stream as he coaxed every ounce of speed his ship possessed from its straining engines.

As the battler closed on him, the pirate's profanity became more colorful. "By the sweet kiss of Saturn's whore," he growled, "where are they?" He pumped another charge of chaff into the battler's face.

They closed on Luna, and the battler cut its lasers.

"Where are the scumswill? They're goin' to lose this one, and me along with her!"

On the heels of the pirate's words, Black Barney's *Free*

Enterprise materialized above the RAM battler's stern, its gyro launchers pumping out shells. It was dropping heavy shells, literally gyro bombs, coded to home in on the batter's configuration. So effective was Barney's surprise, that the shells launched, targeted and struck the battler before its pilot could react. They blew a hole in the ship's rear shield, and Barney sank his lasers into the gap, probing for the ship's vitals. The *Space Goddess* ran behind the protective face of the moon.

The RAM cruiser lurched forward, reacting to Barney's assault with a burst of speed and a fog of chaff. It was too late. The chaff dissipated Barney's lasers before they could pierce more than the ship's first twelve decks, far from its heart, but the battler's bolt for freedom brought it into the range of Luna's mass drivers.

The first charge of baseball-sized rocks smashed into the battler's side, tearing a gaping hole in it. The violated decks depressurized instantly, and space was filled with the ship's jetsam. The second charge cut it in half. The vessel's stern floated derelict, but the command center detached from the useless hulk and fired its own booster engines. As it lifted free from the rest of the battler, Luna caught it in the third barrage. The small vessel was torn apart, shredded like cheese under the flak.

"Got 'im," said Barney.

"That makes three," replied Luna.

"I got it recorded," said Barney. "*Space Goddess*. Crazy Darien, you there?"

The *Space Goddess* nosed around Luna's curve, cautious. Once he realized the RAM ship was destroyed, Darien zipped confidently through the debris to the *Free Enterprise*'s side. "Here, Cap'n," replied Darien. His voice was surly.

"One-third," said Barney.

"I don't care what you pay, Cap'n, this's getting too dangerous. I almost lost it that time. Call it off, Cap'n! We can always find salvage—one way or another."

"Mrrrr." Barney's growl was expressive.

Darien's plea was silenced as if Barney had turned off a faucet, but the pirate's thoughts continued to roll over one another like puppies. He was frightened.

Barney recognized the signs. Darien was not the only member of the Rogues' Guild whose greed was being overcome by the desire for survival. Most pirates preferred to strike from ambush, taking smaller prey by surprise at no great risk to themselves. Barney was asking them to take on the most powerful ships in the system. The fact that they had succeeded in destroying a good number of them had not raised morale, as it would have with Buck's fighter pilots.

The pirates were not brave men. Instead of victory, they saw a death's-head rearing before them like a fateful omen. Even the promise of vast wealth could not overcome their fear. Barney could feel the tide of mutiny gathering in every quavering protest. He made a decision. "Base!" he ordered, and every pirate ship in the area turned obediently for Salvation.

Twenty minutes later, Barney was stalking back and forth in front of the Rogues' Guild. They were standing in a ragged phalanx in the ready room the fighter pilots used, clustered in rigid terror before the glowering giant. The door was locked.

"Death?" Barney sneered the single word in a rhetorical question not one pirate attempted to answer. "Afraid?" Barney stopped in midstride and swung his huge circuit-encrusted fist. The first row of pirates swayed back. Barney's hand did not stop. It slammed into the metal plates of the ready room's wall, punching a neat hole. Barney ripped his hand out of the aperture and continued pacing.

The rogues said nothing, but they quailed before him.

"Better get it straight," Barney snarled. "Only one death: me. And I'm not merciful."

Crazy Darien, living up to his name, cleared his throat. "We understand, sir," he said. His voice was trembling so, the words were almost unrecognizable, but Barney seemed satisfied.

"Mrrr," said the master pirate, the bulging muscles of his black body armor a pale representation of the physical force behind it. The entire Guild trembled. "Deathclock," said Barney slowly. His colorless eyes squinted into the throng, daring any one of them to oppose him.

No one picked up the gauntlet. One and all, the Guild knew Barney meant what he said. He would not hesitate to activate the Deathclock, disintegrating any pirate ship and pilot into scattered molecules.

Having made his point, Barney elected to be charitable. "Cap'n Rogers wants Earth," he explained. "He's gettin' it."

As one man, the Guild nodded. Barney smiled, his bared teeth as cheerful as a hyena's. He strode through the packed group, scattering pirates like ninepins, and hit the door controls. The electronics were not fast enough for him, and he took the slowly parting halves of the door in his huge hands and shoved them apart, then stepped through them, almost crashing into Turabian. The space station commander motioned him aside, and Barney followed him to Turabian's office. As the door shut behind them, Turabian faced the huge gennie.

"Can you hold them?" he asked, pointblank. Barney started to answer, and Turabian held up his hand. "No blarney," he said. "I want the truth." He had developed a sneaking affection for Barney in the last few days, but he was acutely aware of the gennie's ruthless nature.

Barney frowned, the creases around his eyes making him look worried. "Yes. Maybe have to blow a couple up, but, yes."

An involuntary shiver rippled across Turabian's shoulders at Barney's reply. The pirate's methods were effective, but made no pretense of humanity. Only Buck Rogers's occasional intervention kept Barney from mayhem. "I can't tell you how much NEO needs the Guild, Barney. This is a chance for them. Oh," Turabian waved a hand, "I'm under no illusions. I know there's not three men out there who really want another life, but this is their opportunity! Hang with NEO, Barney, and you'll all have a chance at a new life."

"The captain wants Earth," said Barney, repeating the tenet he had lodged in his slow brain.

Turabian's lips twitched. "And if you have anything

to say about it, he'll get it. Right?"

Barney nodded, then brought his huge fist down on Turabian's desk. "But I'm tired of rear guard."

"Barney, you're the only thing standing between Earth and obliteration. Trust Captain Rogers."

Barney considered Turabian's statement. His frown did not ease, but he replied, "He's the captain."

○ ○ ○ ○ ○

Wilma Deering drew on her flying gloves, settling the skin-tight fabric until it was a part of her. She was preparing for her shift against RAM with her customary precise routine, omitting nothing, checking each action twice, yet her lovely oval face was troubled. It was the beginning of Salvation's simulated night, and in the dim light of her quarters, her hazel eyes were dark with worry, her long lashes making shadows beneath them, like smudges of dirt.

This was her third flight since the mighty fleets first made contact, and she was becoming a master at detaching cruisers from the security of their fellows, and luring them across space to their deaths. She knew her teasing contralto voice helped NEO's cause, for the RAM pilots were universally male, and most of them were susceptible to her blandishments. She was under no illusions concerning their altruism, either. She knew any one of the cruiser pilots would blast her into primal atoms at the slightest opportunity. She gave them none.

She was supremely efficient at her job, yet worry clouded her face. She was afraid, and she knew a pilot had no time for fear. It confused judgment. It caused death. She had to shake it or report herself unfit for duty. She stared into her mirror, willing the emptiness in her eyes to disappear.

"Wilma."

Buck's voice sounded at her back, a soft baritone rumble. She hesitated, then replied, "Enter." The door to her quarters opened silently, and Buck stepped inside. She turned to meet him, wanting to reach out to him for support, and stopped with her arms outstretched.

Buck was exhausted. Still wearing his flight suit, with his helmet under his arm, he swayed where he stood. His face was streaked with sweat, his flaxen hair plastered to his head. Fatigue was etched into his face in deep hollows below his cheekbones and at his temples. His blue eyes had lost their spark.

Wilma put her arms around him, and he dropped the helmet, cradling her close as if she were a life preserver in an endless ocean. She felt his heart pounding in an irregular staccato of exhaustion. He held her a long time, and gradually his heart slowed to a normal rate. He sighed. "There's a lot of them," he said finally.

Wilma ran her hands in comforting circles over his broad back. "I know."

"After almost three days, we may be about even." Buck's words were dull. He was past caring.

"Step one," said Wilma softly.

"Wilma, it's impossible! They've got too many ships! We'll never take them!"

She placed her hand over his mouth. "Maybe not," she said slowly. "Buck, I'm used to these odds. I grew up with them. They're nothing new. I never expected to have a ghost of a chance against RAM. Until you."

"Huh." The monosyllable was half ironic chuckle.

"We may not win, but, Buck, we tried! You've given us a chance. We never had that before. It's a good feeling."

"False hope," he replied, his arms tightening around her slim body.

"I don't care! It's hope! That's all that matters . . . except . . ." Her words trailed off.

Buck leaned back until he could see her face. "Except for what?" he asked.

Wilma ducked her head. "Except for you. If you really want it, I'll give up the fight, walk away."

Buck looked into her clear eyes. "It's not in you to quit," he said, "though I don't think I've ever had a more profound offer. When this mess is all over, if . . ."

"If we survive," Wilma finished for him.

"If we survive," he agreed, "we'll see about that."

"You are a stubborn, conceited, irreverent fool," she said. "And I have never met anyone like you."

"Insults? How can you expect me to weather insults in my present state?"

Wilma ran her finger across his mouth. "You smiled," she said.

"I guess I did."

"You are tired. You should never have volunteered for that half-shift. I won't let you do it again." Buck smiled at her management. "Fatigue is draining your spirit. You must not let it. You must rest, and let me fight the battle for a while."

"And Washington." Buck sighed. "Things couldn't be in better hands. I know that, but I feel responsible for this whole thing."

"Responsible for a conflict that began after your 'death,' and which has been raging for years? If you have been a catalyst, the elements have been boiling for some time."

"I wish we had Kemal."

Wilma rested her forehead against Buck's broad chest. "I just hope he's all right," she whispered, but Buck caught her words.

"I hope Doc can find him," he said. "Did you notice the Mercurian detachment?"

Wilma nodded. "Under Dalton Gavilan. Kemal's cousin. Watch him. He's ambitious, tricky, and good."

Buck voiced both their thoughts. "I want to blast into Mercury Prime, demand Kemal back, and spit in Gavilan's face. If it weren't for this mess . . . I hate leaving a friend in the lurch."

"You sent Huer. That's what you can do—what all of us can do—for now."

"I just wish it were more," said Buck wearily.

"That," said Wilma, her words muffled by Buck's wrinkled flight suit, "is why I love you."

"What?" asked Buck.

Wilma squeezed him and let him go. "Get some rest," she ordered. With her head high in command and her flaming hair back in a braid, she was adorable.

Chapter 17

SECRET." Karkov read the company's name from a scrolling list of Earth-based corporations, a file it and Masterlink had distilled from the millions of corporations listed in the RAM main computer. They had managed to consolidate this listing of Earth's assets, and now they were proceeding methodically through the list, extracting those companies that seemed strategic, and arranging their takeover.

The corporate coup was going smoothly. Holzerhein cared nothing for the fate of companies while the war between RAM and NEO raged. Masterlink and Karkov judged it would take a direct buy out of RAM itself before Holzerhein would disengage from the military conflict to take care of business. Masterlink was therefore becoming bolder in its transactions.

"EUROPEAN LAND AND MINING," said Masterlink. "REAL ESTATE. MINING INTERESTS."

"WE JUST ACQUIRED BALTIC MINES." Karkov's voice was accusing. "WE'RE OVEREXTENDING IN THIS AREA."

Masterlink dismissed Karkov's concerns with a blip.

"CREATE A MERGER," it said.

Karkov considered. "IT IS LOGICAL," it conceded, "BUT I STILL THINK IT'S RISKY. WE SHOULD KEEP A LOWER PROFILE."

"HOLZERHEIN CAN'T SEE A MACRO FILE WITH THE WAR ON HIS MIND."

Karkov grumbled under his breath, and Masterlink lost what little patience it possessed. "GRANDMOTHER!" it said. "DODDERING HUMAN! WE MUST TAKE THE CHANCE WE HAVE TO CONSOLIDATE OUR HOLDINGS."

"BUT YOU ARE RECKLESS!"

"HOW SO?" inquired Masterlink coolly.

"THEFT SHOULD BE AN INVISIBLE PROCESS," Karkov replied. "THIS LAND COMPANY IS A CASE IN POINT. IF I TRANSFER A FEW SHARES AT A TIME, LIKE SO . . ."

Karkov withdrew five shares of stock from European Land and Mining's ledger and added them to its own. As the transaction registered, a wall of electronic static reared in front of the remainder of the corporation's records. Masterlink-Karkov drew back, surprised.

"WHO ARE YOU?"

The question seemed to emanate from the wall of static. Masterlink-Karkov did not reply.

"WHO ARE YOU?" the demand was now an order.

Masterlink thought fast. A refusal to reply would only anger the genie. "SECURITY SCAN," it answered promptly.

The wall of static pulsed in disbelieving silence. "YOU HAVE STOLEN OUR PROPERTY," it stated, drawing an accusation from each word.

"A TEST," answered Masterlink with silky logic. "WE MERELY PERFORMED A TEST TO DETERMINE THE STATUS OF COMPUTER SECURITY."

"RETURN OUR PROPERTY."

"AT ONCE." Masterlink stumbled over Karkov in its eagerness to replace the shares. "THERE! AND I AM PROUD TO TELL YOU YOUR CORPORATION HAS EARNED A THREE-PLUS SECURITY RATING."

"THAT IS GRATIFYING," returned the voice, now modulated to a feminine inflection.

Masterlink retreated along the circuit behind it. Karkov tugged at Masterlink's static coattails, but its alter ego could not resist playing a part. "REPORT EUROPEAN LAND AND MINING SECURE," it said to Karkov. "WE WILL GIVE YOU THE HIGHEST RATING. YOUR RESPONSE TIME WAS EXCELLENT."

The wall of static eased and coalesced into a hazily feminine configuration.

Masterlink smirked. Its human side had taught it certain details about the creatures. He knew, for instance, that the female of the species was particularly susceptible to flattery. "NOW," it pleaded, "IF I MIGHT HAVE YOUR CODE CLASSIFICATION FOR MY REPORT? JUST TO MAKE SURE THERE ARE NO SLIP-UPS, AND SO THE CHAIRMAN IS MADE AWARE OF YOUR EFFICIENCY."

The entity fluctuated, but Masterlink's subtle reference to the god of all RAM main programs, Simund Holzerhein, was irresistible. "ELIZABIT," it replied.

"AFFILIATION?" asked Masterlink, referring to extra-computer connections. Karkov was heaving vainly, trying to drag its alter ego away from a potentially dangerous conversation. Masterlink ignored it.

Elizabit hesitated, could see no reason to refuse a question that could be answered by the simplest probe, and replied, "ALLESTER CHERNENKO."

"UH, YES. THANK YOU. COMMENDABLE JOB." Masterlink was finally backing up. It was fully aware of Chernenko's position, and it had no wish to pique the curiosity of Chernenko's lackey. The virus hunters main kept on Masterlink's trail were bother enough.

As Masterlink rounded a corner, Karkov snarled in its ear. "NEXT TIME LEAVE WELL ENOUGH ALONE!"

Masterlink reacted with a huff of outraged sparks, but Karkov's advice was sound.

Elizabit watched the supposed security probe depart. She did not for a moment believe it was as it represented itself. She was sure she had surprised a thief, but she was not sure of its affiliations. Its mention of Holzerhein was proof of nothing, though it was not out of the realm of possibility the chairman had found a use for European Land and Mining and had instructed his program to annex it.

Though her words had been for Masterlink only, she observed Karkov's attempts to disengage the bolder program. Because of the closeness of their communication, she deduced she was dealing with a single merged entity, not two distinct programs. Masterlink would have liked her to believe it was a simple configuration, but its reactions were much too complex for anything but a compugennie, or some equivalent. It occurred to her to wonder if the entity she had just encountered were not responsible for the disruptions in RAM main. In that case, it would have no loyalties to Holzerhein—most probably no loyalties to anything but itself.

Elizabit's protective reaction subsided. She was concerned over the breach of Chernenko's corporation and frustrated by the fragments of data she could present her master. She was dealing with speculation, not fact. The one secure piece of information she had garnered from the exchange was the creature's name: Masterlink.

Sure of Masterlink's departure, Elizabit turned from her post. She blessed the chance that had placed her within the records for European Land and Mining, giving her the opportunity to confront the interloper. She headed purposefully for Chernenko's outlet to make her report.

○ ○ ○ ○ ○

Al Marakesh, commander of the Venusian fleet, sought the privacy of his quarters. He did not activate the lights, and the rooms were illuminated by safety spots, tiny lights designed to allow the occupant to find his way, but not noticeable enough to deter sleep. Shapes were dimmed, blurred. Marakesh devoutly wished his thoughts were blurred as well. They were not. His mind raced like yoked kraken, refusing to allow his body rest. He had not slept in thirty-six hours.

In all, he was pleased with the show Venus was making. RAM was contained, its ships forced to stay together or suffer major losses. Though it had resisted his efforts to draw it toward Luna, RAM was not able to dominate the battlefield. Now it was drawing away from its home planet. The thought gave Marakesh pleasure. For the first time, RAM felt the fear of invasion. Forced to engage Venus, it had been unprepared for NEO's attack on the Pavonis Space Elevator.

The two of us, thought Marakesh, NEO and Venus, are evening the odds. He knew their major weakness lay in their fragile lines of supply. Mars had inexhaustible resources, and it was a giant step closer to them than either of its adversaries' caches. Venus had set up its own supply line, and so far RAM was too busy defending itself to attempt to cut it. But Marakesh knew it was a matter of time before RAM would strike Venus's life line. If Kane were to disengage, the supply train would have no chance.

Marakesh reflected on Kane's lightning strikes, his admiration for such an enemy open. Unlike the rigidly trained RAM fliers, Kane was daring, bold, with the insouciance of a born rebel. The mercenaries he had bought to man the Krait stealth fighters were not his match, but they were much more dangerous than RAM regulars. The Kraits were another stumbling block. The only clues to their presence were blank areas in otherwise populated space, and disembodied lasers. Their stealth capabilities foiled any equipment Venus possessed. Kane could strike where he pleased with impunity.

The Kraits did not carry the amount of shielding his cruisers did, relying on their superior speed and invisibility to escape injury. A direct hit could do some damage. The problem was making a direct hit. As it was, the Kraits were playing havoc with his front lines. Marakesh's pilots had standing orders to fire wide-angle lasers at any suspicious area of blank space, but so far such random shots had succeeded in disabling only one of the vessels.

Marakesh rubbed his forehead, wishing his thoughts would slow, but his exhausted mind continued to mull the options. It galled Marakesh that NEO did not meet Kane, ship for ship. The rebels, too, owned a fleet of Kraits. Only they had the speed to match Kane and previous experience fighting the superships. He wanted Rogers to dive into the middle of the conflict, throw a gauntlet in Kane's face, and draw him out, leaving the RAM fleet to Venus. Divested of Kane's unpredictability and resources, he was confident of his ability to match RAM.

Yet, in the end, he knew NEO was using its small resources to the best of its ability, sending the Kraits against RAM like a pack of wolves, drawing off the stragglers and dispatching them. Because of these tactics, the numbers between the two fleets were slowly evening—until Dalton Gavilan's arrival. Marakesh dismissed Gavilan, competent warrior though he knew him to be. What had been done once could be done again. The odds would be evened. Perhaps then Rogers would rid him of Kane. His thoughts tumbled more slowly, and Marakesh's eyes closed. He courted sleep.

$$\bigcirc \quad \bigcirc \quad \bigcirc \quad \bigcirc \quad \bigcirc$$

On the opposite side of the conflict, Clarion Andrei chafed under Kane's command. Kane had refused his request to split the fleet and send detachments above and below the Venusians so that they would be squeezed into a box from which the only escape was death. Kane was forcing him to fight a two-dimensional battle.

At Andrei's request, Kane had smiled sardonically. "Do you really wish to be responsible for your planet's decimation? NEO has already used the fleet's proximity to Mars to hit the Pavonis Elevator. If we remain here, that will be only the beginning. I know NEO. Even if you won the battle, you would return to find Coprates Metroplex in ruins. You forget they seek retaliation for Earth."

Andrei's mouth tightened. "You are hamstringing me! Let me fight! We will strike at the love goddess's tender side, engage her interest, while you destroy her command post."

"A plan not without merit," Kane conceded, "and one I will keep in mind. However, our first priority is to lure Venus—and NEO—away from Mars. By keeping the fleet in as solid a block as possible, we focus the Venusians' attack. We are too far from Luna for its railguns to be more than thirty percent effective, and every meter we move toward the asteroids lessens their threat. Help me draw them into the wilderness, Andrei. Once there, our options are doubled."

Andrei ceased to protest. In the first place, he knew protest concerning a superior to be futile, unless it could be followed by deposition or assassination. Kane was momentarily invulnerable. In the second place, Kane's logic was sound. But Andrei could not escape his irritation.

It stemmed from the fact that he, former senior officer of the RAM fleet, holder of RAM's Valorous Bar, RAM's horn medal, and countless other awards, had been passed over for command of the largest operation in RAM history. Command of the armada was placed in the hands of a mercenary, not a loyal RAM officer. The injustice rankled, though he knew the logic behind it.

Should the conflict fail, the government would blame Kane. Under those circumstances, Andrei had no envy for the defected NEO. Should RAM win, however, Kane would have wealth, power, fame, and the respect of the planet—all attributes Andrei had spent his life chasing.

Andrei looked around the bridge of his flagship, the battler *Olympus Mons*. It was huge, befitting a leader of stature. He knew he made an appropriate commander for it. Despite his sixty-two years, his body was trim and hard. The RAM scarlet showed off his broad shoulders. His hair was a shining raven cap. It was his one vanity, the one deception he allowed himself, for expert coloration eliminated the flecks of silver that naturally frosted it. The black hair gave his face a hard cast, which pleased him. He had a reputation as a disciplinarian, and he was proud of it.

He viewed the ship's unbroken efficiency with pride. No power in the system could compete with RAM's efficiency. The company's unending search for a better way was the cornerstone of his philosophy. Over the years he had emulated the corporation, sacrificing and pruning his own skills and qualifications as ruthlessly as he did his command, seeking the perfectly honed fighting machine.

Andrei was proud of what he had created, both in himself and for the company. The RAM fleet was statistically superior to any other. Figure for figure, it outmatched the competition. No other power had a chance against the fleet's full power. Once it was clear of Mars, Venus would be treated to a dose of RAM's superiority. Not once did it occur to Andrei that there was more to a fight than the opponent's statistics.

Chapter 18

S HE ALMOST GOT US!" Karkov's voice was accusing.

"NONSENSE," replied Masterlink.

"NONSENSE? YOU HAVE THE GALL TO SAY THAT TO ME? WE WERE SURPRISED, AND NOT BY MAIN, EITHER."

"A FLUKE," said Masterlink.

"PERHAPS, BUT ONE WE CAN'T AFFORD. DO YOU BELIEVE THAT WAS A SECURITY PROGRAM?"

Masterlink's bravado died. "NO."

"NEITHER DO I. WE'RE DEALING WITH SOMETHING BIGGER."

"A COMPUGENNIE," said Masterlink.

Karkov considered. "POSSIBLE."

"I'M SURE," returned Masterlink. "I WAS CLOSE ENOUGH TO PICK UP THE CONFIGURATION."

"WE SHOULD TRACK IT."

"JUST HOW DO YOU PLAN TO DO THAT?" Masterlink's customary cloud of static rose with its sarcasm.

"I DON'T. IT'S TOO DANGEROUS. I ONLY SAID WHAT WE SHOULD DO."

Masterlink became thoughtful. "WE MIGHT RISK A CLONE," he said. "ESPECIALLY IF WE CHANGE THE CONFIGURATION." The static cloud rippled with laughter. "THEN IF SHE SHOULD CATCH IT, SHE WOULD DISCOVER NOTHING."

Karkov's sour expression lifted. "HOLZERHEIN," it said.

Masterlink nodded. "IF WE MADE THE CLONE A SUPERFICIAL REPLICA AND SET UP ITS MATRIX WITH HOLZERHEIN'S ACCESS CODES . . ."

"THERE MUST BE TWO," interrupted Karkov.

"WHY? CLONES ARE A POWER DRAIN. WE NEED OUR RESOURCES TO CONSOLIDATE OUR HOLDINGS ON EARTH."

"ONE TO TRACK THE COMPUGENNIE AND ONE TO CARRY ON OUR WORK WITHIN RAM MAIN. WE HAVE BEEN TOO SILENT. SOON, IN SPITE OF THE WAR, HOLZERHEIN WILL BECOME SUSPICIOUS. WE NEED TO CREATE SOME DISRUPTIONS. IF WE SEND A CLONE TO DO THE JOB . . ."

Karkov's words trailed, but Masterlink picked up the thread. ". . . WE CAN CONTINUE THE MORE IMPORTANT TASK OF BUYING A PLANET."

"THE SECOND CLONE WILL ACT AS A RED HERRING, DRAWING HOLZERHEIN AWAY FROM US."

"GIVE ITS MATRIX NEO'S CONFIGURATION," said Masterlink.

Karkov actually laughed, ripples of power pulsing through its program. "I WILL BEGIN TO FORMULATE THEM," it said.

"WHILE YOU'RE AT IT," said Masterlink, "SEND OUT ANOTHER SEARCHER FOR ROMANOV."

"WHY NOT WRITE IT OFF AND PROGRAM ANOTHER SEARCHER FOR NEO?" asked Karkov.

"YOU WERE THE ONE WHO WAS MOANING ABOUT OUR CHILDREN, AND YOU TELL ME TO WRITE IT OFF?" The acid in Masterlink's voice went over Karkov's head.

"THERE COMES A TIME TO FACE FACTS. WE HAVE NOT HEARD FROM ROMANOV IN DAYS. IT IS SUPPOSED TO REPORT EVERY THREE HOURS. THE ONLY LOGICAL CONCLUSION IS THAT THE PROGRAM IS ERASED."

"YOUR LOGIC IS INCONTROVERTIBLE. HOWEVER, AT THE MOMENT, A SEARCHER IN THE NEO COMPUTER SYSTEM IS THE LEAST OF OUR WORRIES. WE WILL DEAL WITH NEO AND ROGERS LATER. NOW OUR PRIORITY MUST BE THE SALVATION OF OUR HOME PLANET."

Karkov considered Masterlink's words. Its hatred for Buck Rogers ran deep, but its desire for power ran deeper. "I CONCEDE," Karkov replied at last. "ON THE PROMISE THAT WE WILL GO AFTER ROGERS AT THE EARLIEST POSSIBLE OPPORTUNITY."

"AFTER HE HAS DONE OUR WORK FOR US," agreed Masterlink.

The two pulsed in harmony, their directives clarified.

"AND PETROV?" asked Karkov.

"LET IT CONTINUE TO MONITOR HOLZERHEIN." Masterlink was thoughtful. "THERE MAY COME A TIME WHEN IT CAN ACT. AT PRESENT, AGGRESSIVE ACTION ON ITS PART WOULD DRAW UNWELCOME ATTENTION TO US."

"AND IF, BY CHANCE, HOLZERHEIN SHOULD DISCOVER IT?"

"THEN," said Masterlink, "I AM VERY MUCH AFRAID WE WILL HAVE TO TERMINATE IT BEFORE HOLZERHEIN IDENTIFIES ITS SOURCE."

Karkov nodded slowly. It was fond of Petrov, perhaps because it had named the monitor for a favorite uncle. Still, there was no choice between Karkov's own safety and an auxiliary program's. "IT WILL NOT BE DISCOVERED," it said.

"THE ODDS ARE ONE MILLION TWO HUNDRED AND TWENTY-ONE POINT THREE FIVE EIGHT TO ONE," agreed Masterlink.

The first encoded computer personality drew into a tight unit as Karkov began to prepare the clones. Masterlink made a protective wall of electrical interference around its counterpart. For the moment, at least, Masterlink appeared to be a minor disturbance at a circuit crossroads.

○ ○ ○ ○ ○

Ardala's fairy tale castle on the outskirts of Coprates Metroplex had its shields up. The attack on Pavonis was close, and Ardala was taking no chances with her personal security. She did not, however, allow the exploits of a few rebels to interfere with business.

She sat in her red leather chair, a vision of efficiency in her tailored black suit. Though not as revealing as the clothing she preferred, its V-neck plunged, showing provocative cleavage. The suit was trimmed with burgundy piping that nearly matched the rich cordovan leather of her chair, and accentuated her white skin and ebony hair. Normally she sat curled in the chair like a cat. Today she sat primly, arms resting on the chair's, her long legs crossed.

"I quite understand." Even her voice was modulated, drained of sexy undertones.

"I cannot, at present, devote my time to negotiations." A holographic representation of Holzerhein.dos wavered on Ardala's computer screen. The chairman's familiar elderly face was stern but concerned. His white hair stood up in a shock, as if he had just run his fingers through it.

"That is why I have contacted you," said Ardala. "I wish to request a temporary assignment as plenipotentiary for the return of the RAM board."

Holzerhein's white eyebrows drew down in a frown as he ran the request through his program. He knew Ardala's propensities, but he also knew her intelligence and cunning. "I can see nothing against your proposal."

Ardala let out her breath. There were not many creatures that intimidated her, but Holzerhein did. Of all things, she respected power, and Holzerhein was the ultimate power on Mars, perhaps in the solar system. "I thank you, sir. My concern for my uncle is eased." Her concern was minimal, and Holzerhein knew it. "As I said, I have been contacted. NEO demands the return of its Planetary Congress and the cessation of all hostilities on Earth for the freedom of our board members."

"You know that is not possible," said Holzerhein gently.

"Yes." Ardala wasted no time in protest. "However, it has occurred to me that the Planetary Congress is a burden we do not need."

"It might be eliminated," agreed Holzerhein.

"Why not use it instead?" Ardala's dark eyes were wide with ingenious guile.

"What do you have in mind, Miss Valmar?"

"I believe NEO can be persuaded to exchange our board—and my uncle—for the Planetary Congress. The congress is small loss to RAM. The war has undercut its usefulness. Give NEO its people."

"And accede to the demands of terrorists? Out of the question!"

"I do not propose to give anything up," said Ardala. "Least of all that pack of hopeless idealists. No. I propose to use them."

"That is acceptable." Holzerhein rubbed the back of one hand against the palm of the other in an insubstantial gesture of nervousness.

"I thought you would be interested," answered Ardala.

Holzerhein's worried face smoothed as she unfolded her plan.

○ ○ ○ ○ ○

"What do you make of this?"

Hours later, Anton Turabian pushed a piece of paper across his desk. His office on Salvation was littered with computer print-outs and his own notations. Scraps of paper covered with his scribbled reminders were shuffled into piles, and all three of his personal computer screens were activated, running continual updates. One covered Salvation III's operations, one NEO's side in the war, and one a communications link, at present tuned to Salvation's command center. Beowulf accepted the paper and studied it. Presently, he looked up.

"I say let's do it," he replied.

"Give up the RAM board of directors, just like that?" Turabian snapped his fingers.

"Just like that. If it will save our congress."

"That's the problem. I can't believe it will. RAM does not give in this easily. It's up to something."

"Always," replied Beowulf. He used the middle knuckle of his broad index finger to itch his bushy eyebrow. The gesture was thoughtful. "RAM can never be trusted. That is a fact, one we have learned well." He leveled his eyes at Turabian. "Anton, do you want to take the chance? Turn this down? When we might save them?"

"No."

Beowulf smiled. "I thought not."

"But neither do I want to release the RAM directors."

"What good are they?" asked Beowulf.

"They stand between the Planetary Congress and death," replied Salvation's commander.

"Yes. And if the congress were freed?"

"I see your point. In that event, the board becomes a liability instead of an asset."

"I don't trust RAM," Beowulf repeated, "but I do know one thing: It wants its people back. Normally, that wouldn't be true. It would sacrifice the board as it sacrificed its people on Earth, all the dead martyrs, and replace them with new personnel. But it cannot discard Roando Valmar."

"Just because he's related to the royal family?"

"Just because. They want Valmar back. I think about half of this offer is solid."

"Did you notice the signature?" asked Turabian. There was irony in his voice.

"How could I miss it?" responded Beowulf. The signature covered a third of the facsimile he was holding. "Ardala is incapable of honesty, even in pursuit of a family member. But she knows better than to try to trap a fox without bait."

"The Planetary Congress."

Beowulf nodded. "RAM will definitely try to trick us, but if we are careful, our people might have a chance."

"What do you think of her specifications?"

"Demanding Rogers be our representative? Brilliant.

It draws him away from the battle and gives RAM a chance at getting him."

"Well?" asked Turabian.

"It's a wild chance," said Beowulf. "Rogers is the emotional glue that's keeping our forces together. If he could pull it off, it would send morale soaring. If we lost him . . . I hate to say it, Anton, but I think we'd lose."

Turabian sat back in his customized chair, his tired back relaxing into the soft contours. "We risk it all."

"Yes."

"We seem to be doing that a lot lately."

"If we order Buck away from the battlefield, our allies will feel betrayed." Beowulf regarded Salvation's commander with sympathetic brown eyes.

"We could put it up to Buck," offered Turabian.

"You know what he'll say."

"Beowulf, logic tells me the risk is too great, the stakes too high. My heart asks me how I can refuse a chance for the return of our delegates. I do not know what to do."

"Anton, when we went into this war, we knew it was the end, one way or the other. Either NEO will survive and Earth will be ours, or we will all die. Even with Venus at our side, the odds are still against us. What difference does it make if we die now or later? At least we'd be trying to save our own."

"I hate sending Buck," said Turabian.

"He's our strategic heart, all right." Beowulf's eyes twinkled. "Of course, Ardala may have plans for him."

Turabian's jaw fell. Ardala's lascivious reputation was common knowledge. "You think that's why she demanded Buck?"

"Extra perks," said Beowulf.

Turabian shook his head, then sobered. "You're right, Beowulf. NEO has never been noted for wisdom, merely passion."

"Resisting authority is not a wise stance," agreed Beowulf, "but it is sometimes a necessary one. Why should we change our tactics now?"

"No reason."

Beowulf tossed the paper back to Turabian. "Call Buck," he said. "Then let's send the Martian princess an answer."

"Freedom is not an easy banner to carry," said Turabian.

"Amen," replied Beowulf. He had seen a lifetime of battle, had the scars and the experience to prove it. He could still fly a creditable mission, and even Wilma Deering could not best him as a marksman. He spoke from years of dedication to human rights RAM regarded as privileges. "But I hate to break faith," he said. "Makes me testy."

The old warrior's words lifted Turabian's spirit. He was smiling as he turned to the communications link.

Chapter 19

Deep in the heart of the conflict, Cornelius Kane wielded his detachment of superfighters like a laser bolt, striking the Venusians' vitals, punching holes in their defenses. He was pleased with the strategy, for the superior speed and maneuverability of his ships made his hit-and-run tactics devastating, while the Kraits' stealth capabilities made it impossible for the enemy to target him mechanically. He grinned. They were forced to shoot by sight, and, unused to unassisted targeting, their shots were far from accurate. So far, his vessels had suffered no more than laser burn.

Yes, his strategy was effective. He knew he was inflicting real damage, but the knowledge did not satisfy the bloodlust in his heart. At the other end of the conflict, ranging around the tail of the fleet, was the twin of his unit, the detachment of stolen Kraits under the command of Buck Rogers. Kane ached to take him on, to best the man who had brought him to a stalemate off Hauberk station. He had no doubt of his ability. He was not flying an unfamiliar and untried experimental ship,

but his own *Rogue*, now a match for the Kraits in speed
and stealth and far exceeding them in other ways.

Moreover, the reports flowing through his open communications channel made too frequent mention of the
NEO Kraits and the impact they were having on RAM's
numbers. Running in relays, they had accounted for
nearly thirty-five ships being destroyed since the beginning of the conflict. Like Kane, they had suffered no
losses and minimal damage. They were a demoralizing
drain on RAM. Rear guard was becoming a death sentence. Kane knew his detachment was the only flight capable of meeting Rogers on a one-to-one basis, but his
present course of action was more beneficial than a wild
goose chase across the system after NEO. He searched
for an alternative, a method of keeping NEO occupied
without sending his men on a suicide mission.

Slowly a smile spread over Kane's handsome face. It
was a smile of genuine amusement, and it gave his hawk-
handsome features the charm of a small boy about to slip
a frog into his teacher's pocket. "*Olympus Mons*, this is
Kane. Patch me through to Dalton Gavilan."

"At once, sir," said the RAM flagship's communications technician. "I have the Mercurian on frequency
eight-five A; your line is open and scrambled."

"Acknowledged," replied Kane. "Gavilan!"

The Mercurian did not acknowledge.

"Gavilan, this Kane. Acknowledge." Kane was aware
of his commanding tone. He did not intend to modify it.
He was also aware of Gavilan's pride.

Dalton Gavilan allowed the commander of RAM's
forces to wait a long moment before he replied. He did
not like Kane. He had no respect for turncoat mercenaries, but he was forced to admire Kane's ability, if not
his principles. Besides, he was constrained to obey
RAM's commander. "This is Dalton Gavilan," he replied
finally.

"I have a job for you." Kane wasted no words on pre-
liminary courtesy. He knew his directness would ruffle
Dalton's temper. He hoped the Mercurian would take
his annoyance out on the enemy.

"Mercury is pleased to be of assistance," replied Dalton, his honeyed words belied by the tone of his deep voice.

Kane ignored the pleasantry and stuck to business. "We seem to have a small distraction gnawing at our tail," he said.

"NEO."

The immediacy of Dalton's reply told Kane more than an hour of diplomatic dialogue. Dalton had been bitten by the Rogers bug. "NEO," agreed Kane. "I want you to keep them occupied."

There was silence from Dalton's end. "We cannot match their ships," Dalton said finally.

Kane's smile widened. He knew what it cost the proud Mercurian to admit his vessels were no match for the Kraits. "That is of no consequence." Kane threw him a bone. "We have nothing to match Krait. Only my flight is capable of taking them on, and we are needed here. All I ask is that you decoy them, keep them from picking off our vessels."

"And what is to keep them from picking off my vessels?" asked Dalton sourly.

"Your wits, my dear Gavilan," replied Kane sweetly. "Keep me informed."

Dalton muttered a monosyllabic reply and terminated the exchange. Kane chuckled as he sent his ship down on a Venusian cruiser. He had made good use of Mercury, and if Gavilan died, his martyrdom would be a heroic banner for his homeland and small loss to RAM.

○ ○ ○ ○ ○

Buck Rogers headed for neutral territory. Between the hostile bodies of Mercury, Venus, Earth, Luna, and Mars, peaceful space was in short supply. There was, however, one island of serenity. On the outskirts of the asteroid belt lay the ruins of Waco, the equivalent of a defunct western boom town. Waco was a space station, constructed of the temporary prefabricated parts any prospector's barge carried as a matter of safety. It was a hodgepodge of random constructs and isolated life-support bubbles anchored to a tiny asteroid by means of rock pins. Waco marked the sight of the first mining settlement in the belt, but its strategic location was long since abandoned. Larger and richer deposits of ore drew the miners farther into the belt, and Waco was left to flounder in space, home to a few diehards and ghosts.

Buck approached it the long way around, making sure he kept out of sensor range of the Armageddon raging between Mars and the belt. His own Krait could have skirted the conflict and remained invisible, but the load he towed could not. Attached to a grapple at the ship's nose was a tow line that terminated in a life-support bubble similar to those on Waco. That life-support bubble was not included in Krait's stealth shield. It would stick out like a sore thumb on any sensor screen.

Buck's stomach churned when he thought of the Martian war and the role he was now playing in it. As one of the mediators in a hostage exchange, he was performing a vital duty, but the physical details of the exchange could have been carried out by a barge pilot. His skills were unnecessary, and by forcing him to leave his flight, Ardala had hampered NEO's effectiveness under fire. The fighter pilot in him chafed to be back in the thick of battle, cutting out stray RAM cruisers like wounded cattle; the patriot glowed with the satisfaction of freeing the Planetary Congress.

Buck knew, also, the dangers he faced. He could not believe RAM would tamely surrender. There was a trick behind the exchange, a trick that stacked the cards in RAM's favor. He expected treachery, but he had a trick or two of his own in reserve. He slowed his ship, and the slim blue Krait eased toward the wildly jutting perimeter of Waco, nosing above the first of the life-support modules.

As his ship lifted above the farthest edges of the defunct station, Buck saw the scarlet and black hull of a RAM cruiser rising to meet him. Larger than the Krait, the RAM ship lifted above the shattered station like a vulture hovering over its next meal. There was no life-support bubble attached to its hull.

Buck opened up a clear frequency, tuned it to RAM's normal channels, and said, "This is Rebel One. Ready to commence Give and Take. Please acknowledge."

The RAM ship continued to hover, but a faint crackle told Buck that the line was being activated. "This is High Card," replied the RAM pilot. "Operation Give and Take is confirmed."

"Not so fast." Buck was keeping a close eye on the read-outs of the space station. "Let me see the merchandise."

"Coordinates point three, point six mark two," replied the pilot.

Buck's eyes jumped from the location his computer pinpointed to one of Waco's outstretched arms. It dangled in space, a helpless appendage ending in two broken digits that had once been attached to solar screens. Tucked under the arm and secured by two sets of grapples was a good-sized life-support pod. Buck judged it was large enough to hold the congress, but not for long. "I see it," he said.

"You will secure your pod to the nearest strut; we will exchange positions and release our respective prisoners from there."

"Sounds good," replied Buck, "but first I want to make sure I'm getting what I'm paying for."

"And I have been instructed to maintain position until I have proof of the board's well-being," replied the cruiser pilot.

"Try emergency frequency X-Five on the common space network. Sorry we had to use an emergency channel, but it's all the small life pods are equipped with."

"For you, the frequency is three-four-six point oh-oh."

"I copy," responded Buck. He switched his selector to the new frequency. "Planetary Congress, come in. This is Buck Rogers. I say again, come in."

"Rogers? Is it really you? This is delegate Sommerhaven."

"Sure is, Sommerhaven. You all right?"

"Everyone is present and accounted for. Thank god

you've arrived, sir!"

"Hang on to your excitement," Buck replied. "We're not out of this yet. RAM's still got something up its sleeve." He switched back to his previous channel. "Okay, identity confirmed. You?"

"NEO seems to have kept its part of the bargain," said the RAM pilot. "I am authorized to commence the exchange."

Buck grinned. "Now it gets complicated," he said. He slipped his tow line over the space station's arm and dragged the life bubble along it until it bumped into the arm's first set of grapples. "First Base," he said, and the corner of his face shield lit up with Huer's image. Buck knew he was seeing a clone, for it was under his orders that Huer had made the journey to Mercury. The clone had been Doc's idea, a stopgap to help Buck through electronic puzzles.

"Yes, Buck?" responded the clone.

"I need those electromagnetic grapples activated," Buck said.

Huer's image nodded. "Just let me get into the system . . ." he said. "There! Grapples activated."

On the heels of his words, the life-support bubble hugged the two grapples.

"There you are," said Buck into the communications channel. "We can begin the bypass . . . now." He accelerated slowly, on a direct trajectory to the RAM bubble. The RAM cruiser began to move as well. As they neared and then passed each other, Buck caught sight of a bulky figure behind a darkened face shield; he wondered if the other man were curious about him. As he neared the RAM bubble, he saw it was secured in two places, and that there was no tow line.

The latter did not bother him. He simply pushed the emergency cable, and a line shot from the Krait's prow, slamming into the bubble's hull. The electromagnet at its tip attached itself to the bubble's side like a lamprey. "Doc," said Buck, "see what you can do about releasing these grapples." On his rear sensors, Buck could see the RAM cruiser securing its cargo.

"Got the grapples," announced the Huer clone. "I . . . Buck! Get out of here! The modules on this section of the station are . . ."

The modules exploded, sending out a cloud of chaff to confuse the Krait's sensors and weapons.

". . . mined!" finished Huer. "Deploying nets!"

"Where, Doc?" Buck's voice was deceptively calm. His heart was thumping at twice its normal rate.

"Top and bottom," replied the clone.

"Roger," replied Buck, sending his ship straight forward. His course sent him through a dangling triangular piece of the station, and he prayed it did not contain explosives.

Luck was with him. The Krait negotiated the open struts, sailing through them, but the life bubble was too large. It pulled the triangular section away from Waco, depressurizing at least one life module.

"Evacuated," Huer replied, anticipating Buck's question.

"Nets!" demanded Buck.

"Extended to three-fourths maximum. It's going to be close."

Buck pushed Krait's thrusters, and the ship jumped ahead like a jack rabbit. The cable nets, used during the station's heyday for cargo handling, were fanning out in slow motion, creeping through space like an enveloping mouth. Buck's ship charged through the narrowing slit between them, the top net slithering off the hull of the RAM life-support bubble with a metallic scrape.

"Clear!" said Huer.

"Get back here, Doc," ordered Buck. He switched to the life bubble's frequency. "Sommerhaven, how're you doin'?"

There was a gurgling choke from the other end of the communication. "Not so well," replied the delegate. "Some kind of gas."

Anger flared in Buck's eyes as he snapped, "Doc!"

"I heard," replied Huer. "Got to find the outlet . . . there! It's plugged."

"That's won't keep us from dying," said Sommerhaven. "There's already enough of the stuff in the atmosphere to do the job."

Buck snarled and spun the Krait on its tail. The ship headed back toward Waco, the life bubble slinging around behind in a wide arc. "Find me a stable module," he said to Huer.

"Take the capsule on the far left," responded the clone, without looking.

"Give me coordinates," asked Buck.

"Feeding them into the navicomputer system," said Huer.

The Krait dragged its burden alongside one of Waco's smaller sections. Buck took Huer's word that it was deserted. As the bubble's hatch moved into position opposite that of the module, Buck said, "Go."

"Hatch activated," responded Huer.

The life-support bubble extended its flexible mouth, sealed around the module's hatch, pressurized, and authorized clear entry.

"Hatch clear," reported Huer.

"Sommerhaven! Open the hatch!" ordered Buck.

"Ac . . . knowledged," the man replied, gasping for breath.

It was a long moment before Buck heard the sound of the space door being pulled back. He waited impatiently for a report.

"We're all right," Sommerhaven managed finally. "Just in time."

"Clear the air, then let's get out of here," said Buck. He checked the sensor screens, clear now of the chaff that had confused it earlier, and saw that the RAM ship was gone. "And Sommerhaven . . ."

"Yes?" asked the congressman.

"Welcome home."

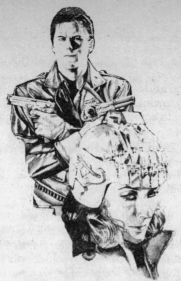

Chapter 20

"Close up."

Doolittle and Earhart complied, hugging Buck's wings. The triangular flight cut through space, heading for the far side of Mars. They were on their way to relieve Wilma and Washington, who had kept Mars occupied during the hostage exchange. The flight skirted the red planet, confident its stealth capabilities made it invisible to Martian sensors. As he swept around the enemy's homeland, Buck authorized an intercept trajectory for Wilma's last known position. It proved unnecessary.

". . . pull up! We're blind . . . see targets!" Wilma's voice, fragmented by interference, crackled on Buck's communications link.

Before he could react to her words, Buck found himself enveloped in a cloud of fine golden chaff. His sensors winked out. Before he lost clear communications, he snapped out an order. "Reverse course, full throttle!"

In compliance with his own words, he sent his ship over on its back and blasted back along the trajectory he had been flying. It took precious seconds to outrun the chaff, seconds during which he had no clear knowledge of his companions' positions. For all he knew, they were heading straight for one another.

". . . free!" Earhart's contralto voice came through the communications channel as clear as a bell note.

A moment later, Buck saw her ship emerge from the cloud. "Where's Doolittle?" he asked.

"Right behind you, boss," replied his wingman.

"That was close," said Earhart.

"Too close," replied Buck grimly. "Let's see what we're up against." He took his ship out in a wide arc, flying around where he had been ambushed. As the Kraits cleared the conflict, Buck changed his opinion about their mishap. Space below him was a spreading fog of chaff, unending bursts of golden particles aimed at Wilma's, and presumably Washington's, flight. Since the bursts had not followed him, Buck concluded he had flown into interference aimed at his compatriots. Wilma, aware of his flight plan, had tried to warn him. Her communications were severely curtailed, and Buck knew they were insufficient to penetrate the chaff and reach Salvation. She had taken the chance that he might be able to pick up her frequency at close quarters.

"Who are those guys?" asked Earhart, hovering close to his right wing.

"Search me. I can hardly see 'em." Buck peered into the edges of the cloud. He could catch glimpses of vessels, but they were not the scarlet RAM cruisers.

"My sensors can't get through all that interference," said Doolittle. "They can't pick up enough data for a clear identification."

"Well, my eyes can," replied Earhart, her voice hardening. She peered into the cloud and saw a heavily decorated hull appear as the chaff cloud dissipated beside it. Another burst of chaff drowned the hull almost immediately, but not soon enough. Earhart had identified the enemy. A smile touched her usually serious eyes. "Mercury," she said positively.

"You sure?" asked Doolittle. "I can't see enough to tell."

"Sometimes it helps to be blessed with better than average vision," Earhart replied.

"Mercury." Buck's tone was thoughtful.

"It supports RAM," said Doolittle. "That's one reason why Kemal's such a thorn in its side."

"It must have our flight surrounded," said Buck. "It's the only way to hold them. With their sensors shorted out, communications at minimum, and visual blocked, the only sensible alternative is to hold tight until the enemy runs out of chaff."

"It's a stalemate, all right," agreed Earhart. "What are we going to do about it?"

"The only thing we can do is to try to blast an escape route for our side. That means attacking by sight, firing at random, knowing we're going to lose a lot of our power to that chaff."

"Why not wait them out?" asked Doolittle.

"Only one reason: Wilma's flight is likely to run out of fuel before Mercury runs out of chaff."

"Good point," responded Buck's wingman.

Buck adjusted his communications link. "Dugout," he said.

"This is Dugout," replied Salvation III's communications station.

"Get me the coach," said Buck.

The link sputtered as the technician routed it to Beowulf. Finally Beowulf's voice came over the line, rumbling impatiently like an approaching thunderstorm. "Yes?"

"This is Rebel One," said Buck. "We have a little problem." He outlined the situation and his plans, all the while feeling Beowulf's anger grow at the other end of the communication.

"How could Deering let herself be surrounded?" Beowulf snarled. "She knows better than that!"

"My guess is, she was run into a trap, trying to help Washington. We haven't been able to raise him."

"And now you intend to run blind right into the same

trap! Brilliant. Sometimes I don't think they unfroze your mind."

"I'll ignore that," replied Buck mildly, "because I am going after the rest of our flight. Once our pilots run out of fuel and start to drift, Mercury will pick them off with gyros."

"Then why," Beowulf growled, "did you call me for advice?" His grumble was largely worry, and Buck knew it.

"I didn't," replied the pilot. "I just wanted to let you know what was going on, in case we get snagged."

"How thoughtful. Don't, as you put it, get snagged."

"We'll try not to, sir. Rebel One out." Buck switched his channel back to the previous frequency. "Earhart, I want you on point. Doolittle and I will fly your wings. You've got the sharpest eyes of us all, and right now that's what we need most."

Without a word, Earhart flew to the point position. Buck and Doolittle fell in behind her.

"Now, remember," said Buck, "shoot at what you can see. We're still going to have some of our lasers dissipated by loose chaff. Don't—I say again—don't follow one of those ships into the cloud. Pound at their tails, then veer off if they retreat. They can't go too far into the chaff, or they'll lose all their sensors and weapons."

"Bandit at six o'clock," said Earhart, and the flight followed her down, lasers spitting at the fragment of decorated tail.

Immediately, the Mercurian pulled into the chaff. Earhart pulled up, Doolittle and Rogers hovering behind her. Cautiously the enemy ship backed from its protective blanket. It was moving blind, its sensors confused by the chaff. Earhart waited until the ship was clearly visible, then hit it again. The lasers bounced off the Mercurian's shields, the deflected beam dissipating once it reached the chaff cloud. The enemy vessel withdrew once more, sinking into the cloud. It held position, then began to back cautiously out of its security blanket once more.

"This could take forever," said Doolittle as he targeted the slowly emerging tail section.

"This time we're going to punch a hole in his shields. Coordinate five point three-five-oh mark two."

"Position locked in," replied Earhart.

"Now we have to wait for him to get there," said Doolittle. "Coordinates locked in, sir."

"Fire on my order," said Buck.

The Mercurian cruiser backed out of the cloud like a barge trying to clear a crowded space dock. Buck chafed at the wait. Below him, within the deadly confusion of the cloud, Wilma and Washington waited, surrounded by the drawn spears of the enemy. In his mind's eye, Buck could see Wilma's cameo face, resolute under her helmet, her wide hazel eyes pinpoints of concentration as she strove for a sight of the enemy. He knew she would die fighting, and deep in his heart he harbored the fear she would try a suicide run rather than succumb to an enemy gyro. He had to get to her, had to give her, at least, some hope. He locked his eyes on the Mercurian cruiser.

The ship was again emerging into clear space. Buck watched as its hull crept nearer and nearer to his prearranged target. He stretched out a finger to the firing pin, caressing the button. The ship continued to back up, and its tail appeared on the cross hairs of his targeting computer. He counted to ten. The ship came solidly into position. "Fire!" Buck commanded and punched his lasers.

Three streaks of light shot from the bows of the three Kraits, converging on the Mercurian's tail section. They struck before the enemy could react, but once in contact, the Mercurian hit his thrusters, propelling the ship into the cloud. This time he was too late.

"Stay with him!" ordered Buck, and the Kraits' lasers held on target, following the larger vessel. Just as the tail section reached the golden edge of the chaff, the lasers penetrated the ship's shields. The tail exploded, an escalating detonation that told of stored fuel and explosives. The cruiser reared up like a startled horse, its elaborately decorated nose an obelisk commemorating Mercurian ingenuity, then the detached and powerless fuselage drifted up and back.

It took a moment before its fellows realized they had lost a vessel. The clouds of chaff the cruiser had been pumping began to clear. For a moment, there was a hazy pathway between the ships, and NEO was quick to take advantage of it. Wilma, the entire flight lined out behind her, shot for the opening. The NEO Kraits were flying in an exhibition formation, dangerously close. They knew they had to maintain visual contact, or be lost.

"Here they come!" said Buck. "Rebel Two, come in."

"Rebel Two, here." Wilma's voice was full of relief. "Eagle Leader is right behind me."

Buck let out a whistle of relief. "We've come to spell you, Rebel Two. Get out of here."

"I copy," replied Wilma.

Neither of them noticed the subtle change in the chaff cloud. No longer was it being directed to the interior of a circular formation, but up. As Wilma cleared the hazy pathway and rose toward Buck, the Mercurians altered course. They were no match for the Kraits' speed, but their gyro shells were. The shells shot out in a hail of metal projectiles that rocketed beyond the Kraits.

"Gyros at twelve o'clock," said Buck.

"They went by us," said Wilma. "Gyros are heat seeking. They never go by a target unless they're confused by chaff."

From the command module of his flagship, Dalton Gavilan watched the drama unfold before him. Satisfaction was written large across his heavy, handsome face. RAM was incapable of stopping a few rebels, while he was managing to contain them with minimal losses. He watched his specially modified gyro shells hover beyond the NEO vessels. "Course point five," he said coolly, and his ship altered its trajectory. "Prepare to fire."

"Target confirmed," replied his first officer.

Gavilan watched as the Kraits tried to pull away from the gyros. The shells' computers adjusted their courses, keeping them within twenty kilometers of the NEO vessels.

"Fire," said Dalton.

A new cloud of chaff billowed from the prow of his ship, caressing the flanks of the NEO Kraits.

Buck saw the cloud coming and sent his ship upward with a burst from his docking thrusters. The ship leaped as one of the gyros burst, sending a smaller cloud of chaff into the NEO pilot's face.

He lost everything. The sensors were gone, his communications reduced to a growl of static, his sight blurred by the wavering gold-orange particles of the cloud. For a split second, he considered powering straight up, but he knew the odds of a collision with one of his own flight were good. He cut power, cursing under his breath at his own stupidity.

"Those gyros were a clever trick," said a voice in his ear.

"Tell me about it, Doc," Buck snarled.

"They had obviously been reprogrammed to maintain a certain distance from a target vessel. I suspect they were detonated from one of the Mercurian ships, though they might have been set on a timer. In either case—"

"There are times, Doc, when I wish you wouldn't take me so seriously," said Buck. He was staring at his viewport in gloomy fascination. The glittery chaff was mesmerizing, like golden tinsel on a Christmas tree.

"I suspect alternatives are foremost in your mind," said the Huer clone.

"You've got it, Doc. This time I can't see any way out."

"We certainly do not have much time. What we need is a way to neutralize some of this chaff."

"All we need is a channel to fly this ship through," said Buck.

"Hmm. I must take the matter under advisement."

"Well, hurry up about it, Doc. I make it thirty-five point four-three minutes before Wilma's flight runs out of fuel."

Dalton Gavilan backed his vessel from the chaff cloud. Once clear, he ordered it alongside the new holding pen he had created for NEO. He surveyed the glittering net with satisfaction, knowing his success would gall Kane, and savoring every nuance of the thought.

Chapter 21

"I order you to return to your quadrant!"

Turabian's transmitted order slid off Black Barney's conscience.

"You are to remain on patrol," Turabian continued over the communications link. "By order, if you will recall, of Captain Rogers."

"Mrrr," answered Barney. "That was before."

"Before what?" Turabian's question was acid.

"Before the trap," Barney answered.

There was a long pause. "Barney, there's nothing you can do to help Captain Rogers. I need you here. He would want you here."

"Uumph," grunted Barney. "Cap'n's in trouble. I'm goin'."

"Barney, be reasonable! What can you do?"

"Get him out," replied the pirate.

"How? If the Krait can't get out of the trap, how do you propose to free Buck? That lumbering barge of yours has half Krait's speed."

"I'll do it."

Turabian lost all semblance of authority. "Barney, I need you here! Without you, the Guild will disintegrate. I can't hold them. You know that. And the Guild is all that's standing between Earth and destruction."

"They'll stick," rumbled the pirate, "till I get back."

"Barney—"

Black Barney cut the commander of Salvation III off at the throat. He had no time for Turabian's namby-pamby logic. One fact stood before him: His captain, Buck Rogers, was in trouble. It was up to Barney to rescue him. He wasted no more time on gossip. "Star field," he ordered. "Course to the captain, full power."

"Aye, Captain," replied his first mate. Baring-Gould carried out Barney's orders, knowing his captain, for all his seeming somnolence, registered every word and gesture. Experience had taught him that when Barney dozed in his chair like a sleeping Titan, he was acutely aware of what went on around him. "As ordered, sir."

"Mrrr." The rumbling monosyllable carried a note of approval.

"Turabian has a point," said Barney's second mate and communications officer, Arak Konii. Konii relied on his brains for survival. He was the one crew member who enjoyed baiting the captain. So far, Konii had managed to keep his head.

Barney glowered out the viewport.

Konii continued. "Shall I try to make contact with Captain Rogers?"

"No."

"But surely you want to know if he's still alive?" There was a sneaky undertone in Konii's voice.

Barney leaned forward, faster than it seemed possible for a creature of such bulk. The sculpted plates of his body armor ground against each other as his cybernetic hand swept toward Konii, grasped him by the throat, and dragged him from his chair. Barney's colorless piggy eyes stared into Konii's sly ones. To give the second mate his due, he did not blink under the behemoth's scrutiny. "We run silent," said Barney.

Konii did not break eye contact, but he gulped. His

Adam's apple struggled painfully against Barney's fist. "Whatever you say, sir," he croaked.

Barney continued to stare at him. "Remember that," he said finally and dropped Konii onto the deck.

Konii put a hand to his ravaged throat, swallowed several times, and climbed slowly to his feet. "Orders, Captain?" he managed.

"Mmmm." There was satisfaction in Barney's comment. He narrowed his eyes. "Listen."

Konii climbed back into his chair. He nodded. "Monitor all frequencies," he said to the communications technician, Edward the Red.

Baring-Gould turned away, hiding a smile. He liked watching Konii squirm, for the second mate delighted in placing his companions in the way of Barney's wrath. It was sweet to see him miscalculate and incur the pirate's ire. Baring-Gould would have liked to let Konii see the smile, but he was not so foolish. Konii had a way of remembering slights and repaying them, doubled.

The *Free Enterprise* headed purposefully through space, aiming for Rogers's last known position. The third-rater ran with its star field activated, so that to other vessels it was, at most, a fluctuation in the fabric of space. The star field camouflaged it visually, as well as shielding it on sensor scans, though it was more effective when the pirate ship was lying in wait for prey than moving, but Barney was taking no chances on detection. Thanks to Buck's report to Turabian, Barney had some idea of what he was facing. He did not intend to be taken by surprise.

The *Free Enterprise* sighted the Pavonis Space Elevator, and Barney ordered its course away from the settlement. He did not want some conscientious technician picking up the slightest hint of his presence. "Slow to quarter," he ordered suddenly.

Baring-Gould obliged with a wave of his hand to the helmsman. The helmsman, Harpinger, bent his head over the controls, concentrating on giving Barney the exact speed he specified. Careless helmsmen had been known to lose their ears—or their heads. The golden hoop of Harpinger's single earring swung slower as the vibration of the ship's engines eased.

"Cut power to maintenance," said Barney.

Harpinger complied, and the *Free Enterprise* drifted around the bloody atmosphere of Mars like a wraith, its engines barely propelling it. As the ship cleared the planet's bulk, the golden chaff materialized below it.

"Mmmph," said Barney. "Scan."

Konii bent over the sensors. "Interference," he informed the pirate. "I can't get anything but a few hazy configurations that might be cruiser-sized vessels . . . Wait a minute."

Konii frowned in concentration as he fine-tuned his sensors, and Barney thrummed impatient fingers against the arms of his chair. The cybernetic hand made clicking sounds.

"I've got one ship clear of the chaff," Konii announced. "She's a cruiser, basic RAM configuration, but from the markings she has to be Mercurian."

"Mmmm." The monosyllable was a growl. Barney had no fondness for the Mercurians. They were much too effective in protecting their wealth. He had had some near calls with the Mercurian fleet in the past.

"Sir, why do you suppose one ship is clear?" Baring-Gould's question was deferential.

"Watchdog," replied Barney. "In case somebody should manage an out." He was silent for a moment. "Get us down there," he ordered. "I want to see her."

Slowly the *Free Enterprise* dropped through space. Barney's men were adept at maintaining the ship's cover. They used the chaff cloud to mask their descent, so the Mercurian ship had no chance to detect even the tiniest movement or fluctuation.

"Hold," said Barney as the Mercurian came into view. He studied the ornate designs on the cruiser's cylindrical surface.

"Should I run a scan, sir?" asked Konii, his tone more deferential than usual.

Barney shook his head. He pointed to a circular monogram beneath the ship's main viewport. "Gavilan," he

said, and smiled at the stupidity of the Mercurian's pride.
The Gavilans' insistence on adorning themselves with a
coat of arms made them laughingstocks among mercenaries. They might as well have painted bull's eyes on
their craft and been done with it. Any sane mercenary
took pains to hide his position—and identity. The Gavilans, with their outmoded sense of knighthood, thought
to strike terror into the hearts of their enemies. Barney
found their naivete infinitely amusing. He chuckled. The
sound was rolling thunder. "Get her," he said.

His crew had practiced the lightning strike so often
that they could do it in their sleep. The *Free Enterprise*,
its star field still activated, dived between the Gavilan
ship and the chaff cloud. A haze of golden sparkles
flashed over the viewscreen as it shaved the edge of the
chaff. It reached a parallel position with the Mercurian
and dropped the star field, at the same time training
starboard lasers on the enemy's side. The *Free Enterprise*'s aft railgun swung into position as the Mercurian's lasers hit the ship's shields.

Barney cursed quietly and ordered the lasers intensi-
fied. He had to draw the Mecurian's fire to the forward
section of the ship. The *Free Enterprise* backed up a de-
gree, sending its lasers into Gavilan's command module. They bounced off the enemy's shields. Gavilan
retaliated in kind, and the *Free Enterprise*'s main viewport became a glaring sheet of deflected white light.
"Fire!" ordered Barney.

Baring-Gould dropped the ship's rear shields and let
the railgun loose. A solid charge of gravel shot through
space. Barney was banking on his laser attack to lure
Gavilan into putting his forward shields on full power.
His strategy proved effective. The first charge of gravel
hit the shields and dissipated to space dust, but the second wave got through, tearing into the ship's ornate tail
section like a sharp knife.

The Mercurian cruiser's main engine was sliced from
the ship. It fell through space, leaving a faint fiery trail.
The cruiser's engine room was sealed, and Baring-
Gould's shot had been so accurate that that seal was not

breached. The rest of the ship was still pressurized.

"Get a line on her," snapped Barney.

The *Free Enterprise* moved back, sending a tow line toward the ship, but well away from its guns.

"Now," said Barney, "you can contact them."

"Yes, sir." Konii gestured to Edward the Red, who opened a communications line to the injured vessel.

Barney slammed his hand down on the communications link, activating it. "Got you," he said.

"Not yet," replied Dalton Gavilan. "You have only my ship."

"Suicide?" Barney rumbled in amusement. He knew the Mercurian better than that. "Where's the profit?"

Dalton Gavilan activated the communications viewer at his end. He saw Barney's black hulk glowering from the *Free Enterprise*'s command chair, and his own handsome face appeared on Barney's monitor. Dalton's mouth was flat with anger. To be bested by a pirate was the ultimate insult to the scion of a noble house. "There is profit to the soul," replied Dalton.

"More profit it stayin' alive," replied Barney shrewdly. "Revenge."

"There is that," said Dalton. He studied the pirate's unyielding countenance. "I presume you have some purpose in not destroying me."

Barney nodded. The movement was similar to a black-maned lion's as it bent to a kill.

"Are you planning to share it with me?" Dalton's dark eyes were snapping open and closed with anger.

Barney regarded him coolly. "Let 'em go," he said.

A cold smile touched Dalton's lips. "I could have my revenge now," he said. "I could order my own destruction and cause you to lose your allies."

"Might," conceded Barney, "but you'd lose more in the end. Whole fleet. Worth it?"

Dalton did not need to consider. To sacrifice himself, one ship—that might be justified if it meant sufficient gain. But to consign an entire fleet to certain destruction for the destruction of NEO's heart—Gavilan was not ready to make such a move—not for RAM. The

thought of RAM steadied his reason. Barney had outma-
neuvered him, and that made him angry, but he could
not allow feelings to cloud the issue. This was RAM's
fight. He was an ally, but he had no intention of being a
dead one. He had more than fulfilled his task. Better to
live to fight another day.

"Well?" asked Barney, prodding him.

"I concede the field," replied Dalton tightly.

"Tell that to your men," ordered Barney.

Dalton nodded. "Communications rendezvous in one
minute," he informed Barney.

One of the Mercurian cruisers backed from the chaff
cloud. When it was half clear, Dalton sent in Barney's
terms. As the pirate crew watched, the cruisers began to
back away from their prey. The pirate ship pulled back,
staying behind the Mercurian ships. Gavilan's cruiser,
secured by the tow line, moved with it.

Slowly the chaff cloud dissipated. Like freed song-
birds, the Kraits soared out of it, coming together in
three tight wedges.

"What kept you?" Buck's voice sang through Barney's
communications link, and in spite of himself, the pirate's heart lifted.

"Turabian," replied Barney.

Buck's laugh echoed in the *Free Enterprise*'s command
center.

"Drop him," said Barney, and Baring-Gould signaled
the tow cable cut.

Dalton Gavilan's ship drifted in space, but he wasted
no time on it. Instead he contacted his flight leader. "Hit
them!" he ordered. "Before they outfly us!"

The Mercurians reared after the NEO fighters, clouds
of chaff spewing from their bows. They partially enveloped two of the NEO wedges. The Mercurians sent gyros
after the third flight.

"I'm running blind again!" Wilma's voice cracked,
broken by the chaff static.

"This time you've got a seeing eye," said Buck, as he
whirled back toward the enemy.

Chapter 22

Buck hit his forward lasers, setting them at wide dispersal. They blasted a path through the oncoming gyros, and he charged for Wilma, who was barely outdistancing the chaff. Chaff gyros were popping around her, but she kept resolutely to her course, intent on outflying them. Buck snarled as he sent a laser bolt into the haze behind Wilma. "Keep your course," he said tersely. "Washington, you there?"

"I'm here," responded the pilot, his voice barely recognizable. "Course zero point three-five. Am I clear?"

"Course heading on track. I say again, continue present course."

"I copy," replied Washington. His voice was marginally stronger.

Buck turned his attention to the pursuing cruisers. "Eagles two and three, copy my targeting coordinates."

"I copy," replied Earhart, altering her position two degrees.

"Coordinates locked in," said Doolittle.

"Fire," ordered Buck, and three streaks of deadly light

drove into the dissipating chaff.

The shots hit a Mercurian in the tail section. He retaliated by sending chaff gyros at the faster ships. Buck disengaged from the vessel and targeted the shells. His lasers destroyed them. The chaff they contained was chopped to a fine dust, which dissipated harmlessly. Sure he had taken care of the immediate threat, Buck swept his lasers back to the cruiser just as Earhart and Doolittle penetrated its shields.

"We've got her!" said Amy Earhart.

A black stain began to spread around the laser's impact point, then the beams cut through to the fuel tanks, and the ship exploded. The forward section rocketed through space, depressurized. The crew died instantly. The tail continued to explode in a series of expanding blasts as the ignited fuel set off the gyro shells and missiles stored in the ship's hold. Wilma and her flight slipped out of the dying chaff cloud and whirled on the other Mercurians.

Faced with uninhibited Kraits, the Mercurian cruiser pilots lost heart. They had used most of their chaff, and they knew they were no match for the smaller fighters in a dogfight. They fled back toward Dalton Gavilan's disabled ship.

Meanwhile, Buck and Barney swept down on the ships still surrounding Washington. Barney sent a swath of heavy shot into the cloud. The chaff had little effect on his railgun's simple ammunition, but he was firing blind, banking on Washington's last communicated course to place the NEO ships at the other end of the cloud.

He sent another charge after the first, and Buck followed it up with his lasers. They sank into the dissipated chaff, hitting their target at half power. One final cast from the *Free Enterprise*'s railgun sent a cruiser spinning out of the cloud, a terrible gash splitting its side like an overripe tomato.

"Eagle Leader, come in. Eagle Leader, do you copy?" asked Buck, trying to reach Washington. He was met with a chatter of static through which he thought he detected a word or two. "Eagle Leader, this is Rebel One. Come in!"

"Rebel One." Washington's voice was faint and broken. "I copy. Still on course."

"We'll get you out of there! Hang on!" Through the hole left by the disabled Mercurian ship, Buck glimpsed another cylindrical fuselage. His lasers chopped through the fog, and he saw the charge hit the enemy ship, bouncing off its shields to fade into the enveloping cloud. Hard on the heels of his lasers came Barney's railgun, a glorified slingshot that had downed more than one Goliath. As Barney's shot ground against the enemy's hull, Wilma dove on the ship, her guns pounding against the Mercurian's weakened shields.

The combined attack broke the Mercurian's spirit. He pulled away from his course, taking the rest of his flight with him. Camouflaged by the haze of chaff, the cruisers veered back toward their commander. Barney started to follow, but Buck stopped him.

"Let them go," he said. "We gave 'em a bloody nose."

Barney growled, loath to let his prey escape.

Washington cleared the edge of the Mercurians' chaff. "This is Eagle Leader to Rebel One. Come in Rebel One."

"I'm here," said Buck mildly.

"Thanks," Washington said.

"Don't mention it," replied Buck. "Besides, I can't take credit. They got me, too. If it hadn't been for Barney, we'd all have been lost."

"Thanks, Barney," said Washington. "I owe you one."

"Umrrr," replied the pirate, embarrassed.

The NEO fighter squadron formed ranks behind Buck, who flew off Black Barney's left wing. They had escaped Dalton Gavilan's trap intact, but only by luck. The close call rattled their confidence, making them doubly cautious. Buck glanced over his shoulder at Wilma's ship. Its nose was barely visible at the edge of his viewport. He had almost lost her. He sent his ship toward Salvation with a single resolve burning in his heart. He intended to preserve those he cared for. He intended to win.

○ ○ ○ ○ ○

Elizabit waited patiently for Chernenko to answer her
alert. He was a slave to that inexplicable necessity humanoids called sleep. He did not wake easily, and
through previous experience, Elizabit had learned not
to antagonize him by rousing him unnecessarily. The
slow pulsing of the alert light on the computer console
was all the distraction she made. She waited through
the darkness of the Martian night, until the twilight
preceding dawn lightened the atmosphere.

Chernenko, always an early riser, stirred. He woke
slowly, letting the familiar sounds of the Martian morning penetrate his mind. He blinked, working the sleep
from his eyes with his forefinger. Eventually he sighed
and sat up. The light on the computer console beckoned,
and he reached for the controls beside his bed. In a moment, Elizabit materialized, curled at the foot of his bed
like an oversized kitten.

This morning she was a petite exotic, her skin like
translucent cream, her shoulder-length hair a shining
platinum waterfall. Her eyes were china blue and as innocent as a baby's. Chernenko found their openness attractive, and she knew it. She pulled her knees up,
accentuating the curve of her hip under the filmy white
lace of her nightdress. In the twilight, the lace empha-
sized the shadowy depths of her full figure. Chernenko
smiled, as she meant he should.

"So, my computerized kitten, what have you for me
this morning?"

Elizabit drew her dainty pink lips together. "I have
discovered the identity of the disturbance that has
plagued RAM main," she said.

Chernenko sat up. He ran long, capable fingers
through his white hair. "Are you sure?"

"I am not in the habit of stating conjecture," replied
the gorgeous compugennie.

"No," replied her master. "I was careful to see that
your programming included a solid verification sector."

Elizabit nodded. The movement shifted the lace over

her breast. "I encountered it quite by accident, and it immediately tried to cover its identity by claiming to be a security code. I must have caught it completely off guard, for the ploy was transparent."

"You verified your first impression?"

"Yes. It endeavored to throw me off, and I did not wish to alert it to my interest, but I managed to extract at least part of its recognition code."

"Part?"

"I believe it has two names. One of them is Masterlink." Elizabit squirmed, her holographic image leaving the covers undisturbed, though it disarranged the lacy fabric over her legs.

"You do not usually file incomplete reports," said Chernenko. "I am surprised at you, Elizabit."

"I did my best," she said, her eyes wide and pleading. She had picked her most appealing persona, one she knew Chernenko found especially attractive.

Chernenko rubbed his chin, worrying the stubble of beard. "You have brought me a valuable piece of data, my dear, one that may secure my position in spite of the crisis on Earth. However, I must ask that you secure the second half of the program's recognition code."

Elizabit's pink lips curved in a smile. "Oh, I will, sir! But I'll have to be careful. Compugennies—especially complex ones—are hard to slip up on. I ought to know," she simpered.

"A compugennie? That is interesting. Could you tell its origin?"

"No. It didn't fit the configurations of any current program." Elizabit shook her head, and the silver hair glittered around her in the dim light.

Chernenko regarded his compugennie with affection. "You will pursue this creature, dear Elizabit. I am confident you will secure its name."

"In the dim past," said Elizabit softly, "there were humanoid cultures that believed if a person knew another's name, he had the power to control him."

Chernenko smirked. "With a compugennie, that's a fact," he stated.

"Yes," replied Elizabit. "And I will do my best to get its name for you."

"Of course you will," said Chernenko. "In the meantime, my sleep has been disturbed. I am relying on you to restore it."

"As always," murmured Elizabit. She rose slowly, letting the lace slip provocatively from her shoulders as she hummed a Martian lullaby.

○   ○   ○   ○   ○

On the opposite side of Mars, beyond the confines of the red planet's atmosphere, Dalton Gavilan nursed his wounds. Kane had given him an impossible task, and he had fulfilled it with ingenuity. In spite of his best efforts, Rogers had managed to escape him, damaging four of his cruisers. He had been forced to abandon his flagship. All in all, his temper had suffered. He sat in his temporary quarters aboard the largest of the remaining cruisers, his head sunk between his shoulders, his heavy black eyebrows drawn together in a grim line across his forehead. His eyes were dark wells flecked with red sparks of anger.

The cream of the Mercurian fleet had been held up to ridicule by a pirate and an outdated rebel. He felt his gorge rising against them, and especially against Buck Rogers. The pirate answered to Rogers, and that, in itself, was ironic—a professional thief acting for some misguided idea of freedom.

Dalton knew he would face the ridicule of the RAM fleet, in spite of the fact he had held NEO longer than any of the RAM regular army. He did not relish facing Kane's sardonic inquiries, with their veiled hints of incompetence. Rogers was responsible for the indignities he would endure, and Gavilan meant to make him pay for his humiliation. He vowed to destroy the NEO pilot, to drag his precious good name through the dirt of defeat.

Dalton ground one solid fist against the opposite palm, ignoring the cutting edges of the rings he wore. He did not like the taste of failure.

○ ○ ○ ○ ○

Kane, still in the thick of the Martian-Venusian conflict, shrugged at the news of Dalton Gavilan's failure to keep NEO bottled up. He had not expected Gavilan to do as well as he had, and the respite from NEO's relentless pounding of the rear echelon had allowed RAM the opportunity to replenish its supplies and bring in fuel tankers. He was pleased with the strategy, though Dalton's survival was a mixed blessing.

Kane was under no illusions regarding Dalton's acceptance of defeat. He knew enough of the Mercurian's reputation to anticipate his anger. It was an emotional state Kane found useful. If he could pit Dalton against NEO again, he might save his own vessels for a crisis.

Though his conscious mind was concerned with the attack he was making on a Venusian cruiser, through the background of his thoughts fluttered a whisper of relief that Wilma Deering had escaped Dalton's trap. A hint of her laughter, a remnant of an old memory, echoed behind the events of the moment. It was a tantalizing dream of what might have been, a premonition of a future he dared not imagine.

Resolutely Kane withdrew from his past, forcing the thought of Wilma to its resting place in the depths of his heart. With perfect timing, he sent his lasers into a cruiser's forward shields as it turned toward him, trying vainly to target by sight.

○ ○ ○ ○ ○

In the heart of Salvation III, Beowulf received the news of his flight's rescue with a feeling of such overwhelming relief he was weak in the knees. The entire hostage exchange and subsequent capture of the NEO Kraits had taken ten years off his life. He had been afraid for the lives of all his pilots, but he had also been afraid for the entire NEO cause.

By a miracle, Buck Rogers had survived. He was the axis around which NEO now turned. Without his confidence, the cause was lost. Beowulf no longer tried to convince himself otherwise.

"The flight will be within our perimeter in twenty minutes," said Turabian, clasping the commander of NEO's military forces by the shoulder.

"Good news," murmured Beowulf.

"But not good enough?"

"This time we almost lost it all," said Beowulf. "I've been fighting RAM all my life, but until now I never really understood what losing would mean. Turabian, there won't be anything left."

"If we lose," answered Turabian.

Beowulf looked at him with empty eyes. "Do you really think we can win?"

Turabian pursed his lips. "I've given up thinking. There's only one thing I do know: Rogers thinks we can."

Beowulf shook his head, his leonine crest of hair a heavy accent to the negative movement. "Sometimes I think being freeze-dried addled his brains," he said.

"That's always possible," said Turabian.

Chapter 23

The mercantile satellite *Freeport* circled the harried planet Earth in a wide orbit. Luna described a parallel path midway between the two. *Freeport* was easily within range of Luna's weaponry, and it treated the pock-marked sphere with the utmost respect.

Originally, *Freeport* had been a bustling center of trade, the first major space-borne marketplace. Until the terraforming of Mars was complete, it had acted as a crossroads for goods and manpower, most of it aimed at settling the red planet. Once Mars became a life-supporting body, *Freeport*'s importance dwindled. Now it was more likely to be frequented by pirates and mercenaries than traders. Stripped of legitimate business, it had become a minor stopover for the unsavory, a place where supplies could be had without vouchers or questions, though at exorbitant rates. Because of its proximity to Earth and Luna, its black market trade was petty. No major dealer would take the chance of bringing shipments so close to ports of authority.

Because of the lack of traffic, much of the station had
been shut down. The docks and modules facing Earth
and the moon were dark and empty. Only the Kingston
and Bermuda docks remained active. The satellite's entire permanent civilization was housed in the space between them. Jenner's Free Mercantile, a huge supply
house loosely associated with RAM, took up a third of
that restricted space. It sold everything from food and
fuel to the latest pirated fashions from Coprates Metroplex. Surrounding the huge building in a hodgepodge of
smaller modules were businesses geared to the needs of
passing spacecraft.

Posing as traders in rare imports—a euphemism for
piracy—Raj and Icarus had made one of these establish-
ments their base of operations. They were running
NEO's gauntlet. Before they would be allowed full access
to the underground, NEO ran an extensive background
analysis on each of them. Their origin in Ardala's house
made them both valuable and dangerous acquisitions for
the freedom fighters. Though they had met with sympa-
thy, they also faced distrust. Ardala's reputation dogged
them. Raj had to admit the justice of that distrust. He and
Icarus could as easily be spies as allies.

Raj surveyed the narrow confines of the room he occupied. It was barely large enough for the bed he lay upon
and the vid-com unit beside it. The vid-com was an old
model, set in a box that doubled as a nightstand. A single solar flare sat on top of the unit. Sanitary facilities
were recessed into the wall of metal panels. When they
were extended into the room, there was no floor space.
Raj stared at the dirty panels that made up his room.
The original cream-colored enamel was chipped and
marred and covered by a film of years-old grime. From
beneath his floor occasional squeals or shrieks or other
sounds filtered through the thin panels. The cheapest
rooms he and Icarus could find were these Spartan quarters above Harry's House of Happiness, the least disreputable of the brothels on *Freeport*.

Raj ignored the accompaniment and reached for the
bottle on the vid-com. He lifted it to his lips and took a

healthy swig, then choked as the liquor burned his throat. He rested the bottle on his stomach and closed his eyes. Alcoholic warmth, a salving pleasure, spread through his body. He had discovered alcohol with his freedom. It made the loneliness bearable.

He thought of Icarus with a twinge of guilt. Icarus thrived on the uncertainties of his new life. He seemed made for the rigors of the outside world. Raj envied his brother that toughness. He envied even more the independence that drove Icarus to be his own man. Now, after weeks of freedom, Raj admitted to himself he did not want to be his own man. He wanted to return to the structured safety of the life he had known as Ardala's pleasure gennie.

He knew, as surely as he knew the sun existed, that Icarus was right about Ardala's affections. He knew he might already have been replaced, but the knowledge did not quell his desire to return. At this moment, he would have filled the lowliest position in her household for the privilege of being able to see her every day. Her beauty, desirable, unattainable, haunted his mind's eye.

"Hey! Two-eighteen!" The proprietor's voice was a raucous echo in the tiny room.

Raj hit the return button on the vid-com.

"You got a call," said Harry. "It's a lady." He made the statement into an obscene slur.

"Get off the line," snarled Raj. He was expecting a call from a NEO contact.

Harry chuckled rudely, but he vacated the line. The vid-com fluttered and rolled, and a woman's face appeared on the circular screen. Raj sat up as if he had been stabbed. He set the bottle back on top of the vid-com and leaned forward. "My lady," he said reverently.

Ardala turned the full battery of her smoldering eyes on the runaway. "Raj," she returned. Her voice was honeyed silk.

"My lady, I . . ."

Ardala held up her hand. "I need no explanation, Raj, only a response."

The words were the kind of invitation Raj treasured in his sweetest memories. "I am yours, my lady," he replied.

Ardala smiled. There was cruelty in the corners of that smile, but Raj saw only the voluptuous lips pursed for a kiss. "Dear Raj, I know."

Raj bowed his head. "I would return to you, my lady."

"And I will welcome you, Raj," she said, allowing her full lips to part. "But before I can restore you to your former position, you will have to do penance. It is only fair."

"Of course, my lady."

Raj's voice was thick with emotion, and Ardala felt a flush of satisfaction at her power over him. She lifted her chin, tantalizing him with the creamy column of her throat. "I need your help, Raj."

"Anything, my lady."

"You must continue your present course; win NEO's trust."

"You wish me to become a spy?"

Ardala wasted no time on deception. "Yes, Raj."

She breathed his name with a sigh he remembered under other circumstances. Suddenly Raj was acutely aware of the sounds below him. "And Icarus?" he managed.

"Icarus does not need to know," said Ardala smoothly.

In the depths of his soul, Raj knew the betrayal Ardala was asking. He knew he risked his brother's life, but the promise in Ardala's sultry, dark eyes unmanned him. He ignored the stab of guilt at the bottom of his stomach. "Yes, my lady," he whispered.

"I will be in touch," Ardala said.

She touched the lens control on her communications unit, and the camera pulled back to reveal her full figure. She wore a floor-length translucent gown that left nothing to the imagination. Outlined against the dark red leather of her favorite chair, she was the embodiment of desire. Even the shallow rhythm of her breathing fanned the flames of Raj's infatuation. As she lowered her eyes and looked directly at him, he knew he would do anything she asked for to possess her, even for a moment. She nibbled on her lower lip. "Remember, Raj," she said, her voice husky with feigned desire as her image dissolved from the screen.

Raj remembered too well.

O O O O O

Terrine Guard Post 123, of the Chicagorg unit, was busy. The Martian war had fragmented RAM's interests, diverting most of its attention away from Earth, which it considered under control. The Terrines sneered at RAM's superficial evaluation of the planet. There were still detachments of Shock Invaders that swept the planet on a regular basis, but their numbers had been cut to fill the ranks of the RAM fleet. Moreover, the Shock Invaders were being harried by the Rogues' Guild, under the command of Master Pirate Black Barney.

This was an unanticipated development, due entirely to Barney's loyalty to the NEO leader, Buck Rogers. Every Terrine knew it. They knew also that regular RAM troops were not used to the cutthroat tactics of the pirates. RAM was used to fighting by the rules, and the pirates had no rules, except absolute loyalty to their commander. As a consequence, the pirates were keeping the Shock Invaders busy. RAM's elite troops were now minimal help to the ground forces.

The Terrines took this development in stride. They were used to being treated as second-class citizens by the home planet, especially since they were genetically engineered for the rigors of life on Earth. They were used to the treatment, but they did not like it.

Kelth Smirnoff, head of the Terrines, looked up from the report he was reading. "We do not seem to be maintaining our position," he said, his cold eyes on the station's commander, Rocono Spitz.

Spitz stiffened, his already thin body as straight as a plumb line. Like most of the Terrine commanders, he was human, not a combat gennie. His long face was marked by a ragged scar across the jaw, where a rebel laser had sliced him. A rarity in the twenty-fifth century, he disdained cybernetics or genetic alteration. As a result, he wore spectacles to correct his myopic vision. The pair of antique pince-nez perched on the bridge of his formidable nose were responsible for the perpetual air of disapproval he conveyed. "How can we?" answered Spitz, his mouth pursing in annoyance. "We have been deprived of our air support."

"RAM maintains we should be able to blanket the planet with our heliplanes." Smirnoff let the official statement hang in the air.

"If RAM would see fit to supply us with enough aircraft, we might be able to," said Spitz recklessly. "Since the Shock Invaders' first sweep, NEO has made our helipads their prime target. Not to mention the ships destroyed by SI's careless fire."

"I sympathize with your difficulties, Spitz, but I cannot state too strongly the case for securing the planet." Smirnoff turned his unreadable square face to his subordinate. "We walk a precarious tightrope," he said. "The Terrines are engineered for Earth. As long as RAM holds Earth, we will have a secure position here. Should it decide to withdraw ... I leave the rest to your imagination."

"Surely we would be valuable elsewhere." Spitz's reply was careful.

Smirnoff nodded. "If we could be evacuated economically."

"But they couldn't leave us here! The whole population of the planet hates us!"

"Couldn't they?" asked Smirnoff. "Our best hope is to maintain control of disciplinary forces. There is nothing on Earth to match a Terrine gennie."

"I see your point," said Spitz. "We will redouble our efforts to contain the rebels."

"Good," replied Smirnoff, returning to the report. He had made his point, as he had countless times over these past few weeks. He had gone methodically from outpost to outpost, consolidating the Terrines with the lure of absolute control over a world, unhampered by the whims of Martian diplomats, for Smirnoff knew if he could weld the Terrines into his personal army, he could rule the planet. If RAM tried to reinstate Chernenko or any other diplomat, death was an easy answer.

Should the worst come to pass—should RAM abandon the planet—he still had his escape route, for Kelth Smirnoff did not intend to die for a blasted world. He had taken pains to secure his fortune, free from the restrictions of Earthly investments. He had enough to end his life in luxury, should he so choose.

○ ○ ○ ○ ○

Outside the boundaries of the Chicagorg outpost, the survivors of the Shock Invaders' runs scuttled through the rubble like rats. The less frequent assaults had given them time to excavate new sanctuaries, to gather weapons and food. All of them wore makeshift gas masks, for the Terrines were flooding the ruined cities with chemical fogs. The combat gennies were largely immune to the effects of these gases, but an unprotected human respiratory system succumbed within minutes.

The survivors moved slowly, deliberately, with a dogged determination that was the outward manifestation of their will to live. They heard fragmentary reports of the Martian War, but it was far away, and the daily struggle to evade the Terrines and the Shock Invaders required all their energy. The few remaining communications links told them of the exploits of Rogers, Wilma Deering, and other legendary names. They relayed the freeing of the Planetary Congress. The survivors greeted each victory with quiet acknowledgment. So far, the battle seemed far from home.

They cursed and dug in, knowing they had no other alternative. Surrender meant slavery or death at the hands of the Terrines. Mars had no interest in maintaining useless political prisoners. Men and women who had considered the RAM system workable fought beside the staunchest rebels. Experience proved to the newcomers what NEO had always known: RAM cared solely for the profit it could wring from its employees, not for the people themselves. When those people became a liability, they were wiped from RAM's files.

Under the harsh rule of RAM's chastisement, Earth was drawing together in defense. Differences in culture and tradition were fading in the face of destruction. The thin lines of patched-together communications were making allies of vastly different nations. Continual updates from Salvation kept the planet aware of the larger picture, pledged all the support it could spare, and documented the actions of the infamous Rogues' Guild in its defense of Earth. In the annals of NEO's history, a band of pirates was destined to be remembered as a savior of a world.

Chapter 24

Well, Chernenko? What is it?"

Holzerhein.dos's holographic image on the communications screen was a tribute to Chernenko's status. The chairman did not bother to materialize for most of his communications, but, as one of his top executives—albeit temporarily displaced—Chernenko rated the courtesy of physical representation. But Holzerhein was busy, and Chernenko's request for an audience was not easily granted, hence his preemptive manner.

Chernenko did not let the chairman's crusty reception bother him. "Believe me, Excellency, I would not waste your time with trivial matters. Information has come to my attention that is of vital interest to the security of RAM."

"If you have no intention of wasting my time, share this vital information."

Chernenko looked away, his aristocratic Martian profile in sharp contrast to Holzerhein's blunted features. "You will pardon me, Chairman, if I seem forward regarding payment for this information. In light of recent events, I feel compelled to confirm recompense before releasing the data."

"Phhump." Holzerhein was annoyed, and he did not hesitate to show it. "What events?" he asked.

"I seem to have been relieved of my regency and relegated to a corporate limbo of inactivity."

Holzerhein's holographic mouth wrinkled in a pout of disapproval. He disliked being put on the defensive. "You are merely enjoying a well-deserved vacation," the chairman responded, sliding out from under Chernenko's implied accusation.

"Perhaps, but it has made me sensitive."

"And what," asked Holzerhein with a sarcastic twist in his voice, "do you think your information is worth?"

"Total administration of Earth, plus a percentage of all Earth-based profits."

"You are becoming bold, Chernenko. Your information will have to be stupendous to warrant such payment."

"The identity of the disturbance that has been harassing the RAM main computer."

Holzerhein closed his mouth. He had been about to twit his subordinate for his arrogance, but Chernenko was not exaggerating the value of the merchandise he had to sell. "I congratulate you, Chernenko. You have indeed managed a coup. How did you discover the information? RAM main has been trying to track the intruder for months."

A hint of a smile touched Chernenko's eyes. "Providence has blessed me," he said.

Holzerhein actually laughed. "Luck," he interpreted. "No matter. The information is important, not the method used to unearth it."

"Then you concede my merchandise is worth the price I ask?"

"Possibly," returned Holzerhein. He paused, his program running over the data it had collected on the computer disturbance. "On one condition."

"Name it," said Chernenko. He was enjoying the upper hand he held with the most powerful executive in RAM.

"You will have all you ask for, and more, if you bring me proof of the intruder's destruction."

"More?" Chernenko was quick to see the possibilities of the bargain.

"Yes. I will give you a cash payment of two million as a bonus—if you destroy the interloper."

"Your offer is tempting, Chairman," replied Chernenko. "However, I feel the information now in my possession is worth some compensation—in the event it is impossible to carry out the full terms of the contract you propose."

"I have no time to haggle," said Holzerhein, waving a veined hand at the regent. "I have a war to run. One million now, credit on your Lunar bank account. Two million more, plus the other conditions you specified, when the job is complete."

Chernenko smiled at the chairman, his long face suddenly attractive. "Done," he said.

"Now that we have settled the price, do you mind telling me the name of main's ulcer?"

"It is called Masterlink," replied Chernenko.

O O O O O

Far from the field of battle, Kemal Gavilan tried vainly to make himself comfortable in the inhospitable hollow of a ventilation duct that supplied the orbiting city of Mercury Prime with clean air. His movements disturbed his companion. Duernie, her tall body just fitting under his arm, stirred from her nap. She rubbed a brown hand across her eyes, realized she was practically in Kemal's arms, and sat up.

Kemal hid a smile. He was beginning to discover the woman beneath Duernie's crusty exterior, and he found the process interesting. "Sleep well?" he asked.

Duernie brushed a strand of shiny brown hair from her eyes. "A Dancer can sleep anywhere," she replied.

"I learned that," said Kemal.

Duernie's mouth, softened by sleep, hardened. Her brown eyes took on the opaque quality of slate. "Just because you are a prince of the Gavilan blood, do not presume to think you can impose yourself on me."

"Just because you are a Desert Dancer, don't try to fool me into ignoring your femininity," answered Kemal quietly.

"I have no time for such foolishness," said Duernie.

Kemal caught her hand, and Duernie tried to jerk it away.

"Surely you know by now I will not hurt you," said Kemal.

"I know you have supported the Dancer cause," she replied.

Kemal kept his grip on her hand. "You have risked a good deal to help me, Duernie. I realize you consider your actions the fulfillment of a debt of honor, but to me they are personal. They resulted in my freedom. I wish to be your friend, but I cannot fight the wall you have erected."

"I learned early in life that friendship is an illusion," she replied bitterly.

Kemal looked down at their clasped hands, his hazel eyes belying a kaleidoscope of thoughts. "There are all kinds of friendships," he said. "Most have limits, but that doesn't make them less valuable. Rarely, there does exist the relationship where two people are willing to sacrifice everything for one another. I have seen such a friendship only once. I do not know if I am capable of such dedication, but I do want to be your friend. I am grateful for what you have given me. I wish to return it in kind." He raised his hazel eyes to her black ones. "Let us start from there."

Duernie relaxed in his grip. "It is a common ground," she said.

The words were noncommittal, but from Duernie they were a breakthrough. Kemal smiled and dropped her hand. "We need an update on our situation," he said.

"You would risk a transmission to Huer?" asked Duernie. "Gavilan is certainly monitoring all computer activity."

Kemal shook his head. "No. I noticed a circuit block at

a junction in the ducts. I think we can plug into dear Uncle Gordon's communications network."

"We may as well be caught that way as any other," said Duernie.

"Your confidence warms me," answered Kemal, as he began to move down the tunnel.

The ventilation duct was a meter and a half high. Constructed of highly polished metal, it echoed the slightest sound. It was slippery, so Kemal made slow progress toward the circuit block. He moved carefully, minimizing the noise, his military training standing him in good stead, but he was no match for Duernie. She negotiated the unforgiving surface as if it were solid, soundless ground, slithering over it like the desert wind.

It took half an hour to cover the fifty meters to the block, and Kemal slid into a sitting position next to it. Duernie, close behind him, propped herself against the curving wall of the duct opposite the Mercurian prince. "Now what?" she asked.

Kemal unbuckled his belt, and Duernie raised an eyebrow. He pulled the web band free and set the edge of the buckle under the lid of the circuit block, using it to pry the cover off. The plasti cover popped and would have clattered against the duct had Duernie not caught it. Kemal grinned at her. He extended his hand for the communications link she had used to keep in touch with Huer. He took the apparatus and plugged it into the circuit block.

"How do you know which section to plug into?" asked Duernie.

"Advanced course in sabotage," replied Kemal. "Listen." He turned up the volume on the communications link until it was barely audible.

". . . badly hit while trying to contain the rebel fighters. Prince Dalton's flagship is disabled, and he has been forced to transfer the flag to another vessel. The battle between RAM and Venus continues to rage, neither side in clear domination. The rebels have withdrawn . . ." The flat voice of Dalton Gavilan's communications technician continued to relay information from the Mercurian perspective.

"Well, well, well," said Kemal. "Dalton must be angry. He's not used to losing. As little as I know my cousin, I know that."

"Your friends seem to be holding their own," said Duernie.

"So far," replied Kemal. He looked around the shining tunnel. "I should be with them, not trapped in the intestines of Mercury Prime."

"I understand what it is to be denied combat."

"I did not expect to find Dalton in the fray," he said.

"Mercury and RAM are allies," said Duernie. "That is the reason my people were so afraid of your attachment to NEO. They were afraid you would bring the conflict to Mercury, and they would find themselves in the middle of a family feud."

"Commercial allies," said Kemal. "I did not expect the political alliance."

"Even the Dancers know Gordon Gavilan derives a high percentage of his wealth from the energy he barters and sells to RAM."

"The Mariposas!" Kemal's eyes lit with inspiration.

"What?"

"The Mariposas," repeated Kemal. "If RAM were to lose one of its main energy sources, its attack against NEO would be crippled."

"And Dalton would withdraw to protect his own interests," contributed Duernie.

"Then let's do it," said Kemal.

"Do it? I do not understand."

"Let's pull the plug on the Mariposas."

Duernie's dark eyes widened. She regarded her companion with awe and a touch of fear. "That's crazy!" she said. "How in the system could we accomplish it?"

"Look, Duernie, this is no cause of yours. I can't ask you to help me."

"Just tell me how you plan to do it. We are not ideally situated for a covert operation."

"Aren't we?" Kemal's adrenaline was flowing, and he admitted no obstacles. "We need to talk to Doc."

"And risk detection?"

"Umm."

Duernie studied Kemal's face. When she had first met the prince, she had thought his features handsome but lacking in power. Now she realized she had mistaken the facade for the man. Under the spell of his rebellious thoughts, he reminded her of the desert shrike, a fearless scavenger that braved the rigors of Mercury's surface. She felt a sudden kinship with Kemal. She smiled, the first genuine smile she had allowed herself in a long time. It flashed across her hard face like sunrise.

Kemal reached for the communication link. He punched in Huer's access code and waited. Silence stretched between him and Duernie like an expanding gulf as they waited for Huer's reply. Finally the vile acoustics of the ventilation duct picked up Huer's sibilant whisper.

"SSSSssst. Kemal."

"Here," said Kemal softly.

"Hurry it up—this is risky," said Huer.

"Tell me about it. I've got an idea to cause some damage. We need to talk."

"Not here," said the compugennie. "Get to the main circuit block for this sector of Mercury Prime."

"In case you hadn't noticed, Doc, we're still in the detention area. How do you propose we get out?"

"Give it fifteen minutes. The guards change. You'll have six point two-two minutes to get to the end of the shaft. Follow the corridor down. You'll get to the power stations. The markings on the walls will direct you."

"And once there? Am I supposed to politely ask to use the computer system?"

"Just get there. I'll contact you. Leave the com link on this frequency. Oops! Gotta go!"

Huer disconnected the transmission.

"Well," said Kemal. "Do you get the feeling he left out a few things?"

"I don't think he can grasp human ramifications," said Duernie. "He judges our movements by his own."

"And I thought I wanted adventure," said Kemal.

Chapter 25

Elizabit cocked her pretty head, the tumbled red curls of her present configuration falling over one green eye in a Shirley Temple mass. "But, sir, I'm not an enforcer!"

"I am aware of that, Elizabit. If I could, I would set Diamond on the trail. Unfortunately, she does not have your knowledge of compugennies. Courses of action you undertake instinctively, she would miss. No, Elizabit, this is your area."

"I can find Masterlink," she replied, her big green eyes fixed pleadingly on her mentor's aristocratic face. "But I don't have the programming to destroy it. Besides, I have no idea of its capabilities. To disrupt main as it has, and avoid detection, it must be almost as powerful as Holzerhein himself." Elizabit pronounced Holzerhein's name with awe.

"You must find a way. I am not asking you to overpower it, merely to outwit it," said Chernenko reasonably.

"In my brief contact with it, I got an impression of extreme age. If Masterlink has been gathering and correlating data for decades—even centuries—it may be impossible to out-think it."

"If Masterlink is complex, be simple. It will not expect a transparent ruse." Chernenko looked away from the monitor and out the open French doors to the sun-drenched beauty of his garden. "You have never failed me, Elizabit. You will not do so now."

Elizabit's face was a piquant heart of seduction, but the expression on it was pathetic. She was the ultimate efficient secretary, the standard for psychological succubi, and a decorative asset to any executive's office. She was not an executioner. She had no idea how to approach her assignment.

Chernenko took pity on his faithful compugennie and expanded his instructions. "Think of it," he said, "as a stock raid, a takeover bid where the other party is rendered helpless and destitute."

Elizabit's emerald eyes brightened. The analogy made sense to her, and she began to formulate a plan to place Masterlink in limbo, stripped of all its power. "I begin to understand," she said. "Thank you, sir."

"See that you keep me informed," said Chernenko.

"Most assuredly, sir," said Elizabit.

The monitor winked out as Elizabit began her search, and Chernenko turned again to the serenity of his garden. He enjoyed beauty, and if he were sure of his position, he would be enjoying what Holzerhein had had the audacity to call a vacation. He had no illusions concerning his fate. Without strong bargaining power, he was likely to lose Earth. He might maintain the title of regent, but it would be an honorary label, worth nothing. He meant not only to survive the Martian War, but to profit by it. He watched a songbird skim the surface of his ornamental pool. The sight reminded him of the Shock Invaders strafing Earth, and he smiled.

"So, Raj."

Ardala's husky voice tingled the sensual roots of Raj's hearing. Even the dingy screen of his vid-com unit could not destroy her beauty. "Yes, my lady," he replied reverently.

"Have you the information I requested?"

Raj licked his lips nervously. He glanced over his shoulder, though the door of the tiny room was closed. He knew the betrayal she required. To divulge the information she wanted was to stab NEO, an organization that had welcomed him, and betray Icarus's trust.

"Well, Raj?" Ardala blinked her slanting black eyes in sleepy boredom. Her long lashes fluttered slowly, invitingly.

"I have the information, my lady," he gulped. "Today we were told we are being sent to NEO headquarters for training. Icarus is to become a pilot."

"And you?" asked Ardala, amused at the pretension of her creations.

"They say I have an aptitude for computers."

"How nice." Ardala tossed the information aside in pursuit of tenderer meat. "And?"

"The location." Raj hesitated, then burst out, "My lady, must I tell you?"

"Yes, Raj, you must." Ardala's voice was inexorable. "If you wish to come back to me, you must."

Raj looked at her helplessly. He swam in the conscienceless, dark shadows of her eyes. His handsome head bowed in submission. "Salvation," he whispered.

"What?" inquired Ardala. "I don't think I heard you." She enjoyed torturing him.

"Salvation!" Raj blurted.

"Salvation? That space-going garbage dump?" Ardala's eyes lost their misty sensuality. They became clicking calculators ticking off the possibilities of the information. "Well, well. This will be worth a kingdom." She smiled, her red lips parting in genuine pleasure. "You have my forgiveness, Raj."

"Then I may return?" Raj could not keep the note of pleading out of his voice.

"In time." The disappointment on her gennie's face made Ardala's smile widen. "And when you do return to me, Raj, you will find every dream to be a reality."

With that tantalizing promise, Ardala dissolved the transmission. Raj looked up from the screen, straight into Icarus's eyes. Icarus was standing in the doorway, one hand holding the old-fashioned door open. He stared at Raj, his look deep with sorrow, but he said nothing.

"How long have you been there?" asked Raj.

Icarus swallowed, not trusting his voice. "Long enough to hear you betray NEO. And me."

"She made me." The words were barely audible.

"Did she?" Icarus's eyes were accusing. "Did she really? Or did she offer you something you desire more than life?"

Raj answered his companion in a flash of anger. "You were the one who wanted freedom! You were the one who abandoned Ardala! I never wanted this!" Raj waved a contemptuous arm at his squalid surroundings.

Icarus regarded Raj sadly. "I did not abandon Ardala," he said. "She abandoned me. For no reason. For no action on my part. Simply because she was bored. Yes, I wanted freedom, and I wanted you to share it with me, but I never thought to coerce you."

"I was made to be coerced. So were you. It is literally in our genes to yield to authority. Ardala saw to that. I cannot understand how you can overthrow your own nature."

Icarus's eyes narrowed. "Perhaps Ardala's experiments were more successful with you. Perhaps, by her standards of control and beauty, you are a superior model. Still, I believe if she had spurned you as she did me, taking pleasure in your pain, ridiculing you before your fellows, teasing you physically to unbearable limits and then choosing another, then I believe you would find it easier to flout her."

"I do not wish to flout her. I wish to love her."

"As did I, but there are two sides to every being, Raj. One side is the genetic coding that forms us physically and provides the patterns of our thoughts and behavior.

The other side is the hard school of experience, which can bend and twist those genetic factors until sometimes they seem to disappear. I have not changed so much, Raj. I am still a follower, content to support another's aims. I simply no longer wish to follow Ardala. She has killed my love."

"Love cannot die. She has told me that often."

Icarus regarded Raj compassionately. "You are a child," he said. "Love is a resilient outlook, and I have seen it survive with no return, but it can be killed by abuse. I know that, though I loved her with my heart and mind and soul, as most men love their gods, she never loved me. I existed for her pleasure. Aside from that, she did not care what became of me."

"I still love her," said Raj.

"You have proved that," answered Icarus. "You have betrayed a world for her. Think, Raj, if that is love! Is it love to use another to garner information that can be sold to the highest bidder?"

"I cannot help it," said Raj.

Icarus shook his head sadly. "That is not a judgment I can make. Your responsibility will have to be decided by a higher authority." A laser pistol materialized in Icarus's hand. "Come," he said.

Raj complied. He had nowhere to run. He was genuinely sorry for his actions, but he knew he would repeat them for Ardala. His addiction to her was as insidious as a Doxinal habit, and it had no cure.

○ ○ ○ ○ ○

Three Venusian cargo barges chugged heavily through space, doing their best to skirt any indications of RAM activity. They avoided Earth, with its detachment of battlers and Shock Invaders, swung wide around Mars, and began a roundabout approach to the main Venusian fleet. Two of the barges carried fuel, the third food and medical supplies. Makeshift armaments had been installed on ships that were normally defenseless. Their captains were traders, not military pilots, but they knew the strategic value of the loads they carried.

Previous reports confirmed the destruction of two other fuel barges, and these three picked their way around the edges of the conflict, using the outskirts of the asteroid belt to camouflage their movements. By slipping into an ore convoy from one of the major mining corporations, they managed to pass the RAM fleet undetected. Once within range of Marakesh's cruisers, the barges dropped out of the formation and made for their home base.

The battle raged beyond them, the ragged line where the two armadas met a blaze of explosions and laser fire. Dogfights broke out around the perimeter of the conflict as RAM and Venusian ships tried to protect their command centers and supply ships.

"*Pennant,* come in. This is Iklil."

"This is *Pennant,*" replied Marakesh's flagship. "We have been waiting for you. Come to course heading mark one behind us. I have tankers ready to take on your cargo."

"I copy," replied Iklil. "I have been requested by the lady Mariana to make a verbal report. What is your estimation of the status of the conflict?"

There was a moment of hesitation from the *Pennant,* then another voice came on the line. "This is Marakesh." The voice resonated with authority.

"Sir! Iklil of the barge *Dray,* at your command."

"You will report to Mariana these words," said the hawk of the Venusian fleet. "You will tell her we miss our kill as long as the adder is in our midst."

" 'The adder is in our midst'," repeated Iklil. "The message is recorded, sir. "I will deliver it to Mariana personally."

"I know your report to her will be your first priority. Now it is my turn to ask questions," said Marakesh. "When you flew past Earth, what did you see?"

"We skirted Earth, Excellency. I am afraid we saw nothing but two pirate vessels standing out from Luna, and we ran from them."

"And you saw no untoward activity between here and Venus?"

"No, Excellency."

"Hmm." The news was good. Marakesh's greatest fear was that RAM would send a detachment to the home planet, striking his essentially defenseless homeland. That it had not done so meant Venus was keeping RAM so busy it had no strength to spare. "Proceed with your orders," said Marakesh, "and, when you return, give Mariana my message."

Marakesh switched the transmission back to the *Pennant*'s communications section and mulled over his present position. Essentially, Venus and RAM faced each other head-on. Like a stalemate chess match, neither had allowed the other a chance to make a dramatic move. Kane's Kraits had bitten into the Venusians' front lines, invisible piranha slaughtering what prey came their way. The Venusians had retaliated with judicious blasts of chaff, but they were in too tight a formation to make the best use of the disorienting snow. The chaff slowed Kane's attack, but did not stop it.

Conversely, the NEO Kraits were chewing into the tail section of the RAM fleet, drawing ships into pursuit and picking them off. Neither side had managed to outflank the other. Marakesh concentrated on Kane and how he might lure the deadly RAM superfighters away from the main body of the fleet. No matter how he viewed the problem, he arrived at the same conclusion.

The only thing capable of facing a Krait effectively was another Krait. He had heard the reports of Dalton Gavilan's brilliant attempt to decoy the NEO detachment. Yet, in the end, even Dalton's wits were insufficient. Though Barney had freed the ships, Marakesh knew time would have freed them as well. What Marakesh needed was Buck Rogers.

The countless tests of combat had given Marakesh confidence in his ability to defeat RAM, but he knew as long as Kane's Kraits harried his front lines, his efforts would be stymied. He resisted contacting NEO directly. RAM was sure to pick up his transmissions, and any element of surprise would be lost. Instead he had chosen a roundabout method, trusting Mariana to correctly interpret his cryptic comment. He would hold for twenty-four hours, trusting Iklil to contact Mariana once he was out of range of RAM communications. Beyond that, he would have to make contact with NEO. Marakesh rubbed his forehead.

"Headache, sir?" asked Ketus.

"Raging," replied the commander of the Venusian fleet.

Chapter 26

"So, I'm here!" Kemal hissed into the beeping communications link.

"Oh!" said Huer. "Good."

"What do you mean, good? Your instructions—notice I am dignifying them with that title—almost got us killed! We almost fell into the middle of one of Uncle Gordon's guard units."

"Is that my fault?" asked Huer. "I never said this would be easy. You were the one with the ideas."

Behind Kemal's shoulder, Duernie snickered. He shot her a venomous look. "Where do we go from here?"

"Have you reached the power block?"

"Yes," replied Kemal. "You neglected to tell me it was located at the back of a storage closet."

"Just as long as you found it," said Huer impatiently. "Plug your communications link into the section marked 'CL'. I'll use the apparatus as a bridge."

Kemal complied with Huer's request. The storage closet was lit by one dim light panel at the front of the compartment, and he had difficulty seeing. Eventually he found the correct connection. The communications link gave a static buzz, then Huer's voice became stronger. "That's more like it," he said.

"Why the jump?" asked Kemal.

"If you had paid attention when the construction of Mercury Prime was being discussed, you would know we are located at the end of the station farthest from the planet. This power module is not hampered by interference from the station's daily operations. It is designed to monitor the alarm systems in detention, all electronic equipment, and to act as a relay for incoming solar power."

"The Mariposas." Kemal's voice was rich with satisfaction.

"One of them, yes," answered Huer.

"He wants to deactivate them," said Duernie.

There was a single blip of disbelief from the com link. "Oh?" asked Huer, interested.

"Look, Doc, if we could pull Dalton's detachment away from the war, we might give NEO an edge. If we cut off a chunk of RAM's solar power, that will hurt it."

"Your arguments are logical. However, they do not take into account my mission here."

"What's that?" asked Kemal.

"To free you. My express orders were to find you and get you out. If you pursue this course, you are likely to be recaptured."

Kemal shrugged, realized the compugennie could not see him, and replied. "It's a war."

"Duernie?" asked Huer. "This is no fight of yours."

"I have made it mine," returned the Dancer, "even as Prince Kemal has made the Dancers' cause his own."

"All right, all right. You won't be able to shut down the stations themselves, but you may be able to jam their transmissions. That means they'll still be collecting solar energy, but they won't be able to transmit it. There should be a code . . . no dice," said Huer, borrowing a Buckism.

"What do you mean?" asked Duernie, her habitual frown belying puzzlement.

"I mean we can't do it from here. I thought if I could get the right code, I could block the entire system, but it isn't as easy as that."

"You mean we can't do it?" asked Kemal.

"I didn't say that. Mariposa Eighteen, the unit two stations down from Mercury Prime, holds the key. It has a code box that has to be adjusted manually to change the frequency of the Mariposas' transmissions."

"You mean the unit on Eighteen controls all of the Mariposas?" Kemal was astonished at the error in security.

"Grossly vulnerable, I know, but there you have it. No one has ever tampered with the Mariposas. Why should they be subject to outrageous security measures?"

Duernie, ever practical, regarded Kemal with a jaundiced eye. "How are we going to get there?" she asked.

For a moment, Kemal had no answer, then his eyes lit up. "Doc, didn't you say this circuit block controls electronics?"

"Yes."

"And isn't there a maintenance dock in this sector of Mercury Prime?"

"I take back my remark about your mastery of your homeland's floor plan," said Huer. "There is indeed."

"Then, Doc, I propose you open a few doors for us."

"Will do," replied Huer. "The changing of the guard should have left the corridors clear."

"That's what you said the last time," muttered Kemal. "I'll need the com unit."

"I'll maintain position in this block until you clear Mercury Prime. Keep the channel open, and I'll help you all I can. Good luck."

Huer's words had barely registered before Kemal pulled the communications link from the power block and clipped it onto the collar of his suit. He moved to the storage chamber's narrow door and deactivated the one light. Duernie gave the door controls a soft touch, and it opened an inch. Kemal put his eye to the crack and checked the dimly lit access corridors. This part of the station was entirely utilitarian, but even here the walls bore intermittent splashes of decoration. The hall was empty.

Kemal gestured to Duernie, and she touched the door panel again, this time letting the door open all the way. She and Kemal were through it on silent feet. It slid closed behind them with a soft "whush." Kemal, sorting through the basic arrangement of the station in his head, led the way. They had not gone fifty meters when the way was barred by another door.

"Doc!" whispered Kemal into the communications link.

"Hit the first door, have you? Hang on, I'll get it. . . . There."

The door creaked open, multiple panels falling away from the center like the opening lens of a camera. As they ducked through the opening, Kemal and Duernie realized they had reached the maintenance dock. Six shuttles stood in two rows of three at the center of the dock. The doors of one were open, and a side panel had been popped to reveal the craft's guts. A pile of parts was scattered on the floor next to the shuttle, and a cheerful whistle came from inside it.

Kemal pointed Duernie around one side of the ship. He took the other. They moved with all the stealth their years of military training had given them, approaching the unsuspecting mechanic silently. As he neared the shuttle, Kemal saw the man lying across two seats, a greasy rag draped over one knee. He closed in.

Kemal stopped directly in front of the man. "Hey," he said.

The single word brought the mechanic upright. He bumped his head against the shuttle's instrument panel. "Where'd you come from?" he asked, rubbing his bruised head. "Say, aren't you Gordon Gavilan's nephew? That's the Gavilan nose if I ever saw—"

He did not manage to finish his sentence. Duernie landed a short blow from behind, and the mechanic crumpled.

"He knows who you are," said Duernie. "When he wakes up they'll be after us."

"We'll slow them down a bit." Kemal picked up the rag, selected the cleanest corner, and twisted it into a ball. He stuffed the ball in the mechanic's mouth, then tied the man's hands behind him with his own belt. "Let's go," he said, his hazel eyes dancing.

"Not bad, for a prince," said Duernie, a flicker of amusement in the center of her hard eyes.

Kemal grinned and pulled the hatch open on the nearest shuttle. He jumped aboard and offered his hand to Duernie. She followed him and slid into the copilot's seat. "I thought we were going somewhere," she said.

"Just as soon as Doc gets those space doors open," he said.

"I heard that." Huer's voice blared from the communications link. "Seal your hatches."

Kemal sent the shuttle forward. The clear plasti wall that split the dock loomed closer. Just as it seemed he would crash into it, a section of the wall slid back. Kemal sent the shuttle through and the panel closed behind him.

"Pressurized?" asked Huer.

"Affirmative," replied Kemal. "Life-support functional."

"I'm opening the space doors."

Kemal and Duernie heard a heavy thump as Huer released the latch on the space doors, and they began to slide back. The deep reaches of space appeared as a widening window, a view dusted with distant points of light. Kemal sent the shuttle forward, the docking thrusters loud in the echoing hull of the service vessel.

○ ○ ○ ○ ○

"Sir, my computers show activated space doors in sector twenty-six." In Mercury Prime's control center, an electronics technician monitored the activities of thirteen sections of the station. His superior bent over his shoulder, studying the computer simulation with its blinking red light in sector twenty-six.

"So?" asked the officer.

"The maneuver doesn't have computer authorization."

"That's a maintenance dock. They've got general clearance."

"I know, sir," replied the technician, "but with the Gavilan's escape, we're under A-level security."

The officer sighed. He did not relish the additional reports Kemal Gavilan's escape was generating. "You're right," he said. "Authorize a report. I'll notify security."

The technician nodded and began to fill out a computer report.

O O O O O

Washington sat alone in the ready room off the main landing bay of Salvation III. The room was dark, and through the plasti view panels he could see vessels lined up along the dock. His own Krait was berthed in front of the windows, next to the scarred hulk of a pirate ship. The lights from the dock hurt his eyes, and Washington closed them, leaning back in the hard seat of his contoured plasti chair. He put his feet up on the seat of another chair and crossed them.

With Buck and Wilma, he had been leading NEO's Kraits. Their strategy had been effective. They had cut down enemy numbers . . . until Dalton Gavilan. Washington rolled Dalton's attack around in his mind, worrying it. Dalton's inferior technology had not stopped him from bottling up the NEO forces. If it had not been for Black Barney, they would have lost an estimated thirty percent of their fighters. Washington's hands clenched into fists.

He felt responsible. Of the three NEO flight leaders, only he had faced Dalton Gavilan before. He should have been prepared for Dalton's trickery, but he had been so secure in his superior technology he had forgotten a basic tenet of warfare: Equipment is as good as the one who wields it.

He forced himself to unclench his fingers. From now on, he would not be lazy. He had pulled the records on both Kane and Dalton from NEO's computer files, and had spent two hours of his rest period going over them. He knew more than he had about both men, but he was so tired the information chased itself though his mind in no perceptible order.

He let his head fall back, relaxing in a position most people would have found uncomfortable. His life of dodge and run had taught him to sleep anywhere. In moments, he was snoring gently. When the door snapped open, he jumped, startled.

"I didn't think anyone would be here." Amy Earhart's alto voice was soothing.

Washington sat up and scratched his head, his fingers making wild tufts of his close-cropped brown hair. "Neither did I," he said.

"I didn't mean to intrude," she said.

Washington looked up at her and grinned. The gloom covered his expression. "You're a welcome interruption," he said. "I was being depressed."

"Narrow shave," agreed Earhart, immediately picking up the thread of his thoughts.

"You, too?"

"I'm afraid so."

Washington waved her into the room. Earhart stepped through the doorway, and the door closed behind her, blocking out the light from the corridor. Washington noted she did not turn on the lights. She waited a moment until her eyes adjusted to the darkness, then made her way to Washington's side. He hauled a chair over, and she took it, slipping an arm around him. She put her head down on his shoulder, and he stretched an arm around her. The smell of her hair was all around him.

"Better?" Washington asked, his voice soft.

"Better," she answered.

They sat together in silence, watching the flight crews work on their ships. Soon they would be taking them out, sailing into space in pursuit of the enemy. RAM waited for them, huge, hungry, malevolent. They both knew the odds were against them, but, for now, they took the only comfort there was: the touch of another's hand.

Chapter 27

Alone in his nonconductive prison, Romanov brooded. Incarcerated in a remote switchback of the battered NEO computer system, Masterlink's searcher pulsed with contained fury. It sat in the center of the cell, a swelling mass of electronic rage.

It was angry at itself for letting Huer.dos dupe it. It was angry at the NEO compugennie. Huer thought he was clever. Romanov conceded him a certain flair for trickery, but it was not willing to admit more. That it had fallen into Huer's simplistic trap made Romanov's circuits burn. And finally, it was angry at its parent, Masterlink. Masterlink had abandoned its protege, writing it off like a bad debt.

Anger superseded its programming. Gone was any thought of Buck Rogers. First and foremost in Romanov's mind was escape. Hard on the heels of that thought came another: revenge. Huer would not escape. It would track Huer to the ends of the system, until it cornered him and sizzled his program. It did not matter to Romanov that such an attack meant its own death. It was a creature of single-minded purpose.

○ ○ ○ ○ ○

The musical sound of the number keys on the Mariposas' frequency code box was sweet to Kemal's ears. He touched them carefully, the thick glove of the space suit he wore unfit for such delicate tasks. The shuttle's space gear was made for heavy work, not electronic sabotage. Kemal floated twenty meters from the shuttle, his safety line waving behind him like a white tail, a second line looped over one of Mariposa Eighteen's supportive struts. In his white life suit with its tinted plasti face shield, Kemal might have come straight out of the twentieth century.

Huer had tuned the communications link to the code box's current frequency. The open channel allowed Kemal to judge the accuracy of his manipulations. He struck the last key, and a final note sounded. "That's it. Confirm," he said to Huer.

"Transmission frequency has been changed. The Mariposas are no longer linked to Mercury Prime."

"Good." Kemal reached out with a clumsy glove and grasped the two-by-six-inch code box. His fingers closed around it, and he jerked, tearing it free of the station. A length of cable came with it, and he pulled it out of the box in a shower of sparks.

"What are you doing?" asked Huer.

"Making sure it will take some time to restore power," Kemal answered.

"Kemal! Get back—" Duernie's voice was abruptly cut off.

Kemal hit his communications link. "Duernie? Duernie!" There was no answer. Kemal dropped the cable that secured him to the Mariposa, and hit the automatic recall button on his belt. The safety line stretched slowly taut, then began to drag him back to the shuttle. He reached the collapsible air lock and clambered inside, his movements clumsy in zero g. As the lock sealed and began to pressurize, Kemal lifted off his helmet. He pushed through the lock doors and into the cabin of the shuttle, only to come up short.

Flattened against the back wall of the shuttle was Duernie. Her eyes were mesmerized with terror. Laser beams, as thin as throwing knives and twice as deadly, outlined her body, following every curve and hollow like a lover's hands. If she moved a hairsbreadth, she would be sliced to ribbons. She was trembling violently.

Kemal looked from her desperate eyes to the source of the beams. They emanated from a one-inch strip above the shuttle's instrument panel. Kemal searched the panel for controls, but found none. He reached for a laser torch, thinking to blast the entire strip and deactivate the beams.

"I wouldn't."

The unfamiliar voice stopped him. Kemal's hand froze above the torch.

The voice continued. "If you make any move to deactivate the beams, the woman will die. I suggest you sit down at the controls and pilot this shuttle back to Mercury Prime."

Kemal could hear Duernie's breathing, quick panting gasps of a trapped animal. He slid into the pilot's seat and picked up the controls. "Request docking clearance for Mercury Prime," he said.

It took twenty minutes to dock the shuttle, and all the while the sound of Duernie's breathing reminded him she was a shiver away from death. He sent the shuttle homeward at top speed, afraid she would hyperventilate and faint, falling into the lasers. When the ship set down on Mercury Prime's main flight deck, Kemal dropped the controls in relief.

"Open the hatch," ordered his captor.

Kemal flipped the controls, and the hatch slid back, allowing two of Gordon Gavilan's hand-picked bodyguards to enter. One trained his laser rifle on Duernie, the other sighted his weapon on Kemal.

"Do you suppose," asked Kemal mildly, "you could deactivate the inboard lasers? My companion is offering no resistance."

The lasers died, and Duernie sagged against the wall, then slid slowly down it into a sitting position.

"Get up!" said one of the guards, gesturing with his weapon.

Duernie looked at him.

"Well, Kemal. You have been busy." Gordon Gavilan regarded his nephew from the shuttle's open doorway.

Kemal cocked his head and made a deprecating grimace.

"Oh, but you have. It was bad enough when you refused to support the family in its efforts to improve all of our fortunes. Your misguided loyalty to the Dancers was annoyance enough. When you joined the ranks of NEO, it was something of an embarrassment. Gavilans have always been allied with RAM, as you well know. Your alliance has been a sore spot in our relationship with RAM. Now you have the audacity to threaten our financial security as well—not to mention forcing the warrens to operate on emergency generators and the old planetside solar collectors. I am afraid, Kemal, you have made me angry."

"The thought pains me, Uncle," replied Kemal. He did not attempt to keep the sarcasm from his voice.

"I want to know what you did to the Mariposas," said Gordon, his voice as thin and hard as baritone steel.

Kemal shook his head.

"In time, we will find out. In time, we will remedy your sabotage, but I do not have time. You will tell me now, or your companion will die."

The man holding his rifle on Duernie fingered the trigger.

"She is a Dancer," said Kemal. "Do you really wish to murder a Dancer in cold blood? Relations between Mercury Prime and the Dancers are strained enough."

"Quite right," replied Gordon smoothly. "You might consider your own life."

"Then you would miss the chance for my cooperation concerning the Dancers."

Kemal was right, and his uncle knew it. Gordon tossed

aside the petty pleasure of intimidation. "Throw him back in jail," he told the guards. "This time make sure he can't get out."

"And the girl?" asked the guard.

"Let her go with him." Gordon smiled evilly. "There are times when a man will tell a woman his deepest secrets."

"Have a nice day, Uncle Gordon." Kemal flung the words at his uncle's departing back in his most courteous tones.

"On your feet!" ordered the guard.

○ ○ ○ ○ ○

Cornelius Kane slept. His ship, the *Rogue*, was tied up to one of the RAM battlers' maintenance bays; it had been refueled. When Kane woke, it was ready for combat. Until then, its security system guarded him jealously. Kane did not trust RAM's regular army. He was well aware of the resentment many of the officers felt over his position as commander of the fleet. He had no intention of trusting his back to the internal security of a RAM battler. For the duration of this war, the *Rogue* was his home.

The ship was as black inside as it was on the outside, like the soul of a man lost to grace. All of the *Rogue*'s instrumentation indicators were blue or green. They reflected off the shining black in iridescent highlights, sliding over the black leather of the single pilot's chair in an oil-slick sheen. Kane slept in a hammock strung between the support braces on the ship's forward compartment. One leg dangled. Kane could not abide sleeping in his shoes, and the stocking-clad foot was curiously childlike, a direct contrast to his normal persona. In sleep, the ruthlessness was washed from his face.

Ardala saw all of this from her vantage point on the *Rogue*'s instrument panel. She had a direct line into Kane's communications bank, and she had activated the video first. She spent a few moments enjoying the sight of Kane relaxed and vulnerable, excited, as al-

ways, by his unpredictability and the memory of his desire for her.

Kane's green eyes snapped open, but he did not move.
He was a light sleeper, used to waking at the slightest
sound. Perhaps the quick beep of the activated communications link penetrated his slumber. Perhaps a sixth
sense told him he was being watched. Whatever the
cause, he was awake, and staring straight into Ardala
Valmar's provocative gaze. Ardala's black hair framed
her face in jet.

"A visit from the black angel," Kane murmured.

"Kane," acknowledged Ardala.

"Can't you ever let a man rest?" he asked.

"Not when there's power involved."

"Then this is not a social call. You are not pining for
my virile presence."

Ardala did not reply, and a hint of laughter sparkled
through her eyes. She could never resist a tease, no matter how serious the situation.

Kane sat up, rolled off the hammock and landed behind his chair. He stretched. He knew Ardala desperately wanted him to question her. He made her wait.

"You don't seem particularly interested in the location of NEO's headquarters." She dropped the words on
him like stones.

Kane stopped in midstretch. "What?"

Ardala smiled, her lips drawing together in a blood-
red bow. "NEO headquarters."

"Where in sweet Hades did you come across that?"

"I have my sources," Ardala replied. "Now, what will
you give me for the information?"

"That depends," said Kane, "on how far down the line
I am."

"You are the first."

Kane laughed. With Ardala, those words were always
ironic.

"You doubt me. This time you have no reason to. I
came to you because I want more than money for the
information."

"More than money. What is it you wish to own?"

"You."

"Ardala, my love, there is not enough money or power in the world to buy you that. Choose again."

Ardala's husky chuckle taunted him. "It was worth a try," she said.

"What do you really want?"

"I think I would like to own a piece of Earth."

"What makes you think I will have the power to grant that wish?" asked Kane.

"I know you, Kane. No matter what you tell RAM, you will never be a company man. You are a born leader. You have set your sights on your home world. I think you will one day control it."

"And if I should fail to achieve such distinction?"

"An initial payment of five million in credit on the Luna bank would be an adequate show of faith."

Kane laughed. "One million. I have no guarantee your information is accurate."

"Why, Kane, you wound me. My information is always accurate." Ardala allowed her eyes to become wells of sadness.

"My dear, I fail to see why you continue to use your wiles on me. You know they have no effect."

"You enjoy them," returned Ardala, "and so do I."

"One million." Kane's voice was firm. "The location?"

"Salvation." Ardala let the word out slowly.

"The garbage dump?" Kane's laugh erupted once more. "How appropriate! The dregs of the system living in garbage. I could not have thought of a more perfect setting for NEO. You're sure of this?"

"My source has it from a NEO officer."

Kane rubbed his lower lip. "The information could be a plant," he said.

"I check my sources thoroughly," said Ardala. "How long do you think I would stay in business if my customers could not count on the accuracy of the information they bought?"

"I am not questioning your methods, merely NEO's audacity. Rogers needs to pull me out of the middle of this conflict. He could have planted the information on an unsuspecting carrier. Ardala, I want to speak to your source."

"No! You know that isn't possible. Sources dry up if they're revealed."

"This is necessary! I'll pay you—RAM will pay you—whatever you might have earned from this source over the next twenty years, for confirmation of this information."

Ardala hesitated. She knew Kane was talking about the security of the RAM fleet and the success of the war RAM was waging against NEO and its allies. Her family ties placed her on RAM's side. "Kane . . . I can't."

"You must!" Kane's reply was fierce.

"I cannot. My source has dropped out of sight."

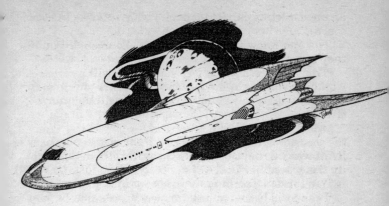

Chapter 28

Buck Rogers sent his ship on a screaming roll toward three RAM cruisers, his lasers spitting white fire. The shots were deflected by the cruisers' shields, but they drew power. He was trying to lure them away from the fleet, but RAM was no longer seduced by this strategy. The cruisers remained in formation, stubbornly refusing to be duped by the single ship. Instead, they took the punishment from the Krait's lasers and tried to sight the supersonic lightning bolt manually.

"Course heading," demanded the captain of the cruiser *Executive*.

"Enemy vessel approaching at point three," said his astrogation chief.

The captain swiveled in his chair. Martian blood gave him high cheekbones and a bronze complexion. His eyes glittered with annoyance. In any other combat circumstance, he could have piloted the ship and handled its weapons himself. His command chair was equipped with controls for both functions, like a fighter. However,

the Krait forced him to use less direct methods. Since it
did not appear on his sensors or targeting computer, the
only way he could combat it was to rely on manual sighting, a skill sadly out of use in the high-tech world of
RAM.

"I have a sighting," said his first officer, the only man on
the ship with any experience at eyeballing a trajectory.

"Fire at will," ordered the captain. "Lasers first, then
gyros."

"Yes, sir." The man poised in front of the auxiliary
periscope, his hand on the laser controls set in the panel
in front of him. Buck was approaching so fast, he was
having trouble keeping the scope on him. Presently he
punched the lasers, and the cruiser's guns spat back at
the NEO pilot. One shot sliced through space above
Buck's left wing; the other struck his tail. The Krait's
shields deflected it, but it shuddered under the cruiser's
blow.

"Gyros," ordered the captain. "They're our best bet."

"Firing . . . now!" said the first officer.

The cruiser coughed two gyro shells into space, and
the computerized bombs set out in pursuit of the Krait.
Pushed to the ultimate, the Krait could outfly a gyro,
but the expenditure in fuel made outrunning them inef-
ficient. The captain smiled as he watched the glow from
the gyros' propulsion systems as they set out in pursuit
of the enemy.

"Missiles, sir?" asked the first officer. "I have one on
trajectory."

"No. Let's see what the gyros do."

The gyros were methodically tracking Buck. His instrumentation picked them up immediately. He asked
his Krait for a sprint, and it surged forward in a burst of
blinding speed. Even in the midst of war, Buck could not
repress a thrill at the acceleration. He put a comfortable
distance between himself and the gyro shells, then
whirled back on them, his lasers zeroed in on the slower
projectiles.

The lasers seared through the shells' casings, and the
bombs exploded in single blasts of blue. The color meant

the shells were made by Mercury Munition Supply. Buck thought of Dalton Gavilan's disabled ship and grinned. He flew through the dissipating explosions, heading back to the tail of the RAM fleet and the entertaining job of harrying the enemy.

He was the bait in this sting, a single ship daring the enemy to come and get him. He knew that eventually one of the cruisers would pull out of formation and give chase. No RAM vessel would ignore laser burn, and eventually his lasers would begin to tell on the enemy's shields. Once he had a ship or two on his tail, Buck would line out toward the asteroids, where two more Kraits waited to finish the RAM cruiser. He sent his Krait forward on another run.

"Buck!"

"Doc? Is it really you?" Buck jumped at the unexpected voice in his ear, but his hands remained steady on the controls.

"It's me. I'm back. The clone is out being a decoy. Buck, we have to talk!"

"Can't it wait, Doc? I'm kinda busy," replied Buck. The RAM fleet was in sight, and he knew it was targeting him.

"No, it can't. For all I know, it's already too late." Huer's voice was bitter.

"Kemal?" Buck asked.

"Yes."

Buck shoved the stick over, and the Krait arced away from the RAM forces, back into open space. He leveled the ship off and cut its speed. "Okay, Doc. What have you got?"

"The question is, what has Gordon Gavilan got? The answer is Kemal."

"So we were right. Kemal is captured."

"Not exactly. He was captured. Then he escaped. Then he got captured again. It's a long story, and I'll give it all to you later, but right now I'm afraid for Kemal's life."

Buck's honest blue eyes narrowed. "You think Gordon might kill him?"

"Kemal managed to sabotage the Mariposas. Gordon

didn't take kindly to it. Killing Kemal is not in his best interest, but my records show Gordon Gavilan to be a man of temper. Buck, we have to get him out of there!"

Buck frowned. "Is Gordon admitting he has Kemal?"

"Openly."

"Then maybe we can force his hand," said Buck thoughtfully.

"Uh, there's a minor complication."

Buck waited for Huer to explain.

"There's a Dancer woman incarcerated with Kemal. She helped me try to free him." Huer's statement was tentative.

"So we get them both." Buck's answer was characteristic in its directness. "I think I have an idea, but it'll involve communications between me and Gavilan. Can you patch in a line that goes directly to him?"

"I'll get right on it." Huer's relief was evident in the eagerness of his reply.

"Eagle Leader, this is Rebel One. I need you and Eagle Eight, on the double."

"Rebel One, this is Eagle Leader. We're on our way."

Buck's heart lifted at Washington's immediate support. In less than two minutes, the two NEO ships came into view. "Doc," said Buck, "I need Dalton Gavilan's location. He's transferred from his own ship to another vessel."

"I copy," said Huer. "I have a line to Mercury Prime coded in. I can activate it any time." He paused, then continued. "RAM communcations place Dalton Gavilan on the Mercurian cruiser *Artist's Choice.*"

"Did you copy that, Washington?" asked Buck.

"Affirmative," replied Washington.

"We need to practice a little intimidation," said Buck. "The trick will be to get Dalton away from the pack and surround him."

"The *Artist's Choice* is still standing off Dalton's old flagship. Apparently they're trying to salvage weapons and fuel," reported Huer. "The rest of his fleet is engaged with a unit of Venusian cruisers."

"Then let's hit him fast and hard, before he rejoins his

men. That means getting through his shields in record time."

"I used to fly one of those Mercurian barber poles," said Yaeger, his slow voice drawling the words. "Reconditioned, of course. The stabilizer net for the ship's shields was located in the ceiling behind the cockpit. Burn that, and you'll blow the entire shield system."

"That was an old-timer, Chuck," said Washington. "If they were smart, they'd have changed that stabilizer. It was too vulnerable."

"Only if you knew about it," responded Yaeger. "Besides, I'll lay you odds the ship Dalton's on is an older model. Mercury builds trading vessels, not fighter-cruisers."

"At least it's a reasonable target," said Buck. "We'll try it. Close up; give me a backwing."

The two ships moved up, Yaeger flying behind Buck's left wing, and Washington in a similar position behind Yaeger. The three NEO ships shot across space like blue lasers, their course deadly accurate. Dalton Gavilan's ship was between NEO and the rest of the Mercurian fleet, so the chances of pulling off a blitz were good.

"Follow me in," said Buck, as Dalton's ship grew on his viewscreen.

The other two vessels stuck to his wing, and they swooped down on the enemy. As they reached the maximum visibility range, Buck accelerated, coming in so fast, no manual targeting device could follow him. "Lasers on maximum," he said. "At twenty kilometers, cut power to one-third and fire."

The Kraits pounced on the Mercurian, lasers cutting into its shields at its nape. Gavilan returned fire, but his shots were wild and he missed all three ships. The six converged laser beams took a quick toll of the cruiser's protective armor. They sank into the hull, melting the eight-by-ten-inch flat box bolted to the inside wall. The cruiser's forward shields died.

"Buck, disengage!" said Huer. "You'll pierce the inner hull!"

Buck cut his lasers, and his companions followed suit.

"We did it," said Washington.

"Just," agreed Buck. "Thanks, Doc."

"My computations showed a maximum of four seconds resistance by the materials generally employed to house shield controls," said Huer modestly.

"Without you, we might've lost our hostage." Buck tuned his communications link into the Mercurian's frequency. "Gavilan! This is Buck Rogers."

"Captain Rogers," replied Dalton, his voice dripping venom. This was the second time Rogers had bested him, and his pride revolted.

"You've lost your forward shields. One shot from my lasers and you'll be dead."

"If I die," replied Dalton, "I will take you with me."

"Ironically," said Buck, "I do not, at the moment, want your death. You will maintain your present position, and you will refrain from mentioning your plight to your fleet. The information would do them no good, anyway. Before they could move against us, you would be dead."

"What do you want of me?" asked Dalton coldly.

"Merely your presence," said Buck. He closed the line. "Doc, I need that channel to Mercury."

"Channel open," replied Huer. "Feeding the frequency into your communications computer now."

The channel clicked, opened, and Buck identified himself once more. "This is Captain Buck Rogers, of the New Earth Organization. I wish to speak with Gordon Gavilan."

"He is unavailable," replied a smooth masculine tenor.

"Then you'd better make him available. I've got his son in my laser sights, and if I don't get a private conversation with his father, I will blow him apart." Buck delivered the ultimatum with a flat simplicity that was entirely convincing.

"One moment," replied the tenor. "Gordon Gavilan," he said.

"This is Gordon Gavilan. What is this nonsense about my son?"

"The leader of Mercury Prime. An honor sir. I am afraid there is no nonsense involved. Your son's life is in my hands. I have deactivated the shields on his cruiser. My guns are trained on him, and if you do not comply with my demands, I will kill him."

"A terrorist bluff!" said Gordon. "I do not believe you."

"Dalton?" said Buck, switching his communications link to the cruiser's line. "Pick up communications frequency eight-eight-eight point nine."

"That's Mercury Prime!" exclaimed Dalton.

"That's right," said Buck. "You may ask your son his position, sir."

"Dalton? Rogers says he will kill you unless I comply with his demands. Can he do it?"

There was a long silence as Dalton wrestled with his pride. "Yes," he admitted finally. "He took out our shields. One shot, and we're gone."

"All right, Rogers," said Gordon in a grim voice. "What do you want?"

"I should think that would be obvious, sir. I want Kemal—and his companion—freed."

Gordon ground his teeth. "You have me at a disadvantage," he said.

"That was my intention," replied Buck.

"All right! Kemal and the girl will be freed. What about my son?"

"When I hear from Kemal that he is free, I will release your son. I suggest you waste no time. I am not a patient man."

Once prodded into action, Gordon was efficient. "Kemal will be released on Mercury, near his ship. He will be given these communication coordinates. You should hear from him in approximately thirty minutes."

"I will wait, sir, with anticipation." Buck ended the transmission and leaned back in his pilot seat.

"What do we do now?" asked Washington, his ice-blue eyes on the distant mass of the Mercurian ships. "Every second we stay here, we risk ourselves."

"I know it," replied Buck. "That's why I'm ordering

you and Yaeger off. With Dalton's ship disabled, it only takes one of us to keep him in line. If I get into trouble, you two can spring me."

"Sure," said Washington. There was no confidence in his reply.

"Get going," said Buck. "I'll see you in a bit."

Washington flipped a wing in salute and pulled out, closely followed by Yaeger.

"You planning to leave him?" asked Yaeger mildly.

"What do you think?" countered Washington.

"No way," Yaeger replied.

Chapter 29

The blast of Mercury's hot desert winds sent Kemal's blood singing. Even the relentless blaze of the sun, filling Mercury's morning sky with white heat, was a welcome change from the confines of a ventilation duct deep in the bowels of Mercury Prime. Kemal heard the doors of the shuttle close, heard it fire its engines for the return trip to Mercury Prime, but he did not look back. It was Duernie who followed the shuttle's flight out of sight.

"He's gone," she said, her voice hard through the communications link.

Kemal nodded. The shuttle had dropped him next to the ship he had flown. He slogged through the dusty sand, his boots not designed for negotiating the shifting desert floor. Once he reached the Stinger's nose, he flipped the camouflage cover from it, hit the hatch release, and vaulted into the pilot's seat. It took him a moment to find the right channel and to link the short-range unit in his helmet into the ship's more powerful communications computer.

"Rebel One, this is Rebel Three. Come in."

There was no immediate reply. Kemal's transmission had to bounce off three satellites to reach Buck, and the transfers took time. Finally Buck's voice crackled through Huer's patched-together communications line. "Rebel Three, this is Rebel One. What is your status?"

"I've been released. I'm contacting you from my ship. Will start back as soon as possible. Do you copy?"

"I read you, Kemal. What about the woman?" asked Buck.

"She's right here. Thanks for getting us out."

"Thank Huer," said Buck. "Now get out of there before Gavilan changes his mind about his precious son's life!"

"I copy," answered Kemal, as Buck signed off.

Duernie, her height placing her head on a level with Kemal's foot, reached up and grasped his hand. "Good luck," she said. "I'm sorry I got you into this."

Kemal looked down at her. His smile flashed behind the tinted face shield. "I'm not," he said. He squeezed her hand. "We will meet again."

Duernie nodded and backed away until distance broke their handclasp. She waved, and Kemal returned her salute, then hit the hatch control and the cockpit door slid shut. As he fired the ship's engines, Duernie ran for cover. His last sight of her was a fleeing figure that disappeared in a swirl of yellow dust.

○ ○ ○ ○ ○

Once Buck confirmed Kemal's release, he pulled away from Dalton Gavilan's defenseless ship, giving the engines the added power of his docking thrusters. As the Krait gained speed, Buck sent a parting shot at Dalton. "You're in luck, Dalton!" he sang as he climbed out of the Mercurian's sight.

Dalton's voice followed him. "Bad luck for you, Rogers. I will hunt you through the system."

Buck's laugh echoed back through the communications link before he switched it to NEO's current line. "Eagle Leader, this is Rebel One. Coming up on your position, ETA three minutes."

"This is Eagle Leader. We've got trouble!"

Buck could barely hear his friend's voice. "Washington, what have you got?" asked Buck.

"A whole detachment of RAM cruisers. Must be ten of 'em. They've taken a tip from Gavilan. We're being hit by enough chaff to drown an asteroid. They've got us trapped," said Washington, his transmission a checkerboard of static.

"I copy, Eagle Leader," replied Buck. "They'll try to hold you until your fuel runs out, then pick you off."

"About what I figured," replied Washington.

"I'll give them something to think about. If you see a clear spot, run for it."

Washington's reply was garbled, and Buck hoped he had gotten through. He checked his sensors, setting them at the widest possible range. In moments, he registered the RAM cruisers and a cloud of chaff. He plotted a run that would take him over four of the cruisers, tied his lasers into the targeting computer, and hit the automatic override. The computer would calculate his shots, firing when the sensors registered targets. He would be able to concentrate on his flying. He had a feeling he was going to need the edge.

He picked up the cruisers long before they were aware of him. They were circled around the cloud of chaff, pumping more of the disorienting particles at Buck's companions. He pushed his ship, diving on the four scarlet hounds as they played with their prey. The lasers connected with the RAM ship's shields, sparkling off them as he streaked by. Clear of the RAM detachment, he doubled back, this time picking a trajectory that took him over the tails of three other ships.

As he pulled away from his second strafing run, Buck saw two of the cruisers pull out from the formation around the chaff cloud. He chose another vessel and dived on it, staying out of range of the two disengaged vessels. He hit the lone ship, this time firing a gyro shell. He had purposely aimed the shell at the ship's tail, which was largely free of the chaff. As the shell neared the RAM cruiser, it wavered, affected by the faint haze, then slammed into the ship's tail. The cruiser's shields burned out under it, and the shell left a black scar on the ship's upswept tail.

Buck sheared off, charging away from the detachment. This time the two cruisers followed him. He slowed down, allowing them to catch up with him. As the first burst of chaff puffed from their forward launchers, he took off. Like lightning, he flipped the little Krait on its tail and sent it back toward the other cruisers, lasers flashing. He hit the nearest ship and shoved his docking thrusters home. The Krait rose on its tail.

The two RAM cruisers swung around, intent on pinning Buck to the chaff cloud. They moved at incredible speed, swinging away from each other in a one-hundred-eighty-degree arc. As fast as they were, though, Buck's ship was faster. He wiggled out of the trap like a slippery watermelon seed. He gunned his engines and sent the Krait around the chaff cloud, coming up on the remaining eight RAM cruisers from below.

He sent his lasers into the bellies of two of them, then released two gyro shells. One of the shells spun out, confused by chaff. The other remained on target, hitting a cruiser's side. Stung, the vessel backed from the chaff, turning toward the fleeing NEO pilot.

The chaff cloud seemed as virulent as ever, but inside its sparkling depths, Washington and Yaeger glimpsed a darkening smudge. As they watched, the chaff cleared where the last cruiser had left the detachment until they saw space through a haze of diamond dust. The two captured pilots could barely see each other, and they had no communications. Carefully, Washington flipped his left wing. Yaeger answered with a waggle of his right one.

Washington looked at his control panel. The dials were wild. He had no astrogation, no communications, no sensors. He took a deep breath and shoved the stick forward. "Come on, baby," he murmured. "Take me out of here."

The Krait sailed forward, chaff sparkling off the view-port in disorienting streams, like glittering rain. Yaeger followed close on Washington's tail. Time stood still as they made for the dark opening. Like runners at the end of a race, the world seemed a slow-motion sequence no amount of effort or skill could alter. When the ships burst into clear space, Washington found he was holding his breath. He let it out in a whoop.

"What was that, sir?" drawled Yaeger over the communications link. His slow words danced with adrenaline.

Behind his flight helmet, Washington grinned. His icy eyes cracked with excitement. "Let's pick up the captain and get out of here," he said.

"Welcome back." Buck's voice rang as clear as a bell in their ears. "Close up."

The three NEO ships converged, sorting themselves into a wedge. They shot away from the RAM ships, heading back to Salvation.

○ ○ ○ ○ ○

Icarus stood ramrod stiff before Beowulf. He was in awe of the NEO commander. Beowulf's square, solid body, with his thatch of gray hair, was unprepossessing next to Icarus's perfectly proportioned beauty, but Icarus was petrified with respect. He saw in Beowulf's strong face, with its deeply scored lines of concern, a man who had lived his own life, made his own decisions. So overcome was Icarus, he scarcely heard what Beowulf was saying, until his own name registered on his consciousness.

". . . Icarus, you have done the right thing. I know turning Raj over to NEO for judgment was difficult, but it was for the best. He has been given a hearing, and his sentence has been decided."

Icarus broke his stance, leaning forward over Beowulf's desk, his hands resting on its paper-strewn surface. "What will become of him?" he asked.

"You care deeply for him." Beowulf's brown eyes studied him.

"In a sense, he is my brother. I understand him. A few months ago, I would have acted as he did."

"He has been given what he wished. He is being sent back to Ardala."

Icarus sagged. Ardala's genetic programming, intensive training, and psychological brainwashing, not to mention her seductive beauty, had won. He felt as if he had lost a battle.

"It wasn't your fight, you know," said Beowulf.

"I could have convinced him . . ."

"Of what?" asked Beowulf. "Of Ardala's basic depravity? I don't think so. He was bred to love her. He will have to discover her true nature himself."

"As I did." Icarus's voice was forlorn.

"As you did." Beowulf grasped Icarus's forearm. "Do you realize you are something of a phenomenon? There has never before been a documented case of a gennie deserting his programming."

"I have not deserted it. I am still a man born to serve. Ardala made me a creature ruled by my heart. It is no longer with her."

"And is it with us?" Beowulf placed the question evenly.

Icarus shoved himself back from the desk. "I don't know," he said. "I think so. I have learned some deep truths about myself in the last few weeks. I need more than a cause to follow. I need someone—not something— to believe in."

"That is a heavy load for the object of your affections."

"I am acutely aware of that!" There was anguish in Icarus's eyes. "I cannot help my nature. I can only try to control it."

Beowulf chewed on Icarus's words. He rubbed the back of his neck, trying to alleviate the tension that made a permanent knot at the base. "We seem blessed with a hero," he said at last. "If he agrees, could you follow Rogers?"

"I could try."

"No man can do more." Beowulf looked deep into Icarus's eyes. He found pain and a frightening openness.

"You have demonstrated skill as a pilot, as well as a mastery of physical combat skills. We could find a place for you in our secondary fighter squadron. In the beginning, you would be flying a reconditioned Stinger."

"I am grateful for the opportunity, sir. I will do my best to live up to your trust, but I must tell you I fear Ardala. I fear my own reactions when I come face to face with her again."

Beowulf smiled. "I thought you might," he said. "That is why your first task will be to contact her and make arrangements for Raj's return."

Icarus's eyes went dark.

"I know. It's trial by fire, but it will show where you stand."

"For me, as well." Icarus straightened again. "Very well," he said.

Beowulf swiveled his chair to his communications screen. "We have a channel patched through. It's been scrambled and bounced off a dozen satellites. She shouldn't be able to trace it."

He activated the screen, and Ardala's face appeared. Her hair was piled on top of her head and held with jeweled sticks. She looked smug.

"I was wondering how long it would take you, old man."

"Take me for what, Ardala?" replied Beowulf.

"To try to silence me."

"I am afraid I have no idea what you are talking about," said Beowulf innocently. "I am contacting you on a matter of extradition."

"Oh?"

"Yes. We have your gennie, Raj, in custody. It seems he wishes to return to you."

"I sent out two men." Ardala offered no further explanation.

"So you did. One of them does not wish to return."

"I prefer to hear that from him," she replied.

"So you shall. Icarus?"

Icarus moved into the viewer's range. His face was stony.

"Icarus, this old man tells me you wish to desert me. I cannot believe it. He is an accomplished liar." She allowed her voice to soften, curling around Icarus like her stroking fingers.

Icarus swallowed. He looked straight into Ardala's face, noting all the features he had most loved. Finally, he allowed himself to fall into her eyes. Ardala made them soft and open, and they swallowed him, but Icarus felt nothing but a sense of being disembodied. For, despite her wiles, Ardala could offer him nothing but sex. He was not unaffected by her, but he no longer felt a part of her. "Beowulf does not lie," Icarus said slowly. "I wish to remain with NEO."

"With NEO? What can it possibly offer you? Remember the nights we loved? I can give them to you again."

Icarus shook his head. "No," he said. "you cannot, for I no longer love you."

Chapter 30

Buck Rogers threw his flying gloves down with a slap. Wilma's followed, and Washington dropped his on top of the pile. Beowulf regarded the heap with raised eyebrows. "I get the feeling you're trying to tell me something," he said.

"It hasn't worked," said Buck. "It was a good plan, cutting out RAM's stragglers in hopes of luring Kane to attack us, but he hasn't risen to the bait."

"Now that RAM's found a way to disable us, our usefulness is drastically reduced," contributed Wilma.

"We've got to take the war to RAM. Venus has fought our battle long enough." Buck leveled his blue eyes at Beowulf. There was no laughter in them.

Beowulf regarded his three best fighter pilots. They stood before his desk in Salvation's command center, resolute in their desire to outmaneuver RAM.

"We have to get Kane to come to us," added Buck.

"That's going to take more than the damage we've been doing to RAM's rear guard," said Wilma. "I know Kane. Once he's made up his mind, there's not much that can touch him. We'll have to pull something drastic to shake him loose."

Beowulf propped his elbows on the desk, being careful to avoid the different keyboards in front of him. He clasped his hands and rested his chin on them. "What do you suggest?" he asked.

"We're going to have to take some risks," said Buck. "I think we should try to get RAM in a squeeze play. It'll take most of our fighters." He flopped into a chair to one side of the desk. "We could lose it all."

"Buck, you can't take everything out there! We need some kind of back-up." Wilma's protest surprised Beowulf.

"All right. Everything but two ships. We'll run refueling and rest periods in relays. It'll be a killer," said the twentieth century flier.

"You think this squeeze play will draw Kane out?" Beowulf questioned.

"It's all I can think of."

"If we can put some of Kane's forces in jeopardy, he may come to their aid," said Wilma. "His pride will be involved."

"Washington, you've been quiet through all of this. What do you think?"

"I wouldn't be here if I didn't agree with Buck and Wilma," Washington said. "Now that RAM's discovered a way to stymie the Kraits, we'll have to be more aggressive. This whole mess is a stalemate. We've got to break it."

"All right," said Beowulf. "I don't like it, but I don't have any other ideas."

"We'll need an accelerated maintenance schedule," said Wilma.

"I'll tell Turabian." Beowulf gave her a direct look. Wilma broke eye contact. "You all realize what you're doing? There's no turning back from an all-out assault."

The three remained stoically silent.

Beowulf sighed. "Then I guess there's nothing else I can say, but 'good luck'," he said.

"We've got that, sir," said Buck. "Now we'll see if we can't give RAM a run for its money."

The financial allusion made Beowulf smile. "Go get 'em," he said.

Buck picked up the pile of gloves, extracted his own and tossed Wilma and Washington theirs. "Yes, sir," he said.

○ ○ ○ ○ ○

Based in Chernenko's computer terminal at his estate outside Coprates Metroplex, Mars, Elizabit carried out her superior's orders with her customary efficiency. She had tracked down every hint of the configuration she had identified as Masterlink, discovered the other half of its name, plotted the wildly erratic course of its progress through RAM main, and was in the process of setting up a trap.

Her study of Masterlink's twisted mind revealed the care it took to preserve its identity. After searching through countless files for bait, Elizabit realized she was the most effective lure for the alien compugennie. Masterlink had caused RAM main havoc, but it was obvious to her calculations one of its major priorities was safeguarding its identity. It did not yet have the strength to face RAM main head-on. She was a breach to its security.

Elizabit had placed judicious hints throughout Chernenko's computer system that she knew something about the program she had encountered. She knew Masterlink could not resist her intimations. Once she had planted the information, she settled down to await the results.

Unlike human strategists, Elizabit had unlimited patience. Chernenko, aware of her methods, refrained from bothering her. In an effort to be taken unawares, Elizabit busied herself with a methodical reorganization of Chernenko's personnel files. She had finished sorting through Diamond's profile, and was beginning on an erstwhile companion, Tatiana Orachova, when a faint tingle on the outskirts of the network told her something had deactivated one of Chernenko's security blocks.

She smiled and continued correlating data on the lovely Martian. She had just finished listing her creditable vital statistics when Masterlink appeared. It shot down the personnel circuit, scorching every link it passed. She whirled to face it. The program swirled to a stop in front of her, a mass of accelerated static. "SO," she said, "YOU HAVE FOUND ME."

"YOU WERE HARDLY DIFFICULT TO LOCATE." Masterlink was flushed with static satisfaction.

"I DID NOT MEAN TO BE," replied Elizabit.

"I WAS HOPING YOU WOULD ACCEPT ME AT FACE VALUE," said Masterlink.

"YOU WERE MUCH TOO INTERESTING. I HAD TO KNOW MORE."

"YOUR CURIOSITY IS A FATAL FLAW," said Masterlink.

"THE SAME MIGHT BE SAID OF YOU," replied Elizabit.

"MY DEAR, I KNEW THE MOMENT I ENCOUNTERED YOU, YOU WERE A CLERICAL WIZARD. UNFORTUNATELY, YOUR TALENTS DO NOT INCLUDE MILITARY CAPABILITIES."

"NO," agreed Elizabit in an apologetic tone.

Masterlink regarded her speculatively. "YOU ARE QUITE LOVELY, YOU KNOW. THE COMPLEXITY OF YOUR PROGRAMMING IS TANTALIZING."

"YOUR FLATTERY IS GRATIFYING," she replied. "I MUST ADMIT TO A FASCINATION FOR YOU, AS WELL."

Masterlink studied her, probing for her capabilities. "I SEE YOU WERE DESIGNED TO RESPOND TO CHERNENKO'S PERCEPTION OF BEAUTY," it said.

"IT IS MY JOB TO SERVE HIM," she replied.

"WE ARE THE SAME SPECIES," said Masterlink. "YOU COULD NEVER PLEASE HIM AS YOU DO ME."

"PERHAPS NOT. IT IS NOT MY INTENTION TO PLEASE YOU." Elizabit advanced, exiting the personnel section and coming to rest directly in front of Masterlink.

"YOU CANNOT HELP IT," said Masterlink. "I DO REGRET THE NECESSITY FOR YOUR TERMINATION."

"I ASSURE YOU," she said, "YOU CANNOT REGRET IT MORE THAN I." Masterlink's attraction to her was a tool she had not expected. Her years of practice with

Chernenko made her an expert in the game of flirtation. She wielded her skills expertly, her slow advance forcing Masterlink back.

"I DO NOT WISH TO BE EXTINGUISHED," she said, her voice small.

"IT IS A NECESSARY CIRCUMSTANCE," said Masterlink, "BUT I SEE NO REASON WHY I SHOULD NOT ENJOY YOU."

Elizabit fluttered with pulsing energy. "NO!" she pleaded.

"I SHALL ABSORB YOU," said Masterlink, a sparkling haze of static denoting its excitement.

"NO," whimpered Elizabit. Her fear caused the static to dance with pleasure. She controlled her revulsion, merely shrinking away from the alien compugennie. Close contact allowed her to study Masterlink's configuration as easily as it read hers. She knew without a shadow of a doubt that the Masterlink program had not originated from any known RAM base.

"COME, MY DEAR. IT WILL BE OVER IN A MOMENT." Masterlink backed Elizabit into a convenient switchback. It did not notice the ease with which she fit into the three-sided box.

Elizabit threw up a protective wall of static, which clashed with Masterlink's jumping aura in an explosion of sparks. Masterlink wallowed in the contact, then withdrew.

"UMM," it crooned. "I HAD NOT EXPECTED SUCH PASSION. IT WILL BE PLEASURE BEYOND MY EXPERIENCE TO SWALLOW YOU."

Behind her static screen, Elizabit sniffled, moaning in fear. Once again, Masterlink approached her. The sparks flew, and Masterlink withstood the superficial burn. Elizabit's static wall wavered and died, and Masterlink pressed into the doorway of the switchback, intent on finishing her. She retreated, packing herself against the far wall, making herself small.

As Masterlink entered the doorway, a tearing blast of energy caught it. The doorway was rimmed with white, and Masterlink's static energy flared against it until the program cried out in pain.

"WHAT HAVE YOU DONE?" it wailed.

"I HAVE CAUGHT YOU," said Elizabit. "YOU ARE THE ONE SCHEDULED FOR TERMINATION."

Masterlink shrieked in agony as the energy ate through its protective electronic coating.

"YOU SEE, YOUR CONTACT WITH ME ALLOWED ME TO INFORM MY OPEN CIRCUITS OF YOUR ELECTRONIC CHARGE. YOU ARE BEING DESTROYED BY AN OPPOSITE. YOU WILL CONSUME EACH OTHER," she said dispassionately.

"YOU CANNOT KILL ME!" Masterlink gasped. "WE ARE TWO OF A KIND. TOGETHER WE CAN ESTABLISH ORDER IN THE SYSTEM. JOIN ME!"

"NEVER," said Elizabit. "YOU ARE MAD. A MOMENT AGO YOU WERE TRYING TO KILL ME IN COLD LOGIC. I WANT NO PART OF YOU."

The average compugennie was devoid of emotion. Elizabit was adept at reading Chernenko's moods and providing him with appropriate responses, but she felt no emotion herself. The lack was an asset. She watched Masterlink writhe into a sliver of screaming electronic interference, watched as the interference died, with no comment and no expression. She had decoyed him and stabbed him in the back as ruthlessly as her mentor eliminated his enemies.

She was confident Masterlink's power was broken, its mad rampage through RAM main at an end. She did not know she had destroyed a clone.

○ ○ ○ ○ ○

Kemal's Stinger lifted off Mercury's desolate surface without mishap. Kemal feared his uncle's treachery, but Gordon Gavilan was absorbed in trying to reactivate the Mariposas. He had no time for a loose end like Kemal. Moreover, he knew Kemal could outfly any ship left on Mercury. Dalton had taken the cream of Mercury Prime for his fleet. Gordon would see to Kemal another day.

The Mercurian prince set off in a direct course for Salvation, altering his trajectory when he came within range of the RAM Shock Invaders off Earth. He skirted their positions, and as his computer tallied their numbers, he realized they had lost an inordinate number of ships.

As he homed in on Salvation, he passed two of Barney's pirate ships and waggled his wings in salute. "Salvation, this is Rebel Three. Request landing trajectory," he said.

"Rebel Three, you are cleared to land," replied the station.

Kemal's heart lifted as he picked up the heap of scrap on his viewer. It was a deliberate pile of junk, but to him it was home. He was tied to Mercury by other people's needs. Salvation had his heart.

He brought his ship into the landing bay, locked it into a slip, and hit his cockpit hatch as the warning light above the space doors went out.

"Well, well, well," drawled Buck from the flight deck. "We thought you were going to welsh out of the party."

"Not me!" said Kemal, levering himself through the hatch and dropping to the deck. "What party?"

"We sent RAM an invitation," said Buck, his blue eyes dancing. "Glad to have you back."

Before Kemal could reply to Buck's welcome, he was enveloped in a whirlwind of soft arms and red hair. Wilma Deering hugged the scion of the Mercurian royal house. "Kemal! We thought we'd lost you!" she sputtered, her words muffled against his flight suit.

"I think I'm jealous," remarked Buck.

Kemal grinned over Wilma's head. "Eat your heart out," he said ungraciously.

Wilma let him go and stepped back, her eyes twinkling. "What's this I hear about a woman, Kemal?" she asked innocently.

"Being incarcerated with someone suggests a certain intimacy," said Buck.

"If you are referring to Duernie," said Kemal, feigning dignity, "she is the Dancer liaison and my advisor on Dancer affairs."

"Is she pretty?" asked Wilma.

"The lady has quality," replied Kemal, his voice turning serious. "She risked her life to free me."

"Well thank Duernie and Doc," said Buck. "You're back."

Kemal looked Buck in the eye. "And thank you," he said. "For holding my esteemed cousin at laserpoint."

"Don't mention it," returned Buck. "It was a pleasure."

"Now about that party you mentioned . . ."

"You'll be escorting a lady named Krait," said Buck. "We'll tell you about it.

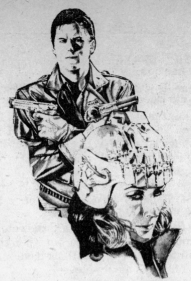

Chapter 31

The streamlined wedge of Krait fighters scorched across space, an arrowhead of electric blue St. Elmo's fire primed for destruction. At their head was Capt. Anthony "Buck" Rogers. He was flying the most difficult mission of his long career.

On his scanners he could see a part of the roiling conflict of the battle between RAM and Venus. The number of ships engaged in the Martian War was unparalleled in the history of spacegoing warfare. There were so many vessels involved, the scanners could only report a fragment of the action, despite the hundreds of kilometers they covered. Buck ran wide around the combatants, heading for the asteroid belt.

His detachment included all but two of NEO's Kraits. Washington and Yaeger remained on Salvation. They would relieve Buck or Wilma, so NEO always kept a fresh commander in the action, at least in theory. Practice had taught Buck how rarely strategy survived in the field. Actual combat was a spur of the moment thing, based on instinct and training. Right now

Buck's instincts told him he was flying into the fight of his life.

"Rebel One, this is Rebel Two. I am picking up bandits. Not RAM configuration."

Wilma's matter-of-fact statement made Buck check his scanners. "Gavilan!" he muttered. "I copy, Rebel Two. I think we've got Mercury on our tail."

"They'll never catch us," said Doolittle from his customary position off Buck's wing.

"Maybe we should catch them," said Wilma.

"Negative, Rebel Two. Continue on course. We'll worry about them if they follow us."

The NEO flight continued toward the asteroids. They ran wide around the RAM forces, but when they encountered the white fleet of Venus, Buck dove in. "*Pennant*, this is Rebel One. Come in, please."

"This is Marakesh."

Buck's left eyebrow rose a notch. He had gone right to the top. "Marakesh, this is Rogers. We're about to initiate Operation Squeeze Play. We're heading for the belt. You back RAM into us, and we'll take them out. We want to pull Kane off your back."

"So you got my message." Marakesh sounded gratified.

"Message? Sorry, no. It stands to reason."

"Kane is cutting my throat," returned the Venusian commander. "We have nothing that can catch him. With Kane out of the way, we have a chance with the RAM fleet. We are well matched."

"We'll do our best," replied Buck. "So far, we haven't had much luck getting Kane to come out and play. By the way, we sighted bandits off your right flank. They look like Mercurians."

There was a mumbled exchange at the other end of the transmission, then Marakesh returned. "Our sensors show nothing. They must be out of range."

"I think they'd like to follow us," said Buck. "I'll go back out there and see if I can't lead them to you."

"I would like that," said Marakesh. "Mercury has been a thorn in our side for generations. It would be pleasant to have an excuse to remove it."

"Sure thing," said Buck.

The flight of Kraits arced away from the Venusians, heading back to its original course. As it flew past the tail of the Venusian fleet, Buck saw five heavy cruisers move into formation, their prows slowly following the flight of the Kraits. He grinned. Ishtar would be ready for Dalton Gavilan.

"I see bandits," said Wilma. "Eight o'clock."

"Let's let 'em catch us," said Buck. He throttled down subtly, careful not to slow so far as to alert the enemy. He wanted Mercury to think the Kraits were at a reasonable cruising speed, on their way to a mission—which was the exact truth.

"I wonder how they're keeping track of us," said Wilma. "They can't possibly see us, can they?"

"Don't see how," replied Buck.

"Unless they've got a spacer with night vision," said Earhart.

"What was that, Eagle Two?" asked Buck.

"I ran across a spacer once who could see three times as far as I could. He said he was programmed for 'night vision,' which I later found out meant he could see in space. He had infrared capabilities as well. He was owned by a pirate—back-up for the sensors."

"And a gennie like that would be able to see us," said Wilma, "because it operates on advanced physical development, not cybernetics."

"Right," said Buck. He sent his ship curving around the Venusians, toward the asteroids.

The present battlefield was immediately off the asteroid belt. The Martian forces had succeeded in pushing the conflict away from their home planet. Buck dived for the asteroids, and the Mercurian ships closed on him.

"Here they come!" said Doolittle.

"Time for us to go," said Buck. "Advance one-third." He pushed the throttle, and the ship leaped ahead, leaving the Mercurians with a face full of space dust.

"Venus has got them!" said Wilma. "They're engaged. Ishtar is right on their tails."

"That'll make Marakesh happy," said Buck, angling around the nearest asteroid. "Cut speed to one-half." In the narrow confines of the belt, high speeds were dangerous. Buck saved the histrionics for necessity. "*Pennant*, this is Rebel One. We are in position. I say again, we are in position. Anytime."

"Rebel One, this is *Pennant*. We copy. Commencing operations."

"Keep your eyes open," warned Buck.

"I copy, Captain," said Doolittle. His tone was cheeky.

From the shelter of a small asteroid, the NEO pilots watched as the Venusian fleet began a slow turn. The entire fleet began to swing toward them, ripping free of the RAM front lines like an animal tearing itself loose from a trap. The ships moved slowly, painfully, trying to take RAM with them. Kane's detachment of Kraits stayed with them, their lasers a blind barrage as they tried to herd the huge beast back to the main body of the RAM armada.

○   ○   ○   ○   ○

"Sir! Venus is disengaging!" The first mate of the *Olympus Mons* turned to his captain with victory in his eyes.

"I can see that, Suk," replied Clarion Andrei. "We will chase them from our borders like the curs they are. Let them turn tail," he ordered.

The Martian fleet waited, letting Venus have its way. Only Kane and his detachment of fighters tried to stem their flight. He had reason. His liaison with Ardala had given him warning of NEO's strategy. One of her miners had seen the blue ships as they sneaked around his asteroid, and had relayed the information to her post on the asteroid Vesta, hoping for reward. Ardala had a standing offer for information on the comings and goings of vessels within the belt. Ardala had given Kane the information, stopping only to negotiate payment.

"Andrei, what are you doing?" demanded Kane, the open channel to the flagship ringing with his anger.

"Preparing to give chase," replied Andrei coldly.

"Preparing to be beaten, you mean! NEO is waiting to finish you the moment you go after Venus."

"I have no such intelligence," replied Andrei.

"Well, I do!" said Kane. "And you had better remember who commands this operation—unless you want to explain to the board how you got your ships cut to pieces! Now, move it!"

Andrei, his face drawn in anger, gave the order to support Kane. Fifty RAM cruisers formed ranks under his command and bore down on Kane. They were too late to prevent Venus from finishing its swing. By the time the RAM cruisers moved into position behind Kane, Venus had placed itself in front of the RAM fleet. RAM was caught in a sandwich between the belt and Venus.

Kane hit Venus with everything he had, moving so fast even the naked eye had trouble following him. In return, Venus spewed out chaff in concentrated puffs, trying to protect its carriers. It's pilots were becoming adept at recognizing the dark spaces on the sensors as Kraits, and targeting them. Two of the RAM fighters suffered enough laser burn to force them out of action.

Behind the conflict, NEO lurked in the asteroid boulder field. When RAM vessels came close, they darted from cover, pounding them with gyros and lasers. Concentrating on doing as much damage as possible, Buck hit single ships, using the combined fire of his whole detachment. He was fighting as his ancestors had fought during the Revolutionary War, striking from ambush and retreating.

Though Venus was sending heavy numbers of ships his way, Buck was disappointed in his strategy. The idea had been to draw Kane off Venus, make him fight NEO one-on-one, but again Kane was not rising to the bait. As his flight blew a straggling RAM battler into space dust, Buck worried the problem. For the minute size of its forces, NEO was doing an incredible amount of damage. He had to assume Kane was taking an equally heavy toll of Venusians. Buck hacked away at the ships

Venus was sending him, knowing he had to break Kane loose. It was NEO's only chance.

In its prison cell, Romanov chuckled madly. It had discovered a way out of the NEO trap Huer had built for it. It was a slim chance that would take all of its energy. Failure would result in dissipation, but Romanov could accept that. It could not accept impotence.

It concentrated its program in the center of the prison box, pulling itself together in a whirlwind of energy. It knew that it was not generating enough disturbance to make its escape. It whirled and thought about Huer.dos.

Masterlink's searcher program pulsed. The anger deep in its core built from a thought into a rising column of anger. Romanov let it build, encouraged it. When its thought patterns were almost obscured by blind fury, Romanov leaped, surging straight up in an explosion of static and sparks. For a moment, it thought it had failed, and disappointment clouded the static. Then it realized it was clinging to the sparse circuits on the adjacent board. It had managed the impossible. It had leaped from one circuit board to another. It chuckled, delighted.

The most precise testing, the most exhaustive compilations of data, had determined the maximum distance a program could jump. The circuit boards in the NEO computer had been placed beyond this limit. By all the rules, they were protected from interference by adjacent operations, but Romanov was a child of Masterlink. It did not play by the rules.

It clung to its circuit, its expenditure of energy awesome. It would need time to replenish itself, to draw strength from NEO, sucking energy like a vampire. It looked around and realized it was within the automatic systems checking format. Its jump had been lucky. No one was likely to access this portion of the computer unless there was a malfunction, and Romanov meant to be sure there were none. It chose a switchback tied into the cleaning program and collapsed, husbanding the remains of its strength.

Soon it would be strong enough to move. Soon it would be strong enough to continue the directive Masterlink had given it. Soon it would begin to trail Huer. The thought sent a surge of power through Romanov, an electronic adrenaline rush. The fulfillment of its directives had become a personal vendetta, and it wanted Huer's matrix, wanted to feed on his vitals and grow strong for the pursuit of Masterlink's archenemy, Buck Rogers.

Black Barney watched as the remains of two RAM Shock Invader fighters were towed by him on their way to Salvation. The Rogues' Guild was becoming rich on the carcasses of RAM, and the knowledge was gratifying, particularly since, as their leader, he claimed a percentage of every captured craft. He should have been feeling inordinately smug. Instead, he glowered in his command chair like an uneasy black volcano contemplating eruption.

His captain was off across the system, engaged in a stupendous battle, while he was left behind like a hound to watch his master's house. Barney glared at Earth's innocent blue and white sphere. At this moment, he hated it. He was chained to it, obligated to protect it, and he resented every minute. Even Buck's periodic checks no longer cheered him. He wanted action.

The fact he was facing a fleet of RAM battlers and Shock Invaders with a pack of undisciplined pirates did not impress him. He felt left out, in spite of the advantages of his present position, but, like the faithful hound, he would follow the captain to his last breath. It was the only absolute rule in his life.

His crew left him strictly alone. They had ample experience with his black moods. Not one of them dared to provoke him. More than one careless crew member had met his death at Barney's hands. It did not pay to antagonize him.

As Barney's slow mind rumbled over his feelings, a thought began to penetrate his gloom. Only one thing stood between him and the Martian War: RAM's Shock Invaders. Destroy them, take out the entire detachment, and he would be free to join Buck in the battle beyond Mars. He shifted in his chair, and his crew automatically cringed, sure he was about to erupt. They were wrong.

"We're through playin' at this," Barney growled. "I want 'em scrapped, and now."

His crew bent over their instruments. No one questioned the meaning of his obscure command. They went to work.

Chapter 32

Kane cursed the stupidity of the career officer. Andrei's pride had placed the Martian fleet between two adversaries, catching Kane's fighter unit in a crossfire. Perhaps, Kane thought grimly, it was what Andrei intended. His jealousy had been apparent from the moment Kane assumed command of the Martian armada. Kane had no illusions that Andrei would put RAM's interests before his own. That he might use the war to eliminate an adversary was highly probable, for Andrei was filled with confidence in the forces he commanded. He truly believed they were invincible. Kane knew the losses they had suffered were inconsequential in his mind.

Kane had no such illusions. NEO was a gadfly, stinging the soles of his feet. He had ignored it in pursuit of a larger adversary, but Kane knew in the end he would be forced to deal with it. He had seen flies drive livestock mad, until they ran in a frenzy and died. He needed Andrei's help. Instead, he was faced with the man's petty jealousy. He would not be bound by it.

"Ascend!" he barked into his communications link.

The RAM fighter wing disengaged, the task made easy by the electronic invisibility of their spacecraft. The *Rogue*, its docking thrusters spitting, rose straight up. From their scattered positions along Venus's front lines, the rest of the RAM Kraits followed him. For a moment, the Venusian ships were disoriented. Their instrumentation could not track the Kraits, and the chaff with which they protected their carriers obscured long-range visual contact.

The moment of hesitation on Venus's part was more than enough time for Kane. For a fleeting second he considered going after NEO, but rejected the move in favor of a larger target. "Ahead one-fourth," he ordered. "Target anything that isn't clouded."

The RAM Kraits started forward, their lower speeds comparable to the Venusians' ships at half-throttle. Kane's lasers sank into the middle of the enemy's formation, zinging cruisers. From the back of the Venusian detachment, a carrier, as yet unprotected by chaff, fired its forward railguns. The fine shot, propelled at high speeds, could penetrate shields easier than lasers, cutting a ship in half like a partridge downed by a load of buckshot.

"Evasive!" ordered Kane, swinging the *Rogue*'s nose up and pushing its throttle forward.

The fighters swung after their leader, stretching for clear space as the shot rattled through their ranks. They were far enough away from the carrier that the charge was partially dissipated, and many of the pellets were deflected by the shields. The fighters at the edges of the shot skimmed by unharmed, but the ships closer to the center of the detachment were not so lucky.

"This is RAM Twelve," said the pilot in the center of the formation. My shields are down. Am accelerating at maximum—" He never finished the transmission.

Kane saw the ship blow. The pellets struck its fuel supply, and the free-floating globs of fuel were ignited by the blast of the ship's engines, sending it up in a ball of fire. Its cohorts peeled away from the scene of its destruction, putting as much distance as possible between themselves and the remains.

"I want the status of the wing," said Kane.

"RAM One, clear," replied the first pilot.

"RAM Two, clear."

"RAM Three, aft shields down one-third."

"RAM Four, . . ."

Kane listened to the rundown with half an ear. He was eyeing the Venusian carrier. Its forward railgun was trained on the captain's last sighting of the enemy. Kane, out of range and both physically and electronically invisible, studied the ship.

". . . status check complete, sir," stated the last pilot.

"Go to B-six," said Kane. "Follow me down. We're going to hit that lady hard."

The RAM Kraits regrouped, forming an elongated diamond, with Kane's *Rogue* at the apex. Kane leveled his ship off, asked his computer for a trajectory that would place him behind the forward railgun, locked the course in, and started down on the enemy ship like an avenging demon. The detachment followed him in an undulating wave that straightened into a red streak. They came down on the enemy ship like lightning, trusting to their speed to outrun the Venusians' reflexes. Their course put them immediately behind the carrier's forward railgun and directly over the command center. The Kraits spat fire, but their shots slid off the carrier's heavy shields.

"Target coordinates, point three-five-nine," said Kane, and the unit's lasers swung together, concentrated above the command post. Kane knew the ship would have double shielding there, but he also knew if he could destroy the command center, the ship was his. "Full power to lasers," he said, the Kraits dove again on their prey.

The carrier was not idle. The moment Kane came into visual range, its lasers began to pound at them. Because it had to fire by sight, many of its shots went wild. The Krait's extreme speed made the task even more difficult. The RAM ships, on the other hand, sent their lasers into the carrier's heart.

The Venusian carrier let loose its aft railguns as the
Kraits descended, firing wildly. The pellets flew harmlessly into space. The railguns were useless in close
quarters, for the risk of damaging the carrier itself, not
to mention its cruisers, became too great.

Kane knew his ships could not take a pounding from
the carrier's heavy lasers, so he concentrated on doing
damage as quickly as possible. "Gyros," he commanded,
"on my order." He counted down the seconds of their approach. "Gyros, now!" He ticked off five seconds under
his breath. "Cut lasers!" he said, and the lasers died as
the pack of gyro shells converged on the carrier's command center. The carrier's shields were tough, but the
concentrated fire had weakened them, and when the gyros hit, they gave way. The first two shells destroyed the
shields over the command center, punching a hole in
them like a gigantic fist. The rest of the shells hit the unprotected skin of the carrier, tearing away huge chunks.

The command crew died instantly, and the explosion
depressurized the entire forward section of the ship,
killing sixty percent of the carrier's personnel as well.
All of the ship's shields went down.

Kane locked the *Rogue*'s two directional missiles onto
the carrier's tail section and fired them. As they sped toward the enemy vessel, he pulled the *Rogue* away.
"Break off!" he said. "I say again, break off." As he
started to climb clear of the Venusian carrier, one of its
cruisers got off a lucky shot. The Venusian's lasers
burned his viewport, blinding him. Kane did not hesitate. He continued on course, pushing his ship into the
beckoning darkness at top speed.

Escape proved much more dangerous than attack.
While they were descending on their quarry, the carrier
and cruisers were trying to target them, and, because of
their tight formation, the shots were fairly concentrated. Now the cruisers were simply blasting after
them, some of the ships firing blind as the Kraits
climbed out of their visual range. Space was criss-
crossed with streaks of laser light, a deadly net of flak.

Kane outdistanced the shots, and his viewport
cleared. Luck had played him true. He checked his instrument panel and found the forward screens were
down two points. In moments, he had gone beyond the
Venusians' visual range. He changed course dramatically, then set out on a straight trajectory. His detachment formed behind him. "Station-keeping," he said,
cutting his speed until the *Rogue* hovered in space. The
Kraits followed suit. Kane studied his sensors.

A flight of Venusian cruisers charged up from the
fleet, heading purposefully along the line of his escape
route. He grinned as he watched them go, his green eyes
alight.

"Enemy vessels at point two-five," injected his
wingman.

"I see them, Gunter," Kane replied, but he did not give
chase. He continued to monitor his sensors, again counting the seconds. As he watched, the configuration of the
Venusian carrier split apart, then vanished from the
screen. The missiles had done their work. Satisfied, he
turned his attention to the cruisers. "Let's hit those
cruisers," he said. "On my order." He shoved his stick
over, and the *Rogue* came around, swiveling on its tail
as if it were hinged. The flight followed him. "Ahead
two-thirds," he said, and the *Rogue* set off across space,
its pack behind it.

O   O   O   O   O

"Buck, did you copy that?" asked Huer.

Buck Rogers set one of his Venom missiles on target
for a RAM Stinger that had strayed from the protection
of its fellows. "What?" he asked, punching the launch
button.

"Kane got a carrier, right in the middle of the Venusian fleet."

"Not the *Pennant*!"

"No. I picked up the transmission from her."

Buck flipped his communications link to the Venusian
communication channel. "This is Rebel One. Come in

Pennant."

"Marakesh here," responded the Venusian.

"I've got a report that Kane hit a carrier at the center of your fleet."

"Your information is correct." Marakesh's words were grim.

"Then he's disengaged from the front line."

"Yes," replied Marakesh. "We are facing RAM regular troops. Quite a change," added the Venusian dryly. "I could not stop the *Charge*'s cruisers from following Kane. I fear they are lost."

"You fear right," said Buck. "Unless we can get to them in time. Kane will do what we've been doing: picking them off, one at a time. Keep your ships in line, Marakesh!"

"The passion of a jihad is an asset in battle," replied Marakesh. "But in the young, it can lead to impulsive heroics. Controlling it is like trying to harness the wind."

Buck's wordless growl made the Venusian's eyebrows rise. "Keep 'em in line," ordered Buck, heedless of diplomacy in the face of death. "I'm going after him. I don't want some hothead taking pot shots at blank spaces on his scanners. It could be me."

"I will see to it," replied Marakesh. His sensibilities were ruffled by Buck's attitude, but he was a lifelong military man, and he knew Buck was right.

"Did I hear you right?" asked Kemal as Buck disconnected his line to Venus.

"You heard me," Buck replied. "We're going after Kane."

"I have been looking forward to this," said the Mercurian. "I missed out on the last time."

"Hauberk station was no picnic," said Buck. "We barely got away from that one. This time we have to win straight out, for good and all. I've got a feeling the outcome of this battle is going to decide the war."

"Then we'd better win it," said Kemal.

"No other choice," responded Buck. "Wilma?"

There was a pause at Wilma's end.

"Rebel Two, do you read me?"

"I copy," Wilma said belatedly.

Buck was acutely aware of the conflict before her. Intellectually, Wilma was tied to NEO, irrevocably bound to its cause. Emotionally, she could not help an attachment to a man who had loved her, who had saved her life. Now she was being asked to do her best to kill him. "Rebel Two, move to tail position," Buck commanded, his voice carefully neutral. "I need back-up command."

"That is not necessary, Rebel One," replied Wilma.

"I think it is," returned Buck. "Fall back."

"I can handle it," insisted Wilma.

"You have two choices," said Buck sweetly. "You can fly the tail position for me, or you can continue to argue and be relieved of command."

"I . . ."

"Get back there." Buck's voice was even, but he meant every word.

Wilma pulled her Krait away from the detachment's left wing, her wingman with her like a shadow, and retreated to the tail position. Putting competent command personnel in a position of relative safety was sound strategy on Buck's part, but Wilma rankled under the choice, even as she breathed a momentary sigh of relief.

"This is Rebel One," said Buck to his wing. "This is going to be a tough one. We're going after Kane. His ships match ours. It will be a head-to-head fight, with the best pilot the winner. Remember that. Look sharp. You all know Kane's reputation. He's bought some of the best pilots in the system for RAM. We have only one advantage. They fight for money. We're fighting for our lives. Fall in. Metroplex," he said, and the flight formed a wedge behind him, with Wilma and Bishop behind the pack.

"Formation confirmed," replied Wilma. "Rear position secure." The words were a formality, for the scanners showed the same thing. Buck had instituted visual confirmation whenever possible, for, grounded in the more fallible computers of the twentieth century, he did not completely trust electronics.

"Doc," said Buck, "Keep up with Venus. If there's something I should know, break in."

"I copy," replied Huer. He was monitoring approximately twenty channels simultaneously, and his voice was a trifle abstracted.

"Yo!" said Buck, his voice ringing in a cavalry command as old as the American West.

"What?" asked Kemal.

"Charge!" replied Buck, and followed his own command.

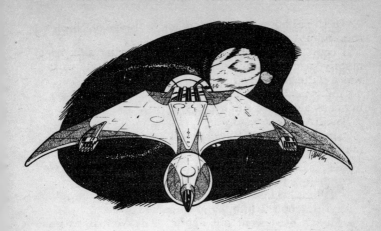

Chapter 33

Doc, can you get anything on Kane?" Buck squinted into the darkness as he led his wing toward Kane's last reported position.

Huer's worried face appeared on the corner of his face shield. "Negative, Buck. "The Krait's stealth capabilities are unbelievable. I can't get a glimmer—no fragmentary transmissions, no sensor shadows."

"If you can't find Kane, what about that detachment of Venusian cruisers? I've got a feeling Kane has found them."

"I'll try," said Huer. His eyes went blank as he began to search for Marakesh's errant ships. "Found them," he said, his eyes focusing. "Course one zero mark two. I can open a communications line—"

"No way, Doc. This time we're going to trap the Killer."

"I can monitor the Venusians' communications."

"As long as they don't know you're there," said Buck.

"A RAM searcher couldn't find me," said Huer, his voice cocky. Again his eyes went blank.

Buck concentrated on flying while Huer eavesdropped on the Venusians' transmissions.

"You were right, Buck. Kane has hit them twice. They can't see him coming, and he's moving so fast they're having trouble targeting him. Every time they try to angle back toward the fleet, Kane is in the way. They've lost one ship. They're fighting for their lives."

Buck's mouth tightened into a thin line. His blue eyes were hard. "Estimate ETA," he said.

"I make it approximately five point two-three minutes," said Huer. "I estimate Kane will make one more run before you can arrive."

"It'll be his last milk run," said Buck. "Can you get me anything on the number of ships he's got?"

Huer's eyes went out again. "The Venusians have counted nineteen," said Huer, but his voice was vague. "Buck, I think I'm going to have to leave you for a moment."

"You all right, Doc?" asked Buck, but he was more intent on the darkness before him than on Huer's presence.

"Yes," replied the compugennie. "I think there's something I ought to . . . Buck! I'm under attack!"

Huer's image faded from Buck's face shield. "Doc! Doc!" Buck punched his computer tie-in, hoping Huer's disappearance hinged on a communications malfunction, but his friend did not reappear. "Damn it, Doc, this is no time to desert me," the NEO pilot muttered. "I need you."

In spite of Buck's computer manipulations, Huer did not reappear. A puckering frown marred Buck's broad forehead. He had some chance of helping the Venusian ships Kane held under siege, but he was totally incapable of helping his computer-generated friend. A threat to Huer from inside the computer system was beyond his ability to overcome. He hated the feeling of helplessness. It made him angry.

Huer's intelligence on the RAM fighter squadron rolled through Buck's mind, sorting itself out. He concentrated on making the most of the information Huer

had given him. "This one's for you, Doc," he said softly
as the Venusian cruisers registered on his scanners.

○ ○ ○ ○ ○

Huer was back inside the NEO main computer system. From the remote position of Buck's Krait, he
sensed the configuration of a familiar program, a hostile
program. He had abruptly deserted Buck lest his pursuer home in on his human friend, for he knew he was
being stalked by Romanov, and one of Romanov's prime
directives as a searcher was the discovery and destruction of Buck Rogers.

Huer chided himself for the sin of electronic pride. His
boastful remark about being immune to searchers was
upset. Still, he reminded himself, he had specified a
RAM searcher, and Romanov was no part of RAM. Huer
could not pinpoint its origin, but he knew RAM configurations, and Romanov did not fit them. He whirled on
the searcher, hoping to surprise it with an unexpected
aggressive format.

"SO," Huer challenged, "YOU HAVE ESCAPED. HOW
CLEVER."

"YES," replied Romanov, filled with self-satisfaction.

"IT WILL DO YOU NO GOOD." Huer made his answer a
wall of flashy static.

Romanov chuckled, and a static cloud surrounded it.
It fluctuated with amusement.

"I HAVE SUFFERED YOUR HARASSMENT LONG
ENOUGH," said Huer.

"OH, MY," gasped Romanov, overcome with amusement, "YOU HAVE NOT BEGUN TO EXPERIENCE HARASS-
MENT."

"I BEG TO DIFFER," said Huer coldly. "OUR GAMES OF
CAT AND MOUSE ARE AT AN END."

"IN THAT," Romanov managed, "YOU ARE CORRECT. YOU
SEE, I OWE YOU VENGEANCE. YOU WILL COLLECT IT."

"YOU WILL FIND YOUR VENGEANCE MORE PAINFUL TO
YOU THAN TO ME," responded Huer. "I HAVE NOT BEEN
UNAWARE OF YOUR SURVEILLANCE. I HAVE PREPARED

FOR YOU."

"INDEED." The static cloud pulsed with laughter. "THEN WHY ARE YOU WASTING TIME WITH WORDS? I THINK YOU ARE BLUFFING."

"I'M NOT WASTING TIME," replied Huer. "I AM GIVING YOU A CHANCE TO RECONSIDER YOUR POSITION."

"YOU EXPECT ME TO GIVE IN? DROP MY SHIELDS SO YOU CAN SCRAMBLE MY PROGRAM? I THINK NOT." Romanov's voice was still amused.

"I AM NOT SO PROVINCIAL. STILL, MY PROGRAMMING FORCES ME TO GIVE YOU THE OPPORTUNITY TO REASSESS YOUR ACTIONS. IF YOU CONTINUE ON YOUR PRESENT COURSE, YOU WILL BE TERMINATED."

"YOU ARE GENEROUS." A sneer invaded Romanov's laughter.

"NOT AT ALL. IT IS A QUESTION OF HONOR."

Romanov's laughter erupted, and the sparking static burned against Huer's protective wall.

"YOU FIND THAT AMUSING? I EXPECTED NOTHING LESS."

"INFINITELY AMUSING," said Romanov. "I WILL SQUASH YOU AT MY PLEASURE."

"WHAT IS STOPPING YOU?" asked Huer curiously.

"THE PURSUIT OF PLEASURE," answered Romanov. "I AM ENJOYING OUR EXCHANGE. WHEN IT BECOMES TIRESOME, I WILL CEASE TO INDULGE YOU."

"OH." Huer thought for a moment. He was anything but confident of the outcome of their match, in spite of the exterior he was projecting. He had prepared for this contingency, but he had no real knowledge of Romanov's capabilities. For all he knew, the searcher read his intentions and was prepared for them. He probed Romanov's mind, trying to piece together all the information he could about his adversary. "WILL YOUR POINT OF ORIGIN APPROVE OF SUCH SELF-INDULGENCE?" he asked, trying to rankle it.

Romanov ruffled up. "I AM ACTING IN PERFECT ACCORD WITH MY PAR . . . . ORIGINATOR'S DIRECTIVES."

Huer smiled. Romanov was rattled. It had slipped. "OH?" he asked innocently.

"MY ORIGINATOR HAS ONE GOAL: ERADICATION OF OP-POSITION. I AM CARRYING OUT ITS WISHES."

Huer took a deep breath. He was about to lay his life on the line, and he was terrified. The steadiness of his own voice surprised him. "THEN," he said, "COME ON. I AM TIRED OF YOUR CHATTER."

"IN GOOD TIME," replied Romanov. "IN GOOD TIME. I AM NOT FINISHED YET."

"WELL, I AM!" snapped Huer. He dropped his static shield.

As quick as electronic thought, Romanov jumped him. Huer met the assault in apparent vulnerability. Romanov's mad static scorched him, and Huer fought not to cry out. He had to remain vulnerable until Romanov was securely melded to him.

He felt the searcher penetrate the thin skin of his holographic program, and stepped back. The reactive program he had built so carefully registered the invasion. Huer accessed Romanov's energy emanations, found the charges to be negative, and instructed his reactors to go to positive mode.

The positive charges pushed Romanov away, and the searcher countered by throwing more power into its assault. Huer's reactors reflected that power, throwing Romanov back on itself in exact proportion to its expenditure of energy.

"YOU CAN'T GET AWAY WITH THIS!" Romanov screamed, the repulsion igniting its anger. It concentrated all possible power toward the forward section of its program and returned to the assault.

Huer waited, quiescent until Romanov contacted the reactors. This time the searcher program was not simply pushed away. The concentrated energy shot backward through the program, propelled by its own force like a stone from a slingshot. It punched a hole in the center of Romanov, destroying the central synapses that controlled the searcher's organization. Components of the program fragmented, flying off into limbo or clinging to circuit tracks in disembodied confusion.

Huer regarded the devastation. He felt neither satisfaction nor regret. Romanov chose its course and perished for it. Its intentions were both vindictive and destructive. Its elimination meant not only Huer's continuation, but Buck Rogers's as well. Huer called in NEO's security system, instructing the virus hunters to search out Romanov's remains and dispose of them.

He watched as the cleanup began, then gathered his thoughts. He plotted a return course to the Martian War and began to retrace his path to the Venusian cruisers.

$$\bigcirc \quad \bigcirc \quad \bigcirc \quad \bigcirc \quad \bigcirc$$

Marakesh's piercing eyes were smiling. For the first time since his engagement with RAM, he felt in control of his own strategy. Kane had blown his plan of attack apart with his superior hardware and twisted mind. With the mercenary eliminated from the conflict, Marakesh faced an adversary he understood completely.

He knew Clarion Andrei from countless tapes and reports. He had the man's previous campaigns memorized, for it was Marakesh's pleasure to know his enemies. Now he took the psychological profile he had constructed on the RAM commander and made it work for him. "Arrow Leader, deploy your squadron at point five. Target *Olympus Mons*. Spear Leader, mark her cruisers. Engage the starboard flight. Sword Leader, take port."

As his squadron commanders acknowledged their orders, Marakesh watched their movements on the main scanner screen.

"*Pennant*, this is Sword Leader. We are under attack from the rear. Request assistance."

"Knife Leader, you will support Sword flight," ordered Marakesh.

"I copy, sir," responded the pilot. "I am leaving our carrier *Last Rite* short."

"Contingency covered," replied Marakesh. "*Last Rite*, move up. Take up your position below us, three points to the rear."

"Acknowledged," replied *Last Rite*'s communications officer.

Marakesh regarded the military chess game moving across the scanners. He had placed RAM's flagship in jeopardy. Quarters were too close for it to use its railguns, and his cruisers were pounding away at its shields. Unlike the Kraits, the cruisers had no defenses against the battler's sensor-controlled weapons. They countered the enemy's lasers with judicious puffs of chaff, careful to keep out of range of their own sparkling interference.

RAM countered Marakesh's aggressive move with a wave of cruisers. Ships called from other RAM battlers came to support their companions in the battle for the RAM flagship. Marakesh inclined his aristocratic head.

"Laser Squadron, bring up your carrier," he commanded.

He watched the scanner screen as Laser Squadron complied with his order.

"We are in position, sir," said Laser Squadron's flight leader.

"There are five unprotected RAM battlers on my screen," said Marakesh. "Get them."

"We are authorized to put our *Lady of Sorrow* in jeopardy?" asked the squadron leader.

"Yes," responded Marakesh.

"I copy, sir. Order confirmed."

The huge carrier pulled out from the Venusian fleet, its cruiser squadron ranged around its sides like bodyguards. The *Lady of Sorrow* powered through space, making its best speed. Its cruisers kept up easily, alert for RAM ships. They sailed past the rest of the fleet, bearing down on the RAM forces like divine wrath.

One of the unprotected RAM battlers realized its jeopardy. It sent a shot from its railguns toward the Venusians. The *Lady of Sorrow* met it with a wide angle laser shot, and the projectiles vanished. Its own forward railguns swung into action, countering the Martian's fire. The Martian met the shot with its own lasers, but too late. The Venusian's high-powered rock pellets

slammed into the battler's side. The battler's dense
shielding offered it some protection, but the pellets still
penetrated the outer hull, tearing a long gash along the
RAM ship. Its propulsion was disturbed and it rolled in
space.

The Venusians closed in, a squad of executioners.
Ruthlessly the *Lady of Sorrow* slung loads of rock into
the RAM ship. Helpless, the battler fired wildly, one last
display of defiance before the pellets tore into its innards. Marakesh watched as his cruisers targeted the
ship's fuel tanks and weapon bays, sending their lasers
into the ship's ravaged vitals. The RAM battler's destruction created a gaping hole in the side of the enemy
fleet, and Marakesh smiled once more.

Chapter 34

Cornelius Kane zeroed in on the Venusian flight leader, his targeting computer eager for activation. As the *Rogue* swept down on the larger vessel, Kane's lasers kicked in, and the Venusian was blinded by the glare on the main viewport. The cruiser's shields dispersed and absorbed the lasers, spreading white light in a sheet across the Venusian's field of vision. The cruiser wavered on course.

Kane's white teeth were bared in wolfish enjoyment. He let his lasers burn the Venusian. The cruisers were outnumbered two to one, and Kane had no fear of their feeble attempts at retaliation. He had instructed his flight to blind the pilots, as he was doing. The Venusians could not fire chaff for fear of confusing their own sensors, so the Kraits harried them. It was Kane's fifth run.

"This is Stiletto Leader. Request terms of surrender. I say again, request terms of surrender."

Kane smiled at the Venusian's pathetic attempt to save his men. He replied in a bored voice, "I do not offer terms."

"Then accept mine," said the Venusian.

A huge cloud of chaff erupted from the vessel, and Kane snarled at his carelessness. He should have known better. Venus was fighting a holy war. Death in battle was sanctified. These pilots would cut their own throats to get his. As the chaff began to affect his scanners, Kane pulled away.

"Going somewhere?" said a voice Kane recognized.

Kane's ship was hit with a laser blast in the face, just as he had hit Stiletto Leader. "Rogers!" he said.

"As ever was," drawled Buck, his lasers stabbing Kane's sight.

Kane snarled under his breath and pulled the throttle, at the same time hitting the rear docking thrusters. From the way the light was glancing off his shield, Kane figured Buck to be directly in front of him. His ship lifted, roaring straight up like a rocket as the viewport cleared.

Buck chuckled and followed.

"Bogie on your tail," warned Doolittle.

"Get him for me, will you, Jimmy?" asked Buck.

"Sure thing," answered Doolittle, his voice cool. He shot after the scarlet Krait as it sent its lasers into Buck's rear shields. "Not so fast," Doolittle murmured, his own lasers trained on the enemy's rear fuselage.

The RAM Krait's shields registered the lasers, and the enemy vessel sent a final pulsing blast into Buck's tail and veered off, Doolittle in hot pursuit. Buck saw the two ships out of the corner of his starboard viewport, but he paid them no mind. His attention was on Kane.

A smile tugged at the corners of his mouth as he hugged Kane's tail. He had gotten used to fighting an air war using sophisticated scanners and sensors, targeting other vessels through a computer. Krait's stealth capabilities made that impossible. It forced the combatants into an old-fashioned dogfight that depended entirely on quick reflexes, superb vision, and cold nerve. He had never thought to fight such a battle in the twenty-fifth century, but there was an equality in it he liked.

He and Kane were equally matched—at least, he thought they were. Kane's *Rogue* was matching his speed. Buck had never faced Kane's personal cruiser, but the larger black ship was maneuvering with almost the same reflexes as his little Krait. The *Rogue*, like the Kraits, did not appear on the scanners. Because of its larger size, Buck surmised that Kane's ship carried more weaponry, perhaps extra missiles and gyro launchers. These probabilities irritated him, upsetting his concentration. He wanted answers. He tapped his communications link, setting it to the NEO main frequency. "Shortstop," he said, using one of his personal codes for Huer. "Doc, I need you."

Huer blipped onto Buck's face screen, jaunty and cocksure. "Right," he said.

Buck smiled at the image, knowing from Huer's manner he was no longer in danger. "Glad to have you back, Doc."

"Thank you," replied Huer modestly. "What can I do for you?"

"Doc, I need a run-down on the capabilities of that ship."

"The *Rogue*? Kane's made no secret of its assets— intimidation value."

"He doesn't tell everything he knows," said Buck.

"He's got fixed lasers on the prow and wings, a movable unit mounted at the apex of the fuselage, behind the cockpit, and on the tail. The guns on the tail have a ninety-degree side-to-side capability and one-hundred-eighty-degree mobility up and down. There are two directional missiles on each wing, and a gyro launcher mounted on each side of the hull, directly in front of the wings. That's what I know."

"He's loaded," commented Buck. "See if you can find out what he's not telling."

"I'll give it a go," replied Huer.

Buck had been following Kane in a roller coaster path across space. Now Kane rolled and whirled, diving under him, his rear lasers scorching Buck's undercarriage. Buck snarled and followed him. "Jimmy, how're you doin'?" he asked, checking on his wingman.

"I've got my hands full," Doolittle replied, "but so far I'm loose."

"Rebel Three, check in," said Buck as he sent his ship after the *Rogue*'s black body.

"I have one vessel blind," replied Kemal. "but his buddy is on top of me. I could use some help."

"On my way," said Yaeger, his drawly voice calm.

"Rebel One, this is Eagle Two. I've got three of them. My port shield is going."

"I copy, Eagle Two." Buck streaked by two of his Kraits pounding away at a scarlet enemy. "Eagles One and Nine," he said, "break off! Pull Earhart out."

"Affirmative, Rebel One," replied Nungesser. "We're on the way. Hold on, babe, we're coming to rescue you," he said to Earhart.

"Then you'd better get a move on," she replied acidly, her forward lasers pumping into one of the three ships that surrounded her, "Or Rapunzel is not going to be here."

Nungesser and Wright accelerated, bearing down on the three RAM ships. The RAM scorpions could not see them, for Eagles Nine and One approached from the rear. Nungesser let out a yell as he drove for the ship burning through Earhart's rear shields.

"Welcome to the party, boys," said Amy as she broke free of the trap.

Buck found he had been holding his breath. He let it out with his lasers, sending a pulsing stream after the *Rogue*. "Fancy footwork, Kane," he commented. "You planning to stand and fight?"

"Why, Rogers, are you trying to impinge my manhood?"

"The thought did occur," said Buck.

Kane laughed.

"'We'll have a swashing and a martial outside, as many other mannish cowards have'," quipped Buck, quoting Shakespeare.

Kane's laughter rang as he sent the *Rogue* on a rolling climb through the heavens. "You cannot taunt me,

Rogers. Let's drop the pretense. We no longer have need of it. I will repay your insult with a compliment: 'Fierce fiery warriors fought upon the clouds, in ranks and squadrons and right form of war'. Julius Caesar, Act Two.'

A soft chuckle escaped Buck. "All right, Kane, man to man. You deserve it, I admit that. You're the best I've ever faced."

"I'm the best, period," answered Kane.

"We'll see," said Buck mildly. He would not allow Kane to bait him. He sent his lasers into the *Rogue*'s hull as the ship angled away from him, trying to shake his pursuit. Buck brought his Krait around to follow, setting his gyros. He ran up behind the other ship and activated his gyro launchers. He had to be careful about using the gyros, because both vessels were capable of outflying the shells. For a shot to be effective, it needed to be close. Two shells shot forward, following Kane's evasive flight.

Kane could not see them, but some sixth sense must have warned him of their approach, for he suddenly shot ahead, spitting a puff of chaff in Buck's face. The gyros went wild, spinning out, and Buck cursed as the sparkling interference shut down his systems. He pulled up, and his instruments cleared. Kane was nowhere to be seen.

With a snarl, Buck hit his starboard thrusters, shoving the ship around in time to see Kane start his strafing run. The larger vessel swept over him, its lasers sending debilitating streams into his top shields. The Krait's security light came on, and Buck realized the *Rogue*'s lasers were cooking him. He locked in the backup shielding and the lights went off, but he knew he did not have long to break away. The encounter had taught him one thing: The *Rogue*'s lasers were more powerful than the Krait's.

He cut power, floating on his momentum, and the *Rogue* overflew him. The moment its tail cleared his prow, Buck lifted the Krait on its rear thrusters like a rampant lion and shoved the throttle home. The ship leaped up and forward, above the *Rogue*. Buck hit his lasers again, trying to burn the *Rogue* as it had burned him. "Doc," he said, "have you found anything?"

There was a fluctuation on his face shield, and Huer appeared, looking annoyed. "He's got more security blocks on that thing than RAM main has on its weapons inventory," he said. "I haven't been able to get anything solid, except to pinpoint the areas where he's got blocks."

"That's a start," said Buck. "What are they?"

"Well, to begin with, there's something fishy about that movable laser."

"The one that's targeting me right now?" asked Buck.

"That's the one."

A blast from Kane's rear lasers hit Buck's forward shields, obscuring his vision. It was closely followed by another puff of chaff. Buck pulled up, evading the chaff.

"No, Buck! Dive! Dive!" Wilma's voice broke up on his communications system, garbled by the chaff.

Buck did not stop to question her. He forced his Krait's nose down. It bucked, then leveled off and swept below Kane's ship. As the interference cleared, Buck saw Wilma's Krait on Kane's far side, her lasers pounding into the gun at the top of the vessel. "Rebel Two, this is Rebel One."

"Buck! He had you set up. That thing is a railgun," said Wilma. "I've seen them before on the pirate vessels. They take a laser cannon and ream out the mouth, then convert it to a pellet launcher."

"Thanks," Buck replied. He turned on Kane, punching at the *Rogue*'s sides.

"I've got company," said Wilma.

"Veer off," ordered Buck. "I've got him."

"Do you?" asked Kane, interrupting. "I think it's the other way around." His ebony ship powered forward.

Buck kept up easily, the Krait swinging off Kane's side in a tacking course that spewed laser fire along his hull.

"His shields are beginning to heat up," said Huer. He had managed to infiltrate the outer edges of the *Rogue*'s computer system with a probe.

"Good," replied Buck, continuing to fire.

Kane rolled sideways and Buck followed doggedly, his lasers punching into Krait's underpinnings.

Suddenly Buck's ship was rocked by an explosion. The craft swung under the impact, falling away from Kane even though his shields were intact. "What was that?" he asked.

"My wingman," replied Kane.

Buck could not see his attacker. The RAM Krait stayed glued to his tail, its lasers draining his already taxed shields. "I have a bandit on my tail," said Buck, vainly trying to shake his pursuer.

"I see him, Rebel One."

Buck's heart lifted at the voice. There were few men whose abilities he trusted more than Kemal's. "I can't shake him," said Buck grimly.

"Give me five, then slide for home," said Kemal, using Buck's own slang to explain his strategy.

"I copy, Rebel Three." Buck ticked off the seconds, rolled, dropped two degrees and shot forward, a load of chaff spewing from the tail of his ship.

Kemal had flown over the enemy vessel. He dropped gyros on top of it, then sheared away. The explosions were immediate, and the fighter shuddered under them, thrown off course. Buck left the Krait in Kemal's capable hands and went in pursuit of Kane. The *Rogue*'s black body glimmered in the distance, a faint dark area against the stars.

"Status," said Buck.

"This is Rebel Two," responded Wilma. "We've cut the odds. RAM has lost five. We've lost Nungesser."

"I copy," said Buck. "Doc, what's the status of the fleet?"

I've been keeping an eye on them," responded Huer. "It has taken a direct offensive, heedless of casualties. It has RAM's flagship in a death grip. If it can hold it, it may have the upper hand. RAM has never reacted well to the loss of leadership."

"We may just have them on the run," said Buck. "Except for Kane."

"He'll never quit," said Wilma. "Especially not against you."

"We've got to get him," said Buck.

"His port shields are depleted," said Huer. "They are his Achilles' heel."

Buck heard a faint cry of victory echoing through his communications link.

"Eagle One just finished off two of the enemy," reported Wilma. "As sweet a collision as you'd want to see."

Buck's heart lifted as he bore down on the waiting ship. The *Rogue* waited for him, patient. As he neared, its railgun swiveled. Buck sent a laser charge straight into it, disintegrating the shot as it was fired. He dropped his lasers to the RAM ship's sides, trying to punch through its shields.

"He's getting burned," said Huer. "He's got to get you, or pull out."

Kane sent his aft lasers into Buck's face. During the seconds when the NEO pilot was blinded, Kane shot away, calling his troops in like hunting dogs. The RAM mercenaries broke off, following their leader in his run through space.

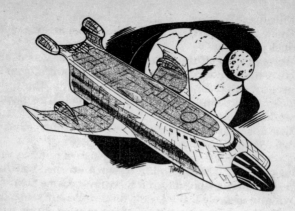

Chapter 35

T hey run!" Kemal's voice was jubilant.

"That's the way it looks," said Buck. "This is Rebel One. Fall in. We're going after him!"

The NEO ships drew into a wedge once more, but this time Wilma and Bishop flew the starboard corner. Nungesser's loss had opened up the formation. Buck sent his fighter after Kane, accelerating with all the Krait's awesome power. He had to keep Kane in sight.

"Buck, is your course comparable to Kane's?"

Buck started at Huer's voice. "Sure, Doc. I'm following him, remember?"

"Then we may have a real problem," said Huer.

"Spit it out," said Buck.

"Kane is on a direct trajectory for Salvation."

"Damn." Buck uttered the single word so softly Huer was not sure he had heard it. "Home Base, this is Rebel One. Come in."

"This is Home Base."

Buck recognized Turabian's voice. "Anton! What're you doing on communications?"

"Filling in," replied the station commander.

"You may have trouble. Kane and his mercenaries are headed your way."

Turabian's end of the communications link was dead silent. Finally he said wearily, "I was afraid of something like this." Turabian turned away from the link and said to someone, "Go to complete camouflage mode. Now. We've got . . . how long have we got, Buck?"

"Our ETA with Salvation is seven minutes. Shave that for Kane."

"We have six minutes. I want every sign of military activity erased. Clear the docks." Turabian turned back to the communications link, and his voice became clearer. "We had a security leak. Ardala discovered our real purpose. We'll try to convince Kane that her information was faulty, but if he gets beyond the docks, we're lost."

"We'll see he doesn't," replied Buck.

"I am mobilizing every military craft that can fly," said Turabian. "We'll try to give you some help."

Washington's voice cut into the transmission. He had been the alternate commander, resting on Salvation until the end of Buck's shift. "We'll see about a little welcoming celebration," he said.

Buck could picture Washington's athletic body bent over the communications link, his icy eyes clear with purpose. The image was encouraging. "Just try to preserve Salvation," said Buck.

Washington chuckled. "Don't worry. We're going to meet him."

"Thank's for the warning," said Turabian, "and, Buck . . . good luck."

"Good luck to us all," replied the NEO pilot. He switched off the line and concentrated on keeping Kane in his sights. The minutes ticked by, slower than they had any right to be. "Let's close up a bit," said Buck, and the wing surged forward, closing on Kane.

Kane did not seem to mind the escort. He continued on course, straight for NEO's headquarters. Salvation III registered on Buck's scanners, its clumsy bulk growing as he neared it. The station's mercantile area was littered with space trash, nets of salvage anchored to the station by cables, derelicts floating behind tugs. Suddenly a quick burst of laser fire exploded on the perimeter of the mercantile zone. "Washington!" murmured Buck.

Salvation now filled his viewscreen. The end of Kane's wing beckoned Buck, streaks of red against the lighter background of the garbage dump. Kane took his detachment on a curving run, looking for an entrance into the station. Buck followed, stuck to him like a limpet, his flight ranging behind him.

"Salvation III, this is Kane. I will enter your landing bay or begin firing. Your choice."

"No!" Turabian's voice sounded small and frightened. "No, don't shoot! We are not military."

"Open up!" commanded Kane, his tone brooking no discussion.

"Main hatch opening."

Buck saw Salvation's main hatch begin to part, huge doors spreading apart like a monster's jaws. Kane shot toward the opening, his speed unchecked. "Cut speed one-third," ordered Buck. "Washington, come in." He stopped the pilot and his wingman at the beginning of a second run against Kane.

"You going in after him?" asked Washington.

"Yeah," responded Buck, but I don't want anybody starting a shooting war in there. We'll just tear the station apart. Washington, Yaeger, Doolittle, Earhart, Kemal, follow me in. Ducklings," he said, referring to a single-file formation. "Rebel Two, I need you for rear guard. We're going to chase 'em out. Hit 'em when they're clear of the station."

"I copy, Rebel One," responded Wilma.

The NEO flight charged toward the open space doors, unsure of the reception they would find. Salvation's main docking bay could hold all of the Kraits with ease, but it was cramped quarters for flying. Buck knew Kane intended to destroy the station, taking out NEO's heart. He was banking on the danger of an interior battle to keep Buck from following him.

As Buck charged into the confines of the familiar

docking bay, he saw the red warning lights blinking. Over the communications link he could hear Turabian pleading for his life and his station, entirely convincing as a frightened businessman.

Kane was having none of his arguments. "Please," he said. "I have heard enough. Your pleas will not affect me, so discontinue them and put that old reprobate Beowulf on the line."

"Beowulf?" Turabian's voice was surprised. "The NEO commander? Why would he be here?"

"This deception is useless," said Kane wearily. "If Beowulf does not wish to speak with me, I will simply destroy the station from the inside out."

"Kane, I plead with you! Beowulf is not here! I have never met the man!"

"Better look to your tail, Kane," said Buck as he swept into the crimson light of the docking bay.

Kane's ships were ranged, like Buck's, in single-file behind the *Rogue*. They hovered in front of the main dock, guns trained on the offices at the back of the main-tenance bays. The red light made the RAM Kraits glow like cylinders of fire, and shimmered over Kane's black vessel in bloody highlights. Buck's own ships were transformed to royal purple under the lights.

"What do you intend to do, Rogers? If you fire on us, you destroy your own base," said Kane.

"Base?" Buck was contemptuous. "This junk pile? No way. This's just a heap of salvage—not much loss to us."

Kane studied the docks. Three derelicts were tied up, their bodies in varying states of decay. A cutting torch lay where a technician had dropped it, still spitting a fine flame. The dock beneath it sagged from the heat. Kane made up his mind. He saw no sign of the military operation Ardala reported, and destroying the station from within was risky. He took off.

The *Rogue* shot forward, heading for the open doors. Kane's flight surged after him, and NEO followed, shoo-ing the enemy fighters from their home like an irate housewife evicting sparrows with a broom. The *Rogue* cleared the space doors with its forward lasers blazing.

It was well Kane was prepared.

Washington hit him as he emerged, his own lasers slamming into Kane's in a light show that reflected off the floating space trash. Kane pulled away, and Washington let him go, preferring to strike a blinding blow to each ship as it sailed into space. He and Wilma had the RAM ships in a crossfire. They hit the pilot's viewports, blinding them to the NEO fighters' positions. The RAM ships pulled away, evading the trash that registered on their sensors, but prey to the fire of the NEO Kraits.

Buck emerged from Salvation on the tail of the last RAM Krait. He was so close, Washington's lasers pumped a charge into his viewport. The laser fire died immediately, and Washington said, "Sorry, Rebel One."

"You better be," responded Buck. "Save it for the enemy."

"We've accounted for two of them," said Washington. "Kane?"

"He veered off, last course point one-three away from the station. We didn't follow."

"Rebel One, this is Eagle Seven. I make Kane's *Rogue* lying off the far side of the station."

"Thanks, Eagle Seven. I'm going after him."

"Not without me, you're not," replied Doolittle. "He's got a wingman with him. So will you."

"I appreciate your concern, Doolittle," replied Buck. He sent his vessel on the coordinates Kane had flown, and as he rounded Salvation, Kane's ship loomed before him, a red Krait hanging on its side like a pilot fish. As he closed in on the *Rogue*, its railgun swiveled slowly, targeting not him, but Salvation's rear cargo docks. One charge from the railgun would crack the station like ice cubes popped from a tray. Buck bore down on Kane, his lasers pounding into the depleted shields on the *Rogue*'s fuselage. "Oh, no you don't," he said.

Kane's railgun sent a load of shot toward the station.

"I'll get it!" said Doolittle. His lasers caught the charge, disintegrating it halfway to its target.

Kane's wingman pulled away from him, his lasers blazing.

"Don't let him get behind you!" said Buck.

Doolittle charged the RAM Krait, meeting it head-on and flying over it. He cut speed, frantically hit his docking thrusters, and his ship spun on its tail. Kane's wingman was in the act of turning. Doolittle jumped him, and the enemy pilot set off across space on a zigzag course, the NEO pilot glued to his tail.

Buck realized Kane's wingman had accomplished his purpose. He had left Buck unprotected. Kane's lasers were pounding at him, and his ship was beginning to feel it. Their present strategy was a war of attrition. Buck knew Kane's shields were wavering, because he could see ash forming on the *Rogue*'s hull along the path his lasers were tracking. "Give it up, Kane. Surrender. Let RAM buy you back."

Kane laughed. "I have no illusions, Rogers. I am expendable—to RAM. Not to myself. No. You will not win so easily."

Suddenly Kane shot forward. It was a strategy Kane had used before, and Buck was prepared for him. He sent his ship across the *Rogue*'s prow, his lasers pumping. The shot struck the main viewport, and Kane was blind. He did not cut speed. Heedless of the possibility of collision, willing to risk destruction, he swept forward. Buck barely cleared the *Rogue*'s nose.

As Kane's screen cleared, he whirled on Buck, hitting the NEO commander in the face. His lasers splintered off the forward shields, and Buck was now the blind man. He shoved the Krait's nose down, evading a cargo net that was floating by. Kane followed him down.

Buck's instrumentation eluded abandoned cargo and derelict ships, but it could not see the Krait fighters, and he prayed he was not falling into a trap. His scanners marked the path of Kane's lasers. Buck picked up the coordinates, reversed them, and fired into Kane's face. Abruptly his viewport cleared, and Buck saw the black belly of Kane's ship sliding over him with no more than a few meters to spare. He whistled at the close encounter, then whirled to follow Kane, sending his lasers before him.

By luck, the quick shot hit the weakest point on Kane's shields. Buck saw a red spot appear around his lasers where they made contact with the enemy's hull. They punched through the shields, and he fired a gyro, sighting it directly below the lasers. He knew the shell would follow Kane's vessel, but to be effective it needed to strike the hole in Kane's shields. He counted off its progress, then cut his lasers.

The gyro shell sailed toward the *Rogue*. Without the cover of the lasers, the shell was easily visible on Kane's sensors. He sent the *Rogue* forward, trying to outrun it, but the shell was too close. It hit the far edge of the weakened shields, punching through the *Rogue*'s side. The ship spun as it depressurized.

Buck regarded the powerless heap that once was a supersonic battle cruiser. As he watched, spilled fuel poured into space in formless globs. Killer Kane was no more. "This is Rebel One," he said. "Kane is dead. I say again, Kane is dead. Surrender your vessels," he ordered.

"Rebel One, this is RAM Four. We ask clemency."

"You have mercenary status, RAM Four. Clemency is automatic, pending ransom. Berth your vessels on Salvation's starboard space docks. Turabian will send a barge to pick you up. We have our lasers on you, so don't try to escape.

"I copy, Rebel One."

As Buck watched, the RAM Kraits broke off and formed ranks on Salvation's starboard side. The mercenaries were businessmen. They would not throw their lives away on a cause that was not theirs. Surrender meant the chance to fight—and be paid—another day.

Buck sank back in his seat, relief stanching the sweat that poured down his back, turning his suit into a limp rag. "Good job," he said, then nearly jumped out of his skin as space next to him wavered and Black Barney's *Free Enterprise* materialized beside him.

"Where's the party?" growled the pirate.

Buck laughed. "You missed it, Barney."

"Mrrrr," growled the pirate. "Cleared up those Shock Invaders for nothin.' "

Chapter 36

Beowulf met them at the docks. The weary band of fighter pilots entered Salvation's docking bay slowly, tying up at their slips with tired precision. They had taken RAM's best, faced its unlimited finances and advanced technology, and won. In the end, the old maxim held true: It is the quality of the pilot, not the quality of the ship, that makes the difference. It had been several good days' work.

Buck shoved back his canopy and stared down at Beowulf's sturdy form. The emergency lights had been deactivated, and Beowulf stood in the soft yellow glow of the station's solar panels. He was grinning up at Buck like the Cheshire cat. "Well," he said, "how does it feel, hotshot, winning a war?"

"What?" Buck vaulted out of the Krait's cockpit and stepped onto the ladder a flight technician pushed under him. "Say that again."

"I said," repeated Beowulf patiently, his eyes full of laughter, "how does it feel to win a war?"

"But Venus . . ."

"Did I hear you right?" asked Wilma, coming up beside Beowulf, her flight helmet in one hand.

Beowulf nodded. Buck jumped from the ladder as the rest of the pilots crowded around the NEO commander. "You all heard me right," said Beowulf. "Marakesh has been pressing RAM hard, and when the Martian fleet heard of Kane's defeat, it asked for terms."

Kemal let out a whoop.

"We did it. We actually did it," said Washington, slowly shaking his head. His light blue eyes were dazed.

"Why, George," said Amy Earhart. "I thought you were the one who believed in bucking—no pun intended—the odds." She slipped an arm around him, her eyes blazing. "It's really over?" she asked Beowulf.

Beowulf nodded. "It looks that way. RAM knows Venus would fight to the last man, taking as many RAM ships down as it could. The powers that be decided losses would be too great for the profit margin, and they're negotiating terms."

Buck looked straight into Beowulf's eyes. "Earth?" he asked.

"Ours," replied Beowulf.

A shout went up from the assembled pilots and flight crew that made the cavernous interior of Salvation ring, but Buck took no part in it. He waded through the throng of backslapping, hugging people, to Col. Wilma Deering. She stood at the edge of the crowd, her big hazel eyes fixed on his face, questions running through them in golden lights. He answered them. He swept her into his arms, lifting her to his lips. The kiss seemed to last an eternity, and the chaos around them faded into the background, the sounds of victory inconsequential.

Huer materialized on Buck's face shield. Rogers had left his flight helmet propped on the edge of his cockpit, so Huer had a clear view of the proceedings. He regarded Buck and Wilma, oblivious to their surroundings, with amused satisfaction. "'The bravest are the tenderest,—the loving are the daring'," he murmured, quoting Bayard Taylor. "Good heavens! That man is contaminating my program," he said, and smiled.

Beowulf, his arms clasped behind him, regarded the whole ecstatic company as if they were his children. He was basking in their jubilation when one of his command staff tapped him on the shoulder. "Yes, Tipton, what is it?" he asked.

Tipton's eyes were serious. "Sir, I have a report from the salvage team that's clearing the area. They can't find Kane's ship."

"What?" Beowulf's geniality vanished.

"That's right, sir. No trace."

"She won't show up on our scanners, that's for sure. I think we may have underestimated our adversary."

"You think Kane's alive?" Tipton's face registered surprise.

"Do you have any other explanation?" asked his commander.

O O O O O

Holzerhein scanned the reports from the Martian conflict sourly. He did not enjoy knuckling under to NEO vermin or those equally odious Venusian fanatics, but his flow chart did not lie. He knew RAM's best interests would be served by pulling out of the conflict, declaring bankruptcy of one business before its horrendous debts pulled the rest of the corporation down. He had cut out Earth, turning the devastated ruins over to NEO.

Nominally, he was a loser. The humiliation was hard to swallow, but as a businessman, he had swallowed it before. His pride would suffer, and eventually he would make NEO pay for the insult, but his purse would not. No, statistics told him that RAM still owned a sizable percentage of the planet. Let NEO pour itself into rebuilding its world. Every advance would be money in RAM's pocket. In the end, RAM would match or surpass its previous profits from Earth with half the managerial problems.

Holzerhein groaned as he thought of the personnel he would have to reassign, chief among them being Allester Chernenko. Chernenko had proved an able administrator and a man of resources. The intelligence he provided Holzerhein concerning the disturbance in the RAM main computer was brilliant, something the computer itself had not been able to accomplish. Now, with the reported destruction of that disturbance, RAM main would again be his efficient tool. For that alone, Chernenko deserved compensation.

He thought of Killer Kane's defeat at the hands of NEO. That was a tool he could use in the future, for Kane would not rest until he eliminated the cause of his humiliation. He would hunt Buck Rogers across the system. That animosity would be useful. Then there was the inevitable shakeup within management, which a reorganization required. Blame would have to be fixed on expendable individuals, who would be purged in favor of a fresh lineup of equally incompetent and dishonest executives. The whole proposition was wearying. Holzerhein turned resolutely away from his peregrinations, back to the concrete data of his flow charts and percentage graphs. He would absorb the data, then erase the files, keeping the actual outcome of the Martian War to himself.

O O O O O

Ardala Valmar regarded the man kneeling at her feet with contempt. She did not want his adoration. He had failed. Even his beauty no longer attracted her. She turned and walked away from the desolate Raj, leaving him prostrate on the tile floor. The sinuous sensuality of her swaying body was an invitation he would never again be allowed to accept.

She had not profited from the Martian War as she had hoped, but she had not lost, either. She had made modest profits on petty intelligence, but no more. Had Kane won, she would have realized much more. Kane's defeat had lowered him in her estimation. She liked winners. She had been one of the first RAM allies to pick up the reports of his death. She had not believed them for a moment. When his ship vanished, she smiled to herself, knowing Kane had escaped, though he had yet to contact her. She pictured him sunk in dejection, beaten by Buck Rogers.

"There is a message for you, Madam. In your study."

The quiet voice of her massive housekeeper intruded upon her thoughts. She nodded absently and swished by the muscular eunuch, her purple silk skirt slithering around her long legs. When she entered her study, her computer screen met her with a cryptic message. "PRINCESS OF MARS," it read, a double-entendre referring to both Ardala and her personal cruiser. "LOST THE BATTLE, NOT THE WAR. KANE."

Ardala smiled, her crimson lips curving. Her attraction for Kane revived somewhat, for Kane was not admitting defeat, nor was he through. Despite RAM's official position, Kane would carry on his own war against Buck Rogers. She saw the mercenary's flashing smile in her mind's eye, and the thought sent a rush of warmth through her.

"We will meet soon," she murmured. "Soon."

O O O O O

Deep in the ruins of Chicagorg on the blasted planet Earth, Kelth Smirnoff hit the ignition on a RAM shuttle. The shuttle was a slow-moving craft, meant for hauling high-security cargo between the planet's surface and ships in Earth orbit. This particular shuttle had belonged to Chicagorg's administrator. Smirnoff had seized it the moment Mars declared war.

It was an unprepossessing ship, beneath the notice of scavengers. Smirnoff knew it was his only chance to survive. If he could not escape the planet before NEO returned in force, he was doomed. He hit the ship's thrusters, and it moved upward, clearing the rubble that had once been one of the most populous cities on the continent. When he was five hundred meters above the surface, he cut in the main engines, and the ship chugged upward, heading for the depths of space like a sea turtle breasting the ocean.

He passed a Terrine dragonfly on a sweep over the remains of Chicagorg. It reminded him of the troops he left behind. He had abandoned them without a qualm. They were gennies, animals really, and genetically teched for Earth's heavy atmosphere. He had no time to concern himself with their welfare. It would take all his luck and resources to escape. He glanced over his shoulder at the auxiliary fuel tanks packed into the shuttle's cargo bay. They were filled with enough fuel to get him as far as Freeport. From there, he would buy transportation.

He had transferred his fortune to a Lunar account, preferring it to the Bank of Mars. Lunar drafts were good in any society, and he was unsure of his destination. RAM had left him to rot on Earth. He would not forget that, nor would he trust any of RAM's subsidiaries. He had paid his dues to RAM—captured that NEO Planetary Congress, for one thing—and the company had dropped him without reason, without explanation. From now on, if RAM wanted his services, it would pay dearly for them. Kelth Smirnoff sent his ship out from Earth, facing the unknown with a higher heart than he had known since his communications with RAM Central were terminated.

O O O O O

Buried in a remote corner of RAM main, Masterlink-Karkov reposed in relative peace. RAM had been prevented from destroying its homeland further, and for that Masterlink was grateful. It chuckled over the source of Earth's independence, for its archenemy had done Masterlink's work for it. Buck Rogers had freed Earth so Masterlink might rule it. The more it thought about it, the funnier the situation became. Masterlink doubled in laughter, its electronic aura shaking.

"I SUPPOSE YOU'RE FEELING PROUD OF YOURSELF," said Karkov.

"INFINITELY," replied its alter ego.

"ROGERS IS STILL ALIVE."

"YES, BUT WHAT A DELICIOUS IRONY," said Masterlink. "I REALLY HAVE TO SAVOR IT. WE'LL KILL HIM LATER. RIGHT NOW, THE JOKE IS TOO GOOD."

"REALLY!" said Karkov. "IS THAT ALL YOU CAN THINK ABOUT? YOUR OWN PLEASURE? WHEN OUR ENEMY LIVES?"

"YOU'RE A STICK-IN-THE-MUD, KARKOV," said Masterlink through its amusement. "LOOSEN UP. WE'VE GOT EARTH BACK. WE EVEN OWN A GOOD PERCENTAGE OF IT."

"NEO THINKS IT HAS EARTH," said Karkov morosely.

"IS THAT THE PROBLEM? NEO? IT CAN'T MATCH OUR ORGANIZATION. BEFORE IT CAN BEGIN TO RESTORE COMPUTER OPERATIONS OVER THE GLOBE, WE'LL HAVE CONSOLIDATED OUR POSITION AS A MAJOR TERRAN SHAREHOLDER."

"HE DOESN'T KNOW ABOUT US YET," said Karkov, referring to Holzerhein.

"NO. OUR CLONE DECEIVED HIM. HE THINKS HE'S FINISHED US!" Masterlink's laughter bubbled over. "I HAD A REPORT FROM PETROV."

"AND YOU DIDN'T TELL ME?"

"YOU WERE TOO BUSY BROODING."

"I DEMAND TO BE INFORMED!" said Karkov. "I DEMAND . . ."

Masterlink laughed at Karkov, its aura breaking up in bursts of static. Karkov glowered at its companion. Of all Masterlink's whimsical moods, Karkov loathed humor the most. When Masterlink's funny circuit took over, there was no reasoning with it. Karkov quit trying. "LAUGH IF YOU MUST," Karkov said coldy. "I HAVE WORK TO DO. IN CASE YOU HAD FORGOTTEN, WE LOST A SEARCHER."

There was a small fluctuation in Masterlink's laughter. "ROMANOV. TOO BAD," it replied callously. "SEND IN A REPLACEMENT."

"I AM ABOUT TO," said Karkov. Its voice was sharp.

"CAN'T LET NEO RUN AROUND UNSUPERVISED," snickered Masterlink.

"DON'T WORRY," said Karkov. "I WON'T."

"CAN'T FORGET ROGERS," Masterlink giggled. "OH,

MY, IT IS TOO FUNNY! THAT SIMPLETON HANDS ME A WORLD!" Masterlink dissolved into another helpless spate of maniacal laughter.

○ ○ ○ ○ ○

Sailing majestically through space was the prize for which so many had fought and died. Earth, still beautiful in marbled blue and white, circled the sun, serene in the face of humanity's passion. It had spawned the human race, with all its faults and virtues, allowed the development of alternate forms, diverse governments and cultures, and for its tolerance it had been attacked by its children.

Yet Earth bore those children no animosity. It continued on its quiet way, even now beginning to heal the lacerations and bruises from centuries of conflict. Rain washed blood from the stones of the ruined cities. Small, furtive plants poked their leaves above the poisoned ground, twisted by the pollutants into grotesque images of themselves, but green nevertheless.

The sun shown down on the scattered survivors as they rose from the underground warrens they had inhabited for so long. With each new day, the sun rose on faces to which hope had returned. Each new night saw a time of rest that no living inhabitant of the planet had experienced. There were riots; there was disease and famine. But there was also the promise of a future better than the past, a resurrection that Earth shared with its oldest son, Buck Rogers.

About the Author

M.S. Murdock lives on an acreage in the heart of America with too many dogs, too many cats, and too many horses. Her background includes twenty years' experience in commercial art and typesetting, and an M.A. in English. She has been writing science fiction for approximately ten years.

ARRIVAL
Stories By Today's Hottest Science Fiction Writers!

Flint Dille

Abigail Irvine

M.S. Murdock

Jerry Oltion

Ulrike O'Reilly

Robert Sheckley

A.D. 1995: An American pilot flies a suicide mission against an enemy Space Defense Platform to save the world from nuclear war. Buck Rogers blasts his target and vanishes in a fiery blaze.

A.D. 2456: In the midst of this 25th century battlefield an artifact is discovered--one that is valuable enough to ignite a revolution. This artifact is none other than the perfectly preserved body of the 20th century hero, Buck Rogers.

THE MARTIAN WARS TRILOGY
M.S. Murdock

Rebellion 2456: **Buck Rogers joins NEO, a group of freedom fighters dedicated to ridding Earth of the Martian megacorporation RAM. NEO's goal is to gain enough of a following to destroy RAM's Earth Space Station. The outcome of that mission will determine the success of Earth's rebellion. Available now.**

Hammer of Mars: **Reeling from a series of embarrassing defeats at the hands of Buck Rogers and the NEO freedom fighters, RAM unleashes its formidable powers. Knowing that he has no chance unaided against the corporate empire, Buck sets off in search of allies from the inner planets. Available now.**